The Trilogy of
Morgalla
PART ONE

DIARY OF A LONELY DEMON

Jon David

OLIVIA-
Never stop being awesome!
JD

Contents

Chapter One: The Vindicator

They say the road to Hell is paved with good intentions.
People like me know better; in reality, it's paved with blood.

In a hallway in Hell, there was a closet. It was hidden at the end of the darkest of corridors, away from the prying eyes of Hell's vermin. It was not used for clothing, hats, or shoes, but was forgotten by everyone. Well, *most* everyone except its owner. It was for this reason that she chose it as her home. The less she was seen, the better, but a low profile could only do so much for one with such a famous father. Like her, the closet was humble in almost every way. She was not content, though, to remain there for the rest of her days.

The first rays of the morning sun came through his window to wake him, as they had on previous days. It had been another all-nighter; he'd slept in his clothes at his desk. He certainly looked and smelled like he had slept there. His eyes hurt from the rays upon his face; his hand went up by instinct. He rose and rubbed the fatigue from his eyes.

What day is it again?

He had to think a moment, and then it came to him. He was a man of advanced years and clearly not human. He had spent his entire life, over a century, fighting, along with everyone else on his home world. Even after he lost his leg the fight continued, only in the science lab now. He hobbled to the coffee machine; the pot was stained and had not been cleaned in days.

Eww.

He looked to the computer, finally noticing the flashing red letters on the screen.

Intruder Alert.

He nearly fell over from the shock. He heard sirens outside, off in the distance, and then voices out in the hallway.

"Only one," a woman's voice said.

He held his chest in fright as he spun around to see her sitting there. The morning light was not shining on that side of the room, but he could see her lavender eyes in the shadows. She was small and humanoid in appearance, and wore all black for stealth. If it wasn't her eyes that screamed what she was, the horns were a dead giveaway. They were black and polished, curving up from her temples to a point. Her hair was long and dark orange; her skin a paler version of the same color.

His eyes were locked upon her, and she could not only see his fear but *feel* it. His blue skin seemed to shock itself into a lighter shade. He looked to the keyboard. One button could summon help.

"You and your friends would not be able to escape," he said.

"There's only me," she replied, sitting in the large chair, her voice completely calm.

"You're too late anyway. You can kill me, but you won't…"

"I'm not here for that," she said, annoyed that he presumed to know the purpose of her presence..

"Revenge, then," he stated. "That's what you're here for."

"Look, if you'll just be quiet for a moment I'd love to have a more productive conversation. Standing looks uncomfortable for you. Why not sit?"

He was stunned, but tried not to show it. He knew, though, that she could tell what he was feeling. He did as she suggested, sitting in the office chair as she sat comfortably across from him.

"How many did you make?" she inquired with great interest.

"The Vindicator has already been given to the authorities. You would need an army to get it back."

"That's not what I asked."

"Why not just take the information from the computer?"

"I'm not good with those things," she admitted. "I'm also clueless when it comes to physics, distorting time and space, crap like that."

"Most of your kind are the same."

"Also," she continued, "I'm not in the mood to spend twenty years learning how to *build* one of those things. Patience is not one of my virtues."

"You're not like other demons," he said. "Others would have tortured me into telling."

"I'll take that as a compliment."

"You know, the Vindicator originally started off as a weapon to kill *your kind*."

He stood and hobbled to the wall where a set of blueprints was hung.

"But *you* found a different purpose, didn't you?"

"Your kind...and *Hell* are connected, aren't they?"

The older ones, yes.

"The less you know, the better," she said, sitting completely still. "Did you make a second one?"

"It would be pointless for me to lie."

"Yes," she assured him.

"You still haven't answered *my* question."

"I'm not here for revenge."

"Surely *Zorach* doesn't want it."

"Don't tell me that *you* can read people's souls now." She smirked, the first sign of emotion.

"No, it's something called *logic*. Your people already took the *first* one."

He looked back at her and was quite confident with his words. Her face changed upon hearing him.

"What?"

"And it's pointless to kill me," he continued. "All information has been copied and we'll share it with whoever wants to defend themselves against *your* kind."

"Wait," she said, standing. "What do you mean?"

"You people already *took* one of them. I'm not sure which one. Security has been doubled around the *other* one."

It was then that he realized just how *short* and young she was. She had to have been barely out of her teens and into young adulthood. The way she spoke made her seem older, though. He watched as she considered who might have taken it. The list was very short.

"What is it?" he asked.

"Dr. Morrow, a hypothetical question for you," she went on, snapping out of her trance. "What if someone from Hell wanted to walk through a door and *lock* it behind them?"

"But…you would not be able to live *here*, on Baladon," he observed, to which she offered no response. "It would be too dangerous. You would need a world with *humans* on it. There's no way you could blend in here."

He knows a lot about my species.

Her eyes moved to the door for a moment upon hearing people running outside in the hall. The doctor's eyes stayed on her.

"All I have to do is call for help," he warned.

"You don't have to do that," she replied. "There's nothing else here for me."

"The Vindicator XI will save my world. Do you intend to use the X2 to save another?"

"I'm not the hero type. I'm just trying to survive."

"You would be a hero to them. The first of your kind, I'm sure."

The door opened and the doctor looked to the security guards who entered with weapons drawn. Doctor Morrow looked back to see that the demon was gone. It was only then that he realized the window was open.

"Doctor, was there someone here?"

"It doesn't matter," he said to the officer. "Today our war with Hell ends."

He felt tired, having missed his morning coffee, and sat to rest his leg. *She could have killed me at any time and she didn't.*

She didn't have much time to get home. They would be using the device soon, and if that happened, she would be trapped on Baladon forever. She mentally ran through a list of names of those who might be daring enough to attempt to grab the second Vindicator. She only hoped her first hunch was right.

✦

They had barely made it home with their prize intact. Limbs were lost but they had already regenerated, though the phantom aches were still there. They all felt light-headed from the blood loss as well, but that too was already being replenished. It would all be worth it when their master saw what they had brought him: a trophy from Baladon, a symbol for what its people had fought and sacrificed. Even though the planet was lost, and was now safe from the hordes of Hell, no other world could get it.

They brought the device in, setting it on the stone floor. The room seemed to be filled with nothing but junk and dust. It was a place where things were stored and quickly forgotten. They wiped the blood away from the housing, exposing the words *Vindicator X2*. Some of the demons collapsed from exhaustion. Only one remained on his feet, and he approached the prize they had attained.

He grinned as he wiped the sweat from his brow. Suddenly, his attention was drawn to the doorway; a small figure stood there in shadow. He could not see this person's features but could smell that it was a female. Though his appearance was monstrous by "normal" standards, she looked upon him without fear, and though he could not see her face, he already knew who she was. More importantly... he knew who her *father* was.

She stepped into the light and removed her hood. While he had never met this person before, he had heard stories and rumors about her. He had heard her name and how skilled she was with a blade. Strange, though, she looked completely different from what he had imagined.

Her skin is orange? I thought it was red.

"Hi there," she began with a bright smile. "Any of you speak English?"

"I do," the alpha answered, though his English was broken and heavily accented.

"Oh, good," she said with relief. "I don't suppose you guys would mind giving that up, would you?"

The alpha looked at the Vindicator and then back to her. He could not believe his ears; at first he thought that he just misunderstood her. He had a firm grasp of the English language, even though he had to repeat the words in his head. He snickered and bellowed out a translation to his comrades, who all joined him in laughter. He then said something else and they looked at her with bewilderment. Hearing her name, Morgalla, at the end of the sentence made it clear what he had just done.

Crap, now they all know who I am.

"This," the alpha said, pointing his sword at the device, "is a *prize* for our master. He will reward us!"

"Or kill you for reminding him of the failure of Baladon." She tried to convince him to see things her way.

"I do not think so."

"I think you should give that to me." She was concentrating now, using every skill she had with her abilities.

"Take it," he dared, as he held his blade to her throat.

Three of his friends stood. Though weakened by the morning's ordeal, they would be damned if someone was going to take the spoils of their hard-fought victory. They drew weapons as they approached.

"Guys, I don't want any violence. I appreciate what you did, going through all that trouble and all…but I *need* that."

"Then you will have to take it from us."

Resigned but reluctant, Morgalla used one of the two weapons hidden beneath her cloak and struck her first opponent. His death was immediate. She had hoped not to resort to the use of these hidden weapons, but, like most every other day, was forced to.

When it was obvious there was no more life in her victim as his body fell to the ground, she turned her attention to the next opponent. He fell almost as easily when her blade cut through his neck. It was a cut worthy of a surgeon.

The alpha put up a fight, their blades clashing. Using the Vindicator as a shield, she leaped over it and then kicked the device into the alpha's body. He fell back and his third friend charged forth with fierce determination. She hurled her weapon through the air and found her mark, impaling the weapon into his skull.

The alpha leaped upon the Vindicator, more determined than ever to defend it. Their fight continued throughout the room and over the corpses of the other demons. She was not only fighting for the key to her future but for her very survival. He was determined to kill her, steadfastly resolute. . Her battle was purely for her physical safety; there was no hate in her face or movements.

He thought for a moment that he might have victory in his grasp, but it was short-lived. Her strength was knowing precisely when to take advantage of her opponents' false sense of dominance. At the first sign that his guard was down, she struck him. He felt the cold of her blade pierce his flesh and go into his heart. His life ended before his body struck the stone floor.

Demons usually died the same way. Once their life ended, their bodies ceased to exist as well; their bodies cannot exist without a soul. Some demons were known to explode or crumble to dust, where others had the rare distinction of turning to stone. Most demons melted at death, their physical forms usually leaving nothing but a disgusting black puddle. No physical part of their bodies were left, not even bones. What possessions they had on their person became engulfed in a black slime. Most would not venture into it to obtain even the most valuable object.

She looked down at the motionless bodies around her. In her heart she felt almost apologetic for their deaths, but it had to be done. She approached the device and ran her hand over the silver housing. The tiniest glimmer of hope crept into her soul as she felt the cold, alien metal. As her hand moved across a panel it came to life and opened before her. A screen appeared with an alien language written across it; it seemed to be intelligent and sensed her touch. A light washed over her and the alien language was replaced by one she could read. Something even stranger happened when the machine spoke: a roadblock came out of nowhere.

"Please enter access code."

"Oh crap," she said aloud.

The Vindicator looked incredibly complex. Her hands went to her head as the blood pulsated within her brain in frustration.

It will take me FOREVER to figure this thing out!

The slain bodies around her began to melt, the life now completely out of them. In the alpha's pocket was some sort of parchment; it looked like rolled reading material. At first she thought it might be a magazine, but that would be silly. She realized what it might be and snatched it up before the alpha's body was completely gone. She opened it, avoiding the black slime on some of the pages. She realized that the Baladonians had left the most important of tools, and her hope returned.

They left instructions. And the alpha brought them with him.

The floor was now filthy with black slime and she felt bad. She had to find something to conceal the device. She searched the room for a cover of some sort and found a tarp. Shelf space was scarce, but she got a brilliant idea (in her mind, anyway). The Vindicator was larger than she was and weighed more, but she was just strong enough to lift it. Although awkward to hoist up, she managed to put it on a stone ledge above the door with sheer will.

She almost forgot her sword, which she had leaned against the wall. Her knife was lost in the sludge that coated the floor and she wasn't going to search for it. She exited the room, looking left and right, her weapon in hand. When she felt confident that she was safe, she sheathed it. The sword changed into a medallion and suddenly hung from a chain around her neck.

She put her hood up and kept a watchful eye out for anything or anyone around her. She should've been able to spot or sense any danger, but in Hell one could never be too careful. The corridor was tall, with pillars on either side. As with most of Hell's architecture, it was big and foreboding. The stone was usually of the darkest red, the shade of a human's blood. The mortar was usually black, and the floor of most hallways and paths was made from the skulls of conquered species. More than likely the skulls were human.

A magical golden light shone down from crystals hung on either side of the hallway. Many things could be hiding in the shadows, for the lights did not reveal much. She was a tiny speck in the mammoth hallway; she did not appear to be a demon at all. One might mistake her for a human.

She arrived at the end; the doors were high and made of thick black wood. There was a series of silver rings on the inside of the doors every two feet, so demons of any height could open them. She had to use all her strength to open one, and she did not bother to close it.

The landscape of Hell was the stuff of nightmares. It resembled precisely what people imagined. At the moment the land before her was barren of life; everyone must have been away at the battle. She heard a commotion off in the distance, the sounds of thousands returning from a glorious victory. She looked to the nexus of the mountainous horizon and felt the euphoria from the beasts there.

They won..

Happiness was always a wonderful feeling to sense from others. In this sense, she wanted nothing to do with their celebration, for she knew the reason *why* they were celebrating. Today, the planet Veradoor had fallen. Morgalla looked at the horrendous skyline. The sky itself appeared to be on fire, red with swirling clouds of black. There was never any snow or rain, only a hot wind that would make her eyes burn and water.

Zorach's castle was adjacent to the cliff on which she stood. The chambers from which she exited were behind it. The castle stretched to the sky, golden light billowing from the windows of the towers. She climbed up the cobblestone, being careful not to be seen. It was either that or face the gorge below, and there was no telling what evil was down there. She made her way to the ledge and inched to the end of the wall. She climbed over it and was glad to see that the courtyard was empty except for two guards at the gates.

She leaped down to the cobblestone courtyard and looked up to the guards who stood at attention. They were large and dressed in black armor, with masks that revealed nothing of their expression. Their eyes were upon her; she just knew they were watching. They were armed with spears gripped by black gauntlets. Their masks obscured their faces completely; nothing but darkness in the eye slits. A lit cigarette hung from one's mouth, protruding from the helmet.

The guards knew who she was, for her size gave her away. She walked with caution to the gate, which led to the outside. They did not attack, but stood at attention doing their job. When clear to the open path, she ran off into the shadows, toward the closet she called home.

Chapter Two: Styx and Stones

Morgalla walked down a tall hallway made of dark red stone. Within the Mountain of Pain there were many tunnels and passageways in which anything could be hidden. It was easy to get lost; that was just one reason she chose it as her place to hide. The ceiling stretched high, like a cathedral. Small gems hung from the wall on both sides and glowed, giving illumination.

A small group of demons lurked in the shadows and watched as Morgalla walked by. They hungered for pleasure, the kind only a female could provide. They thought they were unnoticed, but Morgalla's senses were attuned to her surroundings. She was completely aware of their presence. She had no idea which clan they belonged to, nor did it matter to her. Their intention was clear.

One demon lunged at her and she spun quickly, with a large knife in her hand. Morgalla stabbed the creature in the chest. It shrieked in pain and fell to the ground. As life left its body, it melted into a puddle of red and black.

Morgalla looked at the others who hid, the large knife clenched tightly in her hand. She could barely see them; their yellow eyes gave off a slight glow from the lighting. The creatures looked on wearily but did not advance, unwilling to make another attempt at her. She sheathed her blade, turned, and walked away.

Continuing on, she walked up to a large wooden door. It had been her home, her sanctuary, since she came of age years before. Her hand touched the doorknob and magically it could tell who she was. Seven locks, magically released one by one, starting at the top. She opened it and walked inside. With a *clump* the door closed, and the locks secured her within her small fortress. She was safe again, locked inside her home.

Those sounds of being sealed within the room gave her the most relief. No longer did she have to put up the facade of a heartless warrior willing to kill all who threatened her. As soon as the seventh lock was secure, the tears came. She took no pleasure in the deaths of others, even if those others meant her great harm.

They left me no choice. Why didn't they just GIVE it to me? I'm sure we could have worked something out.

Her hand covered her eyes and her mouth tightened as grief took control of her. Her weapons slicing and piercing through flesh were terrible to experience. But to actually *feel* someone's life end was often unbearable.

The room was very small; there was only a bed, a small decaying wooden desk and a dresser. There was also a small shower, with a curtain that would pull closed. Morgalla removed her cloak and hung it on the wall, revealing her attractive features. She'd never considered herself attractive or sexy—not by demon standards, anyway. All the males she knew merely lusted for her, nothing more. Humans sometimes did the same, but she never showed her true face to them. What human would find a woman with *horns* attractive?

Her ears were large and slightly pointed, twice the size of those of a human. Her horns extended from her temples, curving and pointed upward at an angle. Her body was tiny compared to many others; she was quite short and not very muscular by demon standards.

Her lovely face hid a soul worn by years of pain and torment. She would think herself lucky, but in reality it had been her wits and abilities that had kept her alive to this day. Her face, usually like stone, showed no emotion to the outside world. Her eyes sparkled like violet gems but would reveal nothing. Her body was strong and her skills were sharp, but deep inside she felt like a little girl.

She was young but felt much older, worn beyond her years. Her mind was filled with many memories she did not want. Her heart felt empty; so much was missing from her life. There was nothing that made her feel happy or joyous. All her life she had known that she was different. No one must have known what she really thought, or how she really felt. If they knew, she shuddered to think what they might have done.

"Dear Diary."

On the old desk there was a large book with a red leather cover. The book opened by itself and her words appeared in bursts of flame that illuminated the darkened room.

"It took me six weeks to even *find* the man responsible for Baladon's victory. I doubt he did it all himself; he must have had a small army of scientists and engineers at his disposal. But it was his brainchild, for sure."

As she was speaking, Morgalla removed her heavy black boots and let them fall to the floor. She lay down upon the bed now, believing that her long day was over, and that brought a great relief. As Morgalla spoke, the words would appear in bursts of flame.

"He didn't have it, though. The thing I've called 'the Gizmo' for weeks now has a name: the Vindicator. It was a grand title for a device that will save his people. Zorach wanted me to attend the conquest of Veradoor today. I hope he didn't notice me missing."

She stopped speaking and her eyes moved to the door. She rose up in the bed, sensing a presence approaching down the hallway. Few had the gall to come down here, and even fewer knew that someone *lived* here. Perhaps the person was lost, but odds were that it was one of the only people who visited on a regular basis.

Delilah.

"Close," Morgalla ordered, and the book slammed shut all by itself.

She wiped her tear-soaked eyes which were red and sore. Morgalla had to concentrate, thinking happy thoughts and filling her heart with the few things in life that made her happy.

Sunshine, chocolate, puppies.

There was a knock at the door. Knowing who it was, Morgalla walked up and opened it without fear. A figure cloaked in shadow stood before her; tall, proud, and confident.

"And where were *you* today?" The figure spoke with a voice as smooth as velvet and filled with confidence.

"I had business to take care of," Morgalla replied, choosing her words carefully.

She could tell if I were lying.

"But of course."

Delilah stepped forward and removed her hood. Stepping into the low light, her face was revealed. Her skin was a dark pink, almost crimson, with scales that were smooth to the touch. Her face was very human-like, with nose, lips, and eyes all where they should be. Her features were striking, lovely, and yet vicious, like those of a predator.

Her ears were large, pointed, and decorated with many piercings of gold. Her full, dark red lips hid a beautiful set of fangs and her eyes shone like gold in the low light. Her hair was long and as white as snow, and it flowed in waves down her back. Like Morgalla, she had horns, but they were like ivory and extended horizontally from her temples. Also like Morgalla, she had the physique of a warrior, one who spent most of her days in battle. Unlike Morgalla, she had the desire to kill and conquer.

"Lord Zorach saw that you were missing today," she said, which made Morgalla's heart sink.

"I'll deal with that," Morgalla replied with fake confidence, looking off to the side as if she were a little girl in trouble at school.

"Don't be a fool!" Delilah was stern this time, spinning around and looking down at the much shorter woman. "What possible excuse could you have for missing the conquest of Veradoor? It was a world that took close to a century to conquer!"

"Delilah, I said I will deal with it."

Morgalla sat back down on the bed. Delilah took her place next to her.

"You play a dangerous game, Morgalla. If it were being played with anyone else I would be impressed."

"It's not your problem to solve anymore."

Delilah gave a look of disapproval; she knew further words would be pointless. From under her cloak came not a hand but a claw. It appeared deadly, yet was soft and delicate, like a woman's hand. She placed a cigarette in her mouth but did not use a lighter. The tips of her fingers had claws which glowed with flame and the cigarette between her lips was lit by their heat. She took a long drag and exhaled straight up. The cloud of smoke appeared gold in the light.

From under her cloak again came two more claws; these, however, only had two large fingers, grotesque by human standards. Upon further inspection, one would find that they were attached to not arms but *wings*, a blessing from her ancestor. They extended from her back, but she often used them as a second pair of hands when she was not flying. The two women sat and enjoyed the silence for a moment. Delilah's two "normal" hands rested on her knees.

Morgalla happened to notice a wound in the claw of her friend's wing. There was a large hole; burns surrounded the edge of the wound. Morgalla could smell the injury as she looked on in shock.

"What happened?" Morgalla asked.

"Oh, damn human weapon. Deadlier one than on other worlds. It was one of those that fire...um, you know, they're like lightning bolts?"

"*Lasers.*"

"Yes...yes," Delilah remembered. She moved her wing to look at the wound, squinting from the slight sear of the injury. "Damn *laser*, the wounds always take longer to heal. You should have seen Necrod today, he looked glorious."

"Did you come here to gloat about your glorious victory today?" Morgalla's mood changed to one of sarcasm. Delilah was one of the few people she could be sarcastic to.

"It was my hope that you would have been part of said glorious victory."

"I was busy, I said so."

"That kind of excuse will not appease Lord Zorach," Delilah lectured, as she had done many times. She stood and looked down at Morgalla, who replied not with words but by rolling her eyes. "Don't roll your eyes at me! He expects you at the castle later today."

"I shall be there."

"Do it for your own good."

Delilah's look was less stern and more compassionate now. Morgalla could feel the woman's soul; it was filled with care for her young apprentice.

"I'll do it for you," Morgalla said.

It was Delilah's turn to roll her eyes as her wing hand brought the cigarette to her lips for another drag.

"Being with humans has made you sympathetic," Delilah commented.

Morgalla smiled, for she knew the truth, despite the words of her trainer. Delilah was relieved.

"Sympathy isn't a *bad* thing, you know."

"Human invention," Delilah said, as she walked to the door. She paused and looked back at her apprentice. "It's no coincidence that within the word *sympathetic* is the word *pathetic*, hmm?"

Morgalla did not reply, but only looked at the floor; she did not have an answer and did not want to continue an argument. Delilah walked out and closed the door behind her, and the magical locks all took their place again. She took one final drag off her cigarette and then tossed it away.

Morgalla sat still on her bed, preparing herself in a mental sense for the coming gathering at the castle.

"Open," she commanded, and as she spoke, the words appeared again in bursts of yellow flame. "Delilah knows I'm up to something, but I don't know how much she knows. I...actually considered asking her to join me. Somehow, though, I know she would never fit in on a human world. She hates them too much. She would never be happy. I can never be happy here, but she would be the only reason I would stay. She's the closest thing I have to a..."

Morgalla didn't finish her thought, for she couldn't bring herself to say the words. She fell back on the bed and her hands went to her face to massage the tension away. She was frustrated from the events of not only the day, but also the past few weeks. A glimmer of hope had come into her life, but she had not worked this hard before. Her hands slid down her face, her weary eyes barely open.

"I hate my life."

✢

She sighed, having stood in a long line for quite a while. The beings around her, of many different sizes and shapes, were also annoyed by the wait. Patience is not a virtue of demons.

"Don't spend it all in one place," a voice said at the head of the long line.

The Banker was an oddity, even among demons. She seemed to be an amalgam of different animals found on countless worlds. She was a female with a powerful physique, though her voice was high-pitched and her movements were as feminine as those of the most elite princess. Her skin was like velvet to the touch and a dark shade of gray.

Her body's overall shape was much like that of a primate, often hunched over. She would stand on two legs but often walk on four. Only three fingers and toes were at the end of her appendages. She had two long necks, much like a snake's body, and they were incredibly flexible. At the end of each neck was a cat-like face. Each face had two lovely orange eyes that peered out at the world. It was the two heads sharing one body that made her an oddity; however, she never wanted to be known as *they*—but *her*.

"Next!" one of the heads shouted.

The large demon in front of Morgalla stepped to the side and her small features were presented to the two sets of eyes.

"Hello again, young orange one!" the second head called. "Dropping off or picking up?"

"I believe Delilah had something brought here," Morgalla said, standing at the marble counter which came up to her collarbone.

"Ah, yes, she did. A special order."

The Banker's powerful arm reached beneath the counter and took out a small bag. The sound of metal came from within. Morgalla in turn gave her an empty sack.

"Sorry the gold is not as much," one of the heads said regretfully. "The spoils were much smaller than anticipated."

"You know you're the *only* person who brings the bags back?" the second head stated with great annoyance.

"I can see how that can be annoying," Morgalla said.

"You have *no* idea."

Morgalla opened the sack that had just been handed to her and looked at its contents. With a pen that was on the counter before her, she reached in and took out a ring.

The other head spoke up. "You always do that. Why don't you ever want jewelry?"

"Personal preference," Morgalla said with a small wave of her hand. "See you next week."

Her last statement was filled with doubt. As she walked past the long line, there were rumblings of disapproval about how long the line was and how the Banker was in a chatty mood today, making the line go even slower.

"Next!" both heads shouted.

Morgalla did not hear one word of English from any of the demons waiting in line. She could, however, feel their anger, hear the disapproval in the tone of their voices, and sense the emotions emanating from their souls. She exited the main chamber. Two massive guards armed with spears stood on either side of the doorway. Night would come soon; she had to make it back to her sanctuary in the Mountain of Pain. Flashes of red decorated the landscape and illuminated those in attendance within the cobblestone courtyard.

She recognized one face immediately; he had an entourage of two. He was dressed handsomely, with the most expensive of clothes. He wore rings on both hands, and a Shadowblade medallion with the emblem of his family on it hung around his neck. He chose to be subtle with his piercings and had only one in each ear. His hair was long and black, and it blew softly in the evening wind. His eyes, as gold as the jewelry he wore, looked upon her. He had done this on many days, as often as he could. His skin was a dark shade of violet, much like the night sky of Hell itself. The subtle claws at his fingertips ran over the medallion around his neck as he smiled at her.

"Hello, Morgalla."

Her face showed as much emotion as a stone statue. She cared not what he had to say, and was annoyed that she could not avoid him. He must have seen her enter and waited for her to exit.

Damn.

"You were missed at the battle today," he said.

So were you.

"Blood doesn't wash out of clothing very easily, Vex."

He gave a slight sneer at her mockery of him.

"We *each* do our part, Morgalla. Besides, I thought *you* were the pacifist. Would you not want someone who shares your views?"

"We *all* kill when necessary." Morgalla smirked now, the first sign of emotion.

He stepped forward, and she exhibited no change in her behavior or mood, though the smirk was gone. He was walking a tightrope with her and he had to be careful. A deadly game of chess was being played; one wrong move could be quite costly. The price of failure might even be his life.

She did her best to hide her intentions and what she happened to be feeling at the moment. It was something she had become accustomed to doing day after day. Her cloak concealed her arms and she might have been hiding a weapon. This was a fact that did not escape him.

"Please accept a gift," he said, as a member of his entourage stepped forward and presented to her a necklace made of gold. "Spoils of war, won earlier today."

More than likely you took it from someone who was already dead.

"No, thank you."

"Infidel! You would deny his gift?"

"Call off your lackey, Vex," she demanded, with her eyes on *him* and not the servant.

"Insolent bitch!" the lackey yelled, drawing his weapon.

Vex was about to warn him, to order him not to attack, but it was too late. Morgalla drew not her Shadowblade but the weapon she had hidden beneath her cloak. Vex's fears were justified as her blade drove through flesh. It was an instrument that was longer and narrower than an average dagger or knife, and she struck her opponent with a surgeon's precision. It found its mark and ended the life of her would-be attacker. He fell to the ground, a lifeless husk.

Morgalla's eyes never left Vex, who kept his distance from her; the only wise move he had made that day. The body, now changing to nothing but a vile black puddle, sent a smell across the air. Already there were sounds in the distance, the wildlife of Hell coming out of hiding from their lairs of darkness. Morgalla did not turn her back to Vex or the lackey standing next to him as she passed. She held out the blade, pointed at the two of them as a warning not to approach.

"Delilah would be proud," he said.

She reached the end of the courtyard and started down the path that would lead her to the Mountain of Pain.

✿

Morgalla had dressed in the uniform of Hell's minions, a requirement of all meetings with their master. Her black leather uniform was tight and uncomfortable; she hated to wear it but had to. It was so…formal, with its high collar. The boots were her least favorite, heavy and metal tipped to provide the maximum amount of damage. The symbols were bright gold, meant to remind her just to whom her body, life, and very soul belonged: her father.

A warm breeze blew over her and all who had gathered. Two massive black wooden doors were at the entrance of Zorach's castle. Golden knockers in the form of skulls hung as decorations. Only four beings stood before the doors, and their decorations were the most elaborate. They were generals who answered to no one in attendance. Their master would be with them momentarily.

Down the steps were loyal warriors and agents, Morgalla and Delilah among them. These demons were dressed the same as Morgalla, many with more symbols of gold to signify their rank among Hell's hierarchy. Delilah's uniform had some of the most gold upon the black; she stood with pride before the massive gates. Standing a full head taller than Morgalla next to her, she and everyone else awaited the arrival of their master.

Behind those of a high rank there were rows upon rows of soldiers who wore a different uniform than Morgalla and Delilah. They were less elaborate and bore only one symbol: that of their master, Zorach. They growled in hunger; the horrible noise amplified by the thousands in attendance. They had little intelligent thought, and walked as men but were somewhere between demonic and human. They were beasts of burden, mindless brawlers, and good for little else.

Surrounding the castle was a terrible wilderness, a forest of jagged black rock. In this wasteland, a howling of Hell's wildlife could be heard. The dracon, who were only motivated by instinct, answered to only the most powerful of demons: in this case, the lord Zorach. When unleashed, they could only be pointed in a direction and let loose to kill and feed.

All those before Zorach's castle were summoned to bow and submit to their master. So far it was an average day. The front rows were reserved for a special audience, a rarity in Hell. They were the leaders of different worlds that had been under Zorach's iron grip. Most were human and though they were dressed in their best, their garbs were rags compared to others. They were forced to stand ahead of all demons, the pawns at head of the chessboard.

Surrounding the castle courtyard was an army of the nameless minority of Hell. This sub-species, just above humans in strength, could barely call Hell their home. They were used as fodder, brawlers in times of war. They played their part.

There was a group to the side who gathered for this meeting as well. They were the aristocrats, not soldiers or warriors at all. Their power and wealth gave them more freedom than anyone else. Delilah happened to glance over to them, standing off to the side and higher up. The youngest of Hell's elite looked down on all, but one was looking her way.

Delilah thought his golden eyes were on her, but it became apparent he was looking at someone else. She looked down at Morgalla, whose eyes were straight ahead; surely she must *feel* his eyes on her. Morgalla indeed felt the gaze, but ignored it and endured the leering; her powers were a curse at times like these. It wasn't just a pair of eyes; she could feel his soul and the lust within it. Delilah smirked and took a step forward to prevent him from looking upon her friend any more.

"Thank you," Morgalla whispered, keeping her eyes forward.

"Anytime," Delilah replied. "He seems a bit upset with you today."

"I...denied his request today."

"A request for what?"

"What do *you* think?" Morgalla asked, though it should have been obvious.

Delilah had to snicker just a little at the thought. She looked at the young Vex and smirked. She could feel his anger directed now at the both of them, but he returned the smirk.

No matter.

They all waited longer than normal for their master to arrive. No complaints were uttered, and they all did their best to conceal their emotions.

Finally, the gates parted and light poured from the entrance. They all felt a freezing wind, so cold that their breath was visible. The lesser beings fell to the ground, first. They groveled to the ground beneath them, their palms and foreheads touching the cold stone. The generals were next as they dropped to one knee; then row by row they all did the same, even the rich elite. Their heads bowed before the figure that emerged from the castle.

It was huge and moved as if darkness itself had suddenly come alive. Cloaks of black flowed from his large form; they were delicate and almost beautiful, with the consistency of smoke. The garments would be frayed where they touched the ground. No limbs were visible beneath his cloak and no face was visible beneath his mask. To gaze into the mask was to stare into an abyss. His soul was so old and consumed by evil that it had become like a shadow. The most impressive physical feature were the horns that ascended from his head, curving up to a point. They resembled Morgalla's, though immensely larger.

He looked at his minions and felt their fear. If he could smile, he would have. All had fallen silent now, not one noise was uttered. He walked down the staircase, and all trembled at his presence. He stopped a moment to look at Morgalla, whose gaze remained focused on the ground like everyone else's. He continued on and his generals followed.

Delilah was the first with the courage to look up and see their master leave. She then looked to Morgalla, whose head was still down. She was the only one still looking down. Everyone else was now leaving, their obligations for today fulfilled. They had expected the worst, Delilah especially, but they all breathed a sigh of relief. He did not show any vengeance for today's loss.

*

Later, Morgalla and Delilah stood on a balcony overlooking a tall hallway. Morgalla gazed down on the countless minions and some demons much like herself coming in from their victories, not just from the dimension Morgalla was in but from many others. Some of her kind were injured or dying, others were celebrating. Morgalla could sense a myriad of emotions and sensations coming from all of them.

"*You* are lucky," Delilah said.

Though she did not show it, Morgalla was relieved. She looked up at her mistress.

"I don't feel lucky."

"Did you get the horde of gold found today? I made sure to leave some, as usual."

"Yes, I got it already. Thanks for making sure there was no—"

"Yes, yes," Delilah cut her off. "No jewelry, only coins."

"I don't like how they feel."

"So what if you can still feel the soul of whoever wore them last? Can you not do the same with coins?"

"Not those that have been freshly melted and remolded," Morgalla said.

Delilah crossed her arms, leaning upon the balcony ledge. Her thoughts went back to the young Vex who had been staring at Morgalla again today.

"You know, you could do worse," Delilah noted.

"What do you mean?"

"Vex. He was looking again today. You could do worse."

"Or I could not 'do' at all." Morgalla was annoyed now, and disgusted by the idea.

"How *high* are your standards? Are you afraid you might not be able to control him?"

"Yeah, let's go with that reason."

"Deep down, Vex is weak. You would be able to control him, I'm sure." Delilah grinned.

"Fine, why don't *you*...'couple' with him?"

"Hmph. Your standards are too high, if you have any at all."

With that, Delilah walked away. They argued many times, especially now that Morgalla was older. Morgalla was about to walk away when she felt a presence. She knew who it was from the sudden chill in the air.

Zorach had emerged from a darkened hallway and minions fled at his presence. He felt the hot wind and heard the sounds of his underlings in the distance. Few demons became as powerful or lived to be as old as Zorach. It was unknown exactly how old he was, but he had seen many centuries. He had also seen people from many different worlds die by his twisted whims. To live the life of a demon one had to be cold-blooded. To live as long as Zorach one had to be an absolute monster, destroying and killing all those in opposition.

Zorach saw Morgalla standing at the edge of the balcony and was about to approach, but turned to see General Darvis approaching him. The General stopped before his master and bowed.

"Lord Zorach, Veradoor is officially ours, master. And we have many survivors."

"Execute the leaders, the injured, and the sick," Zorach commanded, looking down at him. "Keep the women for sport, and keep the males and children as slave labor."

"Yes, Lord," the general said, then he bowed and walked away.

Morgalla stood alone, feeling the cold chill of her father's approach. She exhaled, seeing the white vapor of her breath.

Damn it. It's always either too hot or too cold here.

She did not turn to see who it was, for she did not have to. If she were blind she would have known. A living shadow passed behind her and Zorach stood there. She acted as if she did not notice him, but his presence was unmistakable.

"Morgalla," he said, his voice above a whisper.

Morgalla slowly turned around and looked up at this beast. She showed no fear whatsoever at his ominous figure.

"Yes?" she said.

"You were not present at the fall of Veradoor this morning."

"It bored me," Morgalla answered.

He must know I'm lying. Maybe he enjoys torturing me.

Zorach gave a slight chuckle at what she said. He found it amusing, for he knew she was lying. He moved to her side, and both of them looked down upon the other demons and minions. All the terrible and glorious things that had happened this day were a culmination of war, death, and destruction. This was everything that Zorach and his kind lived for.

From his cloak came a gauntlet made of metal and cold to the touch. It was rare that he would show one of his hands to anyone, but Morgalla was special to him.

"You are young," Zorach said. "You know little of war. But you will join them soon."

"Is my contribution not good enough for the cause?"

"It appeases me, but soon I shall require more from you."

"Yes...Father."

Zorach's claw hand slowly ran down Morgalla's hair, his touch making her feel uncomfortable. She looked down to those whose lust for the kill had ruled their entire life. She saw the pain they put themselves through, all for the glory of Hell and their master. Some were in celebration, but many were in misery from their wounds.

"All of this," he continued, referring to the beings before them, "is for the glory of the *Dark One.*"

Go away! Leave me alone! Don't touch me!

She could not stand it anymore, so she abandoned the balcony and ran off into the darkness. She did not care where she went, but she had to get away from him. As usual, Zorach showed no emotion, even for one who shared his blood. It did not matter to him at all what her reaction would be.

You will see in time, young one.

Morgalla opened the large wooden door and slammed it shut behind her. She removed her hooded cloak, tears in her eyes. She began to cry, and removed any emblem of her demon heritage from her uniform. This sanctuary, her home, was the only place she felt safe. She got a hold of herself once more, controlling the tears.

"Dear Diary," Morgalla said, and suddenly the large red leather book opened. Small flames burst on the page, leaving the words *Dear Diary.* As Morgalla spoke, the words appeared on the page.

"Father noticed that I wasn't at the battle. I'm submitting my report soon on the world I was assigned to. They'll be curious about the typical things, how valuable the world is or is not. Mine is not incredibly valuable, thank goodness."

She sat on her bed and removed her boots.

"Had that dream last night. I'm not complaining, I'm just curious about what it could mean. Wish real life could be like it. Father will expect me to start taking a more 'hands-on' approach to the family business when we invade the next world."

Morgalla reached under the bed for her security blanket, a large plush elephant worn by many years. One eye was missing and the ear was crooked, the wire inside it bent beyond repair. Grasping it tightly, she held it close to her chest, curling her legs up and then falling on her side on the bed. Crouched in a fetal position, she closed her eyes and let out a sigh. She tried to block out the sights, sounds, and feelings of the already terrible day.

A folder made of red leather was there in front of her when her eyes opened. It was her report on her assigned world, thick with all the basic information her superiors would be requiring. She took hold of it and tossed it to the desk. There was a ten-digit number on the folder, and beneath it was written one word: *EARTH*.

Morgalla closed her eyes again.

"I gotta get out of here."

Chapter Three: Jasper Davis

On a planet called Earth, there was a town. It was just a small dot in a large landscape, with many people ignorant of the universe around them and of the terror at their back door. Lately the sky was nothing but gray, and all the color seemed to be drained from the town. The mood was abysmal and melancholy, a sea of frowns and sneers on every crowd. One young man, late for his appointment, seemed unflappable despite the sour mood around him..

A long red nail tapped with impatience on a tabletop. The nail's owner looked at her watch again. She would have left, but she had to get this over with. She didn't look at the waitress who walked up and refilled her coffee cup. She saw him run up to the window suddenly; he smiled and waved at her, and she sighed.

About damn time!

He ran in and she stood to meet him, but only for a brief moment. He gave her a kiss on her cheek, though it was unwelcome.

"Hi, sorry I'm late."

"I've been waiting for twenty minutes, *Jazz!*"

"I know, I know, I'm sorry, Mariette! I got you something!" They both sat down and Jasper held up a large, thick envelope holding many papers. "I finished it!"

"Finished what?" she said, her head resting on her hand.

"My latest essay. Another draft, anyway." Jasper's smile could not get any bigger; he was so anxious for her to read what he had just finished. "I was up half the night finishing it. I hope Mr. Kent likes it. I swear, that guy is impossible to please."

"And this is draft, what number again?" Mariette's question was filled with contempt for Jasper's craft.

"Oh, well, I don't know, I lost count. But I think I got it this time!" He set the envelope in front of her, but she showed absolutely no interest in it.

"Look, Jazz, I just don't *care* about this, okay?" Mariette said, pushing the envelope back across the table to him.

Jasper's smile was gone in an instant. He was confused as to what was happening.

"You don't want to read it?" he asked.

Mariette was frustrated and becoming angry.

"I just don't want this anymore, okay?" she exclaimed. She tried to keep her voice down, but he was making it difficult.

"This? You want me to write something else?"

"Damn it, you're getting dumped, you moron!"

All eyes were on the two of them for a moment and the coffee house was silent. All emotion was gone from Jasper's face as his eyes clouded.

"You…you're dumping me."

"Duh!"

"Well," he continued, "it sure was an interesting two and a half dates."

"I don't have the *time* to go into it in detail."

"No detail is necessary," he replied, as he gathered his papers and was about to leave.

"I thought it was sweet at first," she said. "That you wanted to be a news guy—"

"*Journalist*," Jasper interjected.

"Whatever. But I didn't know you *sucked* at it! You're never going to get a *job* doing this!"

"What?" he said in disbelief, angering. "I'll have you know—"

"Then there's your car," Mariette interrupted him. "It's a piece of crap, Jazz. And don't get me started on your apartment!"

There was the honk of a horn and they both looked out to see a shiny red sports car. A man behind the wheel waved and pointed to his watch. Mariette stood and threw her purse over her shoulder.

"Look, there's my ride," she went on. Jasper's jaw dropped again. "Face it, Jazz, you're going nowhere. I found a man with a future."

He should have said something and he knew it, but he kept his mouth shut. He had every right to yell at her and call her a name, but didn't. As always, he remained silent.

She walked out of the coffee shop and Jasper slouched in the chair. He was helpless, watching the shiny red sports car driving away with tires squealing. The waitress walked by, setting the check down on the table.

✢

He was good at school but hated to go, too many negative people and too much pointless work. Jasper sat numbly in Mr. Kent's class at the local community college. He was still in shock over the morning's events.

How could I have been so blind?

Jasper never thought he would get ensnared in the web spun by a ravenous female. He was just a fly to her, and this particular black widow had tossed him aside for bigger game. He didn't see it now, but he was better off. Though the relationship was still in its infancy, Jasper saw it as love. He shouldn't have.

This was the class that he hated most. Not because of its subject matter, but because of the teacher. Mr. Kent seemed to be completely unsatisfied with most people's work and hardly ever handed out high marks to anyone. Jasper did notice, though, that the two most physically attractive ladies in the class often got good grades. He never lingered on such things, though he wasn't the only one who noticed.

Mr. Kent was an oddity among the teaching staff at the school. Where other teachers would wear slacks, he would wear jeans with holes in them. Other teachers would wear dress shirts; he would wear shirts of the same style, but wrinkled and with the sleeves rolled up. Though he was often told to wear a tie, he simply refused, much to the annoyance of the dean. What hair he had left was gray, and he kept it long and wore it in a ponytail.

The teacher looked at the class. Some students did not care much for what he had to say. Jasper Davis was on the edge of his seat, quite anxious. Mr. Kent had collected their latest assignment and was passing back the one he had just graded.

"Some of your work was so riveting I couldn't put it down," Mr. Kent said. "I was quite impressed with your latest assignment. For the most part."

Jazz let out a sigh and sank a bit more in his chair. His teacher handed him a paper, facedown and slightly folded so that everyone else could not see the grade. It was pointless, though, since Jasper immediately flipped it over to see that his teacher had failed him. A failing grade, after all that work.

What?

Mr. Kent then looked at the attractive Missy Rider. He smiled at her and she gave him a wink.

"In this class, people," Mr. Kent continued, "we think with compassion and with open minds."

As Kent spoke, Jasper flipped through the latest essay that was graded. He was reading the handwritten notes, each a great annoyance.

You gotta be kidding me!

"Today we're going to talk about the United Nations," Mr. Kent began his lecture. "Its history, impact upon the world, and how it is important to all nations on this planet."

Jasper could not concentrate, hearing only the title, "United Nations," as the lecture began. His eyes went to the paper he had turned in today, in the large pile on the teacher's desk. He thought about how hard he had worked on *that* one, too. His heart sank, for it probably would be another failing grade.

After class, Jasper sat slouched in a chair in Mr. Kent's office. It was just a bit bigger than a closet, with a desk and a bookshelf. The walls were white and mostly covered with banners sporting the circular peace sign. There was also a poster from President Fletch's campaign, a fake smile on a two-dimensional figure.

Jasper sat alone in a broken chair, awaiting his teacher's appearance. He was aggravated by his grade, and what annoyed him most was the fact that he went out of his way to make his writings as politically neutral as possible. He saw now what he would have to do to get any high grade in the class.

Finally, Mr. Kent made an appearance and shuffled into the room. He sat behind his desk looking over Jasper's grades.

"You didn't like *this* draft either?" Jasper sounded almost desperate for some good news on this black day.

"It could have been better," Mr. Kent replied.

Jasper was more frustrated with himself than anything. He honestly thought he had gotten it right this time.

"I've lost count of how many drafts I've made."

"And it's still not right," Mr. Kent repeated.

"Ironic that you use that word."

"Look, Jazz, I'm just not satisfied with your essays or any of your writings."

"Because I disagree with you," Jasper observed.

Their faces were locked in a silent battle. Neither was going to back down, but it was clear that Mr. Kent had the upper hand.

"Have you given any thought to another major?" Mr. Kent asked.

"Everything in my essay was *factual*," Jasper said, bringing the subject back to the matter at hand.

"Look, you might not have been aware of this, but we're calling them the founding *framers* these days. Not fathers."

"Are you saying that I should give up?" Jasper asked. "I need this class for my degree."

"SCC doesn't offer a journalism degree."

"I'm going for an *English* degree," Jasper continued. "I need that to transfer and I need this class—"

"Yes, yes," Mr. Kent interrupted. "Jasper...can I call you Jazz?"

No.

Jasper remained silent. As with Mariette, he found that arguing would be a pointless venture.

"Jazz, listen," Mr. Kent continued. "I've tried to have you see things in a certain way. Is it *my* fault that you haven't?"

"If I fail this class it will ruin everything," Jasper exaggerated. "Not to mention it will bring my GPA down."

"Not unless you drop it," Kent suggested. "And as I suggested, Jazz, you can always change your major."

Bastard.

Jasper left Mr. Kent's office. The talk they had didn't help at all. In fact, it only filled his head with confusion as to what he was going to do. One man stood in the way of his education aspirations, and he just didn't know what to do next. As he left the office he saw Missy Rider standing there, leaning against the wall. She gave him a smirk.

"You are unbelievable," she said.

Jasper said nothing. He zipped up his jacket and put his bag over his shoulder. Missy watched as he walked away, shaking her head in disgust.

"Pathetic," she muttered.

Missy looked at Mr. Kent, who motioned for her to enter his office. She entered and he then closed the door.

Jasper stepped out of the building and looked at the campus. He glanced at the sign on the building, which read: *Sp ingd le Community Co l ge.* For years it had been like that, with the administration never making the effort to replace the missing letters. The crumbling red bricks of the building made the concrete below turn red. The sky was painted with many shades of gray, not a patch of blue to be seen.

The sun was setting, though you wouldn't know it. Many thoughts ran through his head, all of which were melancholy. He sighed as a cold wind blew over him and through the uncared-for grass filled with weeds. With his bag over his shoulder Jasper headed for the parking lot, looking forward to ending his day.

✻

Jasper walked through the crowded gym. Many large body-builder-like men and attractive women were working out there. He wore shorts and a T-shirt, his typical work-out gear. So much of what had happened that day was on his mind that he almost bumped into one woman.

"Excuse me," he said, sounding apologetic, but then realized the woman was Missy Rider.

She ignored him and walked another way, up to her boyfriend Steve. He was a large, incredibly muscular man. They gave each other a kiss and Steve put his hands on Missy's rear. She knew that sort of thing annoyed Jasper greatly.

Jasper tried to shrug it off as he continued to the front desk. His friend Meggan was there, sitting behind the large counter. She was working on the computer, looking intently at the screen.

Meggan was a petite woman with the physique of a personal trainer. Before Jasper met Meggan Miller he was considered a *toothpick*, no muscle on him whatsoever. She saw hidden potential, and despite Jasper's negative attitude, Meggan thought that with the right combination of tough love and brutal honesty, she could make him stand up and fight for himself.

As Jasper stepped up she saw him out of the corner of her eye. Her hand ran through her long black hair as she stared at the screen. She continued to work on the computer as she talked to him.

"Twenty-five looks to be too light for you," she advised. "Go to thirty."

"I don't know, my arms have been feeling like jelly lately, thanks to you!" Jasper replied.

Meggan finished her work and looked at Jasper. "If you wanna get big, you gotta lift heavy!" She smiled, but Jasper merely rolled his eyes. "Something *else* bugging you?"

"Got some bad news from my journalism teacher."

"Is that the underworked, overpaid teacher?"

"*All* my teachers are," Jasper noted, his cynical attitude shining through.

"Anyway, what did he say?"

"I should change my major."

"Ouch." Meggan's look turned to one of pain, feeling sympathy for him.

"Translation: you suck."

An attractive young woman walked up to the counter and signed in, standing right next to Jasper. He took a step to the side, nervously. He looked at her shyly and managed to smile.

"You know," Meggan went on, "before you started dating Mariette I would have said that you needed twenty or so pounds more muscle. And a better car. And a better job, and—"

"Your point?"

"Confidence," Meggan said with a smile. "I mean, yeah, you got the girl, Jazz, but now you just need the confidence to keep her."

"I think I might be better off with a sports car."

"Sports car?"

"Never mind."

Jasper finished his workout and changed back into street clothes. As he walked out of the gym, a backpack over one shoulder, he held the door open for two women walking in. They continued their conversation, not noticing Jasper at all or his kind gesture.

"You're welcome," he said under his breath.

While walking to his car, Jasper searched for his keys. He stepped up to his car just as he located his keys and promptly dropped them. He reached down to pick them up. When he stood up, he suddenly felt a presence behind him. Jasper spun around quickly in surprise. For all he knew there was someone who was going to mug him. He saw three men standing there, one of them Missy Rider's boyfriend Steve. He was the biggest and most muscular of the three. The other two were standing on either side of him. Jasper relaxed when he saw the three familiar faces, expecting instead to find a stranger.

"Uh…hi," Jasper said.

Steve stood with his large arms folded; he did not look happy.

"Stay away from my girlfriend," Steve said with a sneer on his face.

"Um…Missy?" Jasper asked, a bit confused.

Steve slowly walked up and looked down at him in an intimidating way. He outweighed Jasper by one hundred pounds easily and there would be no contest if a fight broke out.

"Look at her again, and I'll break your face," Steve said. This time he pounded his fist into his palm for emphasis.

Steve held up his fist and clenched it, cracking his knuckles. Jasper tried to back up a bit, but his car was behind him and Steve's friends were on either side. There was nowhere to run, and Jasper looked intimidated.

"I'll break you in half, you geek."

Steve walked away, confident that he had done something important. His friends, who acted more like minions, followed, giving Jasper a smug look. As they walked away, Jasper could not help but notice Missy Rider standing next to Steve's expensive sports car. She smugly looked at Jasper and then kissed her boyfriend passionately.

Jasper breathed a sigh of both relief and frustration at what had just happened. He turned around, looking at his old, beat-up car. His day was certainly not going well.

✣

Jasper arrived at work, running in through the front doors of Springdale Public Library. He almost ran into people exiting, apologizing to them as he ran past. There was a young woman in a purple long coat, her hair long and the color of raspberries, almost the shade of burgundy. She was looking about the latest magazines.

"'Scuse me!" he said to which she gave a jump.

The short woman looked to the person who startled her only to see that he had run into the office.

Who the hell was that?!

Jasper looked to the clock only to see that he had just made it without being late. He saw Andy's desk was empty and Sherry had already left for the day.

"Wilbur is looking for you."

Jasper looked to see Cynthia standing in the doorway. She was smiling. He took a deep breath and prepared for the verbal assault from his boss as he walked to the circulation desk. He walked slow and prepared for the onslaught.

The short woman with dark red hair had found a few periodicals and was sitting on one of the couches. Jasper saw how content she was. He was jealous.

Chapter Four: A Normal Night at Shenanigans

Shenanigans was often the place where many people in Springdale would come to unwind after a long day. It was busy for a week-night; not too surprising, since the weather was getting colder by the day. Jasper was at the entrance and many people had been flooding in. He looked at his watch; he had been waiting for a while and it was getting dark. He finally saw Andy, a young man of the same age he had known for years through school and work, running up to the door.

"Where's Meggan?"

"She had something to do at work, she'll join us later," Andy replied. He noticed that Jasper was alone. "Where's Mariette?"

"Long story. I've had the *worst* day."

They entered and walked toward the area where the billiard tables were. There weren't many tables left in the smoke-filled area. Though early in the evening, the alcohol was flowing and people were forgetting their day, whether it had been good or bad.

Andy pointed out an open table that was in view of the old-fashioned jukebox and they made a claim on it. Jasper accidentally bumped shoulders with a large man.

"Sorry," he said, as the person turned to look down at him.

This beast of a man looked like a troglodyte. He was incredibly muscular and tall, like a brick wall that had started walking and talking. His hair was messy and unclean, and his forehead sloped like a caveman's. Bloodshot eyes looked down as he sneered at the intimidated Jasper, who had to take a step back. He could have sworn he saw fangs in his oversized teeth.

"Watch it, *human*," the beast of a man growled at him.

"Jeez, sorry."

Jasper and Andy continued on, noticing the man turning to look back at the billiard tables, almost as if he were watching someone.

"*What* the hell is *that* guy?" Andy whispered.

They got situated at their table and ordered a first round from the waitress. It would be the only round, actually, since it was a weeknight. Jasper told Andy all that had occurred that day so far. His friend could barely believe his ears about what Mariette had done. She had always given Andy a bad feeling, like she wasn't to be trusted. Andy knew how his friend thought and that he wouldn't want to talk about the dumping incident at all. He decided to focus on the goings-on at school instead.

"Your teacher's a douche."

"Yeah, I've been aware of that for some time now." Jasper's attention was on the table, trying to decide which ball to aim for. "Honestly, I don't know what the *hell* this guy wants."

"Uh-huh," Andy replied, with a pool cue in one hand and his cell phone in the other.

Andy was only pretending to listen now; his thumb moved at the speed of light, texting while Jasper vented his frustrations. Jasper took aim at the cue ball and connected, only to miss his shot.

"Write what you know," Jasper said, repeating the words of his teacher in a mocking way. "That's what he's always saying. Well, sorry, I've never met someone who's looking to conquer the world."

"Uh-huh," Andy replied, as his thumb moved as fast as it could on the keys.

"It's your turn."

"Oh, um…yeah," Andy said, putting his phone away. He stepped up to the table, looking for a shot. "So maybe he wants you to start off small. You know, get your feet wet or something."

"Yeah, I guess," Jasper said. "But does he have to be so obnoxious about it?"

Andy took a shot and made it into the pocket. He then looked around for another shot.

"Most of our teachers have always been jerks. You're stripes."

"But there's something about him," Jasper continued, as Andy looked at the table. "I can't put my finger on it, but I can just *tell* that there's something 'off' about the guy. You know what I mean?"

"No," Andy said, looking up.

"Never mind."

Jasper could not find the words to express himself, and he found it ironic in a tragic sort of way. While Andy took his shot, Jasper couldn't help but see the massive beast of a man still standing near the bar and looking in their general direction. He swallowed hard and tried not to show that he had noticed. They waited a little longer and finally Meggan showed up.

"You boys ready to get your butts whupped?" she proclaimed, with the fake confidence of a person who hardly ever plays. "We're not playing pro rules, are we?"

"Hell no," Andy said.

"Oh, good."

"It will have to be cutthroat," Jasper added.

Meggan didn't notice Jasper's words, but instead that he was still wearing his tie from work and his sleeves were not rolled up. In fact, he looked like a manager of Shenanigans. Meggan immediately walked over to loosen the tie, regardless of what Jasper thought.

"My headache's gone!" Jasper joked, which made Meggan laugh.

"You know, I've been thinking," Meggan said. "For your two-month anniversary you should take Mariette to the place you had your first date."

It was then that she noticed Andy standing behind Jasper, waving both arms and shaking his head, desperately trying to indicate that she had just made a huge mistake.

"Mariette won't be coming," Jasper said.

"Tonight?" Meggan was confused.

"*Ever.*"

Jasper looked to the billiard table, wanting only to play the game and forget about the crap that had happened that day. Meggan realized that she had put her foot in her mouth.

"She's a bitch. You can do *so* much better!" she exclaimed, changing her attitude about Jasper's now *ex*-girlfriend.

"Thank you," Jasper muttered, as he lined up to break.

As Jasper broke Meggan gave Andy's shoulder a smack.

"Hey! I tried to tell you," he said. "Check your texts!"

"Don't worry, we'll get you back on the horse," Meggan stated.

"I'm fine, thank you," Jasper lied, his voice showing absolutely no interest in dating, or even talking about it. "We only went out on a couple of dates. Really, it's better to have it end now instead of later."

"Is there anything *else* I should be aware of?" Meggan asked Andy, not wanting any more surprises.

"No," Andy replied, shaking his head quickly. "Still, not as bad as that girl who tried to get him to join the cult. Hey, what was her name again?"

"I don't remember," Meggan admitted.

Andy was now practically yelling across the table, the alcohol having removed all good sense from him.

"Hey, dude, who was that girl who tried to get you to join the cult?"

"Alice," Jasper replied, as he walked back to them. "Your shot."

"Where is she now?" Andy asked.

"Getting her head shaved, how the hell should I know?"

"I had a guy dump me through e-mail once," Meggan added. "Didn't you have a girl do the same thing, Jazz?"

Their game passed, and both Andy and Meggan were glad when the nachos arrived. Jasper didn't have much of an appetite. He sat at one of the tall tables, his chin resting on his palm. Meggan was in the middle of a story about what had happened at work that day.

"So we spend an hour unloading this damn thing. The box was the size of a refrigerator. And finally we get the thing out and start to assemble it, and can you believe it? It's already broken! It must have happened during delivery!"

"Didn't you wait a month for that machine?" Jasper asked, his disbelief matching Meggan's.

"Yeah!" Meggan continued, her face turning red. "Now we gotta put the damn thing back together and ship it back to the company!"

"That sucks," Jasper said, as Andy looked at the table, trying to pick a shot.

They had finished their first game of cutthroat. Andy and Meggan began rehashing what had happened that day with Jasper and his teacher, Jasper was annoyed. He always hated being the center of attention.

"He's going to *fail* you just because you don't agree with his politics?" Meggan asked.

"Why not just agree with him for the time being?" Andy suggested. "Don't you need this class?"

"Yeah, I need to pass it for my English degree," Jasper said. "I won't finish my degree until next semester, though."

"How about retaking the class?" Meggan suggested. She smiled, thinking she had come up with a breakthrough idea. "You can drop this one and retake it."

"He's the only professor who teaches this class."

"Oh my God! You're kidding," Meggan said, her hope crushed.

"I can retake the class and just fail that one too."

"I say again," Andy interjected, as he was about to take a shot, "just *agree* with the guy in order to get a good grade."

"Great. So I write a bunch of propaganda that I don't agree with just for a passing grade? Is this how the press is run these days?"

"Yes," Meggan said, in between sips of her Long Island iced tea. "Hey, how come you didn't tell me that Steve threatened to beat you up?"

"Steve is an ape," Andy observed. "He's also all talk, so I wouldn't worry. He only did that because of his bitch girlfriend. He obeys every single one of her commands!"

"When a woman offers a man sex, he'll do anything," Jasper said. "Besides, that ape can break me in half—literally. I don't want to antagonize him!"

"You should really stand up to him," Meggan suggested. "I mean, what's he going to do? Seriously, Jazz, if he touches you, just have the schmuck arrested! Besides, is he really going to beat you up in the parking lot in view of other people?"

"Well, I guess not," Jasper said.

"Women love confidence, Jasper. I mean, if I saw a guy like you standing up to a guy twice his size, that would be a *huge* turn-on!"

"Hey!" Andy interjected.

"I'm just using that as an example, baby! Relax!"

"Oh, come on, a *huge* turn-on?" Jasper found her statement hard to believe.

"Well, certainly better than seeing him cower," Meggan said. "What does Missy have against you, anyway?"

"She's had it in for him since the ninth grade," Andy said. "We always had a joke that she was really one of Satan's illegitimate kids!"

"Doesn't matter," Jasper added.

"Maybe you should go buy a girl a drink," Meggan suggested.

"You want me to find a new girlfriend in a *bar*?" Jasper replied incredulously

"What's wrong with that?" Andy asked.

"Let me count the ways."

"Not a new girlfriend," Andy continued. "Just ask a girl to have a drink with us."

Jasper didn't say anything at first, but he gave a brief look around the area.

"They all have boyfriends," Jasper said. He noticed that, besides the guy who sneered at him earlier, there were a bunch of *couples* around the tables and at the bar.

"That one doesn't." Meggan pointed to a woman on the other side of the room.

Jasper looked over his shoulder to see a small form "dancing" in front of the jukebox. She was quite short, with long red hair that flowed down her back. She certainly had two left feet. Jasper raised an eyebrow. He looked back at his friends; deep down, he knew they were right. He never had any confidence or courage, especially when it came to women.

"You're serious?" Jasper again could not believe what his friends were suggesting.

"Well, I *have* been drinking so my judgment is a *tad* impaired," Andy replied.

"Um, well, I don't know," Jasper sighed, hearing the advice from his friends. "So why her?"

"Why not?" Meggan replied with a shrug.

"I thought you were using women's intuition."

"Just *go* already, will you?" Meggan was insistent, and Jasper sighed again.

He finished the liquid confidence, what little was left. Never before had he approached a stranger at a bar. He walked toward this woman. To say she looked like a tomboy would be an understatement, judging only her appearance from behind. She wore a dark violet coat that fell to her ankles. Her hair was thick, straight, and long, and a dark shade of raspberry.

Jasper swallowed hard and took a deep breath.

Oh, what the hell.

"Hi," he said, to which she spun around as if she were a child caught in the cookie jar.

Her hand went to her pocket as if she were ready to draw a weapon. Jasper took a step back; if he didn't, he felt that he might have been seen as *creepy.*

"Who are you?" she demanded of this stranger before her.

Seeing her face he would remember her from the library, the woman who he was so jealous of, sitting content reading magazines.

"Um, I'm Jasper."

She faced him now and he could see her attractive features. She was much shorter than him; her head came to his shoulder. Her clothes hid the physique of a professional athlete. Her apparel was conservative, humble, and informal. With her coat open, Jasper could see that she wore a red baby T-shirt with no markings. She also wore jeans that hugged her hips and upper legs, but were loose at the ankles. Worn red and white sneakers decorated her feet.

He looked into her lovely emerald eyes and took in her face. Her complexion was flawless and she wore no makeup. She looked young, but when she spoke it was clear that she was older. She gave Jasper the once-over from head to toe, seemingly bewildered by his bold introduction.

"Where did you come from?" she asked.

"Over there," he replied, jerking his thumb over his shoulder.

"Oh, great. He sent you to spy on me, didn't he?"

"Who?"

"And *who* are you?" she asked, accusingly.

"I'm...Jasper."

"*Jasper*, huh?"

She stood defiantly, with a hand on her hip. She took one long sip of her frozen drink and then stopped. One eye shut and her face contorted, with her lips tightening. Her palm went to her temple and her head trembled slightly.

"Are you okay?" Jasper asked, concerned. "Brain...*freeze*," she moaned, and then her face returned to a more normal state. "Ow, don't you just *hate* it when that happens?"

He looked at the table next to the jukebox and noticed a glass that was almost empty. The cocktail waitress just happened to be walking by.

"Say, you want another? What were you drinking?"

"*You* are going to buy *me* a drink?" she said with surprise.

"Yeah, why not?"

"Virgin daiquiri," she shrugged.

With her drink order put in, Jasper stood with his hands in his pockets. He found her choice of '70s music on the jukebox to be unique.

"And here I thought the whole point of your mission was to remain hidden and not let me see you."

"Mission? Excuse me?" Jasper exclaimed with confusion.

"Playing innocent, are we?" She smirked at him now. "You don't look familiar, so you must not work for my father. Maybe you serve my aunt, and she loaned you out to do a favor for him?"

Jasper's hands were still in his pockets and he was nodding with a fake smile. The cocktail waitress came back with the daiquiri and Jasper reached for his wallet. The woman held the drink and sniffed it, not sure what to think. She finally took a sip of it, but not until after she gave him a suspicious glance.

"Keep the change," he said to the waitress, and made sure to leave an extra-large tip.

Damn, she didn't notice.

"Yummy," she said with a small smile.

"So…my friends were playing pool…"

She looked around him to see two people there. Andy raised his beer bottle in a salute and Meggan gave a small wave. There was something about them that she found unusual and unexpected; she could feel their souls quite easily, especially the male, since he had been drinking.

"They're not with you," she said confidently. "What, did you pay two humans to *pretend* to be with you?"

"O-kay, you have a great night now!" Jasper turned and was about to walk away, convinced that she was mental.

He had gone two steps when she walked around and put her index finger on his chest. She had a point to make and she wanted to make it clearly.

"Look," she said, "you're pretty good at hiding your soul from me, I'll give you that. I mean, I can't sense anything from you."

"Uh-huh." Jasper was smiling and nodding along with her, trying to figure out a way to remove himself from the situation.

That daiquiri wasn't virgin.

"But I don't need a bodyguard and I'll be home in an hour or so. So…you don't need to worry about me. You or your ugly friend at the bar."

"Walking over here was a big mistake and I just wanna go back to my friends, okay?" he said, pointing to Andy and Meggan.

She looked over at the couple he pointed to. She could feel a myriad of emotions, especially from the one that had been drinking. Their souls were like those of most human beings, unguarded and open to her.

Oh my God, they're human, which means THIS guy…

"You're human," she said, looking back at him.

"Well, duh."

"Oh my *GOD*, you're human!" Her hand went to her mouth at the realization and she was at a loss for words.

"Are you okay? Seriously," Jasper said with concern.

"I'm sorry, I didn't mean to…"

Through her mind raced a hundred and one thoughts. She blushed and her hand went to her forehead.

Just how could a human sneak up on me like that? How could he hide his soul? Is he a wizard? Nah, wizards don't live on Earth.

Her questions would go unanswered for the time being; someone came up to interrupt them. It was a human male, a suitor much bigger than this person before her. He had long flowing hair and wore a T-shirt and jeans stretched over a massive and powerful physique.

"Hey there," he smiled at the redhead before him, a beer in one hand and a pool cue in the other. "This guy bugging you?"

Jasper rolled his eyes and was about to walk away, but this wall of a human being stood in his way. It was clear that he had been drinking, and judging from his demeanor and smell, he must have been drinking for a while.

Oh God.

"Why not take a hike, pal?" the rival asked. "A real man's gonna show her a good time."

Jasper was intimidated but he didn't show it. The girl couldn't tell what he was feeling at all; it was as if there was a wall between her and his soul. Jasper took a deep breath and thought for only a second what to do.

"Well, don't you think that's up to her?" he asked.

"How 'bout I kick your ass?"

"How 'bout I call the cops?"

"Screw you." In the rival's drunken-buzz state it was the only comeback he could come up with.

With her keen perception, Morgalla could tell precisely what this other guy was feeling. Alcohol often would open one's soul and make it vulnerable to her. The intentions of this other person were nefarious indeed. It was simply lust at first, clearly directed at her, but now there was anger. This anger must be directed at the man he saw standing in his way.

"Oh crap," said Andy, when he saw the much bigger man standing before Jasper. "The redhead has a boyfriend."

Hearing her boyfriend's words and seeing that the redhead's "boyfriend" meant business, Meggan grabbed her purse and dug around in it.

"I should still have mace in here," she said, in a frantic rush to find the only weapon she had.

The rival's friends tried to pull him away; the entire situation wasn't worth getting into a fight over. He disagreed, though, and pushed his friends away, ready to hit anyone with the pool cue in his hand.

"No, no," he went on, his speech slightly slurred. He gripped the pool cue tighter and pointed it at Jasper. "Listen, punk, the lady's gonna have a drink with me. Get lost or get your ass kicked."

The girl, on the other hand, was confused. Though she could not feel Jasper's soul, she could hear his heart beating, for he was so close *and* it was beating very fast. With the advice of his friend Meggan still fresh in his mind, Jasper had to think of a plan—and fast. The place was crowded; no *way* was this guy actually going to start something in front of all those witnesses.

Maybe this girl would be impressed with a little courage.

Jasper was trying to be polite and not agitate the drunkard, but at the same time he couldn't back down.

"Look, friend, there's no way you're gonna try anything in front of all these people."

"Yes, he would," the girl interjected, being able to feel the violent intentions of Jasper's rival.

Her instincts were overtaking her, and she reached behind her coat to her back pocket. Her favorite weapon waited there: a pair of nunchakus. A sober friend put a hand on the bully's shoulder, trying to bring sense to him, but the hand was slapped away. The redhead stepped up to Jasper's ear.

"You should leave," she advised. "Seriously, he wants to kill you."

"What?" Jasper was shocked by her words. "You're kidding me. How do you know?"

"It's a gift." The redhead's words and tone were serious. "You better get out of here."

As the anger grew within the rival, Jasper took a step back, realizing that maybe standing up to him was a mistake. It seemed to have just poured gas on the fire. He saw his friends approaching; Meggan had a small can of mace in her hand and Andy held a pool cue tightly.

"Goddamned punk." The drunk and angry bully gave Jasper a shove intended to provoke him into throwing a punch.

And then, just as Jasper's rival swung the billiard cue to strike again, Morgalla pushed Jasperout of the way. If she were any taller she would have been struck; lucky for her, she was very short. Instead, the pool cue hit one of the bully's sober friends, causing him to fall back into the cocktail waitress, who in turn dropped an entire tray of beer on a total stranger playing billiards on a neighboring table.

"Oh crap," Meggan said.

"Oh crap," Morgalla repeated.

The entire room was shocked as the last domino fell, and it was on. The beer-soaked patron and his friends all turned to the culprits responsible. Jasper, still on the floor, looked at the standoff in shock. There was only enough time for everyone to take a deep breath before the brawl began. The cocktail waitress screamed as the fists flew. Pool cues and beer bottles became makeshift weapons as the two factions, some drunk and some sober, did battle among a field of green felt and secondhand smoke.

"Jazz!" Andy yelled over the commotion, as he and Meggan sought cover.

There was a barrage of battling bodies between Jasper and his friends. He looked up to see the redhead take out her nunchakus and split in half the pool cue being wielded by the drunken rival. With a mighty kick, this beast of a man was thrown across the room. She was so fast and strong that surely she could not be human.

Jasper looked on in shock at her skill and daring. He then noticed the cocktail waitress, screaming in fright and in a fetal position to avoid physical harm. The brawl now encompassed all of Shenanigans, having spread within a matter of seconds. Jasper crawled over to the waitress, being careful of any bodies or debris, and helped her to safety. His actions were not unnoticed by the redhead. If she didn't know it before, she was sure now that he was human.

She saw Jasper, the waitress, and his friends make their way to the fire exit. There was a mass of bodies between them, and she knew she would have to make her way through the crowd to the entrance. She dodged and evaded others until she ran into a figure that stood in her way.

"Hello, Morgalla," the male sneered at her.

They stood frozen and gazed upon each other. She gripped her weapon, ready to strike the unknown being before her. He was massive and horrific for a human, and it took only a moment to know *what* he was.

A demon in human form. Few are capable of that.

It was his bloodshot eyes that gave him away. She recognized them belonging to a well-known thrall of Zorach. She said nothing, for words were pointless. Out of the corner of her eye she saw an object coming at them, and thanks to her superior reflexes she ducked. The chair hit him and shattered, and he stood there completely unharmed. He shook off the shock and splinters and looked to see that Morgalla was gone.

She ran out of the building and heard the sound of sirens in the distance. She could see the red and blue lights easily in the night's horizon. There were many people fleeing the building now and she did the same. Something caught her eye, though, under the parking lot's lights: a wallet made of black leather. She thought little of it as she put it in her coat pocket.

*

Later, on the way home, Jasper sat in the backseat of Andy's car. Andy was driving and Meggan sat next to him in the passenger seat and looked in the backseat and saw that Jasper was sulking.

"So," Meggan said, to break the uncomfortable silence, "did you get her phone number?"

Jasper was silent, opting to sulk. Meggan realized that her joke didn't go over well.

Jasper pinched the bridge of his nose in apprehension; words could not describe his relief that this day was finally over. It wasn't until he got home that he realized he had lost his wallet somewhere at *Shenanigans*.

Chapter Five: Boring Meetings

They towered over her so high that she did not know they were alive at first. She peered up with lilac eyes through her black hood as her orange hands gripped the plush elephant as large as she was. This new power she was discovering told her things about other demons that she did not have to ask. Not everything, but certainly enough to read their emotions clearly. . The four that surrounded her were somewhat afraid, but determined to do their duty. Today their duty was her protection.

They were in uniforms of black leather trimmed with gold symbols. Though they were the same species, they all appeared different. She could not see their faces; she thought they were very tall, but in reality she was simply very short. Four warriors of the greatest skill were charged with her protection.

She held the elephant tightly as she looked on with concern. Though she felt secure that no harm was would come to her from *these* four, she was still not sure why she was here. Two more figures entered the chamber, one dressed in extravagant robes decorated with gold. His hair was long and curly, as was his beard. It was white due to his advanced age, and the deep wrinkles in his scarlet skin gave more clues as to how ancient he was. Four horns were atop his head, coming through the thick hair.

His pink eyes looked down at the child before him and she could not return his gaze. She looked down at the marble floor, afraid to look at the strange beings before her. The souls presented to her were quite alien and she did not want to know what they were feeling. Looking at the marble floor, though, would not help.

"Lord Udo," the servant said, "this is the child—"

"But of *course*, fool."

"Y-yes, Lord," the servant stammered.

Lord Udo looked down upon the child, his fingertips together on his chest.

"So you are the one, hmm?" he pondered, and smiled. "Do you speak, child?"

The girl said nothing, for she had nothing to say.

"Look upon me, young one," Udo commanded. She could not explain why, but she felt an urge to gaze at him, regardless of how afraid she was. "Do you know your father?"

The girl shook her head. He stepped up, and she wanted so much to be away from him, to be away from here.

"He is a powerful being. The most powerful...next to the *Dark One*. You are most fortunate that you have his blood flowing through you. *You* will grow to be powerful and take your place at your father's side. But until then, your life is in danger."

The chamber door opened again and a figure entered, dressed in black, her features concealed. Surely it was a woman by the way she strolled in with such confidence and delicacy. The little one felt a pair of eyes on her, but she could not see who was peering down. The person was happy to see her; such joy filled her heart.

"Hello, little one," the figure called in a soft voice.

The child gave a small smile.

"You are very lovely indeed," she continued, as she lifted her hood. "Do not be afraid, young one, I shall not harm you."

Scarlet features were then visible, pale red scales on the woman's face. She had white horns that stretched high behind her head. Her lips, full and vibrant, were black and shone in the light. Her hair was the most beautiful she had ever seen, flowing long and white. Flickers of blue shone upon her radiant locks. The yellow eyes that looked upon her made the young girl gasp.

Her words helped, and the young girl felt her soul. She felt happiness and joy; she was excited to see her. Lord Udo spoke, but the woman did not look at him. Her gaze was on the young orange-skinned girl.

"Mistress Delilah, do you swear in the name of the *Dark One* to watch over this girl? To protect her? To teach her our ways and give her the power she will need in the coming years?"

"Yes," she said, smiling and exposing the glistening white fangs beneath her black lips. "A name. She needs a name."

"Indeed."

"Something grand," Delilah said. "Something that...means something."

"Um...yes," Udo replied. "I have given much thought to this and have decided upon a name that will honor our Lord Zorach and the *Dark One* as well!"

Delilah's gaze never left the young girl. She rolled her eyes briefly at Udo's grandstanding, which made the little girl give a slight giggle.

"I have searched through the ancient texts in languages as old as the girl's father and I have found a name that..."

He rambled on, to the annoyance of Delilah and the confusion of the little girl. Delilah knelt down to her, close enough so that only she would hear.

"He *can* talk a bit too much, can't he?" Delilah whispered, and winked.

Delilah made a couple of funny faces that caused the little girl to burst out in laughter.

"You know, I never thought about having children," the crimson-skinned woman went on. "But seeing you and the potential that you have, the potential that I shall see you fulfill."

"Morgalla!" Udo bellowed.

"Hmm?" Delilah replied, looking back at him.

"The child's name. From this day forth may all know you as…
Morgalla!"

During Udo's vain rambling neither heard the meaning of the
girl's name, something from a long-dead language. But to Delilah it
did not matter. She looked back at the little girl and smiled again. She
stood and the girl stood close, almost hugging the woman's leg. Delilah
moved her cloak to envelop the child. It was a simple cloth and yet to
the child, it was stronger than any armor. Delilah swelled with pride.

"Morgalla."

✢

Morgalla awoke and gave the command for her diary to open.

> *Dear Diary,*
>
> *My full report on Earth is due today. It's not worth
> their time, really. Finally, they'll get off my back.*
>
> *But still…*
>
> *I was at a bar last night. Never again. Every single
> guy hit on me. I just made them go away, but it was
> really annoying anyway. There was this one guy, though.
> I thought he was demon too, sent by my father to check
> up on me. He's done that a couple of times before. Turns
> out he was a human and none of my powers would work
> on him. It was like staring at a blank wall. Clearly he
> had a soul, but I could not feel anything from it. Only
> a powerful demon could do that…or maybe a human
> could, but only if he knew what I was. Hmm.*

He was cute, though, I guess. Maybe I should have talked to him. I'm such an idiot!

✿

She glanced at the clock, sighing heavily. She never had enough time in the morning. Getting dressed in her uncomfortable uniform, the tight leather, the revealing midriff, the heavy boots, the golden runes, she left her room ready for anything, as usual. At least due to her low rank she did not have many runes on her collar. If she were anywhere but Hell she would not mind tight or revealing clothes, but here she could not stand the many eyes of Hell's vermin, undressing her.

She arrived at the end of the long corridor. Her destination was a twelve-foot-high door made of black wood with a silver doorknob in the shape of a skull. She made a quick adjustment to the uncomfortable leather uniform. Pulling the hood over her head, she got into character, willing herself to think like a typical demon. *Think mean thoughts. Kill, kill, kill.*

It was not far from the truth, really. If any demons or minions dared to attack her, she would kill them, but the big difference was she would not take pleasure from it. One of Delilah's many lessons that she taught Morgalla was "never show fear." The opponent could smell fear, even humans. All creatures of Hell, even the lowest of slime, could smell fear quite easily.

She took a deep breath and twisted the doorknob. Morgalla emerged from the darkened hallway to see the inferno that was Hell's sky.

Everything about her changed; she had a scowl on her face and a hateful gaze, ready to stare down anyone who looked at her. The image of Vex appeared in her mind's eye. She became a bit nauseous, but mostly hate flowed through her. She imagined smashing his smug smile with her foot. Her anger swelled within her heart and could be felt by all who might be lurking. Her walk changed too, slower and more confident. Her hooded cloak flowed in the hot wind. One hand was on the strap of her bag; the other clenched a medallion ready to transform into a deadly weapon.

The journey was not long, thank goodness. Morgalla's closet was just within reach of her father. He liked keeping her close, and her home was not far from the portal chamber and Zorach's castle. The castle was the only place she was required to go, and the portal chamber was the only place she ever wished to go. As she made her way through the path, the castle courtyard was presented. There was a field filled with life; skin tones of shades of red and burgundy.

Today's visit to Zorach's castle, like all her visits, was mandatory; she was to give her report to the generals. A cobblestone path made of human skulls led up to the courtyard where a fountain stood. She approached the fountain of blood in front of the black castle. A statue made of marble in the fountain was of Zorach, holding a severed human head in his claws.

Blood gushed forth from the eye sockets and from the bottom of the severed head. A permanent cloud of heavy smoke loomed above the castle, and red lightning crashed down periodically. The black stone held together with red seemed to have been grown from the black dirt. As trees grew wild in an undisturbed forest, so did the monstrosity before her. It was thick at the base and curved, narrowing at the middle like an hourglass. Towers extended like claws to the veil of darkness that hung above it. Everything there was a monolith to her father's tremendous ego.

Another demon, a bit younger than Morgalla walked by. She saw him and smiled; it was a fake smile, one to convey the sudden rush of sarcasm flowing through her.

"A villain lives here, can't you tell?"

He gave her a weird look and walked on to the entrance. She sighed again, thinking the sooner this meeting began, the better. Delilah was waiting at the entrance to the chamber. She had been pacing, waiting for Morgalla. When she saw her, she gave a look of annoyance.

"About time you showed up," Delilah said.

"So I'm not early. I'm not upset about it." Her reply came without looking her mentor in the eye.

The two women walked among the different clans that occupied Hell. There were the Swamp Devils who were notorious for wearing the skins of the dire gator. The Hellbenders required their members to cut out an eye before joining. Since demons regrew limbs and organs, many found it to be rather pointless.

The Hexcog Nine were from a province that no longer existed. There were only nine of them, but there was a weight and age requirement. Their size and power was enough to deter most other clans. Troop 666 was a group of children that were hired assassins and the Cougars were all women of a certain age that kept younger male demons and humans as *pets*.

Delilah took her by the arm and zealously led her inside the chamber. She practically had to shove her apprentice into the room. Many demons were around, not unlike Morgalla and Delilah, and many of the males were giving the two of them the usual looks.

"So *Delilah*," one demon called, making sure to bring attention to her name. "How does one with a *human* name get to be such a—"

His words were cut short. Delilah and Morgalla were walking past him and it appeared as if they would ignore him completely. Morgalla knew her mentor and trainer too well, though. She ducked even before Delilah's claws were on her weapon. In a silver flash it came from her belt, and by the time it came around to the demon's neck it was a blade. It sliced across his neck and his lifeless body fell to the cold red stone.

Morgalla had seen this on more than one occasion; luckily, Delilah was of a high enough rank to get away with killing someone who was unarmed, and in front of so many witnesses. Her reputation preceded her and her temper was legendary. The most sensitive of Delilah's quirks was that her name was not to be ridiculed. Yes, it was a human name, but she had been given it because of her dragon grandmother.

"My name," Delilah said, her golden gaze looking over the crowd as Morgalla rose behind her, "is *not* human! She is a noble creature. One of power and beauty!"

Sheathing her weapon, the two of them continued into the chamber. Morgalla sighed, for this was not the first time she had witnessed Delilah killing someone. The two women walked away, but as soon as their backs were turned Morgalla could tell what someone behind her was feeling. One demon gazed at her with lust, and his long tongue slithered out. Every now and then Morgalla had to give an example to others, just to send the message that she was not to deter any potential attackers.

Thank you.

She spun around, her medallion changing into a short blade. She pointed the short sword to the beast, the tip against the soft pink flesh of his tongue.

"Put it away," she commanded.

"Yes, ma'am!" he replied, and all courage was drained from his body.

Delilah laughed, not just because it was funny but more importantly to mock him. Later, Morgalla sat in a large conference room, a chamber large and circular made of dark red stone. Hundreds of demons of human size sat in attendance. The mumbles among the creatures were a mixture of many different dialogues. If one concentrated on the sounds, one probably could not understand any of the words being spoken. Morgalla sat at the end of one of the rows of demons. There were a few feet between her and the others; she did this on purpose. Delilah was standing in the aisle; the claw at the end of her little finger was scraping away between her fangs.

"I think I wanna learn French next," Delilah said. "How is it?"

"You won't like it," Morgalla replied.

"Really? Depressing. How's my accent sounding?"

"Nice, you sound English."

"Sweet!"

✻

Oh Lord, do I hate meetings. It's bad enough that I have to be around any one of these creeps, but an entire roomful is intolerable. At least Delilah is here. I'm glad there is at least one I can rely on. Even though I can only understand one or two words spoken by many of the demons here, I can tell what's on their minds. What's ALWAYS on their minds.

I think hardly anyone is speaking English today. Not many demons speak that language. I think Delilah chose it because she thought it sounded regal. And because she spoke it, that's the language I picked up. I don't remember much of any other demonic language, only that there must be at least over two hundred different kinds.

✻

As with everything demonic the room was huge, larger than it had to be. Morgalla went and sat in the back row, in the shadow of a column deep in the darkness, not to be seen.

Silence filled the room as Zorach entered. The breath of all present as white vapor in the air as all warmth was drained. He did not simply command respect, but instead demanded it upon penalty of death. Silently, they all rose to their feet. He strode across the stone and took his place at the wall farthest from the door. He faced his minions as Delilah walked over to stand next to him. He spoke and all understood his words, regardless of what dialect they spoke.

"Be seated."

They did as he commanded and Vex took his place in the center of the room. There, in the middle of the room, the magical image of a planet appeared, and afterward images of the civilization that lived there. There were images depicting its people, technology, magic, and knowledge.

Vex stood near the center of the chamber as three demon generals faced him. Zorach stood off to one side, listening, and Delilah stood next to him. She yawned, bored with the goings-on. Morgalla also sat yawning.

Delilah looked up to her master, Zorach the Unholy, and not just in the literal sense. She hoped to be like him someday, with every living being either terrified of her or serving as her obedient slave. Part of her was jealous of Morgalla for being the flesh and blood of Zorach. She always thought how glorious it must have been, knowing that his very blood flowed through her veins.

If she only knew the truth.

Delilah was scared of Zorach, but so was everyone else, so she felt no shame in it. If anything, she felt it was a sign of respect to her lord and master.

Vex was in the middle of his presentation to the generals.

"There are numerous and well-organized armies, with highly advanced weaponry."

"There are multiple portals on this world, correct?" General Darvis inquired with great interest.

"Yes," Vex replied. "They are aware of other dimensions and have defenses against such invaders."

"Would they have such defenses against us?" General Zeethros asked, almost confused, for all the different worlds were bleeding together.

"Against the lesser demon population, yes," Vex continued. "The casualties would be great."

"Although we were successful in our last conquest," General Makraka added, "we suffered many losses."

"A large army would be required," Vex said.

"Would they invade *us?*" Darvis asked with a slight tone of concern.

"They're unaware of our realm," Vex answered. "We recently came into possession of some technology from a conquered world, though, which is similar to theirs."

"What technology is that?" Darvis inquired.

"An explosive device which closes dimensional gates." His words caught Morgalla's attention and she scribbled down a note, remembering the technology Delilah had captured from their most recent conquest. "Many humans are acquiring this kind of technology. It is believed that it might be stolen from other dimensions or shared."

"Shared?" Darvis asked with a tone of shock in his voice. "The humans are scared of us. They choose not to face us in battle, so they hide on their worlds!"

"That *must* be it, my lord!" Vex said in complete agreement.

Morgalla was annoyed at Vex's comment.

Full suck-up mode on.

Time passed and Morgalla was now standing in front of the generals, who seemed a bit bored by her and her report.

"So," Darvis said.

"Nothing much else to say, really."

"They have a large population," Zeethros observed.

"Very low on resources, though, which would be valuable to us," Morgalla reported.

"They are completely unaware of our presence," Makraka added. "We would have the element of surprise."

"But if they needed to, they would use weapons of mass destruction that would obliterate an entire army," Morgalla said.

"So it is your recommendation that this world is not worth our time?" Darvis asked, finally bringing the point of Morgalla's presentation to light.

"Yes, that is exactly what I'm saying."

"Are they *entirely* unaware of Hell?" Makraka asked. This Earth seemed familiar to him.

Morgalla paused a moment, knowing they would know if she were stating an outright lie.

"Yes, they *are* aware of Hell," Morgalla continued. "Or should I say that the majority of them *believe* in Hell."

"Elaborate," Zeethros commanded.

"Well, it's your classic case, really," Morgalla continued. "Many people there think that if you're bad in life your soul goes to Hell when you die."

"Oh, it's one of *those* places," Makraka replied.

"You may sit." Darvis gestured to her, with a sense that her presentation was a pointless waste of time.

Morgalla took her seat as Zorach's gaze followed her. Delilah noticed Zorach watching Morgalla and wondered if there was something wrong. She felt a bit concerned for her young apprentice.

✿

Fall's in full swing.

Autumn always depressed Jasper, especially in this town. He took the long way to work; though it added ten minutes, as the roads were in better condition and saved wear on his car. It was Jasper's turn to drive this morning, with Andy riding shotgun. Andy was talking about...something, but Jasper wasn't paying attention. He usually caught half of what Andy said because he had to pay attention to driving, but lately he had more on his mind. The radio was playing; currently it was on a news break about the latest thing that President Fletch was doing. Neither of them gave any attention to the sound bites.

They arrived at the Springdale Public Library. Like many things within the town it was old and run-down. The parking lot was filled with holes and cracks and the sidewalk wasn't any better. The brick was crumbling and left red dust wherever it fell, and the building didn't even have a ramp for the handicapped.

They walked through the back door, an employee entrance, since the building wasn't open yet. Jasper swiped his employee ID to the card reader and unlocked the door. He and Andy each put on a fake smile to deal with their baby-boomer co-workers. They found it ironic that it was cloudy both outside *and* inside.

"Hi Barbara," they said as they walked past one desk, only to get no reply whatsoever.

"How you doing?" Jasper stopped to ask, but still got no reply. "Have a great day!"

"Hi there, boys."

They both looked to see the face of Sandy, the only ray of sunshine within the building.

"Hi." They both replied to her.

"Say, I don't suppose one of you strong boys could help an old woman out with something?"

"Only because you flatter us." Andy replied.

"There are some boxes on the back dock I need brought up here."

"You got it, Sandy." Jasper said.

"Thanks, guys. No rush, just sometime before lunch."

They walked on to the break room for their morning coffee. It might not have been as good as at a coffee house, but at least it was free, and in their condition they had to be fiscally responsible.

"There's no *way* that woman was at Woodstock," Andy muttered.

"Yeah, tell me about it," Jasper replied. He still did his best to prevent anyone else from bringing his good mood down, even if it was completely fake.

Another familiar face exited the break room, full coffee mug in hand.

"Hiya, Ron, how you doin'?" Jasper asked with a genuine smile.

"Shitty," was the reply he got. "Bunch of crap from the higher-ups. They're making me be the bad guy. Just irks me, you know?"

"Irks?" Jasper asked.

"Irks." Ron replied.

"Irks." Andy said with a nod.

As Ron walked off Andy had to hold back the laughter. Even though Ron completely disrespected him, he still found the situation humorous. Ron was actually closer to their age, but years of alcohol and smoking had taken their toll on him. In his youth he was skinny, but his horrible diet had made him balloon up to over two hundred pounds.

"He's irked." Andy said.

"I'm gonna stop asking," Jasper said.

"Yeah, that's the only reply you ever get from the jerk."

"Hey, Walker!" Ron yelled from down the hall. "Sherry needs you in the office, pronto!"

"Can it wait?" Andy replied with frustration, for he looked forward to the coffee first.

"What does the word *pronto* mean to you?" Ron replied with aggravation.

"Okay, fine." Andy was angry, but held back the urge to call Ron a name to his face.

"Sorry, dude." Jasper said.

Jasper continued on to the break room. He was glad to see that he was the only one there, welcoming some peace and quiet before what was sure to be another rough day.

The aroma of Colombia's finest beans flowed through Jasper's nose. That and the warmth of the coffee cup were emotional therapy. He tried his best to think positively, determined to keep that mind-set for the entire day.

"Davis!" a voice bellowed.

Of course, it was too good to last.

He had not noticed Wilbur walk into the break room. You would think that someone with bones as old as his would make more of a "creaking" noise. Jasper did not want to snap out of his aroma-induced trance, but he'd rather not be yelled at anymore.

"Davis!" Wilbur yelled again.

Jasper turned to look at him, a man of at most eighty pounds and an entire head shorter. The man's age had brought a hump to his back and his face was contorted into a permanent scowl. His bones were so feeble that Jasper was afraid to shake his hand the day they met, out of fear of breaking it. It took less than a day for Jasper to learn to hate him.

"Yes?" Jasper asked, holding back every bit of frustration.

"I left papers on your desk," the old man snapped. "I want it done by the end of the day!"

"How many papers?" Jasper asked out of curiosity.

Wilbur was about to turn and leave, but Jasper's question—stupid, in the old man's opinion—made him stop and give a look that clearly implied "I can't believe you just said that."

"*You* don't have to worry about that!" Wilbur yelled. "Just do it!"

"Sure thing," Jasper muttered, his voice soft. Then he took a sip of his coffee.

"Watch yourself, or I'll find *more* work for you!" Wilbur sneered at him, and left.

Jasper rolled his eyes and shook his head in frustration. Normally he would state his frustration to the man who was difficult to work for, but he was afraid that if he raised his voice higher than a whisper he might scare the man to death—literally. He could talk to Sherry, their mutual boss, but that was hopeless too. She did not want anything to do with the problem.

The Springdale Public Library was a place run by the greedy, lazy, and unethical. Years of dust covered the tops of the bookshelves. Outdated materials, including an encyclopedia set twelve years old, sat among the crumbling reference section. There were history books that didn't tell how the Cold War ended and technical journals that didn't mention the Internet. Patches of carpet were worn to the floor, and some fluorescent lights flickered and were in need of replacing. Tables meant for study were scarred with people's initials and the undersides were littered with a few decades' worth of gum. Years of abuse had taken their toll on the library. Working in a place such as this was a match made in Jasper's worst nightmare.

He went to his desk behind circulation, and sure enough, there was a pile of paperwork at least two feet high.

Oh, come on! You're too freaking old to know how to use a computer properly, so I have to do most of your work?

His fist clenched for a brief moment as if he were about to explode, but he sighed and his shoulders slumped. In his mind there was nothing he could do. Jasper sat at the desk; it faced Wilbur's office, and he could see him from the side staring at his computer. It took the old man half the day just to type a memo. Jasper looked up from his work every now and then to sneak a peek at Wilbur. Every time, he was at his computer, just *staring* at the screen.

Wilbur Wellington, the man who made other workaholics look lazy. It was common knowledge that he had served in one of the major wars. He said it was World War II, but many speculated that it was actually World War I. He claimed once to know Eisenhower, but someone joked that he actually knew Lincoln. Wilbur was there at the construction of the library many years ago, but again jokes and speculation ran amok.

"His desk was the first thing in and he was working at the same time as the construction workers!" one woman joked. "They built the library *around* him!"

These jokes and mockery would be all over the break room. Jasper would never join in when he first started working there. He thought it was disrespectful to talk that way about someone behind his or her back. It took only a couple of hours on his first day of work before his pity for the man died a mercy death. He still did not join in the jokes, though, for someone might get him in trouble. Who knew working in a library was so cutthroat?

Jasper came across another file that confused him. The numbers for the budget really weren't adding up, from his perspective. He was by no means an accountant, and staring at numbers all day gave him a headache. All of these records really should be in the hands of Wilbur, due to his authority.

He got up and walked through the open door of Wilbur's office. He did not speak out of fear of startling the old man. With file in hand he approached, hoping that his boss would notice him out of the corner of his eye.

"Um...Wil—er, Mr. Wellington?" Jasper said in a soft voice, but there was no movement or sound from the old man.

Damn it. He's fallen asleep at the computer again.

"Mr. Wellington?" Jasper asked again, just a tad louder.

The last time he woke the old man he regretted it. He startled Wilbur, though it was unintentional. Jasper thought the unthinkable, but he had to be sure. His hand, gentle as could be, touched Wilbur's shoulder. The old man slumped forward, and his face fell flat against the computer screen.

✢

Morgalla walked out of the bookstore, a small bag in her hand. She looked to the sky and saw the black clouds approaching fast. She put her new book in her pocket.

Damn.

She walked at a quickened pace for home, hoping that she could make it. As the rain came, she put up her hood and buried her hands deep in her pockets.

"DAMN!"

She stopped under the canopy of a diner and hoped the water pouring from the heavens would stop before it got too late. Besides the light from the diner, the only color would be the red and green of the traffic light.

Jasper was on his way home. His stomach rumbling, he thought what might sound good for a late dinner. As he stopped at the red light, he couldn't help but notice the small form in front of the diner. He recognized her.

Jasper looked forward, the bright red light taking forever to change. He looked at her and then back to the light. He rolled down his window.

"Hey!"

Morgalla looked to the source. Not feeling the presence of a soul from the vehicle, she had a hunch as to who it was. She stepped as close as she could to the edge of the awning and saw Jasper's face bathed in red light.

"You waiting on a ride?" he asked.

"Um...no, it's okay!"

"You *got* a ride?"

"Really, it's okay."

"Look, it's no trouble if you need a ride."

She crossed her arms and shivered slightly as the night air blew. The rain was coming down hard now and she had no confidence that it would let up any time soon. She was over a mile from the portal to Hell.

"Would it help if I told you that I'm harmless?" Jasper asked.

"That's *not* my concern," she replied with a smirk.

"It's cold and rainy. I'm headed up that way, I can drop you if you want."

The way in which Jasper pointed *was* the same way she was going and the thought of dealing with a long rainy walk was unappealing. Morgalla ran to the car, hopped in the passenger seat and rolled up the window. Taking down her hood she managed a smile at him.

"So where are you going?" Jasper asked.

"About a mile up the road."

"Sure. By the way, I'm Jasper."

The young woman looked forward, rubbing her hands together for warmth.

"I'm...Morgalla."

"My friends call me Jazz."

"Thanks, Jasper."

It was rare for her to converse with anyone, but this was strange to her. Usually she could feel the soul of the person she was with, but Jasper was a virtual blank.

"You live up at the apartment complex?" Jasper asked.

She thought a moment and figured out that he was speaking about the apartments next to the construction site where the portal to Hell was.

"Oh, yeah."

"Cool place. My friend Andy and I looked into moving into there."

The rain only came down harder now, forcing Jasper to drive slower and turn the wipers on fast. Morgalla didn't want to admit it, but she was glad she wasn't walking in it.

"Looks like I came along at the right time," he said.

Morgalla looked to his smiling face.

"Yeah, my hero."

"Look, how did you know about that guy at the bar?"

"I just have a pretty good sense about violence, I guess."

"I guess that can come in handy sometimes."

"More often than you know," she said as she looked out the window.

"You don't get out much, do you?"

"Oh, I get out all the time."

"I mean with people."

"What makes you say that?" she asked.

"Just an observation, a hunch. I've seen you at the library, haven't I?"

"Yeah, it's quiet."

"Quiet is an understatement. Sometimes the place can be a tomb."

"But sometimes the people there can be really tense," she said. "It can be...aggravating."

"You have no idea," he muttered under his breath.

"And it's always the people who *work* there, for the most part."

Jasper laughed and shook his head which made Morgalla look at him.

"What is it?"

"It *is* the people who work there who are the most tense. I thought working at a library would be easy."

"Well, you look like the kind of person who can handle a little stress."

"Oh, I can handle it," he said with a smirk. "Just don't expect me to like it."

The rain continued to pour down, making it hard for Jasper to see even with the windshield wipers going at full speed. The car could only move at a crawl.

"So where do you work?" he asked.

"Oh, here and there," she replied with nervousness in her voice.

He saw the lights of the apartment complex and pulled into the parking lot. Thankfully there was a covering for the parking spots as Jasper pulled in.

"Thanks," she said as she ran her hand through her raspberry hair. "Let me ask you something: Why did you do that?"

"It's pouring rain, why wouldn't I?"

His words and the look on his face had the greatest of sincerity. She could not tell from his soul if he was telling the truth, she only had what was before her.

"I...forget I asked. Again, thank you."

She got out of the car. In his mind, Jasper shrugged. Pulling out of the parking lot, Morgalla saw the red lights of his car pull away into the night. She waited there for a while longer before the rain let up and then continued on to the construction site and then to home.

✡

Everyone has nightmares, but only little children are supposed to be disturbed by them.

A beautiful woman with long dark hair rolled over in the king-sized bed; her dark hair all messed up from a long night's sleep. She woke completely when she felt nobody next to her.

"James?" she said, looking around, her English accent as lovely as she was.

She heard a sound coming from the bathroom, the familiar sound of water running and splashing. She rose and reached for her silk robe, and walked to the bathroom to find him there, hunched over the sink. He was splashing cold water on his face and running it through his hair. He gave a sound of misery, though it was muffled because his hands were on his face.

"God." was the only word he said that she understood.

"Happened again?"

"This morning was the worst one yet."

"This isn't going to get any better, James," she said with concern. "You should see a doctor."

"I *have* seen doctors," he groaned, looking up at her, his hair and face soaking wet. "I've taken every medical test and spoken with a hundred shrinks."

"And all they do is prescribe drugs which do little to nothing."

He rose and reached for a towel to dry himself off. He rested against the tile wall and she walked up to him, her gentle hands on his chest for comfort.

"Don't worry about me, Rebecca. It's my problem, I have to get over it."

"You wake up almost every morning as if you're hung-over, even though you don't drink." Her voice was stern. "The nightmares finally started going away until a few weeks ago. What could it all mean?"

"I don't know."

"I think you *do*, James. And it's time to call in your father."

"He has enough problems." He hung his head now.

"James." She held his chin and made him look up at her. "Was it him? Was it that *thing* again?"

He didn't reply at first, but she knew the answer, looking in his eyes. A wife can tell sometimes.

"Yes," he said with melancholy. "It was him again."

"If it isn't in your head, and it isn't medical, then what could it be?" she asked. His silence frightened her. "James, what if it's a warning? A warning that it might be coming back!"

"No…it can't be." James was in denial and shook his head.

"James…please. You *must* go to your father."

✻

The family of Smythe was once a grand army of holy knights and wizards who studied the magical arts. Centuries ago, they fought the forces of Hell from invading their world. In recent years the Smythe fortune was not as great as it used to be and the family itself had dwindled down to barely a dozen. Three still studied the ways of the family's proud heritage; spending what time they had to prepare for a judgment they were sure would come.

Richard would also be troubled with a nightmare this late morning. It started off nice enough, with smells he had not smelled in a long time. It was his wife's perfume and the smell of her hair as they slept together. It was something he had not experienced for two decades. The nightmare continued with a woman's scream, and black liquid enveloped him like a living shadow.

He woke up in a king-sized bed in a clutter-filled room. He just lay there for a few minutes, the images and feelings of the dream running through his head. Words could not come to his mind, for the shock was still too new and fresh.

He found the strength to get out of bed and found his robe. With a wave of his hand the bed folded up into the wall, to reveal a bookcase in its place. He walked over to the desk that was covered with the oldest of books. There was also an array of strange objects that resembled pieces from a chemistry set.

The entire room was filled with objects that were ancient and appeared to have no value. There were stacks of books on the floor, overflowing from the shelves. There were rolls of parchment and bottles, some filled and some empty. In an umbrella stand there were staffs of wood, some of which were too short to be used for anything. They all were old and engraved by expert hands that were long dead.

This was the only room the maids were not allowed in, and it showed from the dust. The man seemed to match the room. Though he was not "old" by any definition—he could not have been more than fifty—his face and body were worn beyond his years. The stress was self-inflicted due to the work he had been doing for two decades. His face was unshaven and he was long overdue for a haircut. The bags under his eyes were scars from the many nightmares that plagued him.

He hit a button on the phone to listen to voice mail. He was still massaging his closed eyes trying to wake himself up.

"Hi, this is yourself speaking." The voice mail made him open his eyes completely. "Reminding you of your meeting today with Fred, the financial guy. You cannot be late."

He looked at the clock and realized he had less than an hour to get to the meeting.

"Damn it."

He showered and dressed as fast as he could. He had no time to choose what to wear, so he went with the first suit he found in the closet. He grabbed a scone for breakfast and ate it as he walked to the front door. He rushed through the extravagant mansion he and generations before him called home. It was virtually deserted except for one of his housekeepers, who was nowhere to be found at the moment.

He walked quickly through the lobby to the front door, which opened by itself. He looked up and was nearly startled out of his mind by a figure that was walking up to the door at the exact same time as he.

"James!" he shouted, startled.

"Sorry," the man before him said. "In a hurry?"

"Meeting our financial advisor," he replied, as he noticed the look on the younger man's face. "Are you all right?"

"I…it's nothing, really, but Rebecca insisted that I come see you."

"Must be important."

"It can wait. You have a meeting to get to."

"*Nothing* is more important that this," he said, as he motioned for James to enter. They retreated to the study. "Is the nightmare back?"

"Yes," James conceded.

"Mine is back, too."

The remark caught James's attention and he looked concerned.

"What could this possibly mean?" the son asked.

The father didn't reply. As they entered the study, James was not surprised to see it in the state of disorder it usually was in. He sat in the chair in front of the desk and his father sat before him on the other side.

"Have you been keeping up on your skills?" Richard asked, as he searched through belongings on the desk.

"Yes, of course, but—"

"Akira said that he and his people are ready at a moment's notice. There are times that I think he's more dedicated to this than we are."

"But what about the—"

Richard picked up the phone and dialed a number. After a few rings, someone finally answered.

"Hi, it's me," Richard stated. "I'm sorry, but I'm going to be a little late. Don't worry, I'll buy you lunch, your choice. I'll call you back."

He hung up before he even got an answer, something that might make other people think he was being rude.

"He's mad, isn't he?" James asked, with only a little concern.

"He'll get over it. I pay him well enough," Richard shrugged with a smile. "Oh, and I found another wizard."

"Where from?"

"China. I want to bring him out here for a talk."

"What about the dream?" James brought up the subject again, but he didn't get an answer, with his father deliberately changing the subject.

"Oh, and I found a new spell—"

"*Father.*"

"Fine." Richard sighed, knowing he had no choice in the matter. "I once had the same dream, years ago, for a few weeks."

"And?"

"It was before your mother died."

James was speechless and he felt the knot in his stomach return. His pulse raced and his skin was clammy. He didn't know what to say next.

"Wh-what do we do?"

"Plan for the worst, James. If they were premonitions before, then this time we *must* act."

"Yes, I know, but—"

"Come here, there's something I need to show you." Richard stood and walked to the window. There was a small table with a medallion in the midst of the thick dust. "What do you think of this?"

"A…talisman of some sort?" James asked, as he was presented the seemingly innocent-looking item.

"More like a deadly weapon."

There was no flash of light, no impressive metamorphosis, but only a quick change and the medallion was now a large and imposing knife in Richard's hand. James was surprised but he didn't show it. After all, through the years he had seen many wondrous things in this mansion.

"My father, the wizard." A smile came over James's face, the first time in a while, upon seeing the amazing use of magic.

"Akira found the spell," Richard said. "A weapon invented by a Japanese sorcerer centuries ago. It's called a Shadowblade."

"Amazing!"

"One combines an ordinary trinket with a magical weapon, now hidden in plain sight. Akira believes that the spell might have been stolen by…*them*. They tried to destroy evidence of its existence, but lucky for us it survived."

Richard handed the blade to James and he held the knife in his hand. It took only a moment to change back into the medallion.

"It doesn't last long out of the intended user's hand, I'm afraid," Richard continued. "This particular weapon is made for my touch and my touch only. Not to worry, I can make one for you and Rebecca for your trip."

"Trip?"

"Yes, you're going somewhere for an investigation."

"And where would we be going?"

"Well, it was the dream again," Richard reiterated, as he went back to his chair. "I cannot explain it, nor was the dream clear with names, but I just *know* of someplace that is in danger."

"But surely if it returns it will be here."

"I don't think so. Call it a hunch or a gut reaction, James, but I just know it."

"But what if you're wrong, Father?" James asked, concerned for his father.

"That's why you and your wife are going. If need be you can call in reinforcements and we'll be there. I've already booked your flight."

"Flying? Why not just use the stones?"

"Because if you were to use magical travel and there were any of *them* there, they would sense your presence. No, best use as much stealth as you can."

There was a silence as James walked to the window, looking out over the sea that he had remembered looking upon since he was a child. He still held the medallion in his hand, looking at the engraved image on it.

"One of these will certainly make it easier to take a *sword* through customs," he smirked.

"Were you just coming here to tell me about the dream?"

"No, it's not just that. There is something new in the dream now."

"Please, tell me," Richard said, leaning forward.

"There was...a roaring of some sort in the distance." James now stared out the window. "Like everyone cheering for something at once. But there was something to it that made it sound horrific. There was a, *lust*, a lust for war."

"An army."

With the word spoken James looked at his father now. He didn't dare speak the word, not even to himself, for it was too terrible to comprehend.

"There was something else. On top of the cheering there was an inhuman roar. There were just as many, they equaled the sound. I don't even want to guess what they were."

"Nor do I," Richard agreed. "I only had one other dream as vivid and lurid and that one came true. This time I vowed to be ready."

✿

The stacks of books were taller than her. But then again, most things were taller than her. The book the child carried was very big and heavy. She didn't even know the subject matter, nor did she care, but its size would fit her needs. She had arranged books into four walls and within she had set the largest book down to sit upon. Within her small fortress of knowledge, Morgalla would fill her mind with lessons that her mistress had commanded.

The ceiling of this chamber was huge with multiple levels. There were shelves that seemed to go on forever atop iron catwalks. Dusty books were about on the floors and shelved in what seemed to be no order. There were no signs of life except for one small figure, a child of twelve.

Virtually all demons by the time they were twelve year old had already executed their first lesser being by then but Delilah had kept Morgalla among the stacks of Hell's library. Delilah had fallen asleep high upon one of the shelves. The sound of the large book plopping down upon the catwalk had woken her. Her limbs, all six, stretched the fatigue from her body and she rose up. She gave her red dragon wings a few flaps to return the circulation and then gave a leap off of the shelf. She glided down to where she had left her apprentice, finding her within the four walls.

"Constructed your own little castle, I see." Delilah noted.

"Uh huh."

"Finish the lesson?"

"Yes, mistress."

"Let's see."

The girl held up a few sheets of parchment; upon the first was her name written many times. Delilah took the sheets in her claws and flipped through them to see many other words spelled out. Morgalla kept her eyes to the book in front of her. Her voice had a sound of aggravation and slipped closer to anger. Delilah, as she looked over the child's writing, couldn't help but notice that the utensil her pupil had been using was digging deeper and deeper into the paper. She found the final page curious, seeing some doodles; a drawing of a woman with red skin and wings, a sword in her hand.

"You're improving, child. Excellent."

"That purple boy made fun of me the other day."

"Oh? What did he do?"

"He told me all about how great his family is and how I'm nothing."

"Striking him might be fulfilling for sure," the dragon-demon said. "But it could cause friction between his family and yours. They are powerful, do not forget."

"I won't. I just...*hate* him..."

"Yes, I know." Delilah assured. "Look at me, child."

Morgalla obeyed, looking up to meet her mistress's eyes. Delilah's clawed hands rested upon the wall of books in front of her.

"He is to never touch you," Delilah stated with conviction. "If he does...you are to tell me. Understand?"

"Are you going to kill him?" Morgalla asked with a look of concern.

"Oh no. I'll just cut off his hand. Don't worry, it will grow back. That will be warning enough."

Morgalla giggled as Delilah gave a smirk and a wink. The woman then crawled down to the floor and made her way through the castle's entrance. Master sat next to student for a moment of silence.

"Morgalla, I mean it. He is not to touch you."

"I understand, mistress."

"Do you think the Master of Knowledge will be angry with your little...redecorating?" Delilah asked, referring to the castle.

"These books were unshelved."

"Librarians love their books. To them, they are the bricks that make up their kingdom."

"I'm making the library look nicer!" The girl proclaimed.

Delilah's laugh filled the high ceiling, making it sound like an ancient cavern. She then looked over to the open book Morgalla had been looking into. There were pictures on the pages of beaches, the sun shining upon the sand and crystal-clear water.

"Where did you find this?" Delilah asked.

"It's pretty."

"I guess. But all that sun? I'm sure it's nice and hot but...too bright."

Delilah's head suddenly snapped and her eyes averted to another part of the chamber. She sensed the presence of others entering as quiet as they could. She stood and looked over the wall of books, then down from the catwalk to the entrance far below.

"I think it would be nice to have a house on the beach. What does the ocean smell like?"

"Shh…" Delilah commanded.

Peering down to the main hall, there was a group of demons that had entered and tried to be as stealthy as possible. They were dressed in black, their features hidden from view but Delilah could with ease feel their souls but their intent was not clear to her.

"There are others here," she whispered to her young apprentice.

"Who?"

"They're from the family of the purple boy."

"Eww."

"Yes." Delilah agreed and extended her hand. "We should go."

"Can I take the book with me?"

"I…I guess. I doubt the Master would notice a book like that missing."

Delilah took the girl in her arms and gave a leap off of the catwalk and glided down through the darkness. By the time the two of them hit the light of the main hall and the group of demons noticed them. Delilah with the child in her arms had already swooped to the main gate and flew out.

The Master of Knowledge had been returning, walking up the cobblestone path that lead to his kingdom. An older demon, one who imposed his will upon the youth of Hell. Instead of joining the many wars fought upon many worlds, he kept his nose in books. Now he had grown in power that demons as young as Delilah dared not cross him directly. Delilah flew past him in a blur, the air tearing as her wings flapped.

"You better not have taken any of my books!" He shouted.

Morgalla held on with both arms and legs as Delilah's powerful limbs kept her apprentice close to her. The book was pressed between their bodies, a new treasure that the child wasn't going to lose. Delilah flew towards Zorach's castle but would land in a court-yard some walking distance away from it. She set Morgalla down and then looked about as if she were searching for something.

"Velleau!" Delilah called out.

"Over here."

Both ladies looked to see a demon step forth from the shadows of stone. He was dressed as if he came from wealth and power, dripping with gold from his expensive robes.

"Did you get it?" Delilah asked.

"Yes, of course. You know I had to pull some favors for this."

"No gratitude for saving your life? And here, I thought you came from one of the more honorable families."

"Do you *always* exploit those in your debt?"

"It's not for me," Delilah said. "It's for her."

"Ah yes. The daughter of Zorach?"

Velleau gave a nod to the girl, who in return gave a little wave. Morgalla never left Delilah's side, staying close and holding onto her coak.

"But you got it, right?" Delilah asked.

"Yes, yes. I got it."

The blue blood held out a small draw-string bag and handed it to Delilah. She knelt and opened the bag, pouring the contents to the ground. A single item fell out. It was a medallion with seem-ingly unimpressive features. Both Delilah and Velleau were careful not to touch the trinket with their bare hands.

"Come," Delilah spoke to her ward. "Hold out your hand."

Morgalla was confused but did as she was told. Delilah took hold of her, making sure that the girl's hand was directly above the medallion. Velleau stood a few feet away, picking something from between his teeth with his pinky claw.

"Now close your eyes."

Again, the child did as she was instructed though her pulse quickened. With the speed of a bullet and the precision of a surgeon, Delilah took out a small blade and made a razor-thin cut upon the child's palm. Morgalla's eyes were open again as she let out a slight cry of pain. Delilah held her wrist, making sure that drop of blood fell upon the trinket at her feet. Morgalla looked at her palm, seeing that the cut had already healed itself thanks to her demonic powers. Delilah took the decoration by its tiny chain and lifted it from the ground.

"Excellent," Delilah said. "Here, take it. It's yours!"

Morgalla took hold of the gift.

"For me?"

Her teacher smiled and nodded. The child would be shocked to see the metal in her hand change to that of a blade as long as she was tall. The sudden weight change surprised her and she dropped the weapon.

"Easy there," Delilah said. "Not to worry, you'll get used to it. Soon it will feel like you're carrying no weight at all."

With both hands the young girl held the sword up. Morgalla could see her reflection upon it. She lost strength in her shoulders and set the blade down. She fell to her knees and set the blade upon her lap, still marveling upon the craftsmanship, a work of art meant to kill.

"There are few things in this life that you can trust, Morgalla."

Morgalla looked up to her mistress with a smile. Delilah did not return it but instead looked upon the weapon.

"I trust you!" The child replied.

"Others cannot be trusted. But this…a weapon in your hands, at your control. You are its mistress. *That* you can trust!"

"I…I don't know."

"I will not always be there for you," Delilah said as she stood. "Do not look to another to save you. Do not look to a male to be your hero. This sword will be your hero."

Morgalla looked again up to her mentor and then back to the gift in her hands. It took only a moment to decide a name for her new friend.

Hero.

✡

As her strawberry-shaped alarm clock woke her, Morgalla realized that she was late for an appointment with her teacher....again. She swore and rushed to get dressed.

There had been many human beings who had sought out Morgalla's father for assistance. The promise of power beyond their wildest imaginations was an enticing seduction for one whose will was weak and whose hate was strong. There were others whose fear was also so strong that they joined him only to avoid being cattle for the slaughter. The idea of being a pet was far more appealing to them. As for Morgalla, though...she wanted neither.

Morgalla was late for practice with her trainer and mentor, Delilah. She walked down a large well-lit hallway. She was in her demon form, dressed in a violet cat suit, which left her arms bare. She also wore a long dark violet coat and a medallion around her neck.

The walls of the hallway were tall and made of dark crimson stone. Large wooden doors lined either side. There were light fixtures attached, with tiny gems magically glowing brightly for light instead of light bulbs or flames.

Morgalla continued to count the doors as she walked down.

When will they number these damn things?

She approached one and was about to enter when suddenly it opened and Necrod stepped out. Morgalla stepped back, grasping her medallion tightly as he looked at her. He smiled wickedly, but she could sense something from him that was different. He was spent, tired from what could have been a hard workout. Putting two and two together she realized what he and Delilah had been doing. She looked slightly disgusted and could feel the bile rise up in her throat.

"Bye-bye, lover!" Delilah yelled to Necrod from inside the room. Her beast of a boyfriend gave a slight look back at Delilah. "Now go."

Necrod did as he was commanded and walked away, and Morgalla stepped into the room. Delilah had a short sword in hand and practiced different moves with it. The room was large, with a high ceiling, and the walls and floor were made of stone. Morgalla removed her long coat and began to stretch her muscles.

"You're *late*."

"They need to number the doors," Morgalla replied.

"You will be practicing your offensive skills. You defend too much."

"Just my style, that's all."

"You will never claim victory with that attitude."

"It's a good thing I was late," Morgalla said. "Otherwise, I might have interrupted something."

"Perhaps," Delilah snickered, as Morgalla continued to prepare herself. "You need not worry. He looks upon you with lust and would have you if he could…but he shall not."

"You do not have to do me any favors," Morgalla assured her.

"It is no favor to you. He is mine! He's lucky I do not punish him for looking at you! Now attack!" Delilah gave a command and took hold of her short sword with both hands.

Delilah was ready for Morgalla's assault. She held up her sword in an offensive manner. Morgalla stretched her hamstrings and appeared to ignore Delilah. She looked over at Delilah, who remained motionless, frozen in her stance. Morgalla rolled her eyes and then slowly rose to her feet. The medallion around her neck transformed into a short sword. As it transformed, it went from around her neck to her hand in a flash. Morgalla warmed up a bit more, twirling the sword. Delilah became impatient, with her eyes fixed on Morgalla.

"Hello?" Delilah called.

"In a minute!" Morgalla knew she was annoying her teacher. She took a deep breath; finally, her preparation was finished. "Okay, now I'm ready!"

Morgalla and Delilah sparred with each other, practicing their dueling skills. They were both masterful, the weapons moving as two blurs of magical steel cutting through the air. Delilah tried to taunt and trick her into attacking, but Morgalla remained in her defensive mode. For years they had sparred with each other. Delilah had taught Morgalla all she knew, but something new must be thrown into the mix to keep her apprentice's skills sharp. They suddenly stopped.

"You're doing it again," Delilah said with annoyance in her voice. "Quit defending and go for the kill!"

Morgalla said nothing. Delilah again lunged forward, attacking. Their movements were quick as they clashed. Morgalla did her best to defend, but Delilah gave her a small cut on her shoulder. Morgalla felt the slight sting and dropped to one knee. She looked at the cut; it healed completely within a few seconds, thanks to her demon powers. Morgalla was more shocked at what Delilah had just done. She looked up and met Delilah's intense gaze.

"Never show mercy," Delilah ordered.

They continued to spar, using masterful skills. Delilah might've been the master, but every now and then Morgalla would surprise her. A kick here or punch there; once she even disarmed her. Today it was Delilah who did the surprising. The cut on Morgalla's shoulder, tiny and already healed, left her wondering. After a long duel they stopped, both women sweating and breathing heavily. The swords then changed back into medallions around their necks.

"Are you trying to *kill* me?" Morgalla exclaimed, almost afraid of the answer.

"Keeping your skills sharp," Delilah replied.

Some time passed, as both women sat on the floor against the wall. They drank water from bottles and Morgalla told Delilah of recent events.

"So did he bleed much?" Delilah inquired.

"I didn't make him *bleed* at all!"

Delilah snickered again at Morgalla's reply and her mood.

"Was he somewhat cute?" Delilah was practically begging for details now. "At least you could have used him once."

"Used?" Morgalla was almost afraid of the answer.

"For pleasure," Delilah said. "Sex with humans is seldom good but often amusing. But the most fun comes at the end, when you kill them."

"Why don't you have that attitude with Necrod?"

"I might kill him...someday," Delilah pondered aloud. "For now he's quite...*valuable*, if you get my drift."

Morgalla winced again in disgust and her teacher laughed.

"You certainly do like the strong and silent type," Morgalla noticed.

Delilah slowly leaned in to her. "Men are to be seen, not heard," she whispered, and then relaxed against the wall. "You know, you're wound up too tight. Have you ever done anything spontaneous? Perhaps taken something that didn't belong to you?"

"I'm not the 'taking' type," Morgalla said, and looked away. "Besides, hasn't the *Dark One* forbidden us from sleeping with humans?"

"I think that's just having a *child* with them," Delilah said. "Besides, the *Dark One* can't see all that we do, hmm?"

"Of course, when I say *something* I actually mean *someone*." As Delilah talked, she drifted off, as if in her own little world. "Humans can be quite amusing during sex. Hearing him scream, in a mixture of pain and pleasure. Feeling his heart pound in his chest, quickly at first, then slower...and slower. As his blood flows from his body, so does his life. He screams at first, then a moan, then a light whimpering. Just like a baby. There was this one time—"

"I gotta go," Morgalla interrupted. She stood and walked to the door, carrying her coat.

"Consider what I said," Delilah ordered, as Morgalla looked back. "I think you'll be better off. For crying out loud, you don't even connect with *me* half the time. Would it *kill* you to connect with someone? If even for a little while?"

Morgalla had nothing to say, no rebuttal, for she knew Delilah was right. She looked away and contemplated.

"I...I guess it wouldn't," Morgalla shrugged.

"Brexus is having a feast tonight at his castle, I've been invited. Why not come?"

"I don't know," Morgalla pondered, as she looked off to the side. "His kids give me the creeps."

"You may have a point there," Delilah replied with a laugh of agreement. "You got Hero?"

"Right here." She replied with a point to the shadowblade medallion around her neck.

Morgalla stepped out into the hallway, closing the door behind her. She put her coat on and walked down the hall with much on her mind. Just when she thought that Delilah might be nice, Morgalla was reminded of how she thinks. Though Delilah's "interests" and way of thinking often disgusted her, she had a point. She also reminded Morgalla just how important it was not to tell anyone what she really thought.

As Morgalla walked, there were three demons in the shadows peering out at her. They were three young males, their minds filled with lust. She walked as if she did not notice them, taking a drink of water.

"Hello there, pretty lady," a voice called.

Morgalla stopped, letting out a sigh. She had hoped they were going to let her pass without incident, but not today. This was only going to end one way. Morgalla turned to see one of the young males standing before her. Her eyebrows rose slightly at the sight of him.

"What's a young tiny thing like you doing all alone here?"

"Tiny?" Morgalla was a bit annoyed by his comment.

"Yes," he said. "One as small as you surely is in need of protection!"

"Judge me by my size, do you?"

Suddenly, one demon leaped out of the shadows at her to attack, but she quickly gave a kick to his face, knocking him to the ground. Quickly, she had her sword out, ready to fight them off as the other two joined the fight. The two attacked, but Morgalla parried with superior skills for which she had Delilah to thank. Weapons clashed as they fought. She kicked one to the side and he fell to the ground. The first one she kicked was up and tackled her to the ground, as another went to hold down her arms.

The first male with all his might tried to spread her legs open, but her ankles grasping his neck thwarted him. With a quick twist, there was a snap and he fell over. With her knee, she hit the other in the face, smashing his nose and causing it to explode with blood. She was up again, grasping her sword, and fought with one of them. He quickly realized that he was outmatched and backed up against the wall. It did not take long for Morgalla to defeat him; his head left his shoulders with a quick swipe of her blade.

The male with the broken nose got up reaching for his sword, his face painted in rage, blood flowing down his mouth and chin. He grasped his sword tightly while Morgalla stood, not letting the same anger control her. She looked at him with a calm face, ready for his attack. He lunged forward and their weapons clashed again. He roared at her, another mistake she would capitalize on. He was enraged as he attacked, roaring and snarling. With superior aptitude, she fought him until finally, with a quick slice of her blade, his arm was cut off just below the elbow. He fell to the ground screaming, his blood flowing black onto the stone floor.

She raised her weapon, ready to finish him, but he held up his other hand in defense.

"Please," he begged, holding up his good limb. "No more!"

Morgalla stopped, feeling pity for him, the very thing Delilah had warned her about. The blood from his severe wound flowed out. As she walked away, his arm began to regenerate. The blood flowed out, taking the form of an arm and hand. He fought the pain, his teeth grinding as Morgalla walked away. She stopped and contemplated whether leaving him was the right thing to do. She gave a brief glance back, knowing his nature and how he and the rest of her species thought. Today he begged for his life, tomorrow he would be back, filled with more lust and anger, and quite possibly more friends.

His hand and arm regenerated and the pain subsided. He breathed a sigh of relief and then looked around for his sword.

Suddenly, he turned to see Morgalla standing over him. She did not make eye contact as she swung her sword quickly again. This time, it was his head that fell instead of his arm.

Vex watched from the shadows, distraught at Morgalla's fighting abilities. He had hoped in the past to win Morgalla's heart, to woo her into thinking she should be his. Since his advances had been met with the cold shoulder he decided to take her as a prize instead. This happened often in the demon world. Morgalla could be owned by Vex, but it would not be easy. He had not known that Delilah had trained her so well. If he were to try and "take" her, she would put up a fight and he stood a good chance of losing. It would appear that he was in need of a third option.

✿

Mmm. . .red meat.

She stared down at the large burger burnt to a crisp, just how she liked it.

It was almost a sacred ritual to her, soaking in the ambiance and aroma of the surrounding area. The tables and chairs made of plastic and wood. All the colors of the rainbow were represented throughout the room and bright neon shone all over the front counter. The best part was the lively spirit within. Everyone appeared to be happy as they ate their delicious, unhealthy, high-calorie meals. Even the employees were happy. It must have been payday.

With a light grip she held the hamburger to her mouth and took the biggest bite she could, with a huge chomp. She sat alone for a while until a small group of teenage girls walked over and sat at the table next to her. Each of them had a cell phone, and each of them spoke with a high-pitched whine that rivaled a dog whistle. Their conversation was benign and annoying. Morgalla could not decipher what they were saying even if she were to concentrate. She rolled her eyes; the air was littered with the sounds of "um," "you know," and "whatever." All three of them pressed a button on their bright pink cell phones and folded them up. It did not matter how close or far away they were, the combined effort of their mediocrity was overwhelming.

"So, like, Robbie bought me these earrings for my birthday," one of them said.

"Oh my God, you're like *so* lucky to have a rich boyfriend."

"I wish *my* boyfriend made more money. As soon as I find someone better, he is, like, *so* gone."

Their voices all blended into one. Morgalla did not look over to see who was talking, for she did not care. Again, her keen hearing was a curse. She rolled her eyes, glancing at the flock of infantile estrogen.

My God, it's a cult.

They all looked alike in Morgalla's eyes. Their hair, clothes, makeup, and sound made them appear as if they had been brainwashed by someone like her father. But Zorach would never have tolerated such...annoyance. Not to mention so much pink.

Morgalla looked away, but could not bring herself to leave just yet; her curiosity got the better of her. The conversation, if one could call it that, was rather pointless, though enlightening from Morgalla's point of view.

The views of the three shallow females on relationships surprised Morgalla in many ways. They viewed males as a commodity, a natural resource to be used as they saw fit.

Morgalla ate the rest of her meal. The banter, though lacking wit, was filled with information. Morgalla dabbed her lips with a napkin and crumpled the empty paper containers.

Her sensitive ears continued to be bombarded by their moronic chitchat.

"You know, um, whatever."

So calm was Morgalla's demeanor and body language that the trio of bimbos never saw her verbal onslaught coming.

"You know, um, whatever."

"SHUT UP!" Morgalla yelled, getting the attention of many in the restaurant. "Shut...the...HELL...up!"

The three girls stared at her, literally lost for words as Morgalla's powers worked remarkably well.

"I have *no* interest in listening to any more of your witless, moronic prattle!"

Morgalla's eyes gazed upon them, the frustrations of her day being unleashed on the three unsuspecting girls.

"You're all shallow, materialistic little bitches who are going to get what you deserve! That's a fat ass, a trailer park home, and five kids from five different fathers! So be thankful that you're young and healthy, try to make yourselves better people by looking past someone's *looks* and money, and quit your complaining! Go finish your burgers, throw them up in the bathroom, and have a nice freaking day!"

She stared for a moment in anger, but just for a moment. She snapped out of her trance and looked around the room. Morgalla regained control and rose to her feet. The three girls were stunned. The reality of her words hit them hard and their eyes glistened, the tears ready to flow at any moment.

Morgalla looked around and decided to make an exit. She stood, the calmness once again taking control of her. She left the restaurant, with everyone else just a tad freaked out from what had just happened. There were many, though, who suddenly realized that Morgalla had just said what they were all thinking.

✼

Morgalla would later find herself in one of her favorite spots in this or any world. The early autumn breeze blew through the leaves of a lone oak tree, tall and powerful against all the challenges of nature. Morgalla sat alone beneath it, her back feeling the strength and stability of the oak. Often she had wished that the oak was not just a living being, but had the ability to talk. It already listened very well.

With the tree at her back and the sunset before her, Morgalla sighed as another day ended. The sun managed to peek just a bit from beneath the gray clouds of Springdale's bleak autumn for a few moments to deliver shades of red and orange. It was not until she saw the stars begin to emerge that she considered leaving, returning to her closet in Hell.

Dear Diary:

I lost control again. This time I told off three little teenage bimbos in my favorite restaurant. It was everything about them that made me lose it, their attitudes in particular. They're just as bad as anyone here, wanting to possess and control people instead of maybe...loving them. If there is such a thing as love. I'm far from an expert, but I can't imagine any relationship lasting that way.

People suck. Both in Hell and on Earth.

Chapter Six: We Meet Again

Jasper sat quietly in a chair in the office of the library. Andy was there, typing at his computer. From inside the conference room they heard the laughter of many women. He looked at the clock, and then went through his proposal again to make sure he had everything perfect.

"Know what you're going to say?" Andy asked as he typed at the keyboard.

"Yeah, I've been thinking of nothing else, really," Jasper replied. "All the ideas I've had for the past two years that Wellington never supported."

"He was too set in his ways."

"Maybe, but I think it was because he didn't like it when people wanted to run his department...or so he said. Is it just me, or is it really a bit *morbid* that the guy has only been dead for a day and we're already interviewing for his *job*?"

Andy looked around to see if anyone else was in the room. Seeing that it was clear, he leaned toward Jasper.

"I think Sherry was waiting for this," he murmured. "I mean, she couldn't fire Wilbur 'cause he had too many friends in high places. Come on, someone could have slammed a door too hard near him and the shock could have killed him."

"Well, it's just weird that people are pouncing on his job like it was solid gold or something."

"You know, maybe on your business cards you should spell your name differently. Instead of *Jasper*, maybe spell it *J-A-Z-Z*."

"Not very professional-sounding, is it? Unless I become a rock star or something."

Andy nodded in agreement and looked back at the computer screen. He tried to continue typing, but nothing happened to the document he was working on. His expression changed to one of annoyance as the computer froze.

"Oh, come on!" he exclaimed, slapping the side of the computer. "Damn it, nothing works around here! I swear, this place, this *town*, is the tenth layer of Hell!"

Jasper sympathized. . He had lost count of how many times the computers at circulation and most of the technology in the building failed. He was about to make a suggestion when one of their co-workers, one of the only ones close to their age, entered the office.

"Good morning, everyone!" He beamed the brightest of smiles.

"Hi, Landon." The young men spoke in unison, sounding disinterested.

"And how are you two this morning?"

"Fine," both men said.

"A great day for the environment," Landon said, newspaper in hand.

"Great day?" Jasper asked. "It's gray and colder than it should be for October."

"But didn't you hear what President Fletch did?" he asked.

His words caught both of their attention. Andy stopped trying to fix his computer and turned to look at him.

"What did His Highness do now?" Andy asked, mocking his former boss.

"They're gonna pass the 'Green Motorists' act," he continued with another smile.

"What act was that?" Jasper asked.

"Oh, Jazz, you really need to read more. I read about four newspapers a day. I've been a fan of President Fletch ever since he was in the Senate."

"No, you haven't," Andy interjected, as he spun around in the office chair to face him. "I remember you weren't a fan until he started pushing all those environmental laws."

"He's doing the right thing."

"Yeah, yeah, that's great," Andy said. "Isn't the 'Green Motorists' act where they penalize people for not driving electric cars or something?"

"*Penalize?*" Landon asked in disbelief. "Andy, it's the first step to saving the planet!"

"What are you talking about?" Jasper asked. Landon handed a newspaper to him.

Jasper stood and held the paper so that he and Andy could read it together. As they read the news about the new act signed into law, both of them felt foolish for not keeping up with what was going on. And then, they felt outrage.

"We'll have to pay *more* to register our license plates?" Jasper said in shock.

"Not if you drive a hybrid," Landon said. "The bigger the car, the more you have to pay."

"Well, thank God that neither of us drives a big car," Andy said.

"But we don't drive hybrids, *and* our cars are older. Look at this." Jasper pointed to another paragraph in the article.

"The older the car, the more someone is charged?" Andy read. "What for?"

"Well, older cars aren't *green*, of course!" Landon added. His tone indicated that Andy had asked a stupid question.

"Landon," Jasper said, "I'm going to be charged a *thousand* dollars a year just because of my car?"

"Jazz, we all have to do our part!"

"Fletch, that bastard, is going to make us drive electric cars that cost a fortune and can only go ten miles an hour!" Andy exclaimed, as he slammed the newspaper on the desk.

"It's not that bad. Just don't drive around so much."

"What do you mean?" Andy asked.

"DMV is going to make us register our odometers," Jasper said, as he slumped back into the chair. "The more you use your car, the more you're charged."

"We're being punished?"

"It's not punishment, it's what we need to do to save the environment!" Landon insisted.

The two men just sat there, both concerned but for different reasons. Andy was angry, feeling that government was abusing its power. Jasper, though, was worried whether or not he would be able to afford these new changes. He had until next summer to make more money. This job interview was now more important than ever.

"What the hell are we going to do?" Jasper asked. Andy looked at him.

"I can't believe you two!" Landon said, and stormed out.

Suddenly, the door opened and two women stepped into the office: Sherry, the head of the library, and Cynthia, one of Jasper's co-workers at the circulation desk. They were laughing together as if they had just come from a party. Jasper looked on with a worried expression on his face at the scene before him.

Oh crap. This can't be good.

Jasper stood, looking at them curiously, but he was ready for his interview. As soon as Sherry turned to see Jasper her smile was gone.

"Come on in," she said.

Jasper entered, sitting in a chair in front of a long table. The table was perpendicular to him, and four other women sat there, two on either side of Sherry. All of the women were older than fifty; many of them had been at the library for decades.

"So…," Sherry said with complete disinterest to the man before her.

"Yes?" Jasper said, smiling nervously.

"This is the part where you start to talk and tell us why you think you deserve the promotion."

"Oh, sorry, I thought you were going to ask me questions," he said.

"No, I don't handle interviews that way," she replied. "You've worked here for how long now?"

"Two years. Never called in sick, never been late."

Jasper looked at the other four women; one read a magazine and one was falling asleep.

"If you're given the job, Jasper, what do you plan to do differently?"

"Well, I have many ideas for how to organize the circulation desk." Jasper went on, opening his folder and taking out papers. "It could be more efficient, and we could start recycling paper for the environment and to save money."

"Uh-huh."

Jasper was silent a moment, seeing their lack of interest. He wondered if maybe this was a waste of time, but then realized that he needed this promotion.

"We could also work with the children's area and perhaps do something fun for kids," Jasper continued. "I mean, we could encourage kids to read and make the library a popular place—"

"Yes, yes. That's enough, *Jazz*. We'll let you know."

Jasper hesitantly put his papers away, got up and walked out. Sherry waited until the door closed and she heard the latch click. She looked at the other women.

"We've already got *one* man working in the office. That's enough."

Jasper was good at his job but he hated it, primarily for the same reason he hated school - he got yelled at a lot by strangers for things that were never his fault. He was still quite young, but part of him felt worn beyond his years. Jasper had done a lot of work at school, his job, and even relationships. The relations with women he felt were the most pointless. In recent years he had put more work into his love life than expected and gotten very little in return, other than regret.

Jasper seemed slow today, a pile of books upon the circulation desk was slowly being checked in. He looked at the time again, only a few minutes had passed. Cynthia was saying something to him but he wasn't paying attention. Finally the sound of a popular 80's song came from his pocket. He took his phone out to see the name "DAD" upon the screen.

"Excuse me." He said and walked to the shelves.

Among the silent bookshelves he answered his phone. A masculine voice was on the other end.

"Hi dad. How's she doing?"

"A lot better and in better spirits."

"What does her doctor say?"

"She's optimistic. She doesn't think it was as bad as some other people thought."

"Thank God for second opinions."

Jasper closed his eyes and took a deep breath.

"You want to talk to her?"

"Of course."

Next a woman's voice was on the phone, the voice weak.

"Hi, mom."

"Jasper!"

He looked over his shoulder to see Cynthia standing there with an angry look.

"I'll be there in a minute." He replied.

"I'm not checking in all these books by myself!"

"Okay, okay!"

He gave a brief farewell to his mother and closed his phone. He walked behind Cynthia, daggers being driven into the woman's back.

✿

Morgalla was on her bed, flat on her back and staring at the blank black slate that was her ceiling. She was still confused about why her powers would not work on Jasper. It was quite curious indeed, but she felt confident that there was nothing dangerous about him. It was a good thing she didn't have to fight her way out of there. The last thing she wanted to deal with was human authority figures.

She needed to cheer herself up. Rising out of bed finally, she headed to the decaying desk against her wall. She opened one of the drawers and took out a folder filled with clippings taken from many different magazines and books. They were all pictures of the beach, the classic white sands and clear blue sky that humans dream about going to and sometimes do. She, on the other hand, didn't have such a luxury.

It was torture, really. The happiness would not last long, though these few moments of imagination and hope would bring her at least some comfort as she flipped through the pages. She saw people surfing, something she had always wanted to try. She felt sure she could do it; it seemed easy enough.

It was like a drug. The feelings of happiness would only last for a little while, and the emptiness afterward was almost too difficult to bear. It wasn't until she saw the photo of the couple holding hands and walking on the beach that she decided to close the folder. Recent events seemed to be haunting her terribly, almost as if a sentient power was torturing her—or maybe guiding.

Morgalla was curious about the way humans dated and courted one another. Would it really hurt if she tried it once? The words of advice from Delilah rang in her ears, to do things she had never done before.

No one would want to date me. Demons only want to control one another. And humans will never accept me.

But in the back of Morgalla's mind there was a tiny voice, a voice of hope that maybe she was wrong. There was a part of her soul she could not explain that made her different from all other beings of Hell. The piece of her heart often spoke to her, as it did today.

Maybe a human could love you.

No they couldn't.

If not love, at least friendship.

A human with a demon for a friend? Or more than just friends? Doubtful. I can just picture me bringing him before my father.

As usual, Morgalla's talent for sarcasm started to shine through.

Hi, Daddy! This is my new boyfriend, a human being! You know, the people you want to torture, kill, and enslave?

Do you wish to spend the rest of your existence here in the closet they've given you as a home, doing nothing but talking to a ceiling?

Morgalla had no reply for that. Maybe…just maybe, the other part of her—the part that was not quite so cynical—was right.

✿

With her official report on the world Earth complete, Morgalla felt like celebrating, but wasn't sure exactly how. Sure, they would more than likely make her do more work, or make her investigate another world, but for now she had no obligations. She thought maybe Delilah would enjoy heading out somewhere, but then remembered how her mentor hated taking on human form. Delilah's age and experience certainly qualified her to have said ability, but the fact of the matter was that she was disgusted with the idea of looking like a human being.

Shenanigans had proven to be much like a demon bar with the violence. She decided that was out of the question; any place that served alcohol would be off her list. Morgalla thought maybe for a moment that visiting a world *other* than Earth might be fun. The beaches of Arani were often quite nice and she longed to feel hot sand on her bare feet again. Drawing attention to herself was not advised, but maybe she would hit it lucky. If someone at the portal chamber were slacking off, then maybe she could get away with sneaking out.

She sneaked into one of the many hallways, avoiding contact with anyone there. The halls branched off like the roots of a tree. They seemed to be assembled in a haphazard way, with no sense of construction or form. All chambers were of different sizes, some more protected than others. She rounded a corner, excited that she was almost there, but froze as a demon lord and his entourage met her.

Brexus.

Morgalla was about to dive for the cover of shadows but there were none. She was frozen as the beast turned to see her. His form was menacing, tall and massive, much like her father's. He was not as old as Zorach, but one could tell that his soul was already plummeting into a black abyss. He was dressed in black with gold decorations, in robes that flowed to the floor and seemed to breathe with unholy life. His face was so inhuman that one could not tell where his mouth or nose would be. But it was his eyes that caught the most attention; empty sockets where black smoke bled forth.

He and his entourage looked at Morgalla. He smiled with black teeth and held up his hands, his thumbs caressing his fingertips. He did not walk but floated toward the much smaller form before him. This beast dwarfed Morgalla, who was clenching her fists in her coat pockets. She did her best to keep calm, but a demon lord as powerful as Brexus would be able to see through any lie.

"Young one," the monstrous being began, "you and I must speak."

Crap.

She did not reply but only looked up at him. Her face did not move in the slightest and remained like stone. The minions of Brexus kept their distance from her, but she could sense their murderous intent. This feeling was apparent in the youngest, a teenager with spiked hair white as snow. He looked at her with a contemptible sneer. She refused to acknowledge him..

"You...went to Baladon," Brexus said.

"I heard it was beautiful this time of year."

He squinted, and less smoke poured from his eyes.

"So you do not deny that you visited a world in which you are *forbidden* to set foot upon? And...*why* were you there in the first place?"

"I sought out someone," she answered. "This person had great information that was needed."

He leaned down to speak softly and try to intimidate her. "And...what would that be?" he asked in a voice so soft that only she could hear.

"It was a pointless venture," she replied. "He knew nothing. Well, *close* to nothing."

"I'm sure," Brexus whispered. "But the fact remains you were present on a world where you should *not* have been."

"It's not like Baladon wasn't aware of our species. That world waged war with us for over a century."

"Mind your attitude, girl," he sneered. "Your father is not here to protect you."

"Funny you should bring that up," she said, and then looked at his minions. "What do you think *he* would do if he were here?"

She could tell nothing from Brexus; neither his black soul nor the look on his face exposed anything. It was the minions behind him that interested her, the youngest especially.

His name…Ter…Tor…Torok, that's it.

The minions were afraid when she brought up the name of her father. That gave a clue as to how safe she was. She was now filled with confidence, a weapon to be used for her defense. It stood to reason that the minions' mood gave something away about their master. She smiled up at the monster before her and he sneered with even more harshness.

"Not to worry," she assured him.

"The portals are *mine* to control, girl," he warned. "You are assigned to…"

"*Earth,* my lord," one minion said, when the name of the planet escaped him.

"Yes," Brexus continued, and looked back to Morgalla. "Remember that, child."

The group walked off, leaving only Morgalla and one minion who worked at the portal chamber. He stood there, clipboard in hand and cigarette dangling from his lip. Morgalla breathed a sigh of relief that she was safe—for now. She certainly wasn't starting her day off very well.

✻

Morgalla had much to do today anyway. She had to get out of the closet and into a civilized environment, returning to Earth just as daybreak came. She changed to her human form just before she passed through the portal to Springdale. The morning was chilly and damp; any colder and there would have been frost on all the leaves. She dressed in human disguise, as always, with her long dark violet coat buttoned up and her knit gloves with the fingers cut off. She put on her shades, making the word look purple, and put her earphones in.

With the push of a button the world turned into a musical only she could hear, with the wonderful melodies of the '70s greatest booming in her ears. With her music, the sun fully up, and herself no longer among Hell's vermin, she smiled. She walked on the broken sidewalks of downtown Springdale; so many people were beginning their day. A school bus was picking up children. She often wondered what they learned there. Many people were leaving for work, and she could tell that some were running late by how quickly they were heading to their cars.

At the shops in the downtown area, many doors were being unlocked and people were flipping over the signs to read Open. Her music being the prime factor for her good mood, the people she passed could not explain why they were suddenly in a good mood as well.

She came to a stop at a corner and waited for the light to turn red. There were three other people there; a father with his toddler in his arms and an empty stroller at his side, and an elderly nun. Morgalla stood there a moment. The nun looked at the young woman who had just walked up. They smiled politely to each other, the nun able to see her reflection in Morgalla's sunglasses, as they were the same height.

The wait seemed to be forever and a day and they wondered if it was ever going to change. It was then that Morgalla could suddenly feel a terrible emotion: fear. She looked in the direction of this emotion and saw a car speeding toward the three of them. The father heard the car approaching and abandoned the empty stroller, diving for safety with his child in his arms. The nun looked in shock at the runaway automobile speeding toward her. Morgalla grasped the nun by the shoulders and leaped back out of the path of the car as it struck the light post with a tremendous *CRASH.*

The father looked up, the baby crying as he held her tight in his arms. The nun's glasses and wimple had fallen off from the impact with the sidewalk. She grasped her chest from the shock, her heard pounding. Morgalla was on the sidewalk next to her.

"Are you all right?" the young redheaded heroine asked her, her voice a little louder. The music was still playing in her ears and her shades were askew.

"I…I…," the nun stuttered.

Morgalla looked to the wreck before them. The front end of the car was destroyed and the driver's airbag had deployed. Many people had come hurrying over to help those involved in the crash, assisting the nun and father up, but Morgalla was fine. She looked at the driver, who was in a state of shock, her entire body trembling as people helped her out of the car.

The driver could not form full sentences, but through what she said it was determined that her brakes had given out and she had lost control. Morgalla could not stay; she could not have attention of any kind from the authorities, even if she had saved a woman's life. She ran off, leaving the nun to forever ponder: *What happened to that redheaded girl?*

✻

"You know, you always bring in these strange gold coins that have nothing on them," the pawn dealer said, being inquisitive.

"And you care…why?" Morgalla asked, removing her shades and putting them away.

"Well, look at it from my point of view," the man noted. "How do I know that these aren't stolen? You could have melted them down somewhere and made them into these coins which can't be traced and then you get cash from me."

Wow, he hit the nail on the head.

"I can say with absolute certainty and honesty that I did not *steal* them."

"Well, I don't know." He scratched his bald head, unsure what to think.

"You're getting pure gold. And I'm not asking for more than what they're worth. I barely ever haggle with you."

"I…I guess you're right."

With that, he walked into the back with the gold. She breathed a sigh of relief; it was getting tougher every time she came in here. She figured that she might have to find another person and start all over. She looked around the shop; the ticking of old clocks filled the dust-covered room. The entire shop was filled with things that once belonged to other people but were turned in for money.

Morgalla looked at the dollhouse, how beautiful it was, and it was lavender too, her favorite color. She looked at the shelves of dolls and wondered who might have held them last. She looked through the glass case in front of her at the expensive-looking watches and wondered if they were all real.

The man returned to the counter with a calculator and a large stack of cash in his hands. He did some calculations and then peeled off some bills to hand to her.

"And…you're sure that's *fair*, right?" she asked. "No need to double check?"

"Yes, of course," he replied with confidence.

"Pleasure doing business with you," she said, taking the large sum of money and putting it in her pocket.

She disliked second-guessing people, especially ones she had done business with before, but it had to be done in her case. He wouldn't know how to hide anything from a demon anyway, even if he knew what she *really* was. Perhaps part of him was dishonest, dealing with someone he barely knew. He *was* dealing with gold that was untraceable, after all. Then again, maybe he needed the business. She probably could have pressed him for more money, but decided against it. She could not afford to draw attention to herself.

She put her shades on again and the earphones in her ears. She was just about to walk off when something caught her attention. There were two people, a man and a woman, walking out of the coffee shop next door hand in hand. She could smell the aroma of their hot beverages, high in caffeine, and could also smell the woman's perfume. Their hands gripped each other's as they stood in the chilly morning air.

They were not the first couple she had ever seen in her life, but were one of those rare couples whose souls emanated a glow just from being with each other. The feeling of true love from another human being was something she had vicariously felt, but never personally experienced. She often wondered what it might feel like. She beamed at them. They didn't even notice her as they walked off. They left her with a frown on her face and a lot to contemplate.

✡

Later on, Jasper sat at the counter of the circulation desk. An irate woman complained to him while her four-year-old child shrieked and fussed next to her. The woman's voice and the child's noises cut through Jasper like a dentist's drill.

"And *then* I got this notice that these books are three weeks late when I'm *sure* I returned them!" the irate woman yelled.

"Well, ma'am," Jasper began.

"I mean, this is *bullshit!*" the woman interrupted. Her screaming could be heard on the other side of the building. "I'm *sure* I returned them!"

Jasper's head turned slightly to the left. He saw one of his co-workers, Cynthia Wall, sitting at the end of the counter. She was a woman in her sixties with short gray hair and an overweight figure. She ate a doughnut and read a newspaper, completely ignoring Jasper's predicament. Exasperated at Cynthia's unwillingness to help, Jasper turned back to the irate woman and tried to defuse the situation without it getting worse.

"Ma'am," Jasper said, trying to calm her down, "I know we can—"

"I am *not* paying sixty goddamn dollars!" she interrupted again, not caring what he was saying.

Jasper rubbed his temples in aggravation as the four-year-old child continued to scream and cry.

"Excuse me," Morgalla said.

Jasper and the irate woman turned to see Morgalla standing there. Jasper's eyes widened at the sight of the redhead from the night before. Morgalla looked down at the misbehaving child.

"Hush," she commanded, and the child immediately went silent.

With a soul so young, he did not stand a chance against Morgalla. With the child now silent, Morgalla turned to look at the woman.

"Give the man sixty dollars," Morgalla ordered the woman.

The woman's attitude suddenly changed to one of calmness. She reached into her purse and took out sixty dollars in cash. She quietly handed it over without complaint to Jasper, who was dumbstruck by what he'd just witnessed. Deep down, the woman knew she was wrong but didn't want to admit it. Morgalla merely made her realize the truth.

"Now apologize to him," Morgalla added.

"I'm very sorry for yelling and cursing. I was out of line," the woman said with a slightly hypnotic expression.

"Okay," Jasper said.

"Now leave." Morgalla ordered.

The woman left, though the child stayed behind. Morgalla looked down at him as she stepped up to the counter.

"How you doing?" she asked the child, who stared up at her.

The child held up both of his middle fingers as a silent reply. Morgalla gave a smirk and looked at Jasper.

"Excuse me," she said, and slowly knelt down to the child, her back to Jasper so he could not see her face.

Now face-to-face with the child, she gave him a smile. Making one so young and whose soul was so weak see something that really was not there would be quite easy. She then hissed, her eyes turning bright yellow and her mouth full of sharp teeth. The child ran away screaming. Morgalla stood and turned to Jasper, her face appearing normal.

Jasper was almost concerned for the child, but managed a smile at seeing him run away. The smile was gone when he looked back at the redheaded woman before him.

"I should have made her apologize for breeding," she said, making a joke at their expense. "Angry people are so easy to control. Anger clouds them."

"Who the *hell* are you?"

"No one of importance," Morgalla replied.

"Okay," Jasper said. "Is there something I can help you find?"

"Um...nope," she said.

Andy Walker walked out from an office in the library. He noticed Morgalla, the woman from last night, talking to his friend. He looked on curiously, not sure what to think, but it was a good sign that they were talking.

"Normally I'm not a mean or violent person," Morgalla rambled, trying to explain her behavior from the night before. "I mean, sometimes I'm forced to be. Just my upbringing, I guess, and where I'm from. I was just having a bad—a *really* bad day. I mean, you could not *imagine* the crap I have to deal with!"

Jasper listened to her rambling, politely nodding and smiling. As Morgalla talked, Andy walked by the counter behind her. He looked at the redhead, and then at Jasper, who shrugged in confusion. Andy took his clipboard, and with a big marker he wrote: *ASK HER OUT.* He held up the clipboard so his friend could see the words. Jasper was surprised by the suggestion.

"It's okay, really," Jasper assured her.

"But I wanted to say I'm sorry," Morgalla rambled on. "I mean, me having a bad day might explain it, but does not excuse it."

"Do it." Andy moved his lips but said nothing.

Jasper was nervous, not knowing what to do. Finally, he opened his mouth and the words came spilling out. "Do you wanna go out sometime?"

Morgalla was surprised and suddenly silent. Andy smiled.

"What?" Morgalla wondered if she heard him right.

"Well, I was just thinking. I mean, I guess I owe you for returning my wallet."

Morgalla turned around at the exact same time that Andy turned and walked away. She then turned back at Jasper, curious about this human.

"Morgalla. That's an unusual name. No offense."

"I'm…not from around here," Morgalla explained, taking his hand gently in hers.

"Oh."

Morgalla slowly leaned in, looking at Jasper's face, which caused him to back away a bit.

"I don't bite," she said.

She snickered, and then squinted to look at him, wondering. She held up her hand with her index finger extended and gestured for him to approach. Jasper slowly and cautiously leaned forward.

"What *is* it with you?"

"What do you mean?" Jasper was equally confused; never had he been treated in such a way.

"Stick out your tongue," she commanded. He did not comply. "Lie on the floor, dance a jig, do *something!*" Morgalla commanded again, frustrated by his lack of cooperation.

"Do you have some obsession with making people do weird things?"

Morgalla was frustrated that none of her powers of suggestion were working on him. He was difficult to read, his soul was closed to her and she could not break through it.

"Ow," Jasper moaned, feeling a headache coming on all of a sudden.

"Sorry." Morgalla realized what she was doing. She would look for words but they would be hard to find. "Look…"

With humans she always used her powers and made them go away. With demons, she either ran away herself if they were too powerful, or took out a large knife and stabbed them in the heart.

She had the deer-in-headlights look as she stared at Jasper. She did not know what to say or do, so she followed her first instinct—she ran. Morgalla ran out of the library as fast as she could. Jasper sat there, too stunned by what he'd just experienced to allow himself to feel rejected again.

"Well, that's new," he said to himself.

Morgalla ran out of the library and suddenly stopped. She paced a bit in concern and contemplation.

Would it KILL you to spend a little time with someone?

She looked back at the library, giving a sigh in frustration, and then entered again.

Jasper was back to working at the counter; he turned around again and was surprised to see Morgalla standing there.

"What would we do on this '*date*'?"

"Movie?" Jasper asked, after a moment or two of contemplation.

"Is that it?"

"Well, if you want to do more—" Jasper was about to suggest, but did not get the opportunity.

"No, that's enough," Morgalla interrupted. "I get to choose the movie, though."

"Fair enough," Jasper said. "Um…do I call you or something?"

"No," Morgalla replied. "I'll find you."

With that, Morgalla left. Jasper looked at her in a mixture of awe and confusion. Though this woman was attractive, she was strange, and that was putting it mildly. Besides, the "I'll find you" comment didn't sit well with him.

✻

Andy was back in the office at his desk typing at his computer as Jasper walked up.

"Why did you do that?" Jasper sounded a bit distressed.

"Did she say *yes?*"

"Yeah," Jasper replied.

"I just got you a date with an attractive redhead," Andy said sarcastically. "Oh yeah, I'm a real bastard."

Andy continued to type and listen to Jasper. He glanced at him every now and then.

"What if she's a psycho? My track record for dates isn't that great." Jasper grew more concerned the more he thought about it. "This girl seems weird to me. If I make *her* mad she might cut my jugular! I don't know. Maybe I should just cancel it."

"Relax," Andy said, trying to comfort him. "Don't talk about sports, sex, or past relationships. Oh, and keep your hands to yourself!"

"And what if she gets violent?" Jasper asked. His friend Andy paused a moment in thought.

"Run."

*

Morgalla was perplexed by what had just transpired at the library. Jasper Davis was still a mystery to her, and she'd surprised herself by agreeing to go out on a date with him.

Hope he doesn't expect me to call him Jazz. I think he was just trying to impress me.

She walked through town to the outskirts where there were many construction sites. She sneaked around the site, being careful not to be seen. She was well trained and if she chose not to be noticed it was easy. There were some people there, not as many as usual, for most of them had gone to lunch. There was a foreman barking directions at his crew..

"Tell that slack-ass that as soon as he's done pouring the concrete, *then* he can go to lunch!" the foreman ordered one worker.

The worker walked away and the foreman looked through some blueprints. Morgalla walked by, but was caught by the foreman out of the corner of his eye. He did a double take, and then gave a curious look. The person did not look familiar, and she was small, so odds were it was not one of his workers.

Morgalla continued to move as the foreman tried to follow. There was a large hole being dug for the foundation of a building. No workers were around. Morgalla leapt down into it, just as the foreman saw her.

"*Hey!*" the foreman yelled at her, but she did not listen.

He ran up to the hole and looked down, and he saw nothing.

Back in Hell, in the portal chamber there was an incredibly large arena-like complex. It was larger than three football fields, and was only one of many within the realm of Hell. There, many demons like Morgalla conducted their reconnaissance, coming and going from different worlds.

In one area of the chamber the ceiling flashed bright red and Morgalla appeared. She dropped down and landed easily on the stone floor. She stood and changed into her demon self. A large demon was there, holding a clipboard and smoking a cigarette. Morgalla signed the sheet and walked to the exit. As she walked along the large corridor, she saw many other small rooms in the chamber. Other demons came and went through the portals in flashes of red light.

Chapter Seven: My Date from Hell

Dear Diary:

Demons don't "date." It's pointless to them, seeing as how they don't believe in love or companionship. I don't know why humans date either. I've seen them and I can tell they have ulterior motives. The women want a husband, the men want sex. The women want to have a baby, the men want sex. The women want money, the men want. . .well, sex.

There's something weird about this human. He's not a wizard and yet he's able to block my abilities somehow. He's worthy of further. . .study. It's just curiosity, that's all it is, I'm sure.

My father has been more protective of late. Advances have been few and far between. It's almost as if he's been. . .influencing the way everyone is thinking. Wouldn't be the first time, but it would be the first time he's done so on my behalf.

✿

Jasper was in his car at a stoplight waiting for it to change. He looked to his left, seeing a couple kissing in the car next to him. He rolled his eyes and then looked away. A happy couple jogged in the crosswalk and his eyes followed them. It was then that he noticed an elderly couple sitting on a bench holding hands.

Oh, brother.

Jasper arrived at the movie theater; long lines were all around the box office. He glanced at the listing of movies and then at the crowd to see if this strange redheaded girl might show up. To be honest, he doubted it very much.

Why the hell am I here?

Jasper had no idea why he agreed to go out with this woman who, judging by first impressions, had some serious issues to deal with. Maybe it was out of anger over what Mariette had done to him, to prove that he didn't need her after all. Maybe because he found the redhead attractive, and deep down he just thought, *What the heck? What's the worst that could happen?*

He stood at the entrance to the movie theater which was small and outdated, but managed to get the latest films. He yawned and looked at his watch. She was only ten minutes late, but he didn't think anything of it. He always made a point to be on time for everything, and he couldn't help but notice that everyone—*everyone*—was always late to meet him. Though just a second or two passed, he checked his watch again out of habit.

Late. No big surprise.

Jasper glanced at the listing of movies playing. He saw the words *sold out* next to most of the movies. With a building that had only ten theaters and the crowd getting larger by the minute, surely the choices were going to be scarce. Of the films available there were only three.

The title of one film, *Untamed Hearts*, disappointed him. He saw that the other movie was titled *Soiree of Blood.* The third film available, *Good-bye Captain Craig*, was promising. Though he had already seen that movie, he wouldn't mind seeing it again.

I doubt she'll want to see the horror flick or the war movie. Looks like I might be seeing the love story.

He had heard the women at work talk about the movie and how romantic it was. Jasper shook his head in frustration, for he was *sure* she would want to see that movie. If she showed up, that is.

"*Untamed Hearts?*"

Jasper heard a voice stained with cynicism and turned to see the attractive and petite redhead standing there.

"Pardon?"

"We are *not* seeing the *love story*," she said.

Thank you, God!

"Um…well, what would you like to see?" he asked.

She looked at the titles. "What's *Good-bye Captain Craig?*"

"It's a war movie. And the other is a horror flick."

"Oh, it's not a comedy?" she asked, having some fun with him.

"Um…yeah, well…"

Not a movie person, I guess.

"Oh, I see." She too looked over the titles, giving a slight frown at *Soiree of Blood.* Jasper was sure what her answer was going to be, but she rolled her eyes at the list of choices.

"You know, we don't *have* to see a movie," he suggested.

"I'll give the war movie a chance," she said, which truly shocked him.

"Excuse me?"

"Do you *want* to see a romance movie?"

"No." His answer was based on instinct. "You don't?"

"That war movie isn't super-gory, is it?" She changed the subject on purpose; he wouldn't want to know her feelings toward such tripe.

"No. Actually, they deleted a bunch of scenes to bring the rating down."

"Okay, I'll give it a shot."

Her interruption was a blessing of sorts to Jasper. Once he got started on a subject he was interested in, very little could stop him. He came to his senses and realized he should shut up.

Don't want to sound like a GEEK on the first date.

"I'll get the tickets, then," he said.

"Here." She reached into her pocket and pulled out a billfold. She took a ten-dollar bill from it and handed it to him. This was met by a look of curiosity.

"Are we going dutch?"

"Dutch?"

"It's okay, I can pay," he said, giving the answer he thought she would want to hear.

"What for?" She was truly confused now, not familiar with any human customs.

"You're...really independent, aren't you?"

"You could say that."

"Okay." He took her money, not wanting an argument.

Never before had a woman done that on a date, which he found curious, but he shrugged it off as he approached the box office. He also breathed a sigh of relief that he didn't have to see the sappy romance movie.

Maybe this won't be so bad after all.

Jasper got in line as Morgalla entered the crowded theater lobby. Much like other places of the sort she felt the good emotions from the people around them who were there for a good time. She managed to smile, but then frowned as she walked by a young couple that was kissing.

"Oh, get a freaking room," she muttered to them.

Such a good idea; it was what they were feeling, anyway. Though unintentional, Morgalla unwittingly influenced their souls to merely follow what they were feeling. The couple left, excited, setting out to do precisely as Morgalla commanded. She walked on, looking for the concession stand.

After she bought some yummy candy, she opened the first box immediately, poured some into her hand, and put it in her mouth. She often thought that chocolate had magical properties, for it always made her feel just a little better. The mere taste was enough to melt away the problems of her day. She surveyed the large room, a lobby of sorts that the theaters branched off from. People seemed to be in a very good mood for the most part; perhaps this was a place she should frequent more often. For a brief moment, she smiled at the good feelings coming over her and she almost lost concentration.

"Here you go," Jasper said, handing her a ticket.

Morgalla gave a small jump; she still could not sense his soul at all. Normally she would be able to feel his comings and goings, but he was a blank slate to her.

Damn!

"Sorry about that," he apologized.

"It's...it's okay. Just announce your arrival next time," Morgalla warned, to which Jasper smiled, but only out of courtesy.

Jasper got two of the only tickets left and the movie was going to start at any moment. Morgalla offered some candy to him but he respectfully declined; he was too nervous to eat anyway.

The opening scenes of *Good Bye Captain Craig* were violent. They depicted a battle that any human with a grasp of world history would have been able to identify, but to Morgalla was only vaguely familiar. The movie, the first Morgalla had ever seen in a theater, reminded her of countless battles she had been forced to witness but thankfully had never had to participate in. She saw the appeal of a story being told in two dimensions on the screen; she could experience the events without feeling anyone's pain. She imagined, but only for a moment, what the emotions might be of the characters before her. She shook her head, coming back to her senses.

Idiot, don't think that.

Morgalla took another handful of chocolate candies and shoveled them into her mouth. Jasper initially worried that she might not like the violence, but she gave no hint that the violence bothered her. When Jasper glanced over at her, she was happily stuffing her face with chocolate candy.

The entire audience was startled at one point by an explosion on-screen. Everyone, that is, except Morgalla. She dug into the box of candy for more chocolate, completely oblivious to what was going on. To her, they were mere images, and having experienced some of the real thing made this seem trivial. Jasper was startled along with the audience, and then looked at Morgalla. He gave her a curious look, noting her lack of fear. She tossed another handful of chocolate into her mouth. Noticing that Jasper was looking at her, she returned his gaze.

"What?" Her voice was muffled since her mouth was full of chocolate candy.

"Nothing."

Morgalla looked back at the screen. The audience again was startled by another scary moment in the film and everyone jumped, Jasper included. Morgalla remained silent and still; the only movement was her chewing on her candy. Jasper raised an eyebrow again.

She must watch a lot of war movies.

After the first twenty minutes of violence, she leaned in to whisper and he in turn got a little closer to hear.

"The entire movie isn't like this, is it?" she asked.

"Oh no, not at all."

His answer made her feel relieved. Jasper was indeed right. In fact, most of the movie was talking—lots of it. Time passed and

Jasper could not help but notice other couples in the audience making out. Morgalla sat there, bored, desensitized by the violence on-screen. She glanced around and also noticed all the couples' romantic activities. She saw one guy who was making passes at a girl. The girl did not like it and tried to push him away. Morgalla then looked casually at Jasper, whose hands were on his lap. She raised an eyebrow.

Maybe he's afraid to make a move.

✿

Jasper and Morgalla walked out of the theater along with the rest of the audience into the crowded lobby.

"Wasn't a bad movie," Jasper said.

"Best part was the ending," Morgalla replied, glad that the movie was actually over, but trying not to hint that she hadn't liked it.

Jasper had a smile on his face, but it suddenly changed to a frown when he saw Missy and Steve walking out of another theater. They both saw Jasper and decided to stop and say hi.

"Oh no," Jasper moaned.

"What is it?" Morgalla asked, but then it became clear that something was wrong.

She could not explain the feeling she had, but it didn't feel right. There was a presence she had never felt before on this world, intense hatred and contempt. Morgalla honestly thought that perhaps someone from Hell had followed her. She spun around, expecting the worst, but saw Missy and Steve there.

"So *Jasper*," Missy began. "I heard that Mariette royally *dumped* you for a lawyer. How surprising." Missy looked at Morgalla. "Oh, *look*," she went on. "He has a date! How much did he pay you?"

Morgalla's eyes started at Missy's feet and made their way up to her face. As the two women made eye contact, Morgalla easily sensed Missy's cocky attitude. Morgalla's eyes narrowed and she appeared to want to start something.

Please make a move.

"Got a problem, bitch?" Missy asked, her hands on her hips and her voice full of attitude.

Morgalla smiled at her comment; Missy had now given her an excuse for violence.

"No, I'm afraid it is *you* with the problem," Morgalla replied. "You're annoying me."

"What?" Missy scoffed at Morgalla's comment.

"I have a question for you. Why are you hitting yourself?"

"What are you—"

Missy's words were cut short by a hand up at her cheek slapping it. She gasped. At first she thought it was Morgalla hitting her, but soon she realized that it was her *own* hand slapping her face. Jasper's jaw dropped at what just happened. Morgalla was actually surprised that her powers were working so well on this girl. They were working just as well as they had on the three bimbos at the restaurant.

"Anything else to say?" Morgalla asked with a smile.

"You…you…," Missy stammered, and again she was silenced by her other hand slapping her own face.

"Hey, Davis, control your woman!" Steve insisted.

Offended by Steve's comment, Morgalla looked up defiantly at the muscular behemoth.

"Shut up," Morgalla commanded.

His own fist connecting to his face suddenly knocked Steve to the floor; he was out cold. By then the commotion had attracted the attention of a manager. Jasper saw him walking their way, and he took Morgalla gently by the shoulders and tried to guide her toward the exit.

"Um, I think we should leave," Jasper said.

"Is there a problem here?" the theater manager asked as he walked up.

"No problem, we were just leaving," Jasper replied.

Jasper guided Morgalla to the exit, while she kept a blank stare on Missy and Steve, ready to thrash either of them. Missy's tears flowed; she did not understand what was going on.

Jasper and Morgalla walked out to the parking lot and away from the theater.

"Okay, what just happened in there?" Jasper's question was more of a demand.

"You won't like the answer. Besides, it's not like you didn't enjoy that. You have interesting friends."

"Those were *not* my friends."

"Never grasped the concept of *sarcasm*, have you?"

"Yeah, well it's just something I'd rather not have happen."

"Why does she hate you? Did you turn her down for a date, or something?"

Jasper laughed.

"Hell no!" He said. "Not that I would have said yes, anyway. Missy is one of those people who thinks that her opinion matters more than others."

"Yeah well dead woopie." Morgalla replied with her index finger raised.

"Pardon?"

"Dead. Woopie." She repeated, again with her index finger raised and motionless.

Jasper found her comment amusing.

✻

The two of them went to eat at Morgalla's favorite fast-food restaurant. It was virtually empty, with just a handful of other patrons besides the two of them.. Jasper nibbled at his food, but

Morgalla held a gigantic hamburger in her hands and took a *huge* bite out of it. Jasper watched, surprised again at her eating habits.

"What?" Morgalla's question again was muffled due to having her mouth full.

"Nothing," Jasper replied.

"This is my fav-rite place to eat," she noted.

"Really?"

She eats her a lot and she's not fat?

"So…what are your parents like?" she inquired.

"Average, I guess," Jasper said, not being too specific. "They nag sometimes, make me do stuff even though I don't live with them. My mom insists on being a *mother.*"

"How terrible for you," she replied. Morgalla's features were blank; she did not feel sorry for Jasper in the least, even though she could tell that he was joking around a little.

"She insists that I don't eat right so she still makes me come over for dinner and such," Jasper said.

"She makes you dinner?" Morgalla asked with jealousy. "You're lucky. What about your dad?"

"Don't see him much. He works a lot."

"My dad is a workaholic, too."

"What's he do?"

Morgalla suddenly had a brief flashback of the latest battle. She remembered so many sentient dying in unspeakable ways.

"Corporate takeovers," she lied.

"My dad is in advertising. What about your mom?"

Morgalla stopped eating immediately and looked at Jasper. She paused a moment or two in thought.

"I…I never knew her," she confessed.

Jasper looked sad and apologetic, realizing that he had touched upon a sensitive subject.

"I'm sorry," he said.

"It's okay."

"Without her you wouldn't be here."

"True," she confessed. "I blame my father for that."

Jasper was more nervous now. He nibbled his fries looking for another topic of discussion. Morgalla looked at him with curiosity. Emotionally he was still a complete blank to her and she could not fathom why. She never encountered a human like this before; usually a demon would be able to block his emotions from her, but by now there would be something she could sense.

"You didn't make a move on me in the theater. Everyone else was lip wrestling."

"It's only our first date," Jasper noted. "I didn't want to come off like a jerk."

"Are you for real?"

"Um…yeah, as far as I know."

Morgalla smiled and shook her head, liking his sense of humor.

"You wouldn't survive where I'm from," she said.

"And where would that be?"

Morgalla decided to change the subject and looked down at the table.

"So, how do you feel about women who are…*different?*"

Jasper wasn't sure what she was talking about.

"Different? How so?"

"Well, what if she were just different from all the girls who *you* know?"

"Well, I don't know," Jasper snickered. "I've known some strange people in my time."

"I don't mean strange. I mean really, *really* different."

"Different isn't a *bad* thing, you know," he observed. "And we don't always choose to show who we really are when we first meet someone."

"And sometimes we can't," Morgalla replied.

"Well, that's the game of dating, don't you think?"

"The word *game* is a strange choice of words."

"Yeah...I suppose so," Jasper smiled.

He buried deep the scars that many women left in the past. It was that comment that caught Morgalla's attention the most. Finally, the first crack in his emotional armor had appeared. It was also the first sign of emotion that she could sense. No longer was he a blank slate; unfortunately, she didn't like what she sensed.

He's hiding something.

He noticed her look of suspicion. He had to look down and make sure he didn't spill ketchup on his shirt.

"What's wrong?"

"It's nothing, really. But I think there's something you're not telling me, Jasper."

"Long story," he said. She just stared, eating her burger and fries. It appeared that she wasn't going to drop the subject. "Look, it doesn't matter, it's in the past. We've all got our romantic history, don't we?"

She did not reply, for her answer would have been *no*.

"See that guy over there?" Morgalla asked, and made a slight gesture to a couple sitting on the other side of the room.

"Yeah," Jasper said, after giving them an inconspicuous glance.

"All he wants from her is sex."

"Duh, he's a guy." Jasper chuckled.

"Okay, I'll admit that one's a little obvious. But the girl knows this."

"And you're suddenly a mind reader?"

"Not quite," Morgalla smirked. He wasn't too far from the truth, but he wouldn't believe her if she told him her *true* power. "She's got a conscience but I think she ignores it. Both of them do, they both do wrong things but they don't care."

"Isn't that the definition of evil?" Jasper was smiling now, happy at Morgalla's enlightened attitude.

"Those two aren't lovers yet."

"And how can you tell *that*?" Jasper inquired, finding it hard to believe that she could have such information.

He thought she might have incredible detective skills, but in reality, when two people were together and were lovers, they seemed to give off a glow that was obvious to Morgalla's kind. She often wondered if maybe that's why demons hated humans so much: pure jealousy at the fact that they seemed to bond much easier than demons did.

"I can just tell, okay?"

"Well, she might not sleep with him at all," Jasper speculated.

"She shouldn't make him jump through hoops like that." Her voice almost had the sound of pity in it.

"And he should want other things besides sex."

"They have more in common than they think," she said, and smiled, for it was something they could agree on.

✡

The two of them finished eating and walked out to the parking lot toward Jasper's car. The lot was almost empty; not one person was in sight.

"Threatened to beat you up, eh? What do that ape and his bitch have against you, anyway?"

"I have *no* idea," Jasper replied. "You'd think it would be a waste of their time. She's had it in for me since high school for *some* stupid reason that makes sense only to her. Which high school did you go to?"

Morgalla was silent, for Jasper was asking too many questions. Normally she would have been forced to kill him, but she did not wish to. She searched for an answer to give him, but could only sigh.

"Look, Jasper," she said. "I really should be going home now."

She asked Jasper to drive her in the direction of the construction site near downtown. He thought it peculiar, for there were hardly any homes there. Jasper played some music on the radio he thought she might like, but she had no reaction to it whatsoever. There was hardly any conversation, which depressed Jasper. He got the vibe that she was not interested in any way.

"You can let me off here," she said.

"Here?" Jasper inquired. He pulled up to the curb, stopped, and looked around. There was hardly anything there, only businesses.

"Yeah. Don't worry about it, I can walk," she replied as she got out.

"Wait," Jasper said, getting out and following. He had almost forgotten to put on the parking break and turn the car off.

"Morgalla, wait!" he called out, and she turned to look at him. "I had a great time tonight."

The look on her face was of apprehension. She had hoped this would not be difficult.

I'm such a liar.

"Yeah, so did I."

I'm such a liar.

"I was wondering if I could call you sometime."

Never before had she been faced with something like this. It had never occurred to her that this might happen.

"Look, Jazz, I don't know quite how to say this…," she said, as Jasper's heart sunk. He sighed heavily, and she knew she had just hurt him.

"You don't have to say anything," he said. "I've heard this before. You just want to be friends, you like me but not in *that* way. I've heard it all before."

She didn't know what to say to him, so she simply said, "I'm sorry."

"Look, are you sure you want to walk home?" he asked out of politeness. "It might be dangerous."

"Yes, I'm sure."

"Then have a good night. Say hi if you're ever at the library."

Jasper then turned, his better judgment winning his internal argument. Instead of yelling at her, the rage of all the years of emotional abuse pouring out at once, he decided to just call it a night.

Morgalla, too, thought it best to part ways. He was indeed a nice person, possibly the best she had ever met, but to try and pursue anything with him would be pointless.

A human could never learn to love a demon.

Chapter Eight: Enlightening Banter

The most expensive of cars one can buy drove up to the front of Smythe Manor. Ignoring his driver, Alistair Smythe stepped out and ran up to the front doors. He took a moment, looking up at his boyhood home, hesitant to enter. He walked toward the large double doors that opened by themselves; he was annoyed by the doors opening by magic but walked in. He saw some familiar faces that were surprised to see him.

He had no time to talk, and walked on in search of his father. There were some new faces as well, people from all over the world speaking in different accents and tongues. There was only one place his father was going to be. He entered his laboratory on the high catwalk with the walls covered in books.

Richard was at his desk, hunched over what appeared to be a strange chemistry set. It had been a few years since they last saw each other. Alistair was about to speak, but held his tongue a moment.

Perhaps this was a bad idea.

He sneaked out the same door he had entered through. Richard, with the greatest of care, poured one liquid into another in a small bottle. When combined they changed into a bright blue color. Sensing the presence of someone in the room, Richard looked up to see his son's back.

Alistair walked through the mansion and came across his father's study. He entered it and a flood of memories rushed to him. He recalled running through here with his little brother James, and finding so many places to hide and play. The manor itself was candy to a child's imagination.

There were some books on the desk, some of the only ones not covered in dust. He walked to one and flipped through it, instantly recognizing it as his brother's journal. He kept it only briefly during the most difficult times of his life, a form of therapy to deal with his pain. He flipped through the pages to see words written by a hand filled with fear and rage.

He saw crude drawings of a creature—black, large, and menacing, with no eyes. Broad-shouldered and massive, it seemed to be a walking shadow towering high. The most noticeable of all features were the horns on its head; large, stretching from its temples and curving upward. He looked on in concern, remembering his and his brother's mourning the death that was the root of it.

"James might be offended if he saw you looking in his journal."

Alistair turned to see his father standing in the doorway. He was speechless; not sure what to say. He closed the book and stared at the black cover.

"How...how are you feeling?" Alistair was very concerned for his father, thinking only the worst.

"Oh, I'm quite fine, thank you," Richard replied. "Why do you ask?"

Alistair looked at him, confused and suddenly angry. "Your... your note sounded important!"

"It is *quite* important indeed," Richard replied. "Did you think I was dying or something?"

Alistair was silent, his mouth hanging open. His father slumped in the chair and a cloud of dust erupted. Alistair's hand went to his forehead in frustration.

"You *did*!" Richard exclaimed. "Look, I'm sorry you felt that way, son, but I only stated that I needed to talk to you very soon."

Alistair only assumed the worst; he hadn't seen his father for a few years, but it felt longer. To Richard it felt as if it were only yesterday; his son had been on his mind every day.

"So…what was it you needed to see me for?" he asked, removing his hand from his face.

Richard took a six-foot wooden staff leaning against the desk and picked it up. Walking over to the wall he set it on a rack filled with other innocent-looking artifacts. In reality, they were deadly weapons in the right hands.

"I…I had another vision," Richard said.

"Were you awake?"

"Sometimes I am, other times I'm not."

"When you're asleep it's called a *dream*, Father." Alistair was now mocking his father's interests, as he had many times before.

"You know, if it weren't for all the physical evidence and all the people here in the house, you'd probably have me committed!"

"Do you *want* another fight? Is that why you asked me here?"

The same old argument brewed again and Richard wanted to diffuse it.

"No, I don't want a fight," he said, as he found a chair and sat across from his son.

"Are you upset with me because James followed you and I did not?"

"No, absolutely not," Richard said. "But if you must know, it was because you never believed me." Alistair did not know how to respond. "This whole time, our family has been right."

"That the world is going to end?"

"No, that there are things human beings chose to forget. That there is hardly anyone on the planet who knows and believes. Alistair, I didn't care, nor do I care now, what you did with your life. I'm proud of you, regardless."

"Is that what you wanted to say to me?"

"Not entirely."

"I've never seen this many people here at one time," Alistair said. "How many are here?"

"Thirty-seven," his father replied with a tone of regret. He wished he could have found more.

"Thirty-seven? To save the world?"

"It was never my intention to go into Hell itself, but instead to stop whoever—or *whatever*—from invading."

"And do you think this will happen? Father, it may *never* happen in your or my lifetime!"

"The point is, we'll be ready!"

"Ready...fine." Alistair had always had doubts. There were two worlds. One he had grown up in, within this manor, learning about magic and all the forgotten things from the world outside. He never had a knack for it, though, what his father and his brother were good at. The other world was the one everyone else grew up in. That's why he kept his home life a complete secret. "If you are not dying, then why have you asked me to come?"

"As always, my visions are vague," Richard admitted. "But recent ones suggest that it might not be here." The last comment got Alistair's attention; he found it very curious. "I...saw a black shadow. I did not recognize it at first, but then I took out James's old journal from years ago. The shadow looked just like his drawings."

"It did?"

"Yes. I remembered seeing the drawings, but this vision was different. It was so real that it felt like I was there."

"Did you see anything else?"

"Yes. I saw a woman. I could not see her clearly but it was definitely a woman. She was young and she was being tortured."

✿

Some demons kill out of necessity, the need to survive. Morgalla was one of these demons. Her father, on the other hand, not only killed because he needed to but because he *wanted* to. It was his viciousness and sheer lust for death that earned him more and more power from his master. He had risen through the ranks of other demons to be granted the title of Demon Lord. He now answered to only one.

Zorach was in a bit of a bind. He was required to conquer so many worlds for his dark master and was behind on his quota. He needed an easy victory, and with so many of his forces being rerouted for many other duties he had to find another way.

He walked down a dark, dimly lit corridor. He was far from where he normally lived, venturing to a region of Hell where the demoness Zorinda reigned.

A minion of Zorinda walked from out a hallway and accidentally bumped into Zorach. The minion fell to the ground unconscious. Zorach continued on his way unscathed; the minion's existence meant nothing to him.

The hallway was long, and the deeper he got, the more guards there were. He finally approached a large black door. There were many statues of naked muscular males decorating the outside. There were many guards there. One of them stepped forward, giving Zorach a bow.

"My lord," the guard said. "You honor us with your presence. How may I assist you?"

"Zorinda," Zorach replied. "I shall see her."

"My mistress is currently indisposed," the guard said. "Perhaps you may—"

The guard's words were cut short by Zorach's claw gliding across his throat. The strike was so quick and subtle that there was no scream, just the sound of the air being torn and then the *clump* of the soldier falling. The others moved away from Zorach and the door, letting him pass. Zorach opened the door and entered a large chamber, which appeared to be a meadow on a beautiful spring day. The door he entered stood alone on the grass. There was a stone path leading to a small pond. He walked to the pond where two minions stood. They both bowed. Zorach ignored them, looking only at the calm water.

Without warning, a hauntingly beautiful form rose up out of the water. Her body was toned and red, and she had long black hair and bright yellow eyes. Two large black horns stretched from her temples and her mouth was filled with gleaming white fangs. Zorinda saw Zorach. She did not look happy.

"Don't you ever knock?"

"We must speak," Zorach insisted.

Zorinda walked through the water to the pond's edge. She rose up and got out, naked, and a minion handed her a black silk robe.

"About what?"

"Death, destruction, and conquest," he replied.

"Fun subjects, then."

"Our supplies are low."

"*Your* supplies are low," Zorinda said. "Besides, it's your fault."

"We are behind in our quota. The *Dark One* demands another world."

"Do you have a world in mind?"

"Perhaps," Zorach said, uncertain. "There are a few possibilities."

"Oh, I know which world you have in mind! Your influence is great there."

"My influence stretches far across many worlds, and is particularly strong in that one. I currently have many humans committing murders in the name of God."

"How deliciously ironic," she laughed.

Zorinda walked another stone path to a small stone pedestal where a black orb rested. Her hand glided over it and the area changed from a spring meadow to a desert at night. The sand was black and there were dark storm clouds in the distance.

"There are few ways victory will be possible," Zorach said.

"Any easy victories?"

"No such thing," he replied.

"And because I have heeded the words of my generals, and because my minions have not died in vain, you wish to use them?" Zorinda asked, as she walked to a large chair and relaxed. One minion poured her a glass of wine.

"You have three battalions. I wish to have them."

"You may have one," she said.

"Two."

"*Half!*" Zorinda snapped back, irritated by his persistence.

They were then both silent. Zorinda glared at him, and then smiled, showing her pearl fangs. Demon lords were puppet masters for the most part. Often they claimed a soul of one who could lead an army of darkness to conquest. Usually this person was non-demon. They took all responsibility for failure, but more often than not they took none of the glory. Victory was never guaranteed and failure was met with an eternity of torment.

"You drive a hard bargain," Zorach confessed. "You have indeed earned the souls you have claimed."

"So, what of that youngest daughter of yours?" Zorinda asked, as she took a sip of wine.

"She will assist us in our next conquest," Zorach replied.

"She knows this? Is she not the pacifist?"

"She is, unfortunately," he said with regret. "It's a shame, really. She is quite skilled and powerful. Something we did not intend nor expect."

"Will she pose a problem?"

"No. She is but one young girl. She will meet her destiny when it comes time to conquer again."

"This will be, what, the third time at least you tried to conquer Earth? You tried to help that one German and he was a damn fool."

"We shall not make the same mistake again. I shall take a hands-on approach to it and be part of the invasion myself."

"What is it you have against this particular world, anyway?" she asked with a look of surprise.

"Their innocence disgusts me."

"You never soil your hands in such a way," she observed. "Besides, neither you nor I could survive on this world. We're too old!"

"Morgalla will be the key to our victory."

"Ah, I see," Zorinda said, smiling again. "Earth has been blessed with ignorance. They know not of our evil. Are you sure that the only *one* portal will be enough?"

"It will have to be. Brexus has not been able to create any new ones or even re-open others enough."

"You may be walking to your doom. How many billions of humans are there?"

"The Dark One demands it. You also have heard our master's call."

"Is that *all* you wanted?" She asked.

"Yes…sister dearest."

"You're welcome…*brother* dearest."

As Zorach exited, the servants of Zorinda moved out of his way. Vex was waiting for the demon lord and soon was following behind him.

"Lord Zorach," Vex said, running to keep up. "Please, my master, a moment of your time! It is in regard to your daughter!"

Zorach was ignoring him until he mentioned his daughter. He stopped and slowly turned to look at Vex, who took a few steps back, intimidated by his massive form. Vex fell to one knee before him. His only defense for his life against his master was to grovel.

"My lord, I have come to ask your permission to officially court your daughter!"

"I do not have time for such trivial matters," Zorach said.

"Have I not been your loyal servant, my lord?" Vex did his best to plead his case. "I fought in your name countless times—"

"Silence," Zorach interrupted. "Young Vex, Morgalla is not to be touched. She is too important to my plans."

"I...I understand," Vex replied in disappointment.

"However," Zorach continued, "perhaps if our next engagement is successful, things may work for you better than you know."

"My lord?"

"Morgalla will be the key to our next victory. Do you understand?"

Vex slowly looked up at him, and realized the gravity of his words. .

"Yes, my lord!" Vex smiled. This was good news indeed.

"If she perishes, then so be it. But if she survives, you have my permission to own her."

Zorach turned, his cloak flowing behind him. Vex gave a wicked smile, and finally rose to his feet.

✶

Many people worked at the site in Springdale where new apartment houses were being built. Morgalla actually did not know what she was going to do when it was done, for the basement of one of the buildings was where the portal to Hell was. One of the workers was Fred, who was running late for a meeting with the foreman. With one knee to the ground, he found a small piece of what appeared to be gold. He was in the large hole being dug for a foundation, the same hole Morgalla used to come and go from Hell. Fred looked at the piece, which was worn by age and from being under the earth. It looked as if skilled hands had shaped it into something of an *L*-shape. Another worker, Joe, noticed what Fred was doing. He looked down into the hole.

"Hey, Fred!" Joe yelled down. "They need you up here!"

Fred stood, put the piece of gold in his pocket quickly, and turned to Joe.

"Yeah, be right there," Fred replied.

✡

Jasper was at work all day, trying to keep his mind on his job. He went through some books on a cart getting ready to shelve them. As he flipped through them, he discovered one book titled *Demons and the Occult*. The book caught his eye. He set the other books down and opened it. He went through it quickly, flipping the pages. He could not explain it, but for some reason this book just seemed... important to him. He did not notice that Andy was behind him.

"So?" Andy startled Jasper and he almost dropped the book. He turned to him, his hand on his heart. "Oh, sorry! A bit jumpy, aren't you? What's wrong?"

"It's nothing," he replied.

"So, out with it. How did it go?"

"It went okay," Jasper said.

"You did what I told you, right?"

"Yes." Jasper rolled his eyes.

"And you didn't make a *move*, did you?"

"Hell no!"

"Hey, maybe we could double date," Andy said, smiling.

"Doubtful," Jasper muttered, his voice sounding uncertain.

"Why not?"

"I don't know if I'll see her again."

"Damn," Andy said, his voice filled with regret. Deep down, he had hoped they would hit it off. "What happened?"

"Everything went okay, seemed normal," Jasper replied, but then looked unsure as his mind replayed the events of last night.

"Completely?"

"Well, I *did* think it was strange that she didn't want to see the chick flick. It was her idea to see *Good-Bye Captain Craig.*"

"I heard that was the bloodiest flick ever."

Looking at Andy, Jasper shook his head; it was definitely *not* the film with the most blood.

"She must work in a morgue or something," Jasper said, and he returned to shelving books. "All the gore didn't bug her at all."

"You don't know where she works?" Andy asked, as he took a book and found its spot on the shelf.

"That's just it, she didn't say. You try to get to know someone and she keeps changing the subject."

"Crap, that's not good."

"You might be the self-proclaimed expert on women here, but even *I* know that's not a good sign."

"So…just a date then, huh?"

"Yeah. One thing's for sure…I'm never going to see her again."

They two of them continued to shelve books until the cart had only the book about demons on it. Andy said nothing about it and they returned to the front desk.

"I should have seen it, really," Jasper said, as he leaned against the desk. "She's incredibly private, not to mention hot."

"Oh yeah, don't have to tell me that. Real natural beauty. I was amazed how little makeup she wore."

"I don't think she wore *any*."

"Any? No way," Andy said, shaking his head. "Woman that good-looking and no boyfriend? You know what that means, right?"

"Drama?"

"Hell yeah," Andy said. "And how."

"That's great," Jasper replied. "What I wouldn't give for a woman with no drama in her life."

"There is *no* such thing," Andy replied, almost laughing. Silence followed as both of them contemplated just what sort of drama Morgalla might have in her life. "Jealous ex-boyfriend?"

"Or *husband*," Jasper said.

"Maybe she's on the lam or something."

"Oh, come on," Jasper said, unable to believe his ears. "You watch too much TV."

"Seriously, maybe she was dating a mobster or something and she ran away. They always run away to small towns!"

"That I find hard to believe," Jasper replied. "Look, I gotta get back to work."

Andy smiled and patted his shoulder, and then walked away. Jasper stood there and sighed. He picked up the book of demons and began to flip through it again. He did not know why, but he was drawn to the subject. He could not put the book down. It had many drawings and a few photographs. One photo was very strange and caught his attention. It was a group of archaeologists standing around what seemed like a dig site; they had unearthed a series of stones positioned in a circle. It reminded him of Stonehenge.

Jasper thought of nothing but Morgalla for the rest of the day. Shelving books was easy; he had done it so many times it had become instinctive. His mind and heart seemed to be in conflict;

his heart wishing she had been more open, and perhaps nicer, while his head justified that Morgalla probably had her reasons for keeping him at a distance.

Jasper was at a desk later in the day, sorting through some paperwork, when his co-worker Cynthia walked up. She stood behind him, her arms folded and a jaded look on her face. Jasper noticed someone behind him and knew it just *had* to be her. He did not give her the satisfaction of turning to face her.

"Something wrong?" Jasper's question was cynical; deep down, he didn't care what she thought.

"Why can't you just do your job?"

"Pardon?"

"You stand at the counter all day, flirting with the young women."

It was that comment that made Jasper turn to face her; surely she could not be talking about him.

"*Me?* Flirt?" Jasper said. "If you're referring to the same people I'm thinking of, they needed help."

"That's the librarian's job," Cynthia snapped.

"They were at lunch, though," Jasper said innocently.

"It could have waited!"

"It took me two minutes."

"You just don't *get* it, do you?" she said, after rolling her eyes. "You are *not* to flirt with patrons!"

Jasper was a bit frustrated by Cynthia's ramblings. He thought that somehow there must be a way to reason with her. But he quickly lost hope for that.

"Cynthia, correct me if I'm wrong, but you're not my boss, are you?"

Cynthia slowly leaned in, smirking confidently. "Soon I will be," she said.

"Pardon?"

"That's right," she gloated. "*I* got the promotion, you didn't."

Cynthia stood again and walked out of the office. Jasper sighed and went back to the computer filing. He had enough on his mind that day anyway. Cynthia did not like Jasper for the simple reason that he was young and thin. She enjoyed finding any and all opportunities to get him in trouble and to boss him around.

Now she would be *entitled* to boss him around. His fist tightened in anger as his face contorted with rage. He couldn't hold it in, so he walked out to the back dock. He looked around to see if anyone was there, but saw no one. Jasper kicked an empty box and it flew across the dock.

How could SHE get the promotion?

Part of him wanted to march into Sherry's office and demand to know *why* Cynthia had been chosen over him. He played the scene in his head.

To hell with you! Yeah, that's what I should say.

This job wasn't much of a career anyway, and he was still quite young. He could find something better, regardless of the bad economy.

I should walk out right now!

Jasper took a deep breath and his fingers stretched out for a moment to relax. His mind went to his car, how it barely ran and how his paycheck kept it running. He remembered his rent, and how he would buy things only on sale because of the meager paycheck he got. As meager as it was, he needed it.

"Jasper? Is there...something wrong?"

A woman's voice startled him; he looked at the entrance to see Sherry standing there.

You know what's wrong.

"Nothing. Why do you ask?"

"Thought I heard something, that's all," Sherry said. "Barbara needs you in her office to move some things around."

"Okay."

He went back to work, his rational mind again taking over and winning the argument. It had always won in the past. Calmness overtook him again. They used him and Andy as pack animals sometimes to do heavy lifting. They were some of the only people strong and healthy enough to do any lifting whatsoever, even though Jasper wasn't the strongest of men.

I need this job. I need to work. Things will get better.

✻

Dear Diary,

The word "love" does not exist in the demon vocabulary. And sometimes I wonder if it's truly in the humans' as well. But sometimes I see a couple holding hands, standing or walking, and I wonder. There is something. . .indescribable between them.

Last night was my first—ONLY—date with the human, Jasper. I had never been on or partaken in the unique ways humans seek out companionship. It wasn't bad, actually. I suppose if demons dated it would have entailed some masochism, some deaths, and one of us dominating the other.

Still, it was nice to connect with someone, even if it was for a little while.

✻

Jasper finished work and was exiting the library. He found his keys and was walking to the parking lot when he suddenly felt a presence behind him. Jasper spun around quickly to see Morgalla standing there in her human form. Startled, Jasper dropped the books he'd been carrying. She was dressed even more casually than normal. She wore a pair of violet overalls under her long dark violet coat and her red and white sneakers that had become almost a trademark.

"I'm sorry," Morgalla apologized.

They both knelt and picked up the books. Morgalla could not help but notice the demonic subject matter. Jasper was a bit embarrassed by them. A thought entered her mind, though: *Could he know?*

"Interesting subject matter," she observed.

"Oh, well, it's for a class," he lied. They stood up and she put the books back in his hands. "What changed your mind?"

"Pardon?"

"I thought you didn't want to see me again."

"Well, I thought it over."

"And simply because *you* change your mind you think we can just pick up where we left off?"

"Oh." The reality of the moment fell into place for her, and she realized that she had not exactly treated him well. "I didn't come here for an argument, *Jazz*. You don't have to be a jerk."

"Okay." Jasper sighed. "I'm sorry."

"So am I."

"Why did you leave all of a sudden?"

"Look, can we talk?" She answered his question with a question. With a gesture Jasper offered a seat on a bench and they both sat down. "I'm sure you're a really great guy."

"You've already said that."

"Yeah, and I've given it a lot of thought, and if you still want to…" Her mind sought the words but they did not come.

"Go out again?" Jasper finished her sentence and could tell in her eyes that he was right.

"Yeah. But I want to set some ground rules first."

"Rules?"

"Well, one big rule, really: I can't tell you everything about me," she said. This was answered with a strange look from Jasper, who was silent for a few seconds.

"Morgalla, you've never been *in* a relationship before, have you?"

Well, I suppose I can answer THAT question.

"No. I can honestly say that I have not."

"I'm far from an expert in relationships," he noted. "But one thing is for sure: two people can't have a successful relationship if there are secrets."

Damn. I can't tell him I'm a DEMON. He won't believe me, and if I show him he'll surely freak!

"I. . ." She managed one word, and for some reason her mouth would not obey what her heart was telling her.

"Well?"

"I, uh. . .look, I think a lot better on a full stomach."

Jasper and Morgalla went to another fast-food restaurant, again her choice. She held a large hamburger and took a huge bite out of it. Jasper looked on with one eyebrow raised. He found her eating habits extremely odd. . He had never seen her driving either; perhaps she didn't own a car. He still wasn't entirely sure she even had a place to live.

"Morgalla, when did you eat last?"

"Lunchtime, why?"

"No reason," he said, as if it were nothing, but in reality there was a very good reason. The way she ate, like someone was about to steal her food, Jasper asked himself if she was able to feed herself. "And just what is it you—"

"Look, let me stop you there," she interrupted him. "Jasper, if you want to know the real reason why I don't talk about myself, it's because I'm a very private person."

"Yes, I've discovered that already."

"There are some things that you are going to know, and some things that you probably never will know."

"You're not part of the mob or in the witness protection program, are you?"

What are those? DAMN, I knew I should have watched more TV!

Jasper's face then changed to one of disappointment.

"You don't already have a boyfriend or *husband*, do you?"

"I can honestly say *no* to that," she said.

"But," Jasper said, shaking his head briefly in frustration, "the whole point of a relationship is that I get to know *you*, and you get to know *me*. We connect!"

"Relationship? That brings me to something else. What is it you're seeking here?"

"Well…" Jasper paused. "What is it *you* want?"

"Well, after my burger I have my eye on that dessert cookie."

"Ah. Anything more long term?"

"Do you mean a boyfriend? Thought never crossed my mind."

"Oh, well, me neither, really. I was just enjoying your company." Jasper was lying, of course. There were many strange things about her that made him hesitate to pursue anything of a romantic nature, but she was very attractive nonetheless. It seemed he was out of luck either way. "Okay. Why spend time with *me*?"

Morgalla contemplated the question for a moment or two.

"Maybe I'd just prefer to spend time with someone I'm not threatened by," she said.

Jasper thought a moment, not sure if he should be insulted.

"Not threatening?"

"I'm not threatened by you in *any* way," she said.

"I don't know if I should be offended or not."

"Oh no, you shouldn't be offended. Really, I mean that. You're the nicest person I've ever met."

"I've heard that many times."

"Jasper, I don't know many…okay, *any* nice people."

"Wow," he replied with surprise.

"So what else do you like to do around here?"

"I'm going to school to be a journalist. But it looks like that's not gonna happen."

"Why not?"

"I don't know if I'm really good at it," he said.

"Your opinion or someone else's?"

"Well, it's my teacher."

"They don't know everything. And they get mad when you prove them wrong."

"Yeah, that's true," he said with a smile. "I'm of the opinion that journalists should use facts and the *truth*, but apparently that's not good enough."

"What else do you like to do?"

"Well, I work out too."

Jasper's last statement got Morgalla's attention, and her eyebrows went up.

Chapter Nine: Unique Experiences

Meggan Miller walked out of the gym office; she stopped in her tracks when she saw Morgalla and Jasper enter. Her eyebrows went up in surprise.

"I'll be right out," Jasper said to Morgalla. "Can I hang your coat up?"

Morgalla took off her long dark violet coat and then removed the overalls, revealing her fit physique. She now wore what she normally did during the training sessions with Delilah. Her garb was skin-tight on her body which left her arms bare. She was very prepared to do some sort of physical activity that evening. She noticed him looking and how, for a moment, he couldn't look away.

"What is it?"

"Nothing," he replied. He was sure that if she wanted to she could kick his butt, judging from the condition of her arms.

She had a feeling that he was thinking something, but she still could not sense anything from his soul. It was one of the most frustrating things she had ever gone through.

From the look on his face Jasper certainly did notice. She handed him her clothes and sat on a stool at the counter. He was more conflicted than ever between how attractive and yet how dangerous she appeared. The term *she-devil* suddenly had new meaning. The argument his rational self tried to make became stronger.

But the horny young male side of Jasper's personality had an opinion too.

Shut up, she's hot! If you mess this up, so help me, I will never forgive you!

Thankfully, no one could hear his inner monologue; otherwise, one might think he was insane, arguing with himself in such a manner.

Meggan could barely hold back the laughter. She gestured for Jasper to go back and change. He left and Meggan stepped up to the counter in front of Morgalla.

"Hi, I'm Meggan."

"Morgalla," she replied, and they shook hands.

"You obviously work out. It shows."

"Thank you. So do you," Morgalla said.

"Making it my profession!" She snickered as she flexed a bicep. "Do you compete?"

Morgalla honestly did not know what Meggan could be talking about.

"Compete in what?"

"Never mind," Meggan replied. "So, Jasper is a great guy, huh?"

"He keeps his hands to himself and doesn't drool," Morgalla noted. "I like that in a man."

"Oh yeah, drool can be a definite turn-off!"

Missy Rider's boyfriend Steve walked into the gym, looking as smug and cocky as ever. . He noticed Morgalla instantly, but only from behind. He did not recognize her from the night he punched his own lights out. There was bruising around his left eye.. His eyes glided up and down Morgalla's body as she and Meggan talked. He smiled, liking what he saw and wondering who this new girl was. Jasper came out of the men's locker room in a T-shirt and shorts. He did not even realize Steve was there; his mind was completely on Morgalla.

"Shall we?" Jasper asked Morgalla after a long, deep breath.

"We shall," she replied.

Steve saw Jasper and Morgalla walking off to the weight area. His jaw dropped in disbelief that *this* was the same girl Jasper had been out on a date with.

"It was nice meeting you," Meggan said.

"You too!" Morgalla called.

Meggan beamed as Morgalla and Jasper walked away. She was happy that Jasper was with someone far nicer than Mariette, though she wondered about Morgalla's question about competition.

"I saw you looking!" Meggan exclaimed to Steve as he walked by, heading for the men's locker room.

Morgalla walked along the racks of free weights. She walked past twenty pounds, past the forty, and past even one hundred. Jasper picked up two twenty-five-pound dumbbells, but looked at Morgalla walking toward the heavier weights. Jasper caught up with Morgalla; she was at the very end where the heaviest of weights were.

"Something wrong?" he asked her.

"Two hundred and forty is the heaviest?"

"That a problem?"

"Um…no! Nothing wrong," Morgalla said, realizing she had better play it safe.

"How strong *are* you?" Jasper asked, trying to keep his voice down.

"That's um…uh…hey, look! What does that thing do?"

Morgalla pointed to a machine and proceeded to examine it as if she were really interested.

Time would pass as Jasper did alternate dumbbell curls with Morgalla spotting him from behind. She watched his arms curl with each rep; they strained against the weight. Morgalla was a bit bored, though; this was certainly different from any workout she ever did. Jasper was lifting as heavy as he could, trying to impress her, though it wasn't working. His contorted face was turning red from the strain.

Ignore the pain, ignore the pain.

Another man walked by, looking at Morgalla and not where he was going. Staring at her, he tripped over a bench. In fact, most every guy in the gym was looking at her. She could feel the eyes, sense the lust, and feel the envy of other women. She rolled her eyes and sighed; it was not her intention to make anyone feel bad. She then looked at Jasper, who was nursing one of his sore biceps.

He's jealous of Jasper.

She was almost flattered. It was her turn, so she stood in front of the mirror and he stood behind her. He was not surprised at all that she could lift weights as heavy as he could but little did he know that she found the weights actually too easy. She could see Jasper standing behind her, his face high over hers. He kept his distance and didn't touch her at all, an action that surprised her again.

They finished with the weights and moved on to a large apparatus she found to be quite alien. It had a bunch of pulleys on it and looked like a cage, with bars high above. Jasper could no longer ignore his thirst; he was pushing himself to keep up with Morgalla.

"You want some water?"

"Oh, sure," she said, and looked with great curiosity at the bars above her.

As Jasper walked back to the counter, Meggan noticed him approaching.

"So, how is it going?"

"Fine," he said. "Two waters, please. *God*, am I going to be sore tomorrow."

"Pushing you that hard, huh?" Meggan was on the verge of laughing as she took two bottles from the refrigerator.

He reached for his wallet and realized it was in the locker.

"Crap, can I owe you after we're done?"

"Yeah, sure," she said, and then something caught her attention. She looked over to see that everyone seemed to be paying a great deal of attention to one area of the gym. "Your new friend is certainly making an impression!"

"What?" he asked. Seeing the look of surprise on her face, he looked over to where he had left Morgalla.

Meggan pointed to the weight area. Jasper looked to the other side and saw that many people had gathered around one area. They were all watching Morgalla doing one-armed pull-ups. Jasper's reaction was of pure disbelief. He almost forgot to take the bottles of water back with him.

Surely this could not be what he was seeing, but indeed, after a few eye blinks he was convinced. His jaw dropped and he looked back at Meggan, who was also looking on in bewilderment.

Jasper ran up to the crowd around Morgalla. They were all watching in amazement that this woman, who was quite small compared to them, seemed to be doing this exercise effortlessly.

"How many is she up to?" one woman asked, sounding equally shocked and envious.

"I don't know," a man replied. "I lost count!"

Jasper made his way through the crowd and stood there, shocked, like everyone else. Morgalla finished and dropped to the floor easily and everyone applauded. She spun around, surprised by the reaction of the people, and then she smiled and made a little curtsy.

Missy Rider walked into the gym and immediately heard the commotion.

"What's going on?" Missy asked Meggan.

Jasper walked past Steve, whose mouth hung open, and stepped up to Morgalla. He sheepishly smiled at everyone who was looking, but not many were looking at him.

"She eats a lot of red meat," Jasper said to the few who were.

Morgalla shrugged it off; for once she was getting positive attention. Missy walked up to the crowd and looked annoyed that Steve was staring at Morgalla.

"Who wants to see the other arm?" Morgalla asked the crowd applauding her.

Missy did not recognize Morgalla until she turned around.

The redhead!

It felt like someone hitting her in the stomach; the fear overwhelmed Missy. She took a step back among the crowd so as not to be noticed by Morgalla. She could not explain the events of last night no matter how much she tried. She saw all the attention Morgalla was getting, and her fear was suddenly replaced by envy. To make things worse, the redhead was with *JASPER.*

The sun had set, but the stars were hidden by the clouds. Morgalla walked out of the gym with her overalls on and her coat over her arm. She felt the cool autumn air hitting her warm and lightly spent body. She had almost finished the cold and refreshing bottle of water Jasper gave her. The wind blew through her raspberry hair, and her head tilted slightly to the side to relieve herself of the crick in her neck.

The condition of her workout partner was completely different. His body was on the verge of collapsing; he had never worked out that hard in his life. His shirt was soaked with sweat, and he didn't bother to change back into his street clothes, for he could barely lift his arms. As healthy and fit as he was, Morgalla pushed him to his physical limits. His face glistened with exhaustion and his gym bag hung at his side. His fist could barely grip it.

"That was fun," she said.

"Um…yeah," he replied, which caught her attention.

That was clearly a lie.

This was her first glimpse into his soul; he was indeed human after all. She took his water bottle and splashed him in the face. On any other occasion he would have been offended, but it actually felt good.

Morgalla could feel a myriad of emotions from all around, but didn't pay much attention to them. If she had, she would have felt the daggers coming from one young woman. Missy looked out the window; her eyes followed the two toward the parking lot. She could not believe what had been happening lately as she looked at them. She was even angrier with herself for being jealous.

Jasper and Morgalla walked through the parking lot to his car. There was a slight rumbling of thunder in the distance. Jasper was still amazed at Morgalla's strength. She smiled at him. She could not help but notice his reaction.

Uh-oh, I think I overdid it.

"So, um, are you hungry again? I sure could go for something," she suggested, trying to take his mind off what he was thinking.

As Morgalla walked ahead of Jasper, he could not help but look at her and have the thoughts men have. He was attracted to this woman and had to look, but he was nervous and tried to be respectful. For a brief moment his thoughts were impure. Coming to his senses, he realized what he was doing and looked the other way.

She stopped, as she sensed fear from him. This time, though, there was something different. She turned around and looked at him curiously. She could feel that he was attracted to her, and she saw the guilt on his face.

"Jasper, what is it with you?"

"Pardon?" Jasper responded, trying to seem as innocent as possible, but it did little good.

Morgalla strolled around him, giving him the once-over.

"Normally I can tell many things about people just by looking at them," she said. "They're an open book to me. But you...*you* are an enigma."

"You can *read* people?" Jasper inquired, wondering what she could mean.

"Call it a gift. But *you* are very different."

"Should I be flattered?" His question was accompanied by a smirk.

"Honestly, I don't know."

"Well, different isn't a bad thing, you know," he said with a smile, and his words caught her attention.

"You really think that?"

"Well, yeah, of course," he said, and the two of them continued walking slowly to Jasper's car. "All my life I've been considered *different* by other people's standards. Now I really don't care one way or the other. It sucks that the bullcrap of high school followed us, you know?"

She looked away a moment due to his high school comment.

"I see," she said, and a question came to mind. "At the movie, why didn't you touch me?"

"Excuse me?" Jasper was surprised by her question. It seemed obvious why he hadn't touched her. To him it would have been inappropriate. "Well, I could give a long explanation, but I suppose all I can say is it would have been wrong."

"You're kidding."

"Kidding? No."

"Every male I've ever known would have taken what they wanted. I thought maybe you didn't want me, but I see it. I see how you look at me. Your pulse goes up when I'm around."

"How...how could you possibly know that?"

I can hear your heart beating.

"Never mind that. Look me in the eye and tell me you're for real."

Her words confused him, like almost everything else about her. He wondered about her past, curious if it was as troubled as he suspected.

"Morgalla, everything I've told you is the truth."

The words of her teacher Delilah rang in her head. Jasper was attractive indeed, and very different from any other male she had known. Morgalla stepped up and kissed him. The kiss was instinct; partly hormones, but mostly driven by her heart.

"I know," she said with a smile. But it was quickly gone when she saw the shock on Jasper's face.

She suddenly pulled away, realizing she should not have done that. Jasper was surprised, not knowing what to think or how to react. Her lips were soft, moist, and warm. A feeling of euphoria ran through his body and all his fear melted away.

"What was that you were saying? About men *taking* what they want? Isn't that what *you* just did?"

"I've…I've never met anyone I wanted. I'm…I'm sorry," she apologized. "I shouldn't have done that."

Jasper looked down at her, the shock of the kiss quickly fading. A hunger built within him, a hunger for another kiss. Morgalla looked at him with concern, not knowing what his reaction was going to be. She felt his fear melt away, which was a good sign. She felt a glow from him, a glow of happiness that melted his fear. She could not help but be overjoyed at his reaction and she smiled back at him. Happiness was something rare in her life, and feeling the sensation was intoxicating. She too hungered for another kiss, to feel more from this man.

"Why did you do it, then?"

She looked at the ground, not knowing what to say. He put his hand on her chin and guided it upward to look her in the eye.

"I will never try to take that which is not given," he said.

"You can't take that which I give freely."

Jasper moved in close and kissed Morgalla. As their lips connected lightly, their arms slowly wrapped around each other's bodies. The sensations brought by one kiss were indescribable. It was as if everything in the world had just drifted away; like a tremendous weight had been lifted from both their hearts and everything was right with the world. One kiss was all it took.

Then the rain began to fall, pouring down in buckets, but they did not care. They continued to kiss even as the rain soaked them.

The hard rain continued as Jasper drove Morgalla to the construction site. He was confused why she asked him to bring her there. He pulled up to the area and stopped.

They both really did not know what to say; there was a silence that was uncomfortable for him. To her words were not necessary, for she felt the happiness pouring from him. They looked at each other and smiled.

"Um, can I drop by the library and visit sometime?"

"Of course," he replied.

"Jasper...*Jazz*, thank you. For everything."

"Don't mention it," he said, smiling. "Are you *sure* you want to be let off here?"

He looked around. There was nothing but buildings in mid-construction.

"Jazz, there are things I can't tell you. Not now, anyway."

"But—"

"Shh," she silenced him. "Please. Don't be concerned, don't be afraid."

He looked at her; the streetlight shining through the window made it look as if rain was pouring down her face. Her eyes were beautiful, like emerald gems. Her words, and the tone she used, brought comfort to his fears.

"Okay," he said.

She put up her hood and went out into the rain. Jasper watched her as she headed into the construction site.

✿

Dear Diary,

Something weird happened today. I don't know why this happened or how, and it doesn't really matter. He's weak compared to me. He's fragile, even by human standards. Maybe I like him because I'm a lot stronger than he is. Or maybe it's because he's the first man in my life to treat me with respect. I think. . .I think I'm falling in love with him. But how do I know? What does love feel like?

✿

The last time Akira Daishi was in England, during the mid-1980s, it was for a business deal that fell through, and he saw little need to return. Today he was sealing the most important business deal of his life, though his partner had always done the traveling. The mansion was as grand as he expected; old, large, and expensive.

Another reason he never returned to England was the weather, of course. The wind blew through his thin silver hair and he bundled up, even though it was only autumn. He walked to the front doors and found a pair of large brass knockers in the shape of lions there, old and in need of polishing. He reached up to the handle and was nearly scared out of his mind when the knockers spoke in unison.

"Who goes there?"

"Cute. Not very original," he replied.

"Attitude will not gain you entry," they said.

The doors opened and he was happy to see a real person standing there. It was a woman, tall and attractive, with long auburn hair.

"Mr. Daishi?" she asked with an unmistakably English accent.

"Please, call me Akira."

"Of course."

She greeted him with a warm smile and he returned it, and they shook hands. He tried to walk to the doorway, but for some reason his feet were frozen to the cement steps. He looked down as the brass lions rambled on, making idle threats.

"What is this?" he inquired, confused as to why he could not move his feet.

"Oh, you can come in."

Those few words from her were all that was needed for him to move again. He stepped into the manor to see a glorious lobby, centuries old. He looked back at the steps, not sure what to think.

"Why couldn't I move?"

"It's a safety feature," she replied. "The lions really don't do much, but my father-in-law hasn't figured out how to shut them up. So years ago he installed a new safety feature to prevent intruders from entering. You must be a member of the family or be *invited* in by a member of the family."

"That simple?"

"Well, in a few minutes the steps would have burst into flame and you would have been killed, "she said dismissively.

"Excuse me?" Akira had to know more. "Has this safety feature ever failed?"

"Only once. Richard is out back in the cemetery."

English autumns were gray, the same color as the tombstones that Richard sat amongst. He glanced between the sea and one stone that meant more to him than all the others.

"She always loved the ocean."

Richard turned to see who was speaking to him. An Asian man of many years, Akira Daishi, was there. He walked up to Richard.

"When did you get here, Akira?"

"Just now," Akira replied.

Standing above Richard now, Akira looked left and right for a place to sit, but there was only tall grass and a few grave markers.

"Still afraid to get your nice clothes dirty?"

Akira remained standing, the wind from the sea blowing against him.

"I understand you had another vision," he said.

"They're becoming more frequent," Richard said. "And intense."

"What do you think they could mean?"

"What else?"

Richard's hand moved over the grave marker, feeling the letters and words in the stone.

"It's as if someone is torturing me," Richard said.

"Haven't you done that enough yourself?"

"You may be right," Richard said, as he looked up at his friend. "How long has it been?"

"Twenty-one years, two weeks, six days."

Akira extended his hand to help Richard up. They started to walk back to Smythe Manor.

"How will they do it?" Akira asked, as they arrived at the back porch.

"Difficult sometimes to tell fact from legend."

"All my family has is legend," Akira said. "That and family tradition."

"Your family's skills. Our magic."

There was a pause as another gust of wind blew. Something was on Akira's mind, but he was reluctant to discuss it for fear of t angering his longtime friend.

"Richard, just how far are you willing to go?"

Richard looked at Akira with curiosity. "As far as I need to go," he said.

"Into Hell itself?"

"We've had this conversation before," Richard said, as he turned his back to him. "And I've had similar conversations with my eldest son."

"But we never seem to finish it," Akira said. Richard remained silent, with his back turned. "I think we should talk about this before—"

"Are you afraid that I'm not in control?" Richard interrupted, spinning around. "Are you afraid that vengeance is blinding me and I'll risk the lives of everyone around me to satisfy my lust for revenge?"

"I'm not saying that at all," Akira said in a calm voice. "It was after your wife's death that your family went back to the old ways." Richard took a deep breath and calmed down. He sighed and looked back to the sea. "I'm just concerned, that's all. About innocent people standing in the way."

"You're worried about collateral damage."

"There are always innocent people who get in the way. Despite our best efforts."

"I realize what you are saying, my friend," Richard said.

"Remember, my friend, there is a big difference between good and evil," Akira said. "And it is our choices that make it so."

"The real challenge is determining which is which," Richard replied.

"I have confidence that you'll know."

✿

Damn. Oh DAMN, that hurts!

Jasper held his tricep muscle and tried to massage the pain away. He was in complete agony from the workout the day before.

Damn, she was really strong.

He could not fathom why and how she was stronger than him, despite her tiny frame. He figured that she must have an intense athletic background. He reached into his desk and took out aspirin for the pain. He was regretting pushing himself so hard the day before. Later on, Jasper sat at the front desk at work, his look a mixture of confusion and depression. Much had happened during the past few days and he was trying to let it all soak in. The many feelings inside him conflicted, still but the argument was different now.

Andy was walking by and could not help but notice Jasper's look. His first thought was that Jasper got dumped again.

"Uh-oh," he said.

"What?" Jasper asked.

"Something doesn't seem right in Jasper World," he replied. "How are things with what's-her-face?"

"Okay, I guess."

"Meggan told me she made quite an impression at the gym!"

"You can say *that* again. This girl...there's something strange about her that I can't put my finger on."

Jasper walked from behind the counter and went toward the bookshelves and Andy followed alongside him.

"You've never had a relationship with a woman before," Andy said. "I mean a *serious* one. Are you sure that you're not just, you know, finding out how women *really* work and think?"

"I'm not entirely clueless you know."

"Yeah, I know, but they can be like aliens sometimes! You should prepare yourself for that."

"Yeah, I know," Jasper said. Then a question popped into his head. "Hey, what's around those buildings being put up downtown?"

"You mean where the slaughterhouse used to be?"

"Yeah, there."

"Um...nothing. There's downtown, the site, and then just the woods."

Does this girl live in the woods?

"Oh, you should have seen her against Missy!" Jasper said gleefully, a smile coming to his face as they entered the break room.

"Really? What happened?"

"Almost came to blows, and trust me, Missy would have gotten her ass kicked!"

"Make sure you have your phone, then," Andy said joyfully. "I want pictures of Missy getting what she deserves!"

They laughed, Jasper especially, at the thought of Morgalla beating up Missy.

"It's weird. It's amazing how different and yet how similar someone can be. You know what I mean?"

"Of course, dude," Andy said. "No matter how many things you have in common with them, they're still women...still different. But then again, that's what makes it exciting! Look, Jasper, I don't know what's going on, but it sounds like things are going okay."

Andy walked away, leaving Jasper alone with this thoughts.

Chapter Ten: A Trek Through Springdale Mall

Morgalla sought out Jasper again at the library, only to find that he had left for the day. She noticed the neighboring college and remembered he had mentioned school, however briefly. She tried her luck, looking around the campus, even passing Missy Rider once. Missy glared at Morgalla with hate and stood aside as the redheaded girl walked by. Morgalla didn't even notice her at all, perhaps the greatest insult anyone could give to the vain young woman.

She continued looking, becoming more and more frustrated. A normal human would be easier to track, but this Jasper was difficult to understand.

Morgalla spent half an hour looking around and was almost ready to give up when she finally saw Jasper walking out of one of the many decaying buildings. She smiled upon seeing him, surprising herself a bit. Jasper noticed her almost immediately, smiled, and waved. To her surprise, she found herself holding her hand up and twiddling her fingers in a flirtatious, long-distance hello.

When they reached each other, Jasper and Morgalla exchanged a few pleasantries and then began to make plans for the evening, as Jasper had the night off of work. As they talked, a small something small was different about Jasper. Morgalla noticed a pin upon the lapel of his black coat that stood out: a pin in the shape of a pink ribbon.

That's new.

Morgalla suggested another visit to the gym, but Jasper wasn't particularly interested given his persistent soreness from the previous visit. Besides, he had a better idea.

✿

The local mall was out of Morgalla's way so she had only been there once before, out of curiosity. It seemed like a nice enough place, with plenty of people in good spirits. Some stores seemed pointless to her, like the boutique for very young girls. To Morgalla, it was just a way for parents to spoil their daughters. She also could not fathom why one shoe store was so big and always filled with women. Jasper blushed as they passed the store that sold women's lingerie. He purposely looked in the opposite direction, not wanting to seem like a typical sex-crazed male.

They stopped by the arcade and played some games. One game was filled with zombies and they had to shoot them with big plastic guns. Jasper did well, as he always did, but for some reason Morgalla just could not hit anything. She could not fathom why; even when she held the gun closer to the screen, still no zombies would die.

"Maybe it's malfunctioning," Jasper suggested.

He gave his gun to her, but again, no matter how hard she tried, no zombies were killed.

"This game is dumb," she said in frustration.

It was the same with the other video games. Morgalla just seemed to be jinxed. They were about to leave when she saw a game with basketballs, *real* basketballs. Jasper, still being sore from their gym experience, wasn't too keen on such a contest. Morgalla was great at it, of course, making every single basket. She saw that the game dispensed tickets; the better one played, the more tickets were won.

"Cool!" she said with a smile.

Jasper just stood back as she played multiple times, beating the high score, and, just like at the gym, she attracted a small audience. With two hands full of tickets she turned them in for prizes: she decided on candy.

"Why don't you become a pro ball player or something?" Jasper asked, as they exited the arcade. "You could be rich!"

"You mean there are people who get paid lots of money for doing that?"

Jasper laughed, thinking she was making a joke, but in reality her question was legitimate. She thought it wise not to press the subject.

They found their way to the bookstore, a place Jasper often went to. They browsed the magazines, and Jasper kept his eyes *away* from the top shelf where the "gentlemen's" periodicals were displayed. Morgalla looked around the magazines but saw nothing that interested her, until she caught sight of a magazine with a sunny beach on the cover. Her hand reached for it by instinct. She held it just to stare at the image.

"Like the beach?" Jasper asked.

"Hmm?"

"The beach," he repeated.

"Oh, well, I've only been there once, a long time ago."

"Whereabouts?"

"It was far from here," she said, being vague on purpose, for the beach she was referring to was on a different world. "I was a little girl. A...um...*friend* took me there."

The demon in disguise thought back to that day when she was a little girl and Delilah had taken her to that beach. It wasn't a vacation, nor did they have any fun. As always, it was business, but it had been a happy day for Morgalla, feeling for the first and only time the hot sand between her toes.

She wasn't making eye contact with Jasper as she put the magazine back on the shelf. Jasper did not pry, but looked on with concern. It was yet another sensitive subject that he had stumbled upon. Though he was frustrated, he remained silent. Morgalla didn't notice the look on his face.

Morgalla's sensation of longing only lasted a moment. It was replaced by a feeling that she was being watched, something she was used to in Hell. She looked around, expecting perhaps the worst, only to discover two teenage girls looking in her direction. As soon as Morgalla looked over her shoulder the two girls looked away. Their giggles annoyed her and she frowned, but then she realized that they were not looking at her. In fact, they were looking at *Jasper*, who was strolling down the rack of magazines.

Morgalla's eyes widened with this realization, but it was her reaction that surprised her more. She bit her lower lip and sneered with her back to the two girls. There was a slight twitch of her eyelid as her pulse raced. Her hands clenched and her eyes, the appropriate color of green, glazed over.

STOP. . .looking. . .at him!

Morgalla found herself on the verge of anger at the two girls staring at Jasper. She had never felt this kind of jealousy before in her life, and she realized she had to do something. She stepped down to Jasper, whose attention was still on the rack of magazines. He took the latest issue of *Hardcore Gamers Weekly* and felt her hand grasping his. He looked down at her and smiled, feeling the warmth of her touch. With Jasper's attention on the magazine in his hand, Morgalla looked back at the two girls and narrowed her eyes. The girls, seeing the look of hate coming from her, decided it best that they leave.

Jasper put the magazine back, holding Morgalla's hand in his. The sensation felt wonderful to him and he couldn't help but smile as they left the bookstore. Things were looking up as they walked among the crowd hand in hand.

It was up in the air as to what to do next. Both of them were getting hungry, so Jasper began leading her to the food court. They passed the office of a travel agent. Morgalla noticed the posters of sandy beaches and perfect blue skies. The store next to it was indeed a curiosity, as it was filled with many strange things and was quite dark. They stopped and she looked up to see the name *STUFF* above the doorway.

"What do they sell here?" she asked.

"Well, *stuff*, obviously," Jasper said, jokingly.

Her curiosity got the better of her and she entered the store, her hand leaving his. He followed and lost her among the rows of strange clothing and knickknacks that human youth found so appealing. Morgalla approached a rack of strange items, not knowing what they were. There was a girl whose back was to her; she was dressed all in black and her clothes were decorated with chains. Morgalla assumed that she worked there, since her wardrobe matched the bleak ambiance of the place.

"Excuse me," Morgalla said, "but what *is* this thing?"

The young woman turned to reveal a face paler than death. Her hair, long and black, hung straight down to the center of her back. There was metal impaled through one eyebrow and one nostril, and many in each ear. The black makeup on her lips and around her eyes was so thick Morgalla thought it had been drawn on using a Magic Marker. Morgalla was shocked and showed it as their eyes met.

"I don't work here," the girl said.

"Oh, sorry," Morgalla replied.

"Hey, there you are," Jasper said, walking up to Morgalla. He then jumped like Morgalla had at the appearance of the girl before them.

"Hey, Jasper," the girl said.

"Becky?" Jasper was surprised to recognize the voice and face, even though both had changed since they last had seen each other.

"My name is *Raven* now," she said. "Because ravens are dark and beautiful."

"They're also scavengers who spread disease," Morgalla interjected.

The introduction was uncomfortable for everyone, but Morgalla and "Raven" shook hands.

"So, do you work here now, Beck—er, Raven?" Jasper asked.

"I *wish*," Raven sighed, her eyes half-open. She seemed incredibly drowsy. "They said that I wasn't *cheery* enough, can you believe that?"

"Wow." Morgalla smirked, wanting to say more to mock her, but decided not to.

Nah, that would be too easy.

"I still work at the black abyss of pain," Raven said.

"Say what?" Morgalla asked.

"Taco Hut," Jasper replied.

"Oh."

"You know, Jasper, you should come meet my new friends," Raven said. "They really opened my eyes to the truth and helped me embrace my inner darkness."

"Yeah, I'll keep that in mind," he said.

"We really should go now," Morgalla said, pulling Jasper's arm. "We have that...*thing*, remember?"

"Oh yeah, now I remember," Jasper replied, as he realized what she meant. "It was nice seeing you, Becky."

The two of them left the store, Morgalla practically dragging Jasper out.

"So how do you *know* that girl?" Morgalla asked.

"Well, we had an art class together and went out a couple of times," he replied.

"You *dated*...that?"

"Take it easy," Jasper replied. "She was different then. I have no idea what happened. She was really sweet and wrote poetry, but now she shops for jewelry at a hardware store."

Morgalla broke out laughing, for she was thinking the same thing. Jasper turned to look at her. He was quite pleased to see her in such a joyous mood. Her face was turning red, and she squeezed her eyes shut as they started to water. Jasper grinned at her, realizing just how beautiful she looked with a smile on her face.

"So, I guess she bought the collar from a *pet* store, then, huh?" Morgalla joked, and made Jasper laugh, too.

They continued their journey to the food court; she took Jasper's hand again. The two of them appeared to be just a regular human couple, nothing more. As they walked, Jasper noticed among the sea of faces two that looked familiar. It was a coincidence that Andy and Meggan were also walking around. They exchanged pleasant hellos and Morgalla could tell from their mood that they were honestly glad to see her. She was humbled and blushed, for normally the only people glad to see her were amorous males.

The trek to the food court continued and a pizza was on the menu. Morgalla was sipping the last of her soda through a straw as she sat across from Andy and Meggan. Andy was in the middle of a story from his past.

"So Stills is aiming at the target and pulling the trigger, but nothing is happening," he said. "He stands up and calls for the sergeant, who walked over yelling at him like he always did. 'You got the safety on, Private!'"

"Something they would teach you on the *first day*, I would think," Jasper said.

"*Second* day," Andy replied, and continued with the story. "Anyway, Stills stands up and the gun goes off, nearly shooting the sarge in the foot!"

As Andy broke out laughing, Meggan seemed annoyed and shook her head. Morgalla looked curious, wondering why he found it funny.

"You're laughing at the fact that someone almost had his foot shot off!" Meggan exclaimed.

"*Almost* being the primary word," Andy noted. "I mean, we were freaked out at first, but it's one of those things we can look back at now and laugh about."

"I take it you don't find mutilation funny?" Morgalla asked, as she noticed Meggan shaking her head again.

"Do *you*?" Meggan replied.

"Depends on who's getting mutilated," Morgalla replied, to which her three companions laughed.

The ironic part was that Morgalla said it with a straight face, though she was glad she made the three of them laugh.

"Well," Jasper observed, "I guess you had to be there."

They enjoyed a silence at the food court table littered with pizza crust, empty plates, and soda cups.

"So," Morgalla said, standing up, "excuse me a moment. I gotta go—"

"Oh, I'll join you," Meggan said. She stood up and reached for her purse.

"What for?" Morgalla asked.

"Ha! You're funny," Meggan said with a smile, thinking that Morgalla was joking.

Morgalla's question was legitimate, for she had no idea what Meggan was talking about. She turned to Andy and Jasper who were still sitting and drinking cola.

"No, seriously, what for?" she asked them.

✡

Meggan checked her makeup in the ladies' room, Morgalla walked up to the sink to wash her hands.

"So what do you use for your hair?" Meggan asked.

"Pardon?"

"Your hair, that's a beautiful shade."

"Thanks, it's a...trade secret," Morgalla lied. She was good enough with her powers that she could make her hair most any color she wanted.

"I'm not gonna *steal* it," Meggan said, and ran her fingers through her own hair. "This is my natural hair color."

Morgalla dried her hands and then turned to see Meggan leaning against the sink, with a big smile on her face and a look of great anticipation.

"What?" Morgalla asked.

"Come on, out with it!" Meggan said.

"Out with what?" Morgalla had no idea what she wanted.

"Dish about *Jasper*, of course!"

"I have *no* idea what you mean."

"Well, how are things going?" Meggan asked.

"Fine. I mean, we've been out a few times—"

"I thought he was going to *kill* himself trying to keep up with you at the gym!"

"Oh, yeah, that concerned me," Morgalla said with sympathy.

"Don't worry about it," Meggan said. "Jasper doesn't have an ego. I think he might be one of the only guys on the *planet* who doesn't have one. An *ego*, that is."

"Yeah, I seem to run into all of the egotistical ones," Morgalla joked.

"Dated a few ego-holics, huh?" Meggan asked.

"*Dated*, no. I just *know* them."

They shared a laugh and Morgalla could feel a fondness coming from Meggan. Morgalla had never bonded before with another woman like this, except for Delilah. But from the human being's soul the demon could feel that this woman truly *wanted* her friendship. The smile on Meggan's face was real.

"How come you don't wear makeup?" Meggan asked.

"Oh…well…" Morgalla sought for an answer.

"I'm not saying you *need* it. You have that natural beauty most women would kill for."

"Kill?"

"Not *me*, of course," Meggan laughed.

"I guess I just never felt the *need* to paint my face," Morgalla said, looking away.

"Paint," Meggan smirked. "I've never heard someone use that word before to describe makeup."

Meggan was actually impressed by the fact that Morgalla's lips, though they had a slight blush to them, did not shine from gloss. Everything about Morgalla's face was lovely and yet humble. Meggan could see why Jasper was attracted to her.

Two teenage girls came in, giggling Morgalla, though, was silent, as was Meggan, who did not want to ask the next question in front of present company. The girls finished and then left, and Morgalla ran her fingers through her hair nervously. Meggan didn't have any superpowers, only her two eyes, two ears, and brain.

"You, um, don't date much, do you?" Meggan asked.

"Is it that obvious?"

"You're closed off," Meggan said.

"I…have reasons to be,"

Morgalla replied, but could not look her new friend in the face. Though both women were about the same height, Morgalla felt very small and vulnerable, like a small child.

"I'm sorry if I'm touching on a sensitive subject," Meggan said with concern.

"No, it's okay," Morgalla, replied. "It's just…quite different from *this* side of the relationship."

"This side?"

"Well, up until now I've always…*observed* relationships. I've never been part of one."

"*Very* different," Meggan observed. "When you're a little girl you're told that when you meet 'Mr. Right' everything will be okay."

"Mr. Right?" Morgalla inquired.

"You know, that *perfect* guy who will sweep you off your feet and make everything all better. I get the feeling that *you* didn't believe in that growing up."

"I can say with certainty that wasn't the case with me," Morgalla replied with no hesitation.

"Girls become adults but they don't grow up. They still believe in that perfect man and then get mad when their boyfriend has flaws."

"How dare they?" Morgalla's sarcasm crept in and they both laughed. "So the truth is…"

"Truth is, even if two people are meant for each other there is still a lot of work."

Oh great.

The look on Morgalla's face showed that this was not good news to her.

"That shouldn't discourage you, though," Meggan corrected herself, seeing Morgalla's expression.

"You've had others before Andy, yes?" Morgalla asked.

"Well, yeah, but they don't matter now. I'm with him."

"Jasper...he's hesitant to be with me. I can feel it."

"You have to understand something," Meggan said. "Jasper is hesitant because he doesn't want to be hurt again."

"I had that feeling," Morgalla said, as she recalled what little she could feel from his soul. "That explains many things."

"Like what?"

"It's nothing, just how he's hesitant, like you said."

Meggan looked at Morgalla, who in turn stared at the tile wall. She thought Morgalla might cry, but her face betrayed none of what her heart felt. Two things were for sure: there was scar tissue beneath Morgalla's pale skin, and she was a woman too proud to show weakness.

"Guys are afraid to lose their freedom," Meggan continued. "*That's* why they fear commitment."

"Personal trainer *and* a relationship expert?" Morgalla smirked, looking back at her.

"Not really," Meggan said with a chuckle. "But I've been thinking of charging for both, what do you think?"

"I think you'd rake in the money," Morgalla laughed, though only for a brief moment, and then they enjoyed another moment of silence.

"I don't mean to pry into your life," Meggan said. "And Jasper isn't the kind of guy to pry either. I don't think he'd make the first move."

"I already know that," Morgalla replied.

"Wait, don't tell me you—"

"Well, maybe." Morgalla gave Meggan only brief look and then looked away, obviously blushing. "I still don't know what came over me."

"Oh yes, you do." Meggan was now smiling, for this was the kind of conversation she was hoping for. "You're not as innocent as you look. So is he a good kisser?"

Morgalla bit her lower lip and nodded.

The ladies returned to the table to see Andy and Jasper still sitting there. Andy had a big smile on his face, but Jasper had wondered where both women had disappeared to.

"What took so—" Jasper said, only to have his words cut off by Andy's foot kicking him in the leg for his own good. "OW!"

As the four of them left, there was a question that was still on Morgalla's mind.

"Andy, you've never actually *been* in combat, have you?"

"No," he replied. "I was just in the National Guard. They taught me how to fight, but I never actually had to. How'd you guess?"

Your soul isn't tainted.

"Just lucky," she replied.

While Morgalla and Andy moved ahead to the mall's exit, Meggan took Jasper by the arm and held him back. There was something important she had to tell him.

"I don't wanna freak you out or anything," Meggan said. "But, um, I got a feeling...just a feeling, about your new girlfriend."

"Well, we're not an official couple yet, we're still—"

"Shut up, Jazz!" she continued. "I just got a feeling. Your girl, I think she's damaged."

"What do you mean?" Unconcerned, Jasper looked at Morgalla, who was still talking to Andy many feet away.

"She's so closed off," Meggan said. "There's a reason for that. There *has* to be."

"Like what?" Jasper's question was accompanied by a look of frustration.

"I'm not saying you shouldn't date her. Only that she's probably got some pain in her past. Maybe a guy broke her heart, maybe worse. All I'm saying is that you should take it slow."

Chapter Eleven: The Dam Breaks

The next day was a regular day at work for Jasper, kind of slow and boring at first but then it picked up as paperwork seemed to come out of nowhere. He was glad that he was able to move without pain again. He was reading a magazine at the front desk when a man walked up.

"Excuse me," the man said. "Can you check something on my record?"

"Sure thing, I just need your card," Jasper said, putting the magazine down. The man handed Jasper his card and he scanned it into the computer. His record came up on the screen, but first Jasper had to ask him a few security questions, following the rules set by his boss Sherry. "What's your last name?"

"Love," the man replied.

Jasper stopped, and his eyes went from the computer screen to the man. "Pardon?"

"My name is God Love," the man replied.

"Says here your name is Morris Pelky," Jasper said, looking at the screen.

"That's not my name!" the man replied, annoyed, raising his voice for other people to hear.

"Well, sorry, I'm just reading the screen."

Morgalla entered the library and stood at the end of the counter. She was, of course, in her human form, as she always was on her trips to Earth. At once God saw her and his mood suddenly changed.

"Demon!" the man screamed, pointing at the woman before him. "Spawn of hell!"

"Say what?" Morgalla was completely confused as she stood at the end of the counter. Her hands went to her temples and ears, checking to see if she really was in her demon form instead and had forgotten.

Andy and everyone else in the library within earshot suddenly stopped what they were doing and looked at the counter. Jasper turned to see Morgalla standing there; he was shocked at what God Love was doing and saying.

"DEMON! DEMON! DEMON!" he screamed, as he ran out of the library.

Andy walked up to the counter, confused and shocked at what had just happened. He looked at Jasper and Morgalla, happy to see her there, but was wondering what the heck had just occurred.

"Hey, don't look at me," Morgalla said, trying to sound as innocent as possible. "I have *no* idea what he's talking about!"

"That guy," Jasper said, breathing a sigh of relief that he was gone. "He's out of his mind or something!" He then shrugged, the nightmare over.

"Hey, Morgalla, how's it going?" Andy asked.

"I'm okay, how are you?"

"Like the song says, '*I can't complain but sometimes I still do.*'"

Morgalla smiled; Jasper's friends were growing on her more and more with each time she saw them.

"Well, if you will excuse me," Andy said, realizing that he was a fifth wheel, "I have...things to do." Andy walked away, out of courtesy to his friend.

"You busy?" Morgalla asked Jasper, as she didn't know how this whole "job" thing worked. "I was hoping to talk more."

"I'm off in an hour," Jasper said.

"Sure thing. I'll come back then."

They heard a woman call out Jasper's name. He cringed at the sound of Cynthia's voice.

"Excuse me," he said to Morgalla.

Jasper turned and walked over to Cynthia. She complained that the latest memo he typed was in the wrong font. To Cynthia it was an important matter, but to Jasper it was quite mundane and trivial.

Jasper was so behind on work, he didn't take any break in the afternoon. He went back to the break room only to get his lunch bag. He came in to see Sandy sitting eating a sandwich. It always amazed him how someone who normally would have retired years before worked so hard.

"Late lunch, Sandy?"

"Yeah was so behind I didn't have time. I'm starved."

"I hear you there."

"You know, I overheard you and Andy talking recently."

"Uh oh."

"Oh go on," she chuckled. "Nothing like that. I just overheard you two talking about a girl."

"Yeah, we went out a couple of times. Seems okay but a little weird."

"Hmm, I wonder what's considered *weird* in this day and age."

Jasper sat next to her, the load off of his feet felt good.

"Well, I guess she just seems really distant, that's all."

"I would give her space. Let her come to you. There's probably a good reason."

"I have, not to worry. We've been hanging out more than anything. Nothing romantic."

"Sometimes it's best to go slow. Get to know a girl and you'll be able to sweep her off of her feet."

"I've never been *that guy*. You know, the kind that can charm any woman."

"Did I ever tell you about how my Frank won my heart?"

"You've said a lot about him, but never that specifically."

"Well, besides him being a first a marine and then a cop..."

"*Again* with the men in uniform." Jasper said with a smirk.

"But on every important night he would play *Old Blue Eyes* for me. Your pop stars of today can't hold a candle to him."

Jasper soaked in the words of wisdom a moment.

"Well I gotta get back to work." He said to which Sandy smiled back at him.

He had opened the door when Sandy has one more thing to ask.

"Say, how's your mom?"

"Oh, she's doing much better, thanks."

"Tell her we miss her."

"Sure thing."

As Jasper walked back up to the circulation desk, he passed the CD collection. He stopped a moment and flipped through "S" section.

About an hour passed as Morgalla sat on one of the couches in the library. She was glancing through a manual of some kind and was confused by some of the technical meanings. She turned the page and saw the words *Chapter Six: Detonator* written in big letters.

"Finally!" Morgalla said with relief.

Jasper walked up, glad to put an end to his workday.

"Ready?"

Morgalla slammed the manual shut, not wanting him to see it. She stood, folded the manual in half, and put it in her coat pocket.

"Yeah," she replied.

"What's that?" Jasper's question referred to the manual, thinking it was a magazine.

"Nothing. I brought it in."

Jasper and Morgalla went to a Chinese take-out restaurant. As they both stood at the counter, many people were hard at work in the kitchen. Morgalla was distressed; there was a lot she wanted to tell Jasper but could not. She didn't know how to tell him he was dating a demon. Deep down, she just knew he would not accept it. Perhaps later…

"Hey, something wrong?" Jasper asked, giving a slight touch to her arm to get her attention.

"Is it that obvious?"

"I think you have a wall up, Morgalla."

"Hmm?"

"A wall. You don't tell people your secrets, you don't let people in."

"You don't read minds, do you?" She squinted and looked inquisitive.

"Um…nope, not that I'm aware of," he said, and smiled.

He thought she was joking, but part of her question was a real inquiry.

"A wall, huh? Okay, I'll make a deal with you. You take down *your* wall a little and I'll do the same."

"Fair enough," he replied, glad that maybe he could finally get to know her better.

She thought for a moment, putting her hand to her chin.

"Hmm," she said, and then an idea came into her head. "Why are you nervous whenever you talk to me?"

Jasper held his breath for a moment, for it was a good question.

"Normally I…find it difficult to talk to women, Morgalla."

"You're talking to me."

"I mean," Jasper stammered, looking for the proper words. "I can't talk to them as women. Like at the bar, Andy and Meggan told me to talk to you. Normally I would never have walked up and talked to a total stranger."

"Oh? Then why did you?"

"They kinda dared me, I suppose. My friends, that is. They suggested I take a chance. I mean, what's the worst that could happen?"

How ironic. That's why I said YES.

"So, you can't talk to women. You mean on a romantic level," she replied. "Why is that?"

"I've had bad experiences with that."

"Maybe it's your approach?"

"I once got sprayed with mace for saying, 'Hi, I'm Jazz.'"

"Yowza," Morgalla said. "That Missy person also has something to do with this, huh?"

"It's funny, Andy and I always joked that she must be the daughter of Satan!" Jasper laughed; he had hoped that she would follow suit, but she looked away.

"I wouldn't doubt it," Morgalla said.

A woman walked up with a large bag and Jasper handed her some money. The car drive was rather quiet, but Jasper pointed out his old elementary school to her as they drove past it. She thought of what it might have been like to have had a normal childhood, like humans do. The two of them went back to Jasper's home just as the sun was setting.

"Where's Andy?"

"He's out," he replied. "He's staying at Meggan's tonight."

Morgalla's eyebrow went up.

"You planning something here tonight?" she asked, messing with him a little.

"Oh…uh, *no!*" Jasper said with innocence. "I'm not planning anything! I swear!"

"I'm joking."

More and more, Jasper's soul was opening up before her, though normally he should have been an open book. She could sense a small level of nervousness, but most of him was happy to have her there. She took it as a good sign.

"I'll set everything up," Jasper said.

"I can help—"

"No, it's okay, I want to surprise you."

Normally, Morgalla didn't like surprises. But Jasper's heart and soul were slowly becoming known to her, and so she decided to trust him. She walked into the living room; only a tiny corner of a wall separated her and Jasper. She heard him doing something and her curiosity grew.

She took off her long coat and looked at the photos on the wall. A feeling of jealousy came over her seeing the happy pictures of Jasper and his family. Other photos were of him and Andy, and some were of Andy and Meggan. She felt a bit of jealousy toward them as well.

"So who did you know first?" she asked, loud enough for him to hear in the other room.

"Pardon?"

"Andy or Meggan?"

"Andy," Jasper said.

Morgalla turned to see Jasper standing behind her. Normally she would have sensed him coming, but again the enigma that was Jasper Davis shielded him from her. She jumped slightly.

"Oh, sorry," Jasper said. "I knew Andy first and he introduced me to Meggan. She was the one who convinced me to hit the gym because I was so skinny."

Morgalla went into the dining room, which was at the end of the kitchen. She was surprised to see nice linen on the table and two candles lit, giving off a nice scent. The lights on the wall and in the living room had violet cloths over them, which gave the room a warm glow. Jasper had to improvise everything, being a working stiff with not much money to throw around. Morgalla was humbled and flattered by his gesture; no one had ever done something like this for her.

"How...how did you know my favorite color?"

"You wear it a lot," he replied. "Just a hunch, really."

Jasper set out the plates, milk, and silverware, and they sat at opposite ends of the kitchen table. Jasper ate slowly, enjoying the meal, while Morgalla ate as if it were her last. He sat up, his right hand grasping the fork gently and his left hand under the table. She was hunched over, her face near the plate. Her right hand gripped the fork and stabbed the plate as if she were murdering her food. Her left took a handful of steamed rice and shoveled it into her mouth.

Jasper watched her blankly. Morgalla saw the look on his face.

"Sowwy," she said with her mouth full. She then tried to mimic his movements, using only the fork and not her bare hands. No hunching over, but instead showing proper posture.

"First time eating Chinese food?"

"Oh no, I enjoy it whenever I can," she replied.

Morgalla noticed the look on Jasper's face.

"Be thankful I'm using utensils," she said.

While she ate, Morgalla saw a framed picture on the wall. The painting was of a truck and appeared to have been done by a young child, with orange and yellow paint. The corner of the painting read *Jasper age 6*. Morgalla smiled at this and thought it was cute.

"Awww," she said.

Jasper looked up and saw that she had noticed the painting. His face turned bright red.

"Oh yeah," he said. He shrugged in modesty and blushed slightly. "My father framed it when I moved in here. It was the first thing I ever made. It's supposed to be a Popsicle truck."

"I used to paint and draw," Morgalla said.

"Oh yeah? What did you make?"

"All sorts of things," she said. "Landscapes, rainbows, puppies...then my dad burned them all."

"Oh. I'm sorry," Jasper said, sounding sympathetic. "That's the first time you've mentioned your parents."

"He said they were a bad influence."

"How could art possibly be a bad influence?!"

"I uh...so what's that thing?"

Morgalla pointed to a large box by the balcony window.

"That's my telescope. I was going to set it up after dinner."

"You're into astronomy?"

"I like looking at the stars and planets. I was thinking of going into it as a career but something got in the way."

"What was that?"

"I'm terrible at science." Jasper chuckled.

After finishing dinner, Jasper set up his telescope on the balcony. Morgalla looked through it at the stars, and they amazed her. Jasper looked at her, not caring what was in the sky that night. She then stood away from the eyepiece and looked up at the sky.

"I don't look at the stars much," she said. "They're kinda bizarre to me, but beautiful."

"Really? Stars are amazing! All those TV shows, movies, books, about spaceships and aliens. And there they are!"

"Maybe they're closer," Morgalla said, looking at him and finding it ironic that there was an alien of sorts right in front of him.

"You mean, like Roswell or something?" he asked with a smile, sitting across from her.

"They're like diamonds," Morgalla said, changing the subject.

She then looked at Jasper who immediately looked up at the sky. She smiled, noticing that he was looking at her a lot more intently than he was at the stars.

"Yeah, I guess they are," he said.

Morgalla reached for her long coat and bundled up, chilly from the autumn air. She sat on a bench hugging her body with her arms.

"I hate the cold," she said, and then let out a violent sneeze.

"Bless you," Jasper said. "Don't you go to warmer places ever?"

"It's difficult for me."

"You don't like flying?"

Morgalla shook her head *very* vigorously, for the thought of flying terrified her.

"I hate the winter," she said.

"Snow can be beautiful."

"How?"

"Well, imagine if you will: middle of the night...fresh, undisturbed snow on the ground.

Looks like frosting on a cake."

"I like cake," Morgalla said smiling.

"The full moon shines, the snow glows a beautiful shade of blue with little sparkles along it. Like the stars themselves."

"That doesn't sound too bad," she said. "You have a way with words."

Jasper sat next to Morgalla, but was careful not to get too close. He did not want her to feel uncomfortable.

"Actually, I would be lying if I said that I liked snow," he said. "Haven't had the best of luck with it. You ever go skiing?"

Morgalla responded by shaking her head.

No way.

"I tried it once, and only once," he continued, thinking back to that one unfortunate weekend. "Broke my leg. Weird, though, it must not have been a serious break. I only had to wear the cast for two weeks."

"You know, you haven't asked me to take down my wall yet," Morgalla said.

"Oh yeah, that's right, I owe you a question." Jasper thought hard about a question he could ask. She was actually nervous. What if he asked a difficult question? "Why did you come to see me after our first date?"

She breathed a sigh of relief, for that question she could answer.

"I. . .don't know many nice people," she said, looking up at the stars for a brief moment and then back to him. "I realized, but not until after I went to bed, what kind of man you are. And how lucky I was to have spent some time with you. I'm sorry that I just left."

"I can understand not trusting people. It can be tough," Jasper said.

"And why did you give me a second chance?"

"Good question," Jasper said, and thought a moment. "Old habits die hard, I suppose. I'm the nice guy, and we never win."

You wouldn't last one day in Hell.

"No, they don't. Though they should."

Jasper sensed that perhaps the conversation was getting too intense. He stood and walked to the telescope.

"Say," he said. "I think I can find the Venus, or Mars. You wanna see?"

"My father raped my mother," Morgalla said. Jasper stopped, stunned by this admission. He turned around; Morgalla's look was blank as he gazed at her with concern. "Nobody ever told me, especially not him. But I just know it. I know *him*. He uses people. I don't even know her name."

Jasper knelt and held her hands. She looked at him, her eyes filled with tears. He didn't know what to do or say, but he knew there was nothing he could do to relieve her pain. Her head pounded from the pressure of all those years denying her own pain.

"I'm so sorry," were the only words he could say.

"It's a sobering experience, the day you find out your father is a monster."

Jasper and Morgalla went inside, into the family room. She sat on the futon and Jasper came over with two drinks. She stared at the carpet, a melancholy look on her face. Jasper was saddened by her mood, wishing he could fix all her problems, but he was powerless. He handed her a drink. The tears were gone, but her eyes were sore from crying.

"Thank you," she said.

Jasper sat at the other end of the futon, quite a ways from her. Morgalla took a sip of her drink and then noticed the distance between them.

"What?" he asked, noticing her gazing at him.

"You don't have to sit *so* far away." She motioned for him to come closer. Jasper slowly scooted down, which made her smile. "Now, is that so bad?"

Jasper smiled, realizing the wisdom of her words.

"Do you want to watch some TV?"

Morgalla looked at him and her hand slowly moved to his.

"I couldn't sense anything from you."

"Pardon?"

"It's, um, nothing important. I'm pretty good at reading people."

I can actually read their souls.

"That's a talent I wish I had," he said. "I think it would have really helped in the past."

"But you were tough," she continued.

"O-kay."

"You are unlike any person I've met before, Jasper Davis, and I had to know what made you tick."

"And have you found out?" His question came with confidence and he had a smirk on his face.

"Um, not all." Morgalla gently ran her fingers through Jasper's hair. "Little by little your own wall has come down. I could feel your strong emotions, like when you were afraid. Or when you were attracted to me."

Jasper was intrigued. She could feel more and more from his soul as he let down his guard.

"What am I feeling now?"

Love. . .I think it's love.

"You know, you're very cute," she said, changing the subject.

"I am?"

"Yes, you are."

"I think you are very beautiful," he said, his eyes locked with hers.

Morgalla set their drinks down on the coffee table. She looked into his eyes as her hand ran through his hair.

"Have you ever danced?" he asked.

"*Danced*? No," she replied, her eyebrows going up in surprise. "Well, by myself, but never with someone else. Me, dance? No way. I have two left feet."

"First time for everything," Jasper said, standing and walking to a small stereo on a shelf by the TV.

With the press of a button, a soft song played. The room filled with the voice of Old Blue Eyes. Jasper walked up to her and offered his hand; she was hesitant at first, but accepted and stood before him. His right hand went to her waist and he guided her left to his shoulder. Their other hands grasped each other as the lavender light illuminated the room. He looked into her eyes as their bodies swayed lightly. She was concerned about stepping on his feet, but with his help she got the hang of dancing.

Slowly, both of her arms went around his neck; his hands were on her back and their bodies came together. Their eyes never lost each other as they got closer and closer. They kissed again, gently at first, then with more and more passion. Morgalla's hand ran over his chest and down his abdomen. Her head rested on his shoulder and he held her hand that rested on his chest. The song ended; the melody had soothed her body. Her eyes met his again, and it was clear in her heart and mind what she wanted to do. Her gaze changed to one of pure desire.

Morgalla sought Jasper's lips again as their hands flowed over their bodies. She gripped his shirt and pulled it from inside his jeans. Her hand then slipped under with a longing to feel his skin. Jasper's eyes flew open in shock, never having had a woman kiss him with such enthusiasm. His hands ran over her back and up to her head, gripping her hair in either hand.

They continued kissing, more passionate now than before. Their lips would release and their breath was quick and feverish. With her hands still on his face, she could feel a burning inside her that was only increasing in intensity. Jasper was releasing a primal beast within her and she could barely control it. Morgalla then took Jasper's hand and guided it to her chest.

"Make love to me, Jazz."

He looked into her eyes and saw something he had never seen before from her or any woman. It was a hunger, a longing for the pleasure only a man could give. The sound of her voice was powerful; Morgalla was not making a request.

"I...I don't want to take advantage of you," he replied.

"You're not."

Without warning, Morgalla gave him a shove and he fell back onto the couch.

"Whoa!" Jasper said in surprise.

Jasper was on his back and Morgalla pounced on him as if he were prey. Her hands moved under his shirt and she helped him out of it. His chest flexed as his hands moved up to explore her body.

"Yes!" Morgalla whispered breathlessly..

Morgalla moved down and kissed him some more. Jasper removed her shirt, and their bare chests pressed against one another. She gently took two handfuls of his hair, gripping it as they kissed. His hands lightly scratched down her back.

They moved into Jasper's bedroom, removing clothing along the way. Moonlight poured through the window, illuminating their bodies in pale blue. Jasper and Morgalla were in a fervent embrace as they made love.

Jasper kissed his demon lover as his hips slowly thrust. He felt the warrior thighs wrapped around his body so that he would be drawn closer to her. The sweat on his back gleamed in the moonlight as her hands scratched down his back. She was strong and could seriously hurt him if she was not careful. It was taking all her willpower not to make her human lover bleed.

Jasper moved down to her neck, tasting the sweat on her flushed skin. Kissing her more, she could feel his breath against her neck and along her ear. Morgalla went rigid, one hand clasping the strong shoulder of her lover. The other hand gripped the sheet, holding it tightly as the muscles in her arm flexed. Finally, the brushfire tore through her. The shock of the sudden sensation made her eyes fly open and then slam shut. A noise escaped her lips, one that sounded almost like a desperate plea.

Jasper could feel her strength all throughout his body. Morgalla momentarily lost control, and her nails dug into the flesh of Jasper's back. He grunted as Morgalla drew blood, but the pleasure far outweighed the pain.

Their bodies went limp, and they lay motionless, recovering from the ecstasy they'd just experienced. They heaved with each breath, their hearts racing in their chests. Slowly, their heartbeats returned to a state of normality.

Jasper sluggishly raised his head. Morgalla looked up at him, their eyes met, and they tenderly kissed again. She trembled slightly; there were tears of joy in her eyes. She felt love for him. Never before had she felt such a sensation in her heart. She never thought she *would* feel for a man this way.

"You…you okay?" Jasper asked in concern.

"Yes," she said, and a small smile crossed her face. Morgalla looked at her hand, seeing blood on her fingernails. She cried out in horror, "I'm…I'm sorry!"

"I'll live," Jasper replied, smiling, his pain a small price to pay.

He rolled over onto his back and Morgalla rested her head on his toned chest. They looked at each other and smiled. She gave him a kiss on the cheek.

"Thank you, Jazz," she said.

"Thank *you*," he replied.

"Are we supposed to talk now?"

"We don't *have* to do anything."

Morgalla chuckled and then lay her head back down on his chest. He kissed her forehead; their bodies were intertwined beneath the sheet. She looked up at the window and saw the full moon in the dark sky. There was no moon in Hell, and it was always wild because it was on fire.

"The sky here, it's so peaceful," she said.

Jasper looked over at the window too, and saw the moon against the indigo sky.

"Yes, I guess it can be," he replied.

The sky was on fire where she was from, and all worlds they conquered turned out the same way. But he was also feeling a little pity for Morgalla. He still knew very little about her, but she hadn't told him anything happy about her life.

Morgalla continued to stare at the moon and then noticed the cross on the window. She moved on top of Jasper and kissed him again. She looked into his eyes, wondering how a man who believed in the Bible could love a demon of Hell. But she also realized how important that symbol in the form of a cross on his wall was.

"Do you think there is a God?" she asked, as she looked up at him.

"Of course, Morgalla," he said, looking at her. "Do you?"

"I…" She stopped, not knowing what to say. "I'm…I'm sorry."

"About what?"

"Your religion. It means a lot to you, doesn't it? I'm sorry that I—"

"It's okay," Jasper said, and kissed her again. "Morgalla, you've obviously been through a lot. I know it's tough to have faith in anything when horrible things happen to you. But there is also a lot of room for faith."

"Sometimes, I wonder what it would be like to believe in God."

Jasper gently held her chin and made her look at him.

"Morgalla, if someone as wonderful as you exists in the world, then surely there is a God."

Morgalla blushed at his comment and kissed him again. The moonlight shone down upon them as they drifted off to a peaceful sleep, naked flesh against flesh, Morgalla's breath hot against

Jasper's chest. She soaked in the warmth of his body and the steady beat of his heart, and smiled.

Maybe there is a God, then.

✿

Elsewhere a young boy screamed. There was a woman, young with long red hair, lying dead on the floor of her home in a pool of her own blood.

"Mommy!" the young boy screamed. A large form walked over to the child cowering in the shadows. His feet thumped on the floor. The child looked up, his eyes filled with tears as the beast chuckled. His long black cloak flowed and his face was obscured. In his arms was a newborn baby; his clawed finger slowly ran down the baby's cheek. "MOMMY!" the boy screamed again, running to his dead mother's body.

James Smythe startled awake on the plane flying over the Atlantic. The cabin was dark and most everyone was asleep, including his wife Rebecca. He panted heavily, sweat on his brow. It had been a while since he had that dream. He gripped the blanket tightly and looked over at his wife. Taking a deep breath, he closed his eyes again and tried to go back to sleep.

✿

In Hell, Zorach confronted his generals to discuss their current situation. They met in a large circular stone chamber, darkened, with only small gems giving illumination. The table at which they sat was circular and made of black wood. Zorach sat in the largest chair, with three generals—Darvis, Zeethros, and Makraka—

seated in the others. The table could actually seat twelve people, but their numbers had been dwindling in recent years.

"During the first day the casualties are estimated at a few million," General Darvis continued his report.

"Only a few million?" Makraka asked.

"Our armies will spread slowly out, encountering very little resistance," Darvis replied. "The location of the event horizon is somewhere remote, not in a major city."

"With the battalions of Zorinda in place and the element of surprise, we cannot fail!" Zeethros added.

"That is still not enough to conquer a planet with six billion humans!" Makraka's comment had the sound of pessimism.

"Our Lord Zorach will be the deciding factor," Zeethros replied. "Morgalla herself reported that the planet does not use, nor do the people on it even believe in magic. When Lord Zorach is ready he will lay waste to entire cities. Half the entire population will be dead within weeks. By the time they realize who's invading them it will all be over!"

"Fool!" Makraka snapped at him. "It will take weeks for the planet to be enveloped by our realm and our Lord Zorach to walk freely!"

"Leave that to me," Zorach interrupted.

Their squabbling suddenly ended and all three looked at Zorach.

"My lord?" Makraka tried to understand his master's comment.

"Morgalla will be the key to our victory," the demon lord said.

Zeethros and Darvis sat unaffected by his words, accepting his wisdom and his orders. Makraka, on the other hand, looked concerned.

"My Lord," Makraka said, "are you planning to use her to—"

"Yes," Zorach interrupted.

"She is your daughter," Makraka said.

"That matters not," Zorach replied. "It was her destiny since before she was born that her life be used as I see fit. Even if that means sacrificing it."

When Zorach and the three generals left the chamber, Delilah was waiting. She looked at them walking by, Darvis and Zeethros with their heads up, but Makraka looking bothered by something. Delilah noticed, but brushed it off. She turned to see Zorach at the doorway.

"You summoned me, my lord?" she said, bowing before him.

"Come inside," Zorach said. "There is much we need to discuss."

Chapter Twelve: The Morning After

Meeko fish are a lovely species known only on one world. They change colors depending on their mood, the only animal known to do so, at least according to Morgalla. Her powers were just emerging and everyone around her sometimes changed color, much like the Meeko fish. Morgalla was mesmerized by them.

"When you face an enemy, you should never show mercy. Morgalla? Morgalla, are you listening to me?"

"Huh? What?" she said, snapping out of her trance. She was sitting on a fallen log and gazing into the stream.

"Are the fish more interesting than me or what I'm trying to teach you?"

"Oh, I'm sorry, Delilah."

"I'm trying to teach you something important! Here I brought you on my scouting mission because I knew you liked—well, places other than Hell."

"Oh yes, I do, and I thank you for bringing me!" Her voice filled with gratitude as she looked back at the stream. "It's just… do we *have* to do any lessons today?"

"Every day is a lesson, young one," Delilah said, extending her clawed hand and helping her young apprentice to her feet. "Now, in life, as with all scenarios, you must strike first if you are to gain the advantage."

"Yes," Morgalla said. She trailed behind, her eyes still on the stream as they walked along the riverbed. Every now and then her hand moved to her temple, giving it a scratch.

"This is true with all creatures, whether they be animal, demon, or...*lesser* beings."

Their black cloaks flowed in the spring breeze. The two figures, one with red scale-like skin and the other a light orange, both stuck out among the green and brown.

"Why doesn't my father try to conquer this world?"

"Bevana Prime has no humans on it," Delilah said. "No sentient life whatsoever, except the occasional dragon."

"Like your grandmother?"

"She might be here for all I know," Delilah said. Morgalla scratched at her temple again, and this time her tutor noticed. "What's wrong with your head? Come, let me see."

Morgalla stepped back, but just for a moment, knowing that when Delilah expected to be obeyed she meant it. Delilah removed the young demon's hood and pushed away her long hair to reveal a small bump on her temple.

"Horns! You're growing horns!"

"But I don't want them!" Morgalla said in disappointment, as she scratched at the two bumps on either side of her head.

"Nonsense!" Delilah replied, standing straight. "They will be a thing of beauty! I can show you how to polish them. Oh, and we'll be able to wear jewelry to special occasions too!"

She brought attention to her own two white horns on her head, small and subtle, but she always found them to be a sign of power. Delilah turned and continued to ramble a bit, giddy like a schoolgirl, about doing her nails and all the fun that she and Morgalla were going to have. Morgalla, on the other hand, put her hood back up and gave the bumps another scratch as she ran to keep up with her mentor. They walked on a fallen log across the river, where Morgalla caught the attention of the Meeko fish again. She stopped and looked at two that turned a bright pink when they swam up to each other.

They look happy.

"Hey!" Delilah yelled. Morgalla's trance was broken again as she looked at her tutor walking up.. "What *is* it with these damn fish, anyway?"

"Well, they just seem so happy, I guess."

Delilah scoffed and raised her lip in a sneer.

This is going to be tougher than I thought.

She sat on the log next to her student, searching for the words to say to convince her otherwise. Morgalla was still quite young and Delilah could manipulate her soul to follow her own, but she had decided years ago that she wasn't going to do that.

Surely there must be some way to convince her.

"Morgalla, they have nothing."

"They have each other. And the river, and no one is trying to kill or hurt them."

"Until an animal or something comes along that has a craving for fish."

"But until then——"

"Stop it!" Delilah interrupted her thought by kicking the water. The Meeko fish changed to bright red and swam away as quickly as they could.

All Morgalla could do was watch as they swam out of sight. She frowned. Delilah knew she had been hard on Morgalla, but she did not care. She was doing her a favor.

✿

Morgalla woke with the sun shining on her face. Her hand went to shield her eyes as the warmth and brightness brought her out of her dream. It had been a while since she thought of Meeko fish. The events of the night before came back to her, and she realized that she had woken up in someone *else's* bed. It was a strange feeling, to be sure, and incredibly new. She rose up and looked over to the sleeping Jasper. The rays of the morning sun shone through the window on his body. The sheet up to his waist, sunlight cascaded over his toned form.

Beautiful.

She wanted to reach out and touch him; to feel the firm flesh she felt on top of her the night before, but decided not to disturb his slumber. She instead rose and reached for her clothes scattered on the floor.

It wouldn't take long for Jasper to awaken with the sunlight in his eyes. Half asleep, his hand moved over to feel if Morgalla was there, but he felt nothing. He woke up completely and looked around. Morgalla then came into the room fully dressed, and she seemed to be in a hurry. She grabbed her long coat and put it on.

"I'm sorry, I gotta go," she said regretfully. "I've never been away from—well, it's getting late."

She caught herself, about to say something she should not have. Jasper was still half-awake as he rubbed his eyes and sat up.

"When can I see you again?" Jasper asked. She did not answer at first.

Oh God, please say I'll see you again!

"I don't know when exactly, but I promise you will."

Jasper stretched out his hand. "Come here…please?" he asked, needing to hold her just once more.

Morgalla sat down on the bed, and she and Jasper looked at each other. She could feel complete relaxation from him, as if all was right with the world. She found him incredibly attractive, even with the morning hair. They embraced. Her hand grazed over the area where her nails had dug in the night before. Neither of them realized that Jasper's wound had completely healed.

"What's wrong?" she asked. As her fingertips moved over his bare skin, she loved the sensation.

"I just needed to hold you one more time."

They released and looked at each other. Her hand moved down his chest to his abdomen. She looked at his body; there was something different about him, but she could not put her finger on it. She liked it, though, seeing him in another light.

"I was wrong," she said.

"About what?"

"You're not kinda cute," she said. She looked down at his chest for a moment and then up at his face. "You're damn sexy!"

The biggest smile that he had ever seen on her crossed her face and they gave each other a small kiss.

Jasper put his robe on and walked Morgalla to the door, and they kissed again. Their hands clasped, not wanting to release each other.

"I'll drive you home."

"No, it's okay, I feel like walking," she said.

"Really?"

"Yeah, it's a beautiful morning! Bye," she said, smiling.

"Bye," Jasper replied, also smiling.

Then he looked at the clock and remembered he had to be at work in less than an hour.

"Damn!" he shouted as he realized the time, and he ran to the bathroom.

Morgalla skipped along the sidewalk; the sun was shining and the birds were singing.. She skipped past two elderly ladies sitting on a bench.

"Good morning!" Morgalla called out enthusiastically.

Morgalla continued to skip down the street happily. The ladies returned her smile, her happiness contagious.

"Awww, that's sweet," one lady said to the other. "She got laid!"

Jasper drove fast to work. He could not make any of the lights, of course, and he had to hit the brakes.

Damn it!

He looked at his watch; it was a sure thing he was going to be late. Sitting alone in his beat-up car, the world seemed a little different to him now. Another car drove up and stopped next to him, and he got a strange sensation, a feeling that was indescribable. At first he thought there was someone in the car with him, but of course, that wasn't the case.

The sensation was still there, though, as if someone was right there with him. He looked to his left and then right, and saw the driver of the car next to him. It was a young woman talking on her phone, and even though he could not hear her or see her lips moving, he could tell what she was feeling.

How. . .how do I know that she's happy?

With a honk of the horn from the car behind him Jasper realized that the light had changed color. He stepped on the gas.

Jasper arrived late and ran into the library, hoping no one would notice him walking in. A woman passed him on the way out and Jasper stopped a moment. He could sense something unusual from her, something he never felt before. It didn't matter to her, for she ignored him as he walked by. Jasper shook it off as he walked to the office. There, he saw one of his co-workers, Catherine.

"Hi, J," she said, smiling.

"Hi," he replied, but then stopped and looked at her.

Jasper then sensed something from Catherine. He stopped, looking at her oddly. It was not a bad sensation, but more like a feeling of happiness. He could tell what she was feeling, and it was happiness. She looked down, wondering if she had spilled something on her outfit.

"What's wrong?" she asked, as she noticed Jasper giving her a weird look.

"Uh…nothing," he said.

What the hell is going on?

Jasper walked out into the main library room. It wasn't crowded at all, and yet it felt like it was. He saw co-workers and total strangers, and yet they all seemed the same to him. His emotions were like a ride, changing moods as soon as someone came close to him. At first he felt calm, then stressed, then calm again. But then there was a sensation of a ray of heat burning into his heart. He felt angry and he turned around to see Cynthia walking up to him. She did *not* look happy.

"You're *late,*" she snapped. "Unless you want to spend the rest of your day looking for a new job you better get your ass in gear!" Jasper's only response was to stare at her, his scowl becoming more and more prominent. Never had he hated this woman more than he did at this moment. "What's your problem?" she demanded, seeing clearly how much he hated her.

"Get…away…from…me!" Jasper said, as his rational mind struggled for control. He walked away from her, fast.

"Get back here!" Cynthia commanded, but he ignored her.

Jasper ran to the men's room; thankfully, it was deserted. He looked at himself in the mirror and splashed cold water on his face. He took deep breaths; finally, the sensations were going away and everything returned to normal. A man walking in interrupted his peace. Jasper closed his eyes, trying to block out what the man was feeling. It did not take much effort, for the man was calm; today was an average day for him.

Jasper walked to the circulation desk, still troubled by the odd sensations he was experiencing. The feelings strengthened as he moved closer to his co-workers. One was angered at his computer, for it had frozen yet again. Jasper had to back away from him as he smacked the side of his outdated computer, the sense of anger almost too overwhelming for Jasper to bear.

All throughout his workday Jasper could sense different things from people. All kinds of emotions: anger, irritation, sadness, depression, and even a little lust, were being picked up by him from people walking by, coming up to the counter, and even some he couldn't see. The people with truly intense emotions almost seemed to glow.

Jasper sat at the front desk, shaken by what was happening to him. He couldn't stop sensing the emotions of the people around him.

It's not mind reading. But I can feel others' emotions by just looking at people, and sometimes I don't have to look at all! How can this be happening?

If he concentrated, he could block out what people were feeling; which was a relief, since he didn't wish to feel sadness, jealousy, or anger.

Jasper reflected on the last couple of days. The night before had been the best night of his life and he had Morgalla to thank. Nothing and no one was going to bring him down today. He found himself daydreaming and blanking everyone out. He thought of Morgalla's face, her body, and her scent. He thought about the pleasure she gave him, and how happy she made him feel. He recalled how her body felt next to his as they slept last night. He didn't even notice Cynthia walking up and nagging him. She became increasingly annoyed and then angry as Jasper blocked out her and the rest of the world.

"JASPER!" Cynthia yelled, snapping him out of his trance.

"Oh, sorry," Jasper said, sounding apologetic. "Souls! I can see people's souls!"

"You know, I'm tired of your slack-ass attitude!" she shouted. "You think you can come in here and do whatever you want!"

"Though I don't know if *seeing* is the right word," he pondered aloud. "It's like a sixth sense."

"Look, I've about had enough." She grasped him by the shoulder and spun him around in the chair.

This was the first time Jasper had spoken to Cynthia since he had become…different. Cynthia was always unattractive to him, and he would look at the ring on her finger and wonder what man could possibly have married her, but now she was truly hideous. Cynthia stood before him, but it was an uglier version of Cynthia.

"Cynthia?" he said, in shock barely recognizing the woman before him.

Cynthia could not help but notice his expression and looked contemptuous in return.

"Do you have a problem?" she demanded.

"No, but *you* sure do!" Jasper replied, taking a step back.

"That does it! The day my promotion is official, you're fired, Davis! You hear me? You're *fired!*"

It took Jasper a moment or two, trying to decipher what was different about Cynthia than everyone else he had sensed so far.

Black, her soul is black. Whose soul is black? HOW could someone's soul be black?

They were questions he was almost afraid to know the answers to. He concentrated, and in the middle of Cynthia's angry tirade she stopped, when a sudden headache came over her. In both of her temples it started and then ran through her entire brain. She then felt an aching in her heart, at first just feeling a slight case of heartburn, but then it got worse and worse.

Jasper saw what he was doing, his new abilities causing Cynthia pain, and he stopped.

"I'm sorry," he said.

"What…what is going on here? What did you do to me?"

Your soul, I was searching it.

Jasper looked at Cynthia in a completely different way now. Before, he thought she was just an old and bitter woman, but it was more than that. Her past was filled with anger and hate, turning her soul black. With more probing he could have found out more, but he might kill her for all he knew, and she was aware that he was causing her pain.

"You...you can't have," Cynthia said, her face turning red.

"Look, Cynthia," Jasper said, "just shut up already, will you? I'll be damned if someone so full of spite will be a boss of *mine*." Cynthia opened her mouth, but no words came out. Jasper then realized that he had just done what Morgalla had done to Missy. A smile came over his face. "Get to work."

With that command, she knew deep down what was right and Cynthia left in a hurry. Jasper thought of what to do next, and one name came to mind.

Sherry was sitting in her office and working at her computer. Jasper opened the door without knocking, his eyes instantly fixed upon her.

"How *dare* you!" Sherry yelled. "You *knock* before you enter my office!"

Closing the door behind him, Jasper casually sat in the chair before Sherry's desk and put his elbows on the edge. Resting his chin on his palms, he stared at Sherry with a smile. Just a peek, he needed, just a peek into her soul to see what lay beneath. Not quite as black as Cynthia, but certainly dark through years of dishonesty and sloth. He had always suspected but now he just knew what kind of person she was deep within: she was lazy and dishonest.

"What, did you blackmail people to get your job?"

Sherry's reaction spoke volumes.

"Oh my God!" Jasper exclaimed. "I was right?"

With hands on his hips, he shook his head and clenched his lip. He wanted to yell at her, to tell her about all the frustrations about his job, but he had more important things to do. Jasper walked out of the office and then the building, heading straight to his car *Morgalla. Something weird is going on here. . .she has to know something!*

✿

Jasper drove to the construction site to look for Morgalla. He looked around there and then looked in the downtown area. He had no way of contacting her; perhaps he should have stayed at work, for she might have gone there. He drove home hoping to find her waiting for him, but she was nowhere to be found. The entire drive home was strange too; he could sense the emotions of all the people around him.

He got home, and Andy still wasn't there. Finally, he had some peace and quiet as he lay down in bed. Without warning, he felt a contraction in all his muscles, as if they were all flexing at once. He grunted at the sensation; he was scared and confused about what was happening.

He fell to his knees, his hands on the carpet. He watched in shock as the veins in his forearms began to bulge. He let out a scream of fear as the muscles in his arms began to grow. His biceps grew to immense sizes, ripping through his sleeves. The veins also bulged and his skin slowly turned orange.

Jasper's ears grew long and pointed like Morgalla's, and his hair turned long and gray. The veins in his neck swelled as the muscles in his neck grew. Fortunately there was no pain, just a burning sensation, the pumped feeling he got when working out, only this was all throughout every muscle in his body and magnified.

His calf muscles swelled to an enormous size, making a ripping and crackling sound. His pants shredded and ripped apart like paper. Jasper screamed again, feeling the sensation flow through his back. His shirt ripped more as his back muscles distended, every one of them growing.

Not only did his muscles grow but his skeleton as well. His bones elongated and thickened with his new body, making a crackling sound, and sending a dull ache throughout his body. Jasper cried out in fear.

He rose up gripping what was left of his shirt and ripping it off. His pectoral muscles expanded to tremendous sizes. Jasper let out another scream; the rest of his lower body matching his new size.

His clothes were now rags scattered on the floor. Jasper fell over; he lay on his side, naked, his new gigantic body heaving. The sensations were then gone and his body relaxed. His new, bigger form heaved with each breath and was sweaty. The damage done from the transformation was suddenly healed; he grunted from the sensation flowing through each muscle.

Every aspect of Jasper was now much larger; unimaginable strength and power flowed through every fiber of his being. His eyes were closed shut as he recovered from the ordeal.

Jasper sluggishly rose up, sore in every part of his body, as if he had worked out to an incredible degree the day before. An unusual sensation then flowed through him as the soreness subsided and his muscles healed from the metamorphosis.

He felt a new power flow through his body as he stood. The mirror in front of him was tall; he could see his entire body, and his jaw dropped at the sight. His body was much bigger, six feet tall and over two hundred pounds heavier, and all of it muscle. It appeared that his body fat was virtually nonexistent. His muscles were incredibly developed and the veins were bulging in places he never knew they could. His skin was orange all over and his hair was long and gray.

He slowly approached the mirror, gazing at his new reflection, and his hands explored his face. He saw his eyes change from brown to a dark lavender color. He let out a gasp of shock.

He looked down at his new body; the sensations of the mammoth muscles were incredible. The strength and power flowed through every inch. His hands ran over his skin, feeling new ridges and bulges everywhere. He smiled at the feelings, at so much power and strength flowing through him.

He then came to his senses, the rational part of his mind taking over again. He looked in the mirror realizing that something not only incredible but horrifying had occurred. His heart pounded from fear and his brow dripped with sweat, and he wished Morgalla were there. He held his breath for a moment, then let out a scream and fainted.

✦

James and Rebecca Smythe had a terrible flight to America; delays and rudeness were abundant. They rented a car and drove into Springdale and parked. They were in the downtown area, which was quite run down. They were both dressed rather conservatively, wearing long coats and appearing as if they were harmless and unarmed, but looks could be deceiving. There were strange medallions around their necks. They stepped out of the car onto the sidewalk. The concrete was cracked and worn, and the street was littered with potholes. Leaves the colors of autumn blew in the bitter wind up and down the street.

"Left side of the car, right side of the road," James said. "That takes some getting used to!"

Rebecca looked around, seeing the very quiet main street of Springdale. A young mother and her son walked by. Rebecca smiled at the child, offering a friendly greeting.

"Hi," she said, smiling.

The boy gave Rebecca the finger. She frowned as the woman and her son walked by. Rebecca turned to James, who was shaking his head. He took a transparent gem from his pocket; it glowed pale white.

"Please tell me we're here to kill that child, so we can go home," she said.

James shook his head, looking at the gem in his hand. "No," he said. "According to this, he's human!"

"Damn," she replied.

James turned, holding the gem out. It glowed slightly pink when he faced one direction, toward the construction site.

"This way," he said.

The two demon slayers walked throughout the town. Finally, they came to the construction site where Morgalla had been coming and going. Since it was Saturday, there were no workers around.

James and Rebecca stood over the foundation where Morgalla had entered and exited this world. The gem in James's hand was glowing a brighter pink.

"So what does that mean?" Rebecca asked, as she looked around the half-built area.

"The trail stops here," James, replied. "Curious. Something indeed *was* here, and recently. Perhaps they'll come back."

"Fancy come coffee?" she asked, noticing the coffee shop within view.

✼

Morgalla lay flat on her bed, like she was passed out, but her eyes were wide open. Her hair flowed around the bed sheets and the light flickered off her polished black horns. She stared at the ceiling; though a blank canvas usually, she pictured Jasper's hand-some face. She pictured him turning to look at her, his boyish face smiling at her and a pair of eyes that said everything was going to be all right.

> *Dear Diary,*
>
> *SIGH...I really don't know where to begin so I'll just say it...I made love to him last night. Jasper Davis, the human...I actually made love to him. I'm happy and glad I did it, really. I never thought I would actu-ally do it with anyone. He was so warm and gentle and passionate...*

She sat up suddenly in the bed; her eyes were still wide, but this time from a painful realization.

> *Oh God...I have to tell him. I have to tell him everything. How long can I lie to him? But will he accept this? Will he accept me?*

Morgalla rose from the bed and stood. She walked to the desk looking at the book. The last words had appeared there. She read them again and then closed the book. Her mind was made up as she walked to the door.

Suddenly, there was a knock at the door. Morgalla looked up, startled. With a wave of her hand the diary slammed shut and she hopped out of bed. She slowly opened the door and it creaked open, with her peeking through the crack. Delilah stood in the open doorway, her face emotionless.

"And where have *you* been?" she asked, almost accusing her of a crime.

"Here and there," Morgalla replied.

"I'm sure," Delilah said. She entered and looked around.

"Looking for something?"

Delilah spun around quickly and gazed into her eyes. Morgalla looked back calmly as if she had nothing to hide whatsoever. She had played the part many times before.

"Time to come clean," Delilah said.

"About what?" Morgalla said innocently. She could not hide her happiness at all from her friend.

Delilah moved in closer; her look was more like that of someone who was interrogating, not inquiring.

"You *know* what I mean!" she whispered in a demanding tone, her eyes practically on fire as she gazed upon Morgalla.

There was a silence; Morgalla smirked and then sighed. Maybe it was because she was trying to play the part that Delilah wanted her to play to get her off her back. Or maybe she wanted to brag to someone of the most incredible night she had.

"Okay, you got me," she said, shrugging. "I had a male last night!"

"Ooh! Was he good?" Delilah's question was accompanied by a wicked smile. She sat on a chair and got comfortable, wanting details.

"Very," Morgalla said, falling backward onto the bed.

"Human?"

Morgalla was not sure how to respond. Delilah would surely know if she were lying.

"Um, yes," she said.

"Did he think that *you* were human?"

"Hey, he thought I was *super*human!" Morgalla said with confidence, pretending to almost brag about her abilities, but merely giving Delilah what she wanted to hear. It must have worked because Delilah laughed out loud in happiness for her.

"You *needed* this, you know? You needed a release. You're so uptight! Did you kill him like I said?"

Morgalla looked at her, disturbed, Delilah's words killing her endorphin buzz. She sat up on the bed giving her an annoyed look.

"You really know how to kill a mood." Morgalla was offended, but Delilah looked on with innocence. She meant no disrespect.

"What? I just wanna know if you enjoyed killing him! Come on, details! Details!"

"Oh, brother," Morgalla said.

"You didn't answer my question."

"Well, he was so good, it would be a *shame*, you know?"

Delilah thought a moment and then gave a look of agreement.

"Well...yeah, I guess I can see that," Delilah said. "There are so *few* males that are good." Suddenly, her smile was gone. "He wasn't a *virgin*, was he?"

"Oh no," Morgalla said. "He couldn't have been!"

"Good," Delilah replied. "Trust me, you would *know* if he were."

"He would have been bad?"

"Let's just say something weird would have happened afterward."

Delilah walked past Morgalla and out the door. Morgalla looked out and saw her walk down the large hallway. When sure that Delilah was gone, Morgalla walked out. She walked quietly through the large hallway, looking over her shoulder and being careful not to be seen. Unknown to her, Necrod and two of his minions were lurking in the shadows, ready to strike.

Morgalla walked as quickly as she could, but quietly too. She then stopped in her tracks, turning to see Necrod and his two lackeys standing less than twenty feet away. Their eyes met for a brief moment, and then Morgalla ran as fast as she could away from them.

The three pursued her down hallways and corridors. Necrod and the two turned one corner and saw a dead end, with Morgalla nowhere in sight. The two lackeys were confused, but Necrod was not. Morgalla was actually over twelve feet off the ground, above them on top of a ledge. Necrod looked up and Morgalla attacked the beast and his two unsuspecting thugs. She kicked one goon, who fell back into Necrod and they dropped. The other minion tried to stop Morgalla, but with a blade she sliced through its neck and it fell to the ground dead.

Morgalla ran away as fast as she could. Necrod pushed the minion off him and galloped after her. Down many hallways, twists, and turns Morgalla ran, making her way to the portal chamber, leaping over and around bystanders that merely turned their heads as she ran by. She barged into the portal chamber, bypassing the guards and the attendant, whose cigarette dropped from his lips. She leaped into the portal to Earth and escaped through it. Necrod ran in just in time to see her go through. Shoving others out of his way, he let out a roar of anger and was ready to pursue.

"Don't!" a voice bellowed, and Necrod turned to see Vex standing there.

Morgalla came out of the portal and landed in Springdale. She took out her blade, ready for anyone who might have followed. Her hand trembled as she waited...but no one came out. She breathed a sigh of relief, for she was safe for the time being. Now on Earth again, she immediately changed into her human form, and looked around to see if anyone had noticed her. She was relieved that she was alone.

✿

Back in Springdale, James and Rebecca sat in a coffee shop. The magic gem lay on the table glowing only slightly white. They each sipped their coffee. All of a sudden the gem flashed a slight red color, signifying that someone, or something, came out of the portal. It then glowed pink, which suggested something demonic was nearby.

Only pink?

James was curious what could have come out. Seeing the red glow he thought the worst, but if the gem was only pink, then it must not have been a demon. James was well aware of the gem's effects; he had read an instruction manual of sorts. It glowed many colors to detect many different things, but the color pink was never mentioned.

The two demon slayers both look at the gem, then at each other, and then out the window at the construction site. Morgalla had changed into her human form and was walking out of the site. Rebecca took out a pair of binoculars and looked at Morgalla. James squinted, trying to see, and his look gave the impression that he had seen a ghost.

"Looks harmless enough," Rebecca said. "But then again, I guess that's the point."

"Give me those!" James said, and took the binoculars from her.

"Excuse me!" she said, a bit offended. James looked through the binoculars at Morgalla. He only got a brief look before she was out of sight. "You mind explaining?"

James did not reply. Setting the binoculars back down on the table, he was dumbstruck and speechless. Only a question came to his mind.

Who was that?

The walk to Jasper's home was the longest walk of her life. Many thoughts ran through her head about what his reaction to her being a demon might be. True, he could compromise her entire secret cover and her operation would be dead, though it had been decided that Earth wasn't worth Hell's time anyway. But if word got out of what she was, then Hell might be discovered.

That would be bad. Not for us, but for Earth. My father would have no other option but to attack and not stop.

That was the worst-case scenario. But in all honesty, they would probably not believe Jasper and he would not want to be with her anymore. She had made up her mind, but the walk was primarily to work up the courage to tell him.

Jazz...I'm a demon. Jazz...don't be afraid, but I'm a demon from Hell. No, that won't work.

She finally got to the apartment complex and froze. She looked up to the window that was Jasper's and just stared at it. The cold autumn wind blew through her raspberry hair.

I'm falling in love with you. Maybe that will work. Jasper, I love you...I'm a demon. Well, here goes nothing.

Morgalla climbed the steps to his floor. She knocked at the door but there was no answer. She twisted the knob and saw that it was unlocked. She opened it and walked in slowly, sensing that something was out of the ordinary. She took a look around, but could not see any sign of Jasper.

"Jasper?"

She entered and closed the door behind her. She looked around for Jasper but could not find him. She went into his room, sensing his presence, but did not see him.

"Morgalla," Jasper said nervously.

Morgalla turned to see a large lump in the corner of the room. Jasper had covered himself with the biggest blanket he could find, concealing every part of his body. Morgalla could barely see his eyes peering out at her.

"I let myself in, hope you don't mind," she said, looking at him a bit confused. "Is this some sort of weird erotic fantasy you've always wanted to play out?"

"We have a *big* problem!" Jasper said, obviously terrified. "What is it?" she asked, and stepped closer to him. "Take off the blanket."

"Something weird has happened!"

Morgalla took hold of the blanket and removed it from his head. She was shocked to see his new orange-skinned face.

"What the *hell?*" she said, shocked at seeing this new form before her. She could feel his soul and could tell that it was indeed Jasper, but could not fathom how this could have happened.

"That's what I said," he replied, on the verge of having a panic attack. His pulse raced and his brow was covered in sweat. "Morgalla, what's happened to me?"

Morgalla stood; she was shocked and confused. She would have to calm Jasper down somehow and explain what was going on.

"Jasper…please. I know this is all very, *very* strange, but you have to calm down and listen to me."

"Listen to you? Morgalla, do you know what's going on here?"

"Please! Quiet!" Morgalla said in a firm voice, and Jasper complied. She closed her eyes and took some deep breaths. With a simple thought, her horns appeared at her temples, her ears grew over twice as large, and her skin and hair turned orange. She opened her eyes, which were now violet, and saw the reaction on Jasper's face. "I'm a demon."

If anyone had happened to be walking by that afternoon they would have heard the scream of a young man in terror. Thankfully, the only person nearby was Jasper's elderly neighbor and her hearing was horrible.

Jasper tried to run out of the door, but the fact remained that he was a demon now; his body was changed, and he was only wearing a bed sheet around his waist.

"Jasper, get back here! Please, I'm not going to hurt you!" Morgalla shouted. Jasper finally found himself gripping the doorknob, but slowly the fear subsided. "Jasper, I'm sorry I didn't tell you, but I couldn't! I just couldn't tell you!"

Jasper breathed heavily. He saw such a strange woman before him, but her eyes; her eyes were the same, even though they were a different color. He realized that just as he could sense the emotions of people all around him during the day, he could now feel Morgalla's as well. She was sincere in her words and he could feel her fear, though he didn't know the source. He slid down the door and sat on the cold linoleum.

"Why...why are you afraid?" Jasper asked with surprise.

He has all the powers I have.

"I...I was afraid to talk to you, Jasper. Afraid to tell you the truth. This is what I've been hiding from you."

"What's happened to me?" Jasper's tone changed a bit and his question was barely audible.

"Jazz, I don't know how or why this has happened." Morgalla's mind sought an answer, but her knowledge of Hell's history was vague. Demons weren't in the habit of writing things down. But then something came to mind and she could have kicked herself. "Wait, the *Dark One* forbade demons from mating with humans."

"What? Who?" Jasper asked, confused.

"Never mind," she said, shaking her head. "I thought it had something to do with cross-breeding, but maybe *this* was it."

"Well, what do we do?" Jasper asked.

Morgalla helped Jasper up; it was only then that she noticed just how big his new demon form was. She took a step back, speechless, and her eyes widened looking at the upper half of his body. Jasper put the blanket around his waist and noticed her gaze.

"Yeah, I know I'm...*big*," he said. "Under other circumstances I wouldn't complain. I wish I could say I was happy about this." Jasper walked back into the hallway between his bedroom and Andy's, and she followed him.

"What do you mean?"

"What if I can't change back?" Jasper looked in the tall mirror before him. Morgalla then stood by his side and took hold of his hand, trying to comfort him. She saw a look of concern and worry on his face and could feel the same emotions. "I'm scared. What am I? What have I turned into?" Jasper held up his other arm; the veins were incredibly defined and bulging. "My arms look like roadmaps!" He was worried, and a tear formed in his eye. Morgalla took his face and gently turned it toward her. Her hand ran down his cheek, and she smiled at him.

"Jasper, relax!" she said gently as she tried to comfort him with her touch. "You have now what you humans would call… superpowers."

"Powers? What kind of powers?"

✡

Back in England, Richard Smythe sat at his desk. He had wiped a thin layer of dust from the framed photo of his late wife. He took out a pen and began writing in a book, but as interrupted by the phone ringing.

"Hello?"

"It's me," James said.

"Found something?"

"Yes." James hesitated a moment; the full truth currently was not warranted.

"How serious? You need help?"

James looked at Rebecca and she shrugged. He had thought she might give some advice on what to do.

"Too soon to tell," James said.

"You sure you're all right?" Richard asked, concerned, sensing something from his son's voice.

"Yes, I'm fine. I'll check back with you."

Richard was not too sure what to think, but he trusted his son. "Very well then," he said.

James turned his cellular phone off. He and Rebecca were in a park. He sat on a bench and hung his head.

"You couldn't tell him?"

"Could *you*?"

James looked a bit upset and kept his head down for a moment. Rebecca tried to comfort him. A woman and her dog ran by. Rebecca smiled at the woman, who returned the gesture. Rebecca waited for her to run by, not wanting the woman to hear their conversation.

"She…she looks just like her," James said.

"But she isn't," Rebecca said. "Why didn't you tell me about the baby?"

"Only my father and I knew. We didn't know what to do or how to handle it, but now we have to."

"Now wait a minute. The beast was only there for a short time. How could he—"

"The beast only needed her body for a little while," James interrupted. "He only needed her womb to…" James was choked up and unable to speak. All those nightmares and the worst of his memories were coming back to him for a moment.

"Look, I can understand how difficult this must be for you," she said. "But if you want me to take care of it, I will."

"You mean kill her!" James said, offended by the comment.

"That *is* why we're here, correct?"

"You *know* who her mother was," James said, frustrated.

"You don't know that for a fact," Rebecca said. "But I *do* know who her father is and where she was raised! What are the odds she takes after *his* side of the family?"

Rebecca sighed, thinking of another alternative to their problem.

"We can track her," he continued. "We need to find out *why* she's here, anyway! And see if she's just the beginning of something larger!"

Chapter Thirteen: Pleasure Practices

Morgalla was atop Jasper in a burning, passionate embrace, making love again in his bed, the sheet up to her waist. They breathed hard, and Jasper's incredibly large and strong arms were around her.

Jasper moved carefully, not wanting to hurt his lover. His incredibly muscular arms contracted slightly as he held her, the veins bulging with blood.

Morgalla's hands explored her lover's body. The muscles felt incredible to the touch; at one point soft, and then with a mere thought, they flexed and took on a different feeling, one of strength and power.

Jasper's hands gripped the sheet; his muscles flexed as Morgalla grasped two handfuls of his now long hair. She smiled at him and he returned the look of happiness. He was uncertain, not wanting to injure her, but not realizing that her small body held great power. He sensed her strength encircling him as a convulsive heave shot through her. He did not know that if she lost control she could still hurt him.

She could feel the power of his body within her as well. Through every inch of her skin she could feel his body and its raw power. It was still difficult to take his might, but she did so with zeal, confidence, and great ability.

Jasper leaned upward slightly and kissed her neck. His one hand now gripped a handful of her orange hair. She felt the inferno approaching and only encouraged it as she moved faster. Morgalla's head flew back and her sweaty hair was tossed against her back. She howled through clenched teeth, the intensity greater than the night before. Every muscle in both of their bodies flexed at once, with sweat gleaming on their beautiful forms.

Morgalla lost all strength in her body as she fell forward. She rested her head on Jasper's massive chest. They both breathed heavily, their bodies sweaty and spent. She rested her head against his chest, the pectorals like pillows of muscle. His hands released the bed sheets and moved around her. They slid up her sweaty and heaving back. He held his lover as gently as he could as they both were brought back to reality.

They said nothing. She trembled; never before had she felt this good in her life. The rest of the world did not matter at all to her; there was only Jasper. He could not see her eyes, for her hair and horns were in the way. But if he could see them, he would have seen a single tear form. Jasper tried to determine how she felt, but she was in such an emotional whirlwind that he could not tell for sure.

Their throats went as dry as the hottest desert as their lungs burned and fought for each precious breath. A couple of small groans came from Jasper and he thought he had pulled more than once muscle. His new body healed the injuries almost immediately, and a sense of relief stole over him.

Morgalla was completely limp; she was a sweaty mess of petite, feminine power. Never before had she allowed herself to become *this* vulnerable at any time in her life.

She looked up at him as he delicately held her face in his hands.

"I'm...spent," Morgalla gasped, and managed a smile.

"I thought I might hurt you."

"Yeah, right!" she replied with a smirk, and kissed his chest multiple times.

Jasper smiled as his hand slowly ran through her hair. She leaned down and kissed him gently on the lips. They gazed into each other's eyes and she gave a low growl, just like a large predatory cat. Jasper looked *more* shocked.

✡

James and Rebecca pulled up in the rental car in front of Jasper's apartment complex. James sat in the passenger side with the large gem glowing red.

"She's in there," he said.

"It's glowing even brighter now. What could they possibly be doing?" she asked. James said nothing as he gazed slowly over to his wife. "Don't answer that. So what do we do now?"

"Wait."

Jasper held Morgalla close, the reality of the situation washing over his mind. Morgalla was sleeping soundly, resting her head against his shoulder and gripping his large arm. Never before had she felt this safe or this good.

Jasper was calm and the events of the day had were starting to catch up with him, and his mind raced. His lust had taken over, but his rational mind had control yet again. As with many times before, his mind and his heart had a debate. Today his lust won the argument hands down, but now it was sleeping, fatigued from the day's events.

She's a demon, I can't date her. I didn't know she was a demon; it seemed like a good idea at the time. I don't think I'll go to Hell for that. Maybe a trip to church wouldn't hurt. She didn't do anything bad to me. She may have seemed a bit strange, but she was nice. There's something to be said for that. Maybe Morgalla had an ulterior motive for being nice. Maybe, but I just don't know. . .what have I become?

Jasper wondered how he would explain this to his family and friends. It was not just whether or not he could possibly love Morgalla, but if he could tell his family and friends.

Hi, Mom and Dad! This is my girlfriend, the DEMON!

Another thought hit him: *What about HER family?*

He couldn't even begin to imagine what her family might look like. Jasper watched Morgalla as she slept soundly, the moon shining on her face. He was troubled by her large ears and horns, and was having trouble seeing past them.

As slowly and as carefully as he could, Jasper got up. He looked around his cluttered floor for something to wear, but everything was now much too small for his larger frame. He looked in the drawer and found a pair of sweatpants which were always too big for him, but now fit just right. He walked into the living room and then to Andy's room, peeking in.

Still not home. Things must be good at Meggan's.

He then walked back to the living room where he saw the large crucifix on the wall. He just stared at it for a moment, and a bit of fear crept into his heart. He held out his hand, and inch by inch he stepped closer to the symbol of his faith on the wall. He touched it—and nothing happened. He breathed a sigh of relief.

Jasper then walked to the porch where he had set up his telescope the night before. He gripped the rail and looked out into the darkness. The only thing he heard was the wind blowing through the trees, and that was also the only movement.

"You're still a little freaked by this, aren't you?"

Jasper turned to see Morgalla standing there. She was wearing one of his shirts, which was much too big for her, but he did not mind. Ironically, he had always dreamed of a woman who would wear only his shirt after a night of lovemaking. He did not know what to say, really.

"I would be lying if I said no," he replied.

"I knew this was going to happen," she said, looking away. "If you want me to leave, I will."

"Leave?" His voice sounded shocked. "Please don't. Stay, Morgalla, I need you." He walked up to her and put his hand gently on her shoulder. "This can't be happening," he went on. "I mean, this just *can't* be real!"

"Why?"

"Well, just...because!"

"Ah, yes," Morgalla said. "The typical '*I know everything*' human attitude. Let me ask you something, how old are you?"

"Twenty-three."

"How old is the human race?"

Jasper shrugged, not knowing the answer.

"Your civilization is in the thousands of years, and not that many thousands. And your species has been walking upright for less than a million. How old is the Earth? How old is the universe? How old is time itself?"

"I'm drawing a blank on all three," Jasper conceded.

"Human beings have only been around for a *very* short period of time compared to the universe. Just because you have not discovered it yet doesn't mean it does not exist!"

Jasper stared blankly, trying to take in all that had happened.

"Is *any* of this sinking in?"

"Yes," he replied. "But it's a *lot* to sink in all at once."

Jasper looked at the crucifix on the wall and thought of what he had been told about God, Hell, and everything else. He had never been less sure about any of it than he was right now. There was only one thing that he was sure of at that moment, and that was Morgalla. He held her close and she did the same. They both decided that the best thing to do for now was just get some rest, so they returned to bed.

Morgalla fell into a peaceful sleep. It felt strange to have a someone else sleeping beside her but it was something she could get used to. She slept more soundly than the night before. Now, her true face was exposed to Jasper and she had a good feeling about the two of them together.

Jasper, on the other hand, was a different story. Though he managed to fall asleep, he had a disturbing dream. He saw nothing but flames encircling him. From the fire, countless demons and minions of Hell circled him. He saw them as only monsters. Morgalla was the only being from Hell that he had ever seen.

They stared as if he was their prey, their eyes bright yellow, and they screeched and screamed at him. Out of nowhere there were two glowing red eyes staring at him, but with no face and no body. Jasper then heard a woman's voice whispering his name.

Jasper's eyes opened and he was instantly awake. He sat up, panting and startled by the nightmare. He looked down at his body and was relieved to see that it had changed back to normal. He had thought that he might not have been able to change back, but since Morgalla could alter her form, why couldn't he? He sighed, and then looked over at Morgalla, who was still sound asleep. Her ear gave a twitch and her eyes moved rapidly. Jasper lay back down, relaxing next to his lover. He looked at her face, which was so peaceful.

Wonder what you're dreaming about.

In Morgalla's dream, she sat on a throne in an extravagant chamber. There were tables all around her with different kinds of chocolate desserts. There were many half-naked, muscular men around her. One massaged her feet, another rubbed her shoulders. Two on either side of her presented plates to her with chocolate desserts on them. She took handful after handful of chocolate and gorged herself.

On the bed, the sleeping Morgalla smiled as Jasper looked on.

✿

The next morning Morgalla woke up and saw that Jasper was not there. Smelling wonderful things coming from the next room, she got dressed. She walked into the kitchen to see Jasper making breakfast. He was dressed and back to looking human, as if nothing weird had happened the day before. They smiled at each other as he set the table. He pulled her chair out and she smiled.

"You keep doing things like this and you're going to spoil me," she said as she sat down.

"It's my pleasure," he said, putting his hands on her shoulders for just a moment and then taking his place across the table. They ate for a bit as Jasper ran through the million and one questions in his head. "Morgalla, what is it like in Hell?"

Morgalla was silent for a moment, searching for the right words.

"Difficult to put into words," she started.

"How can you have an American accent?"

"Practice," she smirked. "Comes with the job. I've been speaking with this accent for so long it's now second nature."

"Your job? You actually have one?"

Damn. Probably should not have said that.

"Jasper, my job is kinda complicated and for now it's best that you don't know what it is. I was actually born here."

"*Here?*" Jasper asked. He wondered if she meant Springdale.

"Earth. There are many different worlds. And the *Dark One* wants every single one of them!"

"All of them? Why?"

"No one really knows why, but I have my suspicions. Human beings live on many worlds that demon kind have ever set foot on. I think demons, especially the *Dark One, hate* humans, as if they believe humans are blessed by the divine itself—if it actually exists."

Jasper frowned, bristling at her comment about *if* God existed. She saw the look on his face.

"Jasper, I have nothing against your faith."

"No, you just don't think it's real."

"I didn't say that! Sometimes I wonder what it would be like to have faith in something good—something great." She suddenly remembered the crucifix hanging on Jasper's wall. "You're one of those Christian religions, aren't you?"

"Um, yeah," he replied. Morgalla sighed, for the truth was not going to make him happy.

"Look, get ready for a shock," she began. "Years upon years ago, one of your people got a glimpse of my home. Just a glimpse."

"Uh-huh," Jasper nodded.

"It was obviously a security...*snafu*, shall we say. Normally no human should see it. So this person's primitive mind searched for explanations for what they had just seen—and hence the whole eternal-damnation-for-your-soul-if-you're-bad theory started."

"Hey, now wait a minute," Jasper said, annoyed. "This is my religion you're talking about here!"

"And my presence before you contradicts everything you believe is in that little holy book of yours! Face it, Jazz, like I said before, your species knows hardly anything about how the universe works!"

Jasper didn't want an argument, so there was another uncomfortable silence. He found it hard to believe what he was hearing. He tried to change the subject, or at least ask a different question.

"Satan and the demons are *jealous* of human beings? So I guess God is the parent and demons are the angry siblings that got less attention?"

"Interesting analogy," she conceded. "Demon lords are the most powerful beings in existence, but my father would not be able to survive here for long."

"Why's that?"

"He's too old, been living in Hell for so long that he's become dependent upon the realm and its evil for survival. Younger demons, though, would be able to live here indefinitely. Heck, my trainer Delilah has a grandparent that's a dragon!"

"A *dragon?*" he exclaimed. "Dragons are real?!"

"Yeah. On other worlds anyway. I think they used to live here, too."

His imagination ran wild again. First it was Morgalla's family; now it was this Delilah, who was part *dragon*. He wondered what she might look like.

"Yeah, she can be a bit of a bitch sometimes," Morgalla said. "But what's sad is that she's the closest thing I have to a friend... or *real* family."

Jasper was disappointed that Morgalla did not call him a friend. She noticed his look.

"Um, I mean in *Hell*, anyway," she said, reassuring him. "Here, I have a friend, too."

She put her hand on his and they both smiled. Jasper was never really religious, but he believed in God, in Heaven, and more importantly at the moment—HELL. The reality that there really was a Hell was sinking in. Maybe that was another reason he had been depressed lately.

"Well, fine." Jasper said. "Why not just come and conquer us all? Why haven't they done it in the past?"

"Centuries ago," she would answer. "There was this wizard who gave up not only his own life, but all of the magic on this world to close the portals to and from Earth. I think he was English."

"Gave up all magic?"

"Yeah, there's no magic on Earth anymore. At least I haven't found any. A big price to pay to be safe from people like my father. It was soon after that Earth put magic behind them and turned towards science and logic."

Later, Morgalla sat on the futon with the television on as Jasper was in the kitchen cleaning up.

"Are you sure I can't help?" she asked, loud enough for him to hear from the next room.

"Yeah, it's fine!" he bellowed back, not wanting to risk disorganization in his kitchen.

Since Jasper wasn't there with her, Morgalla reached over to her coat, which had been thrown over the couch arm. She reached into the pocket and found the manual she had been reading over the past few days.

There was a television documentary about World War II on, but she did not pay much attention to it. The television showed Adolph Hitler giving a speech. She looked as if it was a familiar face, but could not place where she had seen it. Her head cocked to one side for a moment, but then she shrugged, thinking nothing of it as Jasper came in. She folded the manual and put it away as Jasper sat down next to her.

They sat on the couch after breakfast and just talked about everything. Morgalla was not too specific about her "job" in Hell because she didn't want to upset Jasper. He was trying to take in all that she was telling him.

"I've always felt part of me belongs here. Certainly not in Hell. I've never exactly fit in there. I've never wanted anything to do with killing or torturing innocents or the souls the demon lords have claimed. I never wanted to conquer worlds. That's *all* they *ever* do!"

Morgalla began to cry, again feeling the emotions overwhelming her. Jasper felt her sadness and became overwhelmed along with her. He sat back down, this time a bit closer to her. The wall that had held her emotions deep within started to give way.

"Morgalla," he said, putting his hand on her shoulder, at a loss for any words of comfort.

He was powerless to help her, as much as he wanted to wish away all her pain. It was especially horrible to feel her pain himself, now that he had these new abilities. It was as if his own soul was in torment because he was so close to her.

"I *hate* it there!" she cried. "I just want to go away, go someplace where they'll never find me. Where I can be left *alone!*"

"Morgalla, I'm sorry," Jasper said.

She got closer as she cried harder. Jasper held her close, and his hand glided over the unusual shape of her ear. This woman he thought was a human being—now, knowing the truth about her made it difficult. Had he not had these new powers, had he not had the ability to *feel* her soul and the connection they had forged, he wondered if he would be this close to her. She cried a bit more and then looked up at her lover.

"I...I'm sorry," she said, as she wiped away a tear.

She saw in his face that he too was in pain, and she knew why. She never wanted to burden anyone else with her problems and had thought that the opportunity would never present itself.

"It's okay," he replied. "*Is* there a way you can leave?"

"I could, but they would just follow."

"There has to be *something*."

"Maybe," Morgalla muttered.

She wiped away her tears and managed to smile again, feeling good that he was there. They both heard the apartment door unlock, open, and then close. Andy walked into the living room, and Jasper looked shocked briefly and then turned to Morgalla. He was relieved to see that she was back to looking human.

"Uh…hi," Andy waved.

"Hi," Jasper and Morgalla replied.

"Excuse me…I gotta do…something."

Andy didn't want to be too specific, though it was obvious to the couple sitting on the couch that he had spent a lot of time at Meggan's and he needed fresh clothes.

"It's cool," Jasper assured him.

Jasper Davis and his new girlfriend Morgalla decided to go out. James and Rebecca were parked in the lot and watched the happy couple walk from the apartment to his car. James looked through his binoculars at Jasper and Morgalla.

"They look happy," James said.

He looked over to see that Rebecca was sound asleep, and no one was listening to him.

✿

He had lived in this town all his life and today it looked alien to him. Jasper sat on a bench and Morgalla joined him. He felt the warmth of her hand in his own and could feel her soul as if they were embraced in the throes of passion. He looked over at her and she smiled back at him. Though the cold autumn air blew dead leaves past them, Jasper did not care—nor did he even notice.

"I can tell what people are feeling!" Jasper exclaimed.

"Yes," Morgalla replied. "It can be a blessing sometimes, and other times it can be a curse."

"I've…noticed," Jasper replied, knowing full well what she was referring to.

"You can tell when they're lying. You can tell when they're angry, happy, or sad, even though they may be acting a different way."

She moved close to him, her hand running down the side of his cheek. He could feel her hand on him but did nothing, as he looked around at the few people that were there.

"This isn't mind reading, is it?"

"No," she replied, and turned his head to look at her. "Demons can feel people's souls."

They smiled at each other, their lips moving closer and closer. Jasper kissed her gently and put his arm around her.

"How much can I control people?" he asked.

"You already figured out how to manipulate them?"

"Yes. Is that what it is?"

"Corruption of the innocent," she said. "Control of the weak."

"Redemption of the guilty?"

"Good luck with *that* one," she answered with cynicism. "What you're able to do now is only that which is within a person to begin with."

"Huh?"

"The woman who was yelling at you, about the sixty dollars? Deep down she knew she was wrong."

"She knew that I was right, and she was still trying to get out of paying."

"Yes," Morgalla assured him.

He thought a moment about what she was saying, and thought back to what he had done already with this new ability. What he was able to do made a little more sense now. Jasper looked around; not many people were there, but he could tell quite a bit about the ones he saw.

"It's not *seeing*," he observed. "I don't know *what* it is."

"I don't know what word would fit. We just know, that's all. Demons are tougher to read than humans, primarily because we can shield ourselves from each other. I can't remember how many times I had to think violent thoughts just to avoid being singled out."

Jasper held her hand as her eyes drifted off to the gray sky. He could see tears forming, as if she had held this in for so long and had had no one to talk to. She looked back at Jasper; she gave a smirk and a shrug.

"Hey, don't worry about me," she said. "I'm used to it."

"Doesn't sound like it. Morgalla, what you described is a horrible place. Surely there has to be something that can be done. Would they notice if you just…disappeared?"

"My father is one of the most powerful, dangerous and *well-known* demons," she said. "The president of the United States, what if *his* daughter suddenly disappeared? They wouldn't stop until she was found."

Jasper sighed, hoping there was an easier solution to the problem. His heart sank; if it wasn't one problem it was another. Morgalla could easily tell what her lover was feeling.

God, it's never that simple, is it?

"Your wall has come completely down," she observed. "You were so closed off, like you had a wall around you. I think that's why I couldn't feel anything from your soul."

"I think you were the same way, too."

"I'm not going to argue with that. When we first met, I thought you were a demon in disguise, or maybe a human who knew how to hide his soul from demons. I still don't know the real reason."

"But now?"

"You're an open book to me."

Jasper then felt apprehensive, the thought of someone able to look into his very soul was troubling.

"It happened over time," she continued. "The more we spent together, the more your soul was revealed to me."

"When did I become an '*open book*'?"

"The night before last."

"That's strange," he said with his eyes in a state of wonder.

"What's that?"

"I...thought I felt something, too."

"Yeah, you *felt* something, all right." She replied with a wink. Jasper smirked.

"That's not what I meant. I could swear, Morgalla. That for a moment, I could tell what you were feeling, as if we were united in some way."

"Demons...they really don't know the blessing that they have."

"No, they don't."

"You need to *not* worry about me," she said, placing her warm hand on his cheek. "Look, this may sound crazy, but I think I have an idea, Jasper. You need to be patient. We both do."

"What is it?"

"You don't need to worry," she said. "Can I meet you later?"

"Of course. Where?"

"The construction site," she said.

"Why *there?*"

"Because that's where the portal to Hell is," she explained, as Jasper looked on in shock. "I'll meet you there at sunset."

They both rose, and though his heart was filled with doubt and fear for her safety, he hugged her and they kissed. As she walked away he only wished she could stay. Questions and strange thoughts filled both of their minds, and Morgalla suddenly remembered something Jasper had told her.

"You broke your leg once," she said, and turned back to him.

"What?" he inquired, only barely hearing her.

"Um, it's nothing," she replied. "I'll see you later."

Jasper didn't want her to leave. Sitting on the cold bench, he wanted her to stay by him. He was willing to say anything to keep her by his side. There was no one else around to hear them, and he had a sudden urge to be honest.

"You were my first!" he shouted.

Morgalla froze in her tracks and turned to look at him.

"What?" she said.

"You…you were my first."

"Your first what?"

"Do I need to *explain* it?" Jasper asked in frustration.

Her jaw dropped as she realized what he meant. She felt foolish, for it was obvious. She came back to the bench and sat down, and they held each other's hands again.

"Are you serious?" she exclaimed.

"Of course. Why would I make that up?"

"I…well…" She saw his point, *and* she would have been able to tell if he were making up such a bold-faced lie. "*I* was your first?"

"You mean you couldn't tell?"

He had a smirk on his face now, and she could not help but notice it. She made a guess as to what he was thinking.

"Oh, don't let it go to your head, Don Juan!" She slapped his shoulder, but he only gave a slight laugh.

"I can't help it," he said with a smile.

"But, wait. You mean, you've…you've never been able to—"

"I've been able," he continued, his smile now gone. "I just never had the opportunity."

"Oh, come on," she said in disbelief.

"Is it so hard to believe?"

"Yes! It is!" Morgalla yelled. "You've spent your whole life here. Surely there have been others—"

"No. There have not." His voice was filled with conviction; he was trying to make her see the truth. "Morgalla, I tried weed as a teenager, just once. I drank when I was nineteen and got damn lucky that nothing bad happened. Maybe it was a wake-up call, but I decided that I wasn't going to rush into anything unless I was ready."

"And you've never been *ready* before?"

"I've seen what's happened to some people who couldn't wait or who threw all caution to the wind."

"So, what are you saying, that sex is *bad*?" she asked, confused.

"No, absolutely not, Morgalla," he replied, holding both her hands. "Being with you has been the most glorious experience of my life."

"Well." She looked away for a moment, closing her eyes as she blushed.

"And I'm sure there are plenty of people who have had nothing but great things happen to them in their love life. Good for them."

"But—" she began, and looked on with concern.

"I've had the opportunity, but with you it just felt right."

"I understand" she replied. "Better than you could ever know."

Her comment made him smile and again they felt the warmth of each other's souls.

"As for me, I just felt that I should be a responsible adult first," he said. "And Morgalla, I'm glad that I waited for you."

They smiled at each other and she realized that time was short.

"Sunset," she repeated. "I'll see you then."

They gave each other a kiss and she got up to walk away. Jasper didn't want her to leave, for he needed her now more than ever, but he didn't want to admit it. She stopped again. Since he was being so honest with her, she decided that he deserved the truth as well.

"Jasper, you...were my first, too."

He didn't say anything, but his smile spoke volumes. With one final glance she turned to walk away.

Damn! Why didn't I say, "I love you"?

All Jasper could do was go about his day as if it were normal. He knew things that no other human did and that disturbed him. He went home, only to see that Andy had left again. He plopped down on the couch and turned on the TV. Jasper sat and contemplated what to do next.

There was a knock at the door. He sprang up and quickly answered it, expecting Morgalla to be there. To his shock, there were minions of Hell leaping through the doorway at him, knocking him to the floor. Before he could let out a call for help, Necrod came up. The last thing Jasper saw was the demon's fist coming at him—and then darkness.

Chapter Fourteen: Betrayal

Zorach stood on a balcony, the same one where he and his daughter had spoken the other day. Today it looked quite different, for there was no movement or sound except the breathing of a thousand sleeping beastly minions. He stood looking out to the darkened cathedral-like hallway. If anyone were to look upon him they might have mistaken him for a statue, lifeless and harmless.

A clawed hand rose up, balled into a fist. The five digits flew open, and in an instant his obedient servants woke. The dracon, the beasts of hell, found themselves starved for the blood and gave an unholy call that filled the chamber. A chain reaction started below the balcony and extended outward in either direction. One by one the pairs of eyes opened upon their master's command. Like beacons of light, their eyes gave off a golden glow. A moment later, an ungodly howl came and filled the chamber with their death cry that begged for blood. Their dark master would oblige their request.

✳

Morgalla walked through the town, heading toward the construction site. James and Rebecca followed her to the edge of the site. She could not sense them, for there were too many people around and their intentions were not murderous.

The demon girl was in a quandary. Never before had she been struck with this kind of problem in her life. She walked back to the construction site, back to the place she called home. She was only a few steps from entering the pit when she sensed something that caused her to stop. There were many worlds she could escape to, some of which were actually considered better than Earth. She was assigned to this world; it was fate that she met the human, Jasper Davis.

She was standing in front of a travel agency and decided to walk in. She asked the woman at the front desk for a pen and paper. Morgalla went to the coffee shop. Ironically, it was the same table at which James and Rebecca had sat earlier. With a pen in her hand, she stared at the blank sheet of paper before her. Her fingers ran through her raspberry hair, and she struggled to find the right words. Finally, after what seemed like an eternity of writer's block, she started the letter. There was no *Dear* in the opening, only a name: *Delilah*.

She finished the letter, folding it up and putting it in her coat. She walked out, returning to the travel agency to give back the pen she had borrowed. She arrived at the site and went through a small hole in the fence. Morgalla changed into her demon self and walked through the construction site to the pit where the portal to Hell was. She looked in the pit and saw nothing, but then felt a presence.

Someone is behind me.

She did not know who to expect, but certainly not the person who was there. She turned around and was startled to see Delilah. There was a brief moment where they just looked at each other. Delilah gave a tiny smirk and Morgalla returned it. Delilah then smacked Morgalla in the face with the back of her hand and she fell into the pit.

Morgalla took her medallion out, ready to defend herself. Delilah leaped down and landed next to Morgalla, and with one kick she disarmed her apprentice. She then kicked Morgalla in the face, sending her into the center. Morgalla came to her senses and saw Delilah standing over her, scowling. She looked up at Delilah, who stood there with a look of contempt and anger on her face. Morgalla could sense something new from her teacher, a rage that was never there before.

"We have her!" Delilah yelled out to seemingly no one, but then the area began its unholy transformation.

Suddenly, the ground began to rumble and shackles broke through the ground, clamping around Morgalla's wrists and neck. She strained against the metal to no avail, for the shackles were magic. She felt pain surge through her body and she cried out.

The earth around Morgalla suddenly lifted up and disintegrated, leaving her surrounded by a circular room made out of red stone. There were golden symbols on the ground, which glowed brightly. Red stone seemed to grow out of the earth and reached high into the sky.

The stone grew higher and higher, changing into a large, foreboding red and black castle. Everyone who saw this screamed and fled in terror. James and Rebecca looked on in shock as they saw the castle come up out of the ground.

Morgalla was trapped in the center of the red circular room. The floor around her and Delilah remained, but the rest turned to blood. Slowly out of the blood rose dozens of Hell's minions, along with Vex and Zorach himself. Necrod was there too, and he looked at Morgalla with a mixture of lust and hate. The blood then changed back to red stone.

Zorach moved toward Morgalla, the living shadow making no sound. He looked down at his daughter and she slowly gazed up at him.

"Foolish little bitch," Zorach whispered. "I had so hoped that you would have sided with me instead of against me."

"No," Morgalla replied. "It...wouldn't have mattered."

"You *will* help us conquer this world. One way or another."

Outside, James and Rebecca both came to their senses, and James helped his wife up. They were both terrified, like everyone else in the town, but their fear was different. They knew what was going on and who was attacking them.

"You all right?" he asked.

"Yes," she replied. "We had better call the reinforcements."

James took out his cellular phone and dialed a number.

In other places of the town, people found their technology interrupted. Internet went down and radios had great interference. Andy's car broke down and he had trouble starting it again. Meggan at work found her computer down completely and the lights at the gym flickered.

Back in the chamber, Morgalla looked at the medallion she had lost. It was only a few feet away, but too far for her shackled wrists. Delilah saw it, approached, and picked it up, putting it around her own neck.

"I believe this was a gift from me, was it not?" Delilah said, as her clawed fingers grazed the beautiful object. "You won't be needing it anymore."

Zorach stepped away from his youngest daughter as Delilah and Vex looked on in disgust. Zorach gave one final look at her and then turned his back. With a wave of his hand a surge of pain flowed through Morgalla; her eyes turned red and her body glowed. She screamed in pain, feeling the very energy of Hell flow through her.

From the dark castle a beam of red energy shot up to the sky. The clouds turned black as smoke and the sky turned red. Like a plague, the evil energy flowed out around the town of Springdale.

Andy walked into Meggan's gym and saw his lover walk from out of the office.

"Hi," Andy said.

"Hi," Meggan replied, and the two kissed hello.

"Did you feel some kind of tremor just a minute ago?" Andy asked.

"Yeah, what the hell was *that*?"

The ground began to quake again, shocking everyone in the gym. They all looked out the windows in horror as they saw the red beam in the distance, and the sky began to turn black and red.

"What in the name of God?" Andy asked. His eyes were glazed over in fear.

Within the castle Zorach was restless. Two of his most loyal servants, Delilah and Vex, were in attendance.

"It will be some time before you can walk the Earth," Delilah told him.

"Yes," Zorach said. "In the meantime—"

"We should attack, shouldn't we?" Vex asked. "I mean, the humans could mobilize and attack us!"

"Let them," proclaimed Zorach with great confidence. "Morgalla's own report on this world states that this village is too far from any armies. Resistance shall be quickly dealt with. By the time the armies come they shall be no match for me!"

Zorach looked at his minions, which filled the room. They awaited his next command. Morgalla lay in the center of the chamber in a fetal position, fighting back the pain. Delilah slowly walked up and knelt before her. Noticing that Morgalla was reaching into her pocket, Delilah, on instinct, grasped her hand, expecting a weapon. To her surprise it was only a folded sheet of paper. She stood with the paper in her hand; Morgalla had not put up a fight to keep it.

"Read it!" Morgalla yelled in desperation, hoping that the words might have an impact and remind Delilah of the bond of their friendship.

Delilah was mildly curious about the contents of the letter, but just then a burst of flame came from her claws. The paper was completely incinerated in an instant. Morgalla was crushed, realizing that the thoughts and feelings she had poured out onto the paper were meaningless.

"It didn't have to be this way," Delilah said to her. "Why couldn't you have helped us? You could have been a queen!"

"Why couldn't *you* have just let me go?"

"Because I'd rather see you die than be *in love* with a human!" Delilah said. Morgalla looked up at her, amazed that she knew. "You really shouldn't write your most private thoughts down. I can't believe you're in *love* with him! Do you think he would ever love you in return?"

I had hoped.

Delilah came close to Morgalla's ear. "Maybe I can have some fun with him before he dies," she whispered. Morgalla balled up her fists in anger. She gazed at her with rage as Delilah stood. "They're beneath us, Morgalla. Every last one of them!"

Delilah walked away, and Morgalla hung her head and began to cry. Vex walked up to her; it was his turn now to gloat and get in some cheap shots.

"You know, we could have been together," he said.

"I...would rather...be dead!" she said with hate in her eyes, fighting the pain.

"You may be soon enough," he replied. "But if you do survive, you'll be more...controllable, for sure. You won't remember any of this."

Vex kicked her in the abdomen and then walked away. She looked up at him in anger. Amazing, really, how she felt then. For years she never *wanted* to kill anyone, and at this point she would have given anything to kill him. The shackles that bound her had drained all but the tiniest bit of her strength, all the power from her body. For the first time in her life she felt a new sensation in her heart: helplessness. The fear crept over her heart and grasped it tightly. She did not feel fear for herself, though. Death would come to her, but it did not matter. Her fear was for Jasper.

Jazz, where are you?

She could sense that he was nearby. That could not be good, for that would mean he was in the clutches of her father. She knew he was alive, though. She just *knew* it.

Vex's hate and contempt she could understand, for he had always been that way. But she was astonished at Delilah, who had been her trainer, a mentor of sorts, and, dare she say it—a *friend*. The only person she would consider a friend and ally had turned against her and she could not begin to fathom why.

There was something different about Delilah. Perhaps her father had convinced her to turn on her. Deep down, Delilah had demon blood flowing through her, through every vein. Of the many aspects of demon kind that Morgalla loathed there was one thing at the top of her list: the demon lust for power was stronger than friendship.

Jasper—run!

Delilah walked up to Zorach and Vex. "Your orders, my lord?" she asked, giving a slight bow.

"Patience for now."

"My lord, the human Morgalla has been with. Something strange has happened to him."

"I care not," her master replied.

"He is like us now."

Those words caught Zorach's attention and he turned to look at her.

"Like us? You are sure of this?" He looked at them both, able to discern that they were telling the truth.

"I have no explanation," Delilah continued. "I am sure that he is not fully demon. He has human weakness within him, I can feel it. But I cannot fathom just *how* this could have happened."

"There is more to the boy than you know," Zorach said. "That is the only explanation possible."

"What do we do with him?" Vex asked.

"What this boy is now is of no consequence," Zorach replied. "Do with him as you wish."

The two demons smiled and walked out.

"So, what did you and Morgalla talk about?" Delilah asked Vex, curiosity getting the better of her.

"Merely telling her future," he replied.

"She has none."

"And here I thought you were her loyal teacher." He replied with a smirk. "What made you change your mind?"

"None of your damn business." Delilah snapped with her back turned to him.

Vex took hold of her arm and she slapped his hand away.

"Keep your hands to yourself, elitist filth!"

Her eyes were intense and her clawed hand was upon her belt, ready to draw a weapon. Demons loyal to her stood behind, where other demons loyal to Vex and his family did the same for him. They all gazed at each other, ready for a fight. Vex held up his hands in a defensive posture.

"Nothing intended, of course!" He said with a smile.

✿

James and Rebecca ran through the town as people were panicking, and ducked into a building for cover.

"I read about this," James said. "Infernal energy is spewing out onto our world! It will take days for it to completely encircle the globe, but we must stop it before then!"

"Right now only minor demons and minions can enter our world, right? Demon lords or any of the high ranks cannot, for they rely on infernal energy."

"But there is something strange. I've never actually *seen* this happen, of course, but the energy is flowing out much faster than what I've read."

"When the world is completely consumed by it, the lords will be able to walk the Earth."

"If that happens, God help us."

✿

With her strength slowly draining and evil power flowing through her, Morgalla tried to fight and hang on, but the energy was overwhelming to her body. She sank into despair. Zorach flowed through the chamber like a shadow dancing on the walls. She could not see them, but could feel his eyes upon her, gazing out from the black helm.

His true motives for keeping her safe all these years were not revealed to her. Delilah's mission was to protect a precious commodity and to give that commodity the means to protect herself. He was quite lucky she was able to defend herself so well; otherwise, his plans would have died before fruition. Since the day she was born her soul had been an open book to him, and now he was reading the most recent chapters of her life. She could not block him in the least, for there was too much pain, which weakened her body and spirits. One person was on her mind, and she was concerned for his life.

He commanded the guards to leave. They complied and exited the chamber. He looked back at his daughter; now alone, he could be honest with her.

"You *love* him," his voice whispered, disgusted.

"What...what do you care?" She defied him, though her blood burned.

"Quite frankly, I don't," he said, as Morgalla's fists clenched even tighter. "Morgalla, bear in mind that it does not matter. It never did, *you* never did. Imagine my amazement when I realized a new way to conquer a world. It may have taken me over twenty years to accomplish, but it's an invention. I'm quite proud of, really. I'll have conquered a world not with an army but with one child. One child bound to this world, for she was born to it with my blood within her."

"The...humans," she whimpered.

"They will die or be my slaves. Thanks to you, Morgalla, they will all kneel before me. Some willingly and some by force."

No! NO! Not another world taken by him. It's all my fault!

"You...you won't be able to leave this castle until the entire planet is enveloped!"

"The people of this *pathetic* world don't know anything about us. They will be all ill-prepared to face Zorach the Unholy!"

Zorach paused a moment in thought, to gloat over his resolve and revel in the relief that his master would be pleased.

He continued his rant. "Earth - So pathetic, not knowing of the evil that lurks so close. I hate their ignorance."

"Ignorance? Or innocence?" Morgalla asked, and Zorach slowly turned to look at her again. "You *hate* them...because they're innocent. They don't know about Hell, about *you* or your kind."

"Don't you mean...*our* kind?"

"I'm *nothing* like you!" she shouted, with tears in her bloodshot eyes.

"*SILENCE!*" he yelled, and with his rage a sudden surge flowed through her blood, making her cry out in pain again. "I *know* you've killed, Morgalla, and enjoyed it! Every death at your hands brought you pleasure!"

"It was done out of necessity."

"It was done out of revenge!"

Silence came to the chamber again as Zorach gazed upon her, and Morgalla shut her eyes. Tears flowed down her cheeks and her body, in a fetal position, fought the pain. In fact, Zorach knew that her nature was never to attack and kill anyone out of sheer blood lust. And Morgalla had to admit that while she often killed other demons purely for survival, there was a tiny part of her which enjoyed making them suffer. It was, indeed, a kind of revenge; punishment for all the times they attacked and attempted to violate her.

"You *know* of our master's demands," he said.

"*Your* master."

"Our master cares not how it is done," he said, ignoring her comment. "Speedy results are all that matters." His tone changed, and she could feel for a brief moment something that she never felt from him: fear. She sensed it only for a fleeting moment before it was gone, but she knew in that moment that Zorach's show of strength was merely a façade. She looked up at her father.

He fears him. That's the only thing, the only person, he is afraid of.

"Morgalla, you have no idea of the burden placed upon me," he said, and with that he chose to make his exit.

"Who was she?" she pleaded, needing to know. He stopped before the chamber door. "My mother, who was she?"

"She was nothing," he replied, looking back at her. "I heard the Dark One's call and was sent to her." His words made Morgalla cry even harder. It was really the answer she should have expected. "You look like her, though."

Zorach left, and the three guards entered again to keep watch over her. She was filled with anger and hate towards her father. She yanked at the chains and they began to buckle.

✡

Jasper awoke, feeling the cold, hard stone beneath him. He tried to stand, but he was too weak. He slowly looked around, seeing nothing but darkness.

He was in his new demon form, wearing only black pants and boots which did not belong to him. The belt around his waist was gray and had strange symbols on it. His eyes became accustomed to the dark and he could now see the walls of stone; the room wasn't too large. He noticed there was a shackle around his left ankle. Attached was a chain, which was then attached to the red-stoned floor itself. He touched the shackle and was flooded with pain, as if he'd just been electrocuted.

"It would be wise not to do that," Delilah said.

Jasper looked up and saw Delilah, Vex, and Necrod stepping into the light. Jasper swallowed, his heart beating quickly, for he knew he was in trouble. He balled up his fists and tried his best to be brave.

"Where's Morgalla?" he demanded, fighting through the fear that was surging in him. Delilah and Vex looked at each other and laughed.

"Quite humorous," Vex commented. "He's trying to be brave!"

Jasper's new powers allowed him to feel a bit of lust and desire from Delilah, but it was sinister and angry. Necrod was pure rage and blood lust; it was doubtful that he thought of much else. Vex, on the other hand—or "the purple one," as Jasper dubbed him—was quite different. Yes, there was anger, but it was a different kind.

At first it made no sense, but then Jasper knew. *He's jealous! But what could this guy be jealous of me for?*

Delilah stepped up and knelt before Jasper while Necrod gazed at the human with hate. Delilah's hand ran down Jasper's cheek, finding him attractive and seeing a possible new…possession.

"Hmm. I can see why she likes you," Delilah said. "You're weak, easy to control. The perfect male. I wonder, boy, if you would consider a different alternative to death."

"What?" Jasper looked on curiously, afraid of what she could possibly be offering.

"Being a slave to my whims certainly would not be that bad, would it?" she asked, now smiling wickedly with her fangs exposed.

"Slave?" he said, incredulously. "Why the *hell* would I ever say *yes* to something like that?!"

"Your body and soul for the rest of your life, of course!"

"You must be Delilah," Jasper said.

"Morgalla has spoken of me?"

"She was right. You *are* a bitch," he said.

Delilah's grin was gone; she stood and gave Jasper a look of contempt. She kicked him in the face and he fell back.

"Stupid male!" she yelled at him. "Your death will be slow!"

Delilah and Vex turned and walked away, but Necrod remained, the lust for blood in his eyes.

"Let me kill him," Vex told Delilah.

"Jealous, are we?" Delilah gloated, rubbing salt in the wound that was Vex's ego. "Jealous that he had Morgalla first?" Vex was angered but said nothing. "I care not which of you kills him, but make him suffer first!"

"Of that you can be certain!" Vex replied. As she turned to leave, he looked back at Jasper and held up a blade. He smiled and fear filled Jasper's heart; the look was that of pure evil.

As the two demons gazed at Jasper with their golden eyes, he could feel their rage, hate, and love of death. The experience was overwhelming, as if a tidal wave was crashing upon his soul. With one kick Necrod knocked Jasper back to the ground, and blood splattered from his mouth. The power of Delilah's beast could kill Jasper with great ease, but he preferred to toy with his prey. He gave a kick and a punch to his helpless opponent, enjoying his pain and his fear. Jasper realized that there was no help coming and he had to come up with a plan—and quickly.

✿

In England, Richard Smythe had rallied his troops after receiving his son's call. They were of all different ages and races, with different fighting skills. Some were trained in martial arts, some in the art of modern warfare and preparing guns. Some were practiced in magical arts, others in sword fighting. Richard frantically searched through his desk for everything he would need for the coming battle. As he searched he set a magical staff down on the desk. He placed gems and various wands into a bag hanging from his shoulder. He looked at the photo of his late wife Margaret and stopped. He picked up the framed photo, wishing she were there; he could use her encouragement right about now.

This day is for you, Margaret!

Richard tightly held the golden crucifix that had belonged to her. He gave the golden luster one last look and put it in his pocket. Richard stepped onto the balcony overlooking the lobby of his manor so everyone could see and hear. The small group of a couple hundred demon slayers all looked up at him.

"For over twenty years we've been preparing for this! I sought you all out not only for your bravery and skill, but also because you believed, just as I did, that this day would come! They will show us no mercy, and we in turn must show them none!"

They all cheered, raising their hands high.

"We will show them that the greatest part of the human spirit is our courage!" Richard continued with zeal for the coming battle. "They *will* regret this day!"

They all cheered again, louder than before. Richard turned to see his son Alistair standing before him, with an expression of disapproval. Richard straightened his back and gave his son a smile.

"Off to claim vengeance?" Alistair's words were thick with contempt.

"I prefer to call it justice," Richard replied, his smile now gone.

"Everyone does. Call it what you wish."

"Not going to wish me—*us*—luck? Anything could happen."

Alistair was silent, realizing that this just *might* be the last time he saw his father.

"Come back alive, Father."

✢

Morgalla was still in the portal chamber, fighting the pain as infernal energy flowed through her body. She looked around the room, seeing that there were three guards. The fear that imprisoned Morgalla's heart was stronger than the metal that bound her neck and wrists, but she fought it. The dark magic of the shackles was powerful, but nothing compared to despair. She managed to get on her knees. The three guards looked at her but thought nothing of it, for they were confident she was not going to break free.

Morgalla looked up at them, her eyes filled with tears and her teeth grinding in anger. Her hands clasped the shackle around her neck and with all her might she fought against its power, trying to break it off. Touching it, she felt the surge of pain flow through her body, but she fought it. Like electrical shocks, the magic flowed up her arms and her hands felt as if they were on fire.

It's only pain! You've felt it a hundred times before, ignore it!

She screamed as she strained against the dark magic that entrapped her neck, her muscles flexing. The guards looked at her with amusement as she tried to break the metal. They thought it was futile and that she was wasting her time. What they didn't realize, though, was that she was slowly succeeding.

✿

One massive kick to his face broke Jasper's nose. He fell to the cold stone floor, spitting out blood as his torturers looked on with fervor. Necrod cracked his knuckles as Vex leaned against the wall with his arms crossed. He let his partner in torture do all the dirty work since he didn't want to get his nice clothes dirty.

"Don't finish him too quickly," Vex said. "I want him to feel pain."

Necrod shrugged. Jasper tried to throw a punch, but he missed as Necrod nimbly moved out of the way. Necrod laughed at Jasper and delivered a few more kicks to his helpless opponent's ribs. Some cracked, and Jasper cried out in pain. Vex took out a large blade, made of black metal , and calmly looked at his own reflection in it, picking food out of his teeth as his ears filled with the sounds of Jasper's agony.

Necrod grasped Jasper's hair and lifted him up. He pummeled Jasper with no mercy again and again, his viciousness overpowering the young man. He finally let go and Jasper fell to the ground. Jasper was bleeding and one eye was swollen shut. Jasper lay there breathing hard, desperately trying to stay conscious enough to come up with a plan..

"That's enough," Vex said, as Necrod sneered back at him. Vex stepped up, looking at the blade and clenching it tightly. He looked down at the heaving mass that was Morgalla's lover. The anger and blind rage at Jasper was overpowering as his golden eyes locked on him. "She...was supposed to be *mine!*"

All doubt as to just *why* this guy hated Jasper was now gone. Vex put a foot on Jasper's chest and knelt down, looking into Jasper's one open eye. He held up the blade and brought the tip down to his chest as slowly as he could. Ever so slowly the blade moved across Jasper's skin, breaking and digging into the flesh. Jasper cried out in pain as Vex made deliberate cuts into his flesh, writing something in his native language.

"Screw *you!*" Jasper yelled at him, defiant and enraged.

"She's going to be mine, one way or another," Vex replied with a voice so calm and in control.

BASTARD!

Jasper's pain fueled his hatred for the demon cutting into his flesh. Vex then stopped, realizing that he was not writing it correctly.

"What am I thinking? You could never read that. With a few swipes of his blade the name *VEX* was engraved in Jasper's chest. He grinned, though it was short-lived.

Jasper looked up at his foe with rage; never before had he hated someone this much. Jasper pulled at the chain but it did not buckle at all. Vex delivered another vicious kick to Jasper's face, and then went back to the wall and leaned against it. He looked at Necrod, who wiped a line of drool from his mouth.

"I want his head," Vex demanded.

✼

All James and Rebecca could do was wait for help to arrive. They had seen some people fleeing for their lives and had brought them into an old bomb shelter in the high school. Children were crying and the room was filled with the sounds of terror. James helped some children and their parents into the room. His adrenaline was rushing, pumping through his veins at a hundred miles an hour.

It's really happening. I can't believe it!

His thoughts were filled with doubt, but he had to stay focused. He had confidence in his family and friends. And he was confident that all human beings everywhere would join in the fight. Most of all, he had faith in a higher power that they would prevail.

Something made him stop a moment, though, as if a powerful force had drained all hope from his soul. He breathed out and white vapor filled the air. Everyone's breath in the room also had changed, and they huddled together for warmth. James felt the fear flow through him, for he had felt the presence one time before. He walked to the exit.

"Where are you going?" Rebecca asked, surprised that he was headed outside.

"I know what I'm doing."

He stepped out onto the parking lot. With a mere thought the medallion around his neck transformed, and it only took a second to be in his hand. He looked around and saw no movement or life within view. He heard the thunder above; looking up, he saw the sky being consumed by Hell's evil. The street the high school was on led to the downtown area, and clearly one could see the stoplights that were still functional. He saw movement and his eyes squinted. A huge shadow appeared, but he could not tell whose. Though it was nearly half a mile away, the beast could feel James and where he stood. James' blood froze and he could feel the eyes of the beast upon him.

I remember you!

His fear transformed into rage, for James *knew* who it was. The vow he had made years ago was renewed that very moment and he gripped his sword tightly. His palms were wet with sweat and his mouth was dry, but he was ready to charge into a fight right then and there. He reminded himself that he needed his family and friends at his side.

On the other end of the long street, Zorach recalled that it had been over twenty years since he had seen Earth's sky. He remembered the sky, blue and dark because it was night. The clouds appeared black, which he found actually quite beautiful, though it was the stars that caught his attention and ruined the perfect dark sky. Today it was very different, though. It was daytime and the sky was nothing but clouds, and even those were being consumed by Hell's evil.

The air seemed to freeze and the wind blew as cold as the coldest January. People everywhere were shaken, scared, and confused. It became clear that the situation was far worse than any of their darkest nightmares.

✡

Morgalla was still building the strength within her to break free from her prison. Many emotions fueled her determination to escape. Her hatred for Vex, the minions and other demons that had made her life Hell—literally. It was also her newfound hatred for Delilah, the friend who had betrayed her. Morgalla knew that billions of people were counting on her escaping and closing the portal. But most importantly, her determination to escape was fueled by her love for Jasper. She longed to see him again, to hold him in her arms.

In Jasper's torture chamber he could hear footsteps walking toward him, and he knew it was the first torturer, breathing like a filthy animal. Though he only had one good eye, he could see Necrod kneel before him. He felt his hair being grasped by Necrod's claws, while a second set of claws gripped Jasper around the chin. A plan, that's what he needed—and fast. A split second before Necrod was about to take his head, Jasper's knee came up and struck Necrod squarely in the groin.

The demonic beast grunted and let out a tiny squeak. He stumbled backward, his hands going to his crotch. His bloodshot eyes bugged out; the pain was unbearable. Vex had been casually cleaning his fingernails when it happened, and the sound his comrade made caught his attention. He looked up in curiosity to see him hunched forward moaning in pain. There was a second kick from Jasper and it was more powerful, hitting Necrod right in the stomach and sending him hurling right into Vex. Both demons crashed into the wall, the stone and some bones cracking. Vex fell to the floor unconscious, but Necrod was only momentarily dazed. Jasper looked up through his one eye, surprised at his own strength. He sat up, gathering his strength, and prayed with all of his might that he'd be powerful enough to free himself. Mustering as much strength as he could, , he pulled, his face contorted in pain. His muscles nearly pulled from his bones with the strain he was putting them under, and the metal began to slowly give way.

He took a break but only to catch his breath, for he noticed that Necrod was coming around. Jasper pulled at the chain harder than before and finally it shattered. The shackle on his leg gave way and Jasper stood. He felt a strange sensation in his face and ribs. The bones and cartilage crackled as they healed themselves within seconds. He found he could see with both eyes again and the swelling was gone. He looked to his chest to see that the cuts upon it were now completely gone, not even leaving scars. His powers were fully restored and he felt his full strength rush back to him.

Necrod was stumbling to his feet and Jasper had no intention of showing him any mercy. Jasper punched him and Necrod hit the wall hard. Jasper kicked him again and again, his rage completely taking over.

"How's that, you bastard?" Jasper yelled, as he unleashed all his might on the beast before him.

Meanwhile, Morgalla's shackle suddenly snapped, and before the guards could reach her, shards of broken metal were thrown every direction. One guard ran up to Morgalla, drawing his sword. She grasped his hand and twisted it, breaking his wrist easily. He screamed in pain as she grabbed his weapon. A second guard ran up; Morgalla threw the body of the first guard into him. She hacked at the shackles that bound her other wrist. The metal finally cracked and the blade shattered. Dropping the sword, she grasped the shackle. The third guard charged at her with weapon drawn.

Morgalla let out a scream of rage as her other arm flew up, the chain broke from the ground and she felt her full strength begin to return. She punched him, knocking him back against the wall and he fell, dazed. Morgalla charged the other guards, attacking them without mercy. She used the chain as a weapon to hack away at her enemies, to parry and disarm them. Taking one weapon that had fallen she killed the remaining demons brutally. She looked down at the dead bodies, her hands stained with their blood.

She stood, her hands clenched in rage. She still had one shackle around her wrist, and with one swipe of a blade she removed it. What was it that they had always wanted from her? To be a cold-blooded killer?

Fine. They've got one!

Red stained-glass windows surrounded the room, and just outside, one demon heard the commotion and looked up just in time to see the injured body of one of his comrades come hurtling through it, smashing the window into a million shards. The injured demon quickly died and his body melted; the other one lay on the floor, dazed and confused. Morgalla leapt through the hole and landed on top of him, feet firmly on the stone floor.

"Hi," she said quite casually, and butted heads with him.

✻

Zorach suddenly looked up, and then toward the castle. His attention was drawn from his tour of the town. He sensed that Morgalla was now free, and saw the red infernal energy now flowing out much slower than before from the castle into Springdale's sky.

Delilah walked the streets; this planet seemed quite different from all other human worlds. She looked at her master and could feel that there was something wrong.

"My lord?"

"To the castle—NOW!" he commanded, and his minions complied, turning and running back to the castle.

Delilah looked to the horizon and noticed, as Zorach had, the energy flowing out much slower now.

"I knew it," she said, realizing that it had been a mistake to underestimate Morgalla. She then took to the air and flew as fast as she could back to the castle.

✻

Jasper was tired from this entire ordeal and kicking Necrod was accomplishing nothing. He knew that he had to get out of there, and soon, for his adversaries were still alive and it would not be long before they were up again and ready to kill him. He looked down to see that Vex was still breathing. He checked the door. It was locked, of course. He kicked it, and then punched it, but nothing happened.

It's just a wooden door! Something is weird about it.

Necrod crawled along the stone floor to the opposite wall. He used it to help himself back up, but he was still dazed. Jasper was contemplating what to do next, but then noticed the cracks in the stone wall which Necrod had been kicked into. He thought a moment, and an idea came to him. He looked at his dazed opponent, then back at the wall, and then at the door. Jasper smiled.

The next thing Necrod knew, Jasper was lifting him into the air. Grasping the demon's belt and a lock of his hair, Jasper drove him headfirst into the door. A makeshift battering ram, Necrod's head smashed into the magically enchanted door again and again. Jasper had the feeling the door was giving way, so he lifted his demonic foe over his head and stood at the other end of the room. With all his might he threw Necrod into the door and it crashed down into the hall.

Necrod's unconscious body slid down to the floor. Jasper leaped through the doorway between the fallen door and his fallen adversary. He didn't stick around for either of his adversaries could wake up in an instant and he didn't want to be there when that happened. He ran as fast as he could away from them, though he did not know where he was going.

Anyplace away from here is fine with me!

✵

Morgalla smashed down a door with ease, sword in her hand and clothes tattered from the fight. The room had an incredible stench to it; the demons that had died there left a horrible mess, and after many days the decay was atrocious. She looked up above the doorway, seeing a tarp there. She climbed up to the top and removed the tarp: the Vindicator was still there and unharmed.

It was heavy, but she could manage quite well if she placed it over her shoulder. In her other hand was a sword, gripped tightly and ready to defend herself. She walked down a large corridor, looking left and right for anyone ready to ambush. One minion leaped out of nowhere but was quickly killed, and two more demons leaped out with weapons. Morgalla battled them, dropping the bomb on the floor. Her sword was knocked out of her hand and it skidded across the stone at their feet. Morgalla dodged the assaults of her attackers and grasped the large, heavy bomb with both hands. She lifted it off the ground and used it to defend herself, their blades not able to break through the bomb's metal casing. She defeated both of them, using the explosive device as a blunt object to smash their bodies.

A dracon saw her and charged on all fours down the hall, drool dripping from its fangs. Morgalla threw the bomb high into the air with both hands directly above her. The minion continued to charge at her with fierce determination to kill. Morgalla took one small leap backward seconds before the beast was about to make a final leap and the large heavy bomb came crashing down upon it, crushing the creature's body and squishing it into a chunky jelly.

✡

Vex had never been this angry before in his life. He had let his guard down for the briefest of moments and Morgalla's lover had escaped. His wounds had healed themselves and he ignored the throbbing pain in his head. He grasped his blade and stood, his fangs exposed in a fury that he had never felt before. His bloodshot eyes burned as his heart screamed for revenge.

"Get up, you fool!" he yelled at Necrod as he exited the room. The two set out to find Jasper and kill him.

It had only been a few minutes before Morgalla came running around the corner. She had been following the trail to where she had last sensed Jasper. His emotions were strong from his fear and the pain caused by Vex. She entered the room and looked around, only to see no people, blood, or remains of a dead demon. She saw the broken chain and the smashed door. Walking up to the chain, she touched it and could feel that this was where Jasper had been.

Vex. . .he tortured Jasper.

She was infuriated, and left the room even more determined to find Jasper and to find Vex—and make him pay! It was only a second after she exited the room that Delilah and her entourage came around a corner. All stopped in their tracks, and student and teacher looked upon each other. For a brief moment it was disbelief, but then their anger quickly returned.

"I knew it," Delilah said. "Zorach was a fool to underestimate you."

"It's over," Morgalla replied.

"Is it now?" Delilah asked, as some demons slowly approached Morgalla, ready to attack. "You're outnumbered six to one, if I'm not mistaken."

Morgalla could feel two minions behind her; they came around the other corner and drew their weapons. All those loyal to Delilah waited for her order; they would not strike until she told them to.

✡

Zorach and many of his followers ran into the portal chamber. Stunned, they say that Morgalla had placed the Vindicator there, and on it was a timer counting down. *Three. . .two. . .one.*

Zorach let out a roar of rage as the minions tried to run out. It was futile, though, as the bomb exploded in a bright blue flash. Zorach's servants vaporized and the explosion enveloped the demon lord's own body. More than just a blue light, it tore through the stone of Zorach's castle, destroying the portal chamber and everyone directly above it. It also tore downward into Hell itself, sealing the portal between the two worlds. The wound on the planet Earth healed in an instant. From the top of the castle, a blue beam of energy erupted into the sky.

Chapter Fifteen: Fighting Back

Delilah and all the others felt tremors in the ground from the explosion. Some fell to the ground from the power of the shock. There was mass confusion as they tried to understand what had happened. Were they under attack? Who would be foolish enough? But Delilah knew better. She saw the look on Morgalla's face and felt her confidence. Morgalla smirked as she looked upon her one-time mentor. After all these years it was Morgalla's turn to be the teacher.

"Now who's outnumbered?" Morgalla asked, mocking Delilah mercilessly. Delilah remembered the Vindicator. "Six *billion* to one, if I'm not mistaken."

"You'll have to go through all my personal bodyguards," Delilah said, and glanced at one who was standing to Morgalla's direct right. "Starting with him."

Without looking at him, Morgalla's arm went up quickly. Her blade sliced across the demon's neck and his head was removed from his shoulders. Delilah watched in disbelief that Morgalla could be so cold-blooded.

"Next," Morgalla said.

"So be it," Delilah replied, and with a wave of her hand her personal bodyguards attacked Morgalla, who defended herself with her exceptional skills.

Delilah backed away as Morgalla fought the five remaining minions. She used her small size as an advantage; small targets were hard to hit, especially when they're moving fast. Delilah made her way from the combat to see if she could find out what was happening elsewhere. She entered a chamber which intersected many corridors. There, General Darvis entered with many of his own subordinates, weapons drawn.

"Mistress, what has happened?" he asked with great concern.

"Morgalla," she replied. "She has been underestimated."

"Underestimated?!" The General yelled back. "*How* could you be so *stupid* to do such a thing? No one else knows her better than you!"

"Listen, you *troll!*" Delilah shouted. "We don't have *time* for this!"

"All stand by, ready to fight. I shall call out—"

"Don't bother," she interrupted.

"Mistress?"

"We're on our own," Delilah said. "Kill everything."

He bowed before her, and both he and the minions exited to prepare for war. Delilah could not explain it, but she could not feel the presence of Zorach any more.

Could Morgalla have dealt with her father that easily? The damn humans must have found a way!

Controlling General Darvis would be easy for Delilah. If Zorach was truly out of the way it would be up to Delilah to conquer this world. This was an opportunity that she had looked forward to for a long time. At last her chance was here.

Morgalla easily defeated the remaining minions while Delilah made her way to the front gates. She passed the demolished areas of the castle; a complete hole had been made from the bottom where the portal chamber was. She looked down and saw nothing but smoking rubble. Looking up, she could see the sky being parted directly above. Earth's sky was taking control again and fighting against Hell's living evil that tried to consume it.

Delilah reached the front gate, where the army had gathered and was ready for their orders. She stepped out first, the gates parting for her. The demonic works of art, made of an alien stone, peered down from the tops of the towers. There were flashes of blue throughout the sky from Morgalla's weapon, but the horizon was still as dark as night.

She leaped into the air and flew up to one of the high towers. She perched on the black stone statue, and immediately sensed something was wrong, a sensation that all demons could feel.

"We have incoming!" Delilah yelled to all who could hear her.

A blue portal opened high in the sky and a dozen wizards flew out. They had medallions and brooches around their necks that glowed, allowing them to fly. They were armed with all sorts of magical weaponry as they swooped down to their waiting foes below them. Dozens of the Smythe and Daishi demon slayer families appeared with weapons drawn, ready for battle.

In the sky, the wizards all had spheres of flame appear in their hands, and dropped them on the army of demons and lesser creatures of Hell. The spheres made contact with the ground and the creatures below exploded in a tremendous inferno. The entire castle seemed to ignite in a glorious firestorm of screaming beasts of Hell. Wings of Zorach's stronghold were destroyed, but the structure still stood.

Many demons charged into the town, only to meet waiting demon slayers armed with all sorts of weaponry. Delilah barely avoided being burned alive by the magical flame. She took to the sky and unsheathed her blade, one of the many works of metallic art on her body changing into a dangerous weapon. She took the life of one wizard who turned, only to see the demoness fly through the smoke cloud.

Delilah looked out into the town and saw flashes of blue appear all around. The resistance was greater than she thought. Demon slayers from all over the world had come with weapons drawn. They ran toward the castle as their demonic foes charged outward. They clashed together like the sea crashing against the beach. Blades of all kinds sliced through demonic enemies and bullets would slay many dracon. All beings attacked as a battle of epic proportions began.

The people of Springdale were shaken and scared. They looked up to the sky and saw it ignite and turn to fire, and the clouds change to black smoke. Just when they thought it could not get worse they saw the winged dracon swoop down. Many screamed and ran for their lives. One cop pulled his weapon and began shooting, but he was quickly killed.

A young woman and her child tripped and fell. Monsters landed by them, its eyes yellow and claws sharp, ready for the kill. The woman and child screamed in terror as the minions struck, but were suddenly stopped by an invisible force. The beasts looked and saw Richard Smythe standing there with his magic staff pointed at him.

Richard smirked and shook his head. With a wave of his hand the minion was thrown into a group of his comrades. All around the town there were flashes of blue light as members of the Smythe and Daishi family appeared. They drew weapons of all kinds and were ready for battle.

Some demon slayers had medallions that changed into swords. Some were magicians with magical staffs, wands, and other magical items. Blue gems hung around their necks in necklaces or were pinned on as brooches; they glowed a pale color. Using these gems, they took to the air to combat the flying dracon.

The Daishi were either martial artists or swordsmen. They were armed with magical gauntlets that could kill a demon from Hell easily. There were even some members armed with guns of all kinds; they drew them and began to slay minions left and right. The beasts of Hell were little match for the combined might of the Smythe and Daishi families, the only advantage of Hell being numbers and their lust for blood.

The army for Earth was less than a hundred people, but they fought with the power and determination of thousands.

✻

Morgalla cut through everyone who came across her path. Lucky for her, she was still in the castle and there were only Hell's warriors before her. She was following the trail of Delilah, but it was getting colder by the second. Delilah was able to escape deeper into the town, but for Morgalla it was like walking through water. She was making strides but could only do it so fast.

Vex was with Necrod only for a short time. The beast of Delilah walked off in search of Jasper. Vex found some warriors and commanded them to follow him. He was going to find both Jasper and Morgalla and kill them both. He only hoped that he could kill one of them in front of the other.

I must decide, though. Which one to kill first?

"You there," he ordered one minion. "Gather as many as you can and bring them to the main gate!" He then looked at a group of others who had just entered. "The rest of you with me!"

They were about to leave the room, heading up a flight of steps. From behind, Morgalla leaped down from the balcony. Everyone spun around to see her rising to her feet. Though the soldiers were not as empathic as their demon superiors, they could feel the anger within her and the raw, seething hatred. Vex knew the anger was directed at him. He remained at the top of the stairs, looking down on her.

Two blades were in her hands, and her grip on them was strong. She looked past the soldiers before her to find her prey. It was Vex and only Vex that she truly wanted.

"Wound her. But the kill is mine," Vex commanded.

She took three steps and found her first opponent, whose skills were substandard. He was killed rather quickly. One by one, Morgalla battled the soldiers, claiming either their limbs or their lives Vex took a step back, realizing that if he stayed he surely would die.

The stone floor was littered with melting dead bodies and weapons lost by soldiers.. With great ease, Morgalla claimed another weapon to continue her battle.

Never before in her life had she felt such a need, a *desire*, to kill. There was hope now, due to Jasper and the Vindicator, that she might escape Hell forever. She would do everything in her power to see this dream come true, and nothing would stop her, certainly not some of her father's minions and especially not Vex. They offered little resistance to her, and she slayed one soldier after the other.

Jasper, on the other hand, was avoiding any confrontation as he sneaked about the castle looking for a way out. His new powers could sense much around him and it was all evil. The lust for death and blood was so ugly, but there was, in the midst of the sounds of death and destruction all around him, a sense that Morgalla's soul was nearby. Jasper moved ahead anxiously.

He entered the room with Vex's back facing him. To his utter shock, he saw Morgalla not only fighting Hell's soldiers but winning. His eyes nearly bugged out of his skull and his jaw dropped. Morgalla would have sensed her lover but she was too busy fighting. Less than half the soldiers remained as Vex stepped back farther, ready to retreat. He did not sense Jasper, for his fear was too great.

Jasper saw the being before him and smiled, knowing just who it was. Vex turned around to find Jasper right in front of him. With a grasp more powerful than his own, the lackey of Zorach felt Jasper grip his throat. He dropped his sword as Jasper lifted him with ease off the stone floor.

Morgalla finished with her adversaries and looked to see Jasper with the helpless Vex in his hand. The demon that had caused her so much grief and pain for years was now gagging and fighting for breath. Jasper and Morgalla looked at each other and he immediately tossed his adversary aside. Unfortunately, Jasper did not know his own strength. Vex hit the wall rather hard and fell helpless to the floor.

He was back up, the demonic blue-blood met now by Morgalla who kicked him back to Jasper. Back and forth the two lovers smacked him again and again, one to the other. Finally he fell to the floor, blood trickling from his nose and mouth.

Jasper and Morgalla ran to each other; she dropped her weapons and they embraced. In one moment all their fear melted away, for they were safe in each other's arms. They kissed with great passion, glad to be alive, and relieved to see the other safe. As their lips came apart and they looked at one another.

"Why didn't you tell me?" he asked, sounding fatigued.

"Tell you what?"

"That you're *Neo*?"

Their celebration was short-lived. Vex was getting back up, angrier than before. With great care and stealth he grabbed a sword, sure that they were unaware of his presence.

"Excuse me a moment," Morgalla said, and broke from Jasper's grasp.

She kicked a blade up to her hand and prepared for Vex's attack. He wasn't even able to make the simplest of maneuvers with his weapon as Morgalla cleaved his arm. Vex felt the burn of her blade and his hand fell to the ground, along with his weapon. He slid to his knees, grasping his life-threatening wound as blood poured from it. The pain was unbearable, and though he tried desperately not to scream, it was futile. Morgalla held her blade to his neck, ready to finish him.

"Morgalla, no!" Jasper yelled.

He was shocked that Morgalla could be so cold and kill someone without mercy. Jasper hated Vex too, but to kill someone was too much for him. He had never seen anyone die and he wasn't ready to be a witness to such a terrible thing, even if this person was a total bastard.

Her shoulders heaved; she was breathing hard and Jasper could sense her fatigue. She looked at him with eyes that he had not seen before. He could feel her intense rage at Vex, and sensed her hate for him. Vex was terrified, his eyes pleading for mercy. Jasper almost felt sorry for him...almost.

"You do *not* want to get between us!" she shouted.

"You...you can't," Jasper said, trying to reason with her.

"Watch me!"

"But he's helpless!"

"He will only be back to try and kill us later! I know him too well! Kill or be killed, Jazz, that's how it works in Hell!"

Jasper was speechless, not sure what else to say. He knew it was pointless to try to convince her to spare Vex's life. Vex's wound was still gushing blood, but his powers were hard at work and his limb was reforming itself. It would only be a few minutes and he would be ready to fight again. Morgalla heard a noise from the neighboring hallway. She knew the sound, and Jasper also could sense something amiss from there.

"Let's go," she said, taking another blade from the floor. Now armed with two, she led Jasper out of the room and he followed without argument. He gave a brief look back at Vex, her words ringing in his head, and wondered if she could be right. "Once they smell blood, there's no stopping them!"

Vex was too preoccupied with his own pain to realize just who was entering the room. He looked at the hallway entrance to see one of the beasts of Hell entering, sniffing the air, hungry for blood. He looked at the other entrance and two more had already entered; he saw their eyes first in the darkness, reflecting the subtle lights. More and more came in, and he reached for a blade with his only remaining hand, but it was too late. The beasts did not care who the prey was, intoxicated as they were with their primal need for blood. They pounced, and it was all over for Vex.

Jasper held Morgalla close, and then he looked back, feeling the terror of Vex's final moments.

Morgalla was walking faster now and Jasper was trying to keep up. He was getting to know this woman, the *real* her and where she was from. Today he was getting a true education on how the real Hell worked, and his instructors were cruel and without mercy. He didn't want to admit it, but he was *glad* Vex was dead.

"Careful with these, they're magical blades," she said, holding up the blade to Jasper. He could hear a slight hum as it went near his skin. "They'll cut through a demon or most anything else like they're nothing." Jasper nodded, having already found out about the blades from Vex. "Come on."

Morgalla walked to the exit and Jasper followed, eager to get out of there and to safety. She wobbled slightly, still weakened from her experience in the portal chamber.

"Morgalla, are you all right?" Jasper asked, his hand going to her shoulder.

"Three battalions, maybe four. That's what they have."

"Only that many?" Jasper was surprised, but then again, he didn't know how large a battalion of Hell was. "That's enough to conquer Earth?"

"No. They…they were using my body as a lens," she replied, leaning against him for support. She needed to catch her breath, but knew they did not have much time before they were discovered. "To focus Hell's energy out onto Earth."

"To what end?"

"The battalions were only backup, support for…for…" She stopped herself before revealing that her father was the main plan of attack, knowing it would scare Jasper completely.

"Backup for what?" he asked, but Morgalla could not answer, for Necrod smashing through a wall of stone interrupted them. The beast let out a roar of pure hate toward the two of them. "You again!"

Charging at full force, the monstrous Necrod wanted to kill them both. Jasper pushed Morgalla out of the way for her protection and prepared for the onslaught, thinking that he might be powerful enough to take him on. He was wrong, though, as both he and Necrod went through the next wall and found themselves falling several stories to the ground outside.

Morgalla got up and ran to the hole in the wall to find Jasper, but debris and smoke clouded her vision. She knew, though, that he was still alive. She looked out into the town and saw the war being waged, and she was consumed with regret as she sensed the suffering of innocent people. Could *she* have prevented this? Even though she played down Earth's importance and said it was not worth her father's time, they still invaded. It didn't matter, for this was going to happen, regardless of what she did.

From behind she was attacked by an ambitious young demon. He had not gone out with the invasion force, but instead sought out Morgalla. Perhaps he wanted to make a name for himself, taking the life of a traitor to their cause. Morgalla actually recognized him from one of the many meetings they had been forced to attend and from passing each other in different places, but he had known then not to try anything with her.

He must have changed his mind today.

She was tackled out the window and the two found themselves plummeting to the ground. She fought him still in midair, but did not want to feel the pain of the fall's sudden stop. She abandoned her weapons only milliseconds before hitting the ground below. Taking hold of her adversary, with one kick she stunned him: she would use his body as a shield. When they landed at the foundation of the castle, the young demon was killed instantly. Morgalla felt the sudden shock of hitting the ground, even though his body shielded her. She remained on top of him as they both slid down the steep hill of gravel and dirt.

They did not stop until the very bottom. The demon's body, killed instantly upon hitting the ground, was now nothing but the ooze from which he was made. Morgalla tried quickly to recover, but she was dazed and weak. Her eyes narrowed; even thought she was nearly unconsciousness, she could see two gleaming objects headed toward her. The weapons she abandoned just seconds earlier came crashing down next to her, just inches from her ears.

She had to regain control, and fast, for there was very little time. Grasping the weapons and pulling herself off the ground, she ran to the closest shelter she could find. Resting for only a few moments she concentrated hard, trying to find Jasper, but there were too many people and creatures around to get a bearing on where he was.

Oh no.

Chapter Sixteen: Invasion

Andy and Meggan were driving, trying to flee the city. The car's radio was dead and try as she might, Meggan's phone wasn't working at all. Andy drove fast, but suddenly he slammed on the brakes. The street was completely blocked by three wrecked cars. From behind the wreckage four dracon appeared; they looked at the two of them with an evil hunger in their eyes. Their claws scraped against the metal of the cars upon which they now stood. Meggan screamed as Andy threw the car into reverse and went full speed in the opposite direction.

He pulled into one alley still going in full reverse and the beasts chased closely behind. He pulled out into another street and the car hit a telephone pole. The airbags deployed and the two of them were jolted by the impact. Meggan quickly came to her senses and could hear the creatures approaching.

"Come on!" she yelled.

The two climbed out of the car, shocked and dazed from the crash but otherwise uninjured. Hearing the snarling of the predators coming down the alley, they fled for their lives. They ran down one alleyway and out onto another street, and were amazed that there was no one around to help, not a single car driving by. Meggan ran ahead, her legs carrying her as fast as they could.

"Don't stop!" Andy shouted, as they both ignored the fire in their lungs and the fatigue in their legs.

Meggan was glad to hear his voice; it was good to hear that he was still there. Andy, though, could tell that the monster behind him was just inches away from his legs. He could hear its hard breathing and its claws scraping against the street. He could feel its hot breath on the back of his legs.

He ran around a building and across the street just as a car came speeding down it. Andy dove, grasping Meggan, and they both went down on the sidewalk. Meggan screamed as the car swerved, not to hit them but the minion, and crushed it. The car sped off as Andy looked behind him to see the monster dead, but he could hear more coming. They could also hear an incredible commotion from the neighboring street; it sounded like a war was going on.

"Over here!" a voice bellowed, and the two of them looked around.

They looked up to see someone standing in a metal doorway. He was motioning for them to hurry and enter the building. They rose and ran through the door and into the building as more dracon came around the corner, charging at them. Once through the doorway, they slammed the door shut behind them. Both Andy and Meggan, joined by total strangers, held the door closed as their monstrous foes outside tried to knock it down. All four of them pushed as hard as they could to slam the door, lock it, and use a deadbolt against the powerful force. They all stood back, hearing the scratching on the metal. Meggan and Andy hugged each other, glad to be alive.

✻

Jasper regained consciousness slowly, hearing the roar of the battle around him. He could also sense more than that, though; years of abuse and pain suddenly flowed through his mind. He could hear Steve's voice, Missy's voice, and the voices of all those who had insulted or belittled him through the years. He could hear the bullies from his childhood, the voices and feelings boiling up from deep within him, ready to explode.

Jasper's eyes suddenly flew open wide, as he felt the strength and power flowing through his body once more. The floodgates of his new power opened, and he was ready to crash like a tidal wave on the first person he saw. When he sat up, he saw Necrod. He looked up and saw the tremendous hole in the ceiling which they had fallen through, and saw that they were in some sort of building. He had no memory of the fall.

The beast Necrod was also staggering back to life; both he and his antagonist were severely broken and bruised. They were both lucky that another enemy had not found them. Jasper got up and walked to the smashed window and saw the battle raging in the place he called home. Businesses that had stood since before he was born were now destroyed. The movie theater in which he and Andy had spent many weekends was gone. It felt almost as if he had lost a friend; this town that he hated so much and wanted to leave was being torn apart before his eyes.

Jasper saw that the battle also continued right around him, and while they ignored him for the moment, he knew it would not stay that way for long.

Who the hell are these people? I gotta get out of here!

Jasper then looked at Necrod and his rage swelled.

Right after that guy gets his ass kicked!

Necrod, the beast of a demon, was dazed but standing, slowly staggering to his feet. Jasper clenched his fists in anger toward the demon who had tried to kill him. Necrod wound his fist back, his anger like a freight train out of control. To his surprise, it stopped in midair as a hand caught it. Jasper flinched, braced for the attack but relieved that someone seemed to have saved him from the fist.

Wait a minute, whose fist is that?

The hand was orange and Jasper's eyes moved over to an arm, which was also orange and muscular. He was shocked beyond words to find that it was his *own* arm and hand that had stopped Necrod's assault. No one was more shocked that Jasper himself, as he found his own hand up due to lightning-fast reflexes. His hand was clasped around Necrod's fist, his grasp strong. Jasper was even more shocked to see that Necrod was fighting like hell to free himself and was losing the struggle. A realization came over Jasper and a smile formed on his face.

"I'm stronger than you are!"

Necrod knew Jasper was right. Jasper gripped Necrod's fist tightly, and the demon let out a groan of pain as his hand was being crushed. Jasper kicked him and the demon fell back. He smiled and looked at his demonic adversary. Necrod was more vicious and had a killer's instinct, which was the only advantage he had over Jasper. Delilah saw the two brawling and was concerned for her lover. He was powerful and vicious but not too bright; also, she wasn't sure how powerful Jasper was. The two of them wrestled in the coliseum as Delilah's looked on with worry. Jasper dropped Necrod easily to the stone floor, then plunged his elbow into the demon's face again and again. Jasper forced Necrod to his feet, and then grabbed him by the neck, punched him and sent him to the ground again. Once more, Jasper picked Necrod up, wound back with his clenched fist and punched the demon again, knocking him to the ground. A third time Jasper grasped his neck, forcing him up. When he released, Necrod was about to fall over but Jasper caught him, holding him up and punching him repeatedly.

✿

Morgalla had been moving from alleyway to alleyway, from building to building, still looking for Jasper. She ran into many soldiers and minions of Hell and killed them easily. She avoided all human contact, for she was afraid they might think she was the enemy.

After defeating two opponents, she could just barely make out the silhouettes of two humans. She could see they were warriors, as they fought other demons with expert skills. She saw the eyes of a man not much older than she. He was looking at her with an unusual expression. She was curious, unable to clearly read the feelings from his soul.

As Morgalla and James made brief eye contact, both of them gripping their weapons tightly, neither of them was sure precisely what the other was going to do. One demon attacked Morgalla and she fought it; James did the same, until they found each other fighting the same foe. The battle went very poorly for the demons, and they began to flee the city, continuing to attack everyone who crossed their paths.

✽

Downtown the battle was raging; Richard aimed his staff up to the sky and fired a bolt of lightning, hitting five winged dracon, killing them instantly. Their bodies melted into puddles of black and red. Richard watched in horror as two monsters killed one of his comrades, and in return he brought the staff down hard on the cement, sending electricity through the street to the two minions, and destroying them both.

Three wolf-like creatures charged at Richard. He pointed his staff of light at them. He was ready to fire another bolt of lightning, but the tip of the staff fizzled out. Frustrated, he tossed it to one of his comrades.

"Recharge it, quickly!" he commanded.

Richard reached into his long coat, took out a red wand, and pointed it at the beasts, who immediately burst into flame. They screamed and died, melting into puddles.

One minion ambushed Richard from behind, but without warning a bullet hit the beast in the head, and it fell to the ground and died. Startled, Richard turned to see a cop standing there with a shotgun, the barrel smoking. They nodded at each other in solidarity.

At the police station, multiple cops in body armor ran around frantically. One of them unlocked a metal cabinet and passed out weapons to the others.

Back downtown, the battle was under control as the Smythes, Daishi, and the police were making quick work of the remaining minions. Two cops fired, killing some minions who dropped dead and melted. Delilah landed behind them, flying in from the sky. She was armed with two black sickles, and with one slash of her arm she decapitated both officers.

Two members of the Smythe family saw Delilah and attacked. She smiled, knowing full well her power was greater than theirs. Their weapons clashed, but she defeated and killed them brutally. She then saw Richard, standing over the body of a wounded family member. He defended him bravely against some minions, killing the creatures just before noticing the female demon. They made eye contact.

Demon. A high rank, if I had to guess.

Her fangs gleaming white and her eyes burning, she licked her lips as she gazed upon the wizard.

Wizard. I smell the leader. This will be fun!

Delilah leapt into the air and flew down at Richard, but he was ready for her. On the back of his left glove was a magical gem glowing pale blue. Delilah landed right in front of him and he blasted her with a blue beam of energy. She was blown back and encased in a block of ice. She was trapped only briefly, but then broke free, sending blocks of ice everywhere and knocking Richard to the ground.

"Fee, fie, fo, fum!" Her words came from behind gleaming fangs, her eyes filled with blood lust. "I smell the blood of an Englishman!"

Richard's comrade tossed his staff of light back to him; its power fully restored. In the background there was another bright blue flash. What appeared to be the section of a street corner fell from the sky, crushing a car. Hans, a wizard member of the Smythe family, came flying out of the sky at Delilah, who saw him coming. Delilah blocked him as she breathed forth dragon flame, creating a wall between the two of them. The wizard fell to the ground, helpless power obviously greater than his own.

One Springdale officer opened fire on Delilah with his shotgun. The bullets were deflected off her body and merely felt like bee stings. She was annoyed as she turned to him.

"Damn humans!" she shouted.

Richard got back up as another blue flash in the background dropped a car onto the street. He saw Delilah fighting his family members and knew he had to help. Delilah sliced through the cop's shotgun easily. He took out a pistol and shot her in the stomach at point-blank range. She knocked the gun out of his hand and grabbed him by the throat, lifting him easily off the ground.

Noticing that Richard was back, she dropped the cop, eager to attack the more valuable prey. She stared at Richard and attacked again; he defended himself using every magical spell that he knew. Delilah grasped the magic staff; he sent surges of electricity through her hands into her body. She fought the pain; their eyes locked in anger. The electricity was no match for her power, though, as she slashed her claws across his face. He fell to the ground injured and she stood victorious over the wizard, ready to bring a finishing blow to him.

Richard looked up at Delilah, whose golden gaze stared back down. Her clawed hand gripped her weapon even tighter and her sneer gleamed. But just before she dealt her final blow, she saw Morgalla standing several feet away. The demon women locked eyes, and Morgalla stood still as Delilah casually strode towards her one-time apprentice.

Richard looked towards Morgalla but could barely see her. He was confused about what was happening, for it was not one of his family members who had come to his rescue. The street seemed to go silent when Morgalla arrived; all eyes were fixed upon her and Delilah.

"So it's come to this?" Delilah approached her one-time apprentice, now completely forgetting the wizard she almost killed. The women circled each other, Morgalla's eyes fixed upon Delilah. Morgalla was stunned by the hate emanating from Delilah and could not understand why she had suddenly turned on her. Flashes of blue decorated the red sky. "You"—Delilah pointed her weapon to her—"and these pathetic creatures will not stop us!"

"You were always a tad overconfident," Morgalla replied, as Delilah smirked. "You're not even going to tell me why you decided to betray me?" Delilah was silent, looking away. "Did my father offer you your own throne? Did he give you Earth?"

"He told me the truth," Delilah replied with her back turned and her voice barely a whisper. "The disgusting truth." She then spun around and yelled at her one-time friend. "And do you honestly think the humans will be gracious to you for your bravery?" Delilah replied with sarcasm. "Applaud you for helping them fight the *evil* demon scourge?"

"It doesn't matter."

"You're right, because *I'm* going to kill you!"

Delilah attacked and Morgalla returned the fight. Their weapons clashed as Richard took out a healing potion. He drank it down and his wounds instantly healed. Neither he nor the other Smythe family members couldn't understand why this demon was fighting *with* them. Who *was* she?

Morgalla leapt up to a rooftop and Delilah followed. They battled with masterful skills as Morgalla went on the defensive and their duel continued over the rooftops.

James, Rebecca, and the other Smythes began to arrive downtown. James helped Richard to his feet.

"What the hell was that?" Richard was in a daze about the being that had just arrived, another demon that seemed to have saved his life.

James and Rebecca looked at each other, not sure how to respond. They all saw more blue light throughout the sky, almost like lightning.

"What's going on?" Rebecca asked, as she looked to the sky.

"Looks to be dimensional instability," Richard said. "How could *that* be happening?"

"*Look!*" James pointed to the sky, seeing that many more winged creatures were flying in from the sea of black and crimson.

"Next wave coming in!" Richard said, trying quickly to come up with a plan.

He looked around, noticing that no one was taking charge of the town. No police officers were there. He had hoped there would be military in this fight and he would just help out where needed, a warrior for Earth. But he was faced with a harsh truth; he had to be in command of this fight.

Morgalla battled Delilah across the rooftops, although she was hesitant to fight the woman who for years had been the only mother figure in her life. She knew she had no choice. There was no more love in Delilah's heart and it was as clear as day what her intentions were.

Delilah disarmed her opponent and was about to go for the kill. She had enough strength in her, but she would have only one shot. Dragon flame came forth, ready to incinerate the woman before her. Morgalla did something unexpected: she leaped above Delilah and in midair she grasped the medallion that was taken earlier in the portal chamber. Morgalla landed, *HERO* in her hand. She motioned to Delilah to advance.

Delilah flew at her but Morgalla quickly dodged, causing her to crash into a brick wall. Delilah smashed into it, and the brick crumbled easily. Morgalla ran to the next rooftop as Delilah came to her senses.

As Morgalla ran, there were more flashes of blue light and more objects fell from the sky. Delilah kicked and pushed the chunks of brick and cement off her and took to the sky again, pursuing Morgalla. There was another bright blue flash in the sky above Morgalla, the biggest yet. A building appeared from the flash and fell to the ground.

Morgalla saw the building coming; knowing she would not survive a building crashing down on her, she stopped immediately and ran in the opposite direction. The building fell upon another, and both were demolished in a colossal crash. A gigantic cloud of dust and debris formed from the impact, enveloping Morgalla and making it nearly impossible to see. Suddenly, Delilah came out of the cloud of dust and struck Morgalla, who fell back. They continued to fight with weapons clashing.

Morgalla could feel the hate flowing through Delilah, who was breaking her own rule: never get angry in a duel, for you will lose. One or two opportunities opened up for Morgalla to capitalize on her opponent's mistakes, but she hesitated, remembering that for the longest time Delilah was the only person she called *friend*.

Anger would be Delilah's weakness in this conflict, where compassion would be Morgalla's.

✡

Jasper dove for cover again as six thousand pounds of metal hurtled past him. It was only inches away, another close call. He felt the hard concrete beneath him. Necrod was atop a car carrier with the semi truck still attached. The vehicle in his claws was awkward and difficult to lift, but soon enough Jasper saw another car being thrown at him.

He rolled out of the way as the car hit the pavement and crashed into more parked cars. Jasper looked up to see his enemy roaring; the beast was enraged and ready for another volley. The machines, clean and with fresh coats of paint, would soon be junk as they were demolished hitting the pavement.

Necrod wound up again, a car high above his head. He slipped in mid-throw and sliced it, the car crashing off to the side, nowhere near Jasper. The explosion was tremendous as gasoline erupted into flame across the parking lot. The other vehicles ignited and the resulting inferno threw both demons back. Necrod landed on the roof of one vehicle, crushing the top and shattering the windows. If they had been human they'd have been killed instantly. Jasper rose up to see a wall of fire between him and Necrod. He felt the intense heat on his skin. For a brief moment he thought he was on fire, but to his relief, his skin and flesh remained intact.

I'm fireproof?

Jasper did not want to test this theory; maybe another day. One theory had to be tested now; if this monster could throw cars and Jasper's strength rivaled his, then Jasper could fight back. He took hold of a car's bumper and began to circle around and around, gripping the bumper tightly. He didn't know where precisely Necrod was, but he could sense his hate through the wall of smoke and fire.

Necrod ignored the heat and took hold of another car. Lifting it high above his head, he leaped up to the top of the car carrier again. He could sense the fear of his prey through the smoke and was ready to strike again. His look changed from rage to shock as he saw a car come hurtling through the smoke right at him. The car smashed into the semi-truck and Necrod fell back. Before losing consciousness, the last thing he saw was the car he was *going* to throw coming down on him. The smoke had started to thin as the flames receded. Jasper he ran off to find Morgalla.

✿

The next wave of Hell's army came swooping out of the clouds. Screeches and flapping wings filled the air. The people felt the rumbling beneath their feet of more animals charging toward the town, heard their roars and screeches, and braced themselves as they listened to the thundering of the demons' claws against dirt, asphalt, and concrete.

"Everyone ready! Wizards by me! Riflemen to the front!"

Everyone did as Richard commanded, the wizards in a line to his right and left. All those with a firearm in their hands moved to the front and knelt down on one knee. All wands and staffs were aimed at the sky, and all firearms in front toward the thundering in the distance. Richard glanced from the street and then to the sky, trying to judge which group of minions would arrive first.

"Ready!" Richard yelled, as the winged beasts swooped down closer and closer. "Wizards aim!" Closer and closer their enemies dove. "FIRE!"

Bolts of lightning discharged from all forms of magical weapons upward, hitting Zorach's flying army. Many creatures died and their black blood rained down. The riflemen of the Smythe and Daishi, joined by some police officers of Springdale, were all vigilant. They kept their aim at the street toward the horde approaching. The monsters came down over buildings and from alleyways, as all firearms released bullets into the coming mass of evil.

The creatures that survived the onslaught from the air and ground charged at the warriors in the town. The police shot at anything that was not human. In the fight, James and Rebecca were back-to-back, their swords slicing into their adversaries.

Chapter Seventeen: To the Rescue

Andy, Meggan, and some other townspeople of Springdale all congregated in a small building. There was a police officer there and Russell Wrath, a member of the Smythe family.

"What the *hell* is going on?" the cop asked, on the verge of having a panic attack.

"You don't know how right you are."

The window shattered and through it three dracon came crashing in. The people screamed in fear as the cop shot at anything that wasn't human. Russell also defended himself, killing one minion rather quickly, but a few more came crawling in through the window, the broken glass crunching beneath their claws and drool dripping from their fangs. The citizens all backed up against the wall near the steel door. More and more beasts came in as the member of Springdale's finest ran out of ammunition.

Just when they thought they were doomed, the steel door came crashing down, crushing one monster. A huge form stepped in from the alleyway through the emergency exit. Everyone looked, including the minions, who backed up sensing danger. They snarled and hissed at the massive being entering. The dust cleared and Jasper stood there in his new demon form.

"Oh shit!" Russell said, thinking that Jasper was just a regular demon who had come to kill him. But Jasper did not look his way at all. Instead, he looked at the foes entering the building, his chin up and muscular chest out. With his hands up he motioned for them to approach.

"Bring it!" he commanded.

The soldiers of Hell attacked, but were little match for Jasper's power. He grabbed one by the neck and slammed it to the floor hard. He kicked another and it went out the broken window and back onto the street. The creature's flight from the building caught the attention of everyone outside. Those who were still in the building, including Andy and Meggan, watched with wonder as this large orange behemoth came to their rescue.

The minions offered no challenge for Jasper; he easily kicked and punched them off him as they tried to pounce. Russell was shocked at this demon fighting the same foes, bewildered by why this was happening. Jasper finished off all enemies in the room; they were either killed by his great strength or found themselves tossed out onto the street.

"Holy shit," Andy said, aghast.

Jasper stood, triumphant, looking over his defeated foes. His chest heaved with each breath. He smiled and then looked at Andy and Meggan.

"You two all right?" Jasper asked his friends, who both looked at him in bewilderment. They recognized his voice but not much else. Jasper realized that his friends did not know of his transformation.

Before he could explain, there was a sudden snarling sound in the room. Jasper looked to the shattered window to see more of Zorach's loyal creatures there, with their gaze locked upon him. He balled up his fists in anger and stared back at them with contempt. He gave a sneer, ready for their onslaught.

Less than a block away the demon casualties were great, thanks to Richard and his troupe. However, everyone was pushed farther and farther back as Hells' cannon fodder circled the humans from every angle, until finally they were huddled together in one group in the middle of the street. They realized that General Darvis' strategy would mean the end of them, and Richard ached with the recognition that he had led them into death.

The slaughter did not come, though; instead, their executioners stopped. Though the beasts of Hell smelled blood, Darvis held them back, for he had a powerful control over them. By his sheer will they held their ground, claws dug into the asphalt, their breathing heavy and wet, their eyes burning with the lust for blood known by no creature of Earth. They kept in a circle around their prey, and while the humans were terrified, they didn't scream. They decided to face their death without showing their fear.

The demons, though, could sense how petrified they were. Darvis relished in these moments and he wanted it to last as long as possible. The humans looked down at the diminutive leader of the invasion standing in triumph.

"No matter how many worlds I conquer, your species never ceases to amaze," he said in a condescending manner to them. He looked at Richard. "How many wizards are there on your world?" he asked, recalling that Morgalla's report had stated there were none. Though he thought Morgalla was lying, in reality she was just ignorant to the fact. No one said anything, though. Richard didn't answer, but Darvis was strong in his powers and could sense his answer regardless. "Not many, are there?"

"You will find no enjoyment. We will resist with our last ounce of strength," Richard said.

"You have only two options, human," General Darvis said. "You will *all* die quickly or you will all die slowly! Choose carefully!"

If I kill him, surely I will die, but maybe Earth will have a chance if their leader is dead.

As Richard contemplated this, he could hear a familiar sound in the distance. If Darvis and his army heard it too, they they chose to ignore it.

There are a lot of them and they're close!

Richard and others saw it on the horizon; like a swarm, human reinforcements were approaching with great speed. James looked to see how close the people were. He stepped behind his father and made sure there was a path for him to the center. Richard had only one option when help arrived and James knew what that option was.

"At least let the parents and children go," Richard said, trying to stall.

"What *is* it with you people and your spawn?" Darvis was disgusted by the human need to *love* one's child.

"Families are our strength," Richard said. "You'll learn that soon enough!"

Darvis rolled his eyes. The sound of roaring engines was getting louder and louder, blades chopping the air.

Richard ran to the center of the human mass. He brought his staff down to the street and prayed that all would be protected from the spell he just cast.

Darvis watched, fearing nothing, but saw the oncoming fleet of army helicopters swooping in for the kill.

"Aw, DAMN." General Darvis's last words were uttered, and a moment later the human weapons slaughtered his minions.

In a blazing inferno the blood of many spawns of Hell spilled. The people of Springdale and their rescuers tried to duck for cover, only to see the black blood of Hell's children splatter along an invisible wall. They could see flame but felt no heat as Richard's spell protected them. The sounds of carnage soon passed, and the dome was stained with blood and turned gray from the smoke.

"DOWN!" Richard yelled, and everyone complied, diving for the ground and seeking what cover there was.

With all the power he could muster he waved the staff above his head. The wall shattered from the inside and exploded out over the street and buildings. Everyone looked at each other, astonished that just moments before they were surrounded by an army and now all that remained was blood, smoke, and silence. Parents held children close and wept. People who'd been strangers just hours before embraced like long lost relatives. The helicopters' engines drifted off into the distance and there was nothing but the sound of the autumn wind.

There was a stir and everyone turned to the source. A lone soldier of Hell rose from the ashes. He was injured and dazed, the rage about to boil over. A shot rang out and he fell dead. People looked to see one of Springdale's finest, his weapon empty.

✻

Hell's winged beasts were feasting nearby when they saw the humans' reinforcements. They saw their own flying warriors and took to the skies. The human pilots had never been up against such opponents. But when they fired, whatever beasts flew into the line of fire were killed immediately. Many flew into the rotor blades and were mangled in a second. A few aircraft were destroyed, crashing to the ground below. Hell's storm rendered all electronic equipment aboard the aircrafts virtually useless. The pilots had to rely upon their basic senses to fight the battle.

The pilots swore as the monsters continued to attack them and tried to break into the cockpits. Some skilled maneuvers shook the beasts loose. With no leader or control over them, the minions of

Hell did not stand a chance. The skies were cleansed of evil thanks to military hardware.

Human soldiers now moved into the town just as another wave of demonic beasts came from all directions. Neither the soldiers on the ground nor their superiors ever imagined just what the threat was. They looked about, seeing the monsters on four legs stepping out into the streets. They came from buildings and alleyways. They peered down from the rooftops at their new prey. Army soldiers were shocked but it was clear they were facing a terrible enemy. No mercy was given from either side.

"Kill them all!" one soldier yelled.

The domino fell as bullets flew in all directions. Beasts charged in and some leaped from the rooftops to meet their end. Hell's army had not anticipated such resistance. The philosophy of "shoot first, ask questions later" rarely applied to the United States Army, but today was the exception, and they killed anything that wasn't human. Many human lives were lost in the battle. While military ammunition was sufficient to overpower the minions, demons of Morgalla's and Delilah's caliber would not be fazed by simple bullets. Bullets would only enrage them. The casualties of the humans would be great, but the humans decided on a strategy. The Smythe and Daishi would concentrate on the greater demons that would only die through magic. The military would make quick work of Hell's soldiers and the beasts that only listened to their lust for blood.

Army training had not prepared them for monsters and beastlike humanoids. It was as if they were battling a pack of wild animals of limitless number. It took more rounds of ammunition than they thought, but each beast eventually fell under volleys of bullets. Hell's soldiers, with their weapons of choice, put up a more vicious struggle. Many of them welcomed the challenge. Humans on this planet *Earth* were not weak.

Richard and the others were continuing their conflict on the streets. Without warning, one dracon came through a wall and rolled to a stop before Richard. The beast was dead at his feet, but he wondered what could have been so powerful to do that. He looked up and saw Jasper come out of the hole in the wall. There was one monster whose teeth were planted firmly on his ankle and another attached to his shoulder. He grasped one by the neck and punched it into submission.

They did not have time to stop and wonder why a demon was on their side. Jasper used his new strength to overpower all demonic monsters that came his way. The street was crowded with all forms of people and creatures, and Jasper didn't realize that Necrod had found him again and was charging at full speed. Grasping the young man, the beast would not let go.

Out of control, Jasper found himself helpless in his grasp and felt two ribs break. He screamed and they both went through another wall, away from the battle of downtown. Necrod released Jasper and hit him again and again, breaking bones and knocking him back through another wall.

✢

Morgalla and Delilah continued their duel on the rooftops of downtown Springdale. Weapons of magical metal clashed, but both women began to feel fatigued. All around them miscellaneous objects fell from the sky, objects being transported from all over the planet. There was a palm tree, a car, and large chunks of earth. Delilah kicked Morgalla, and she fell off the roof of one building and landed hard on another. Quickly, she was up on her feet as Delilah glided down to the rooftop.

"You would side against us, Morgalla? Side with the humans? They're weak and will be crushed easily!"

Morgalla gripped her sword tightly, ready for the advance of her opponent.

"Funny thing about humans," Morgalla said. "They have an uncanny ability to bind together when facing a common enemy!"

"Your point being?"

"They're stronger than you think!"

They dueled some more as flashes of bright blue decorated the dark sky. A car landed next to the building and exploded, knocking them back. In the darkness they clashed more, with flashes of blue above them. As they fought, the metal created sparks. Pushing against one another, they glared into each other's eyes with hatred.

"You always were a pacifist, Morgalla! We had such high hopes for you. But what can you expect from someone who's half *human?*"

Morgalla was caught off guard by Delilah's comment; her eyes grew wide for a brief moment. Delilah kicked her hard again, and Morgalla went flying back and skidded to a stop on the roof of Springdale High School. She shook off the pain, looking around to see where Delilah could be. Out of nowhere Delilah came from the sky, flying down. Pouncing on Morgalla, she drove her through the roof into the gymnasium.

Morgalla came down hard on the wooden floor, cracking the planks and injuring her back. Delilah landed easily as debris rained down, covering them both in dust. There was hardly any light in the room at all. Natural light poured through the hole in the ceiling, the only light within the room. Delilah was confident that Morgalla was sufficiently injured not to fight back. Slowly, she walked up to her fallen adversary in an arrogant strut. She stared at Morgalla's motionless body with a smirk.

Without warning, Morgalla's hand came slashing across the air, cutting Delilah's abdomen severely. Delilah fell back, grasping her wound in pain as blood poured out. Morgalla staggered to her feet; her back was injured, but her powers quickly worked to heal her. Delilah looked down at her injury and with one leap she was up into the rafters of the gymnasium. Her powers too were hard at work, trying to heal the deep cut. Morgalla looked around among the rafters, waiting for Delilah to come out, but it was too dark to see her.

"Who was my mother?" Morgalla shouted. Her demand echoed in the large room.

"You expect me to tell you everything?" Delilah yelled back from the darkness, mocking Morgalla's pain. "This was planned well before you were born!" Delilah looked down and saw that her wound was almost completely healed. "The whole reason you exist was to conquer this world! It was the only way! How do you think you were able to take human form so easily? Usually a demon would have to be twice as old to do it. At first I thought you were just incredibly talented, or that perhaps it was my teaching. How wrong I was."

"You knew all along and you didn't tell me?" Morgalla screamed in rage. She still couldn't see Delilah in the rafters, and couldn't pinpoint where the voice was coming from because of the echo. "Actually, no. Your father told me earlier today! Imagine my surprise, me befriending someone who had filthy human blood flowing through her!"

That's why she hates me now.

Delilah had always looked down on humans, even hated them. Morgalla had never understood why; maybe it was because humans could be found on countless worlds. It almost seemed like the human race, regardless of which world they were on, were blessed by the divine. Jasper was right; this was why demons hated humans. Morgalla looked around the gymnasium for any kind of advantage, and came across a small panel on the wall, and grabbed a fire extinguisher from it.

"The last world we tried to conquer took close to a century!" Delilah continued, yelling from somewhere up near the ceiling. "So we found an easier way, even though it would take over twenty years for your body to be strong enough."

Delilah noticed a small object out of the corner of her eye. She looked over to see the fire extinguisher being thrown into the air by Morgalla. Then a sword was hurled at it, slicing through the metal quite easily, and the extinguisher exploded, causing Delilah to fall from the rafters. She landed smoothly on the floor of the gym but was momentarily blinded. Morgalla came out of the white cloud and kicked her weapon from her hand.

Now unarmed, the two women battled hand-to-hand, fighting with expert skills. Delilah was still partially blinded, Morgalla held her arm behind her back. Overcoming Delilah, Morgalla's other arm got her adversary in a headlock.

"Who was she?" Morgalla yelled, demanding to know, and she wasn't going to let go until she did.

"Take a guess," Delilah mocked. Morgalla punched her out of rage, knocking her back against the wall. "Yes!" Delilah wiped blood from her lip with a sadistic smile. "That's it! That's the killer instinct we've been looking for!"

"Who is she?"

"She's *dead*! So what does it matter?"

Morgalla's fists clenched in anger and her eyes closed; she was unsure what to think or feel. Her entire life she had felt like an outsider, as if she did not belong, and this was proof that she never did. Delilah regained her strength and was ready to fight again as

Morgalla opened her eyes. She let out a scream of rage and charged at Delilah. The two fought more and Delilah flew up through the hole in the ceiling again. Morgalla saw the weapons still on the gym floor and took them. She pursued her one-time friend as she flew away. Morgalla kicked down a door, adrenaline flowing through her fueled by anger. She saw that Delilah was making her way back downtown and she pursued.

Delilah flew off from Morgalla, her fangs exposed in a nefarious grin. She froze in the air, her wings flapping with furious power to keep her in the air. She was shocked at what she saw looking over the town. An army of the humans had arrived, and not just the small band of wizards and swordsmen. She saw strange vehicles, alien in appearance but clearly human-made. Their function was also quite obvious: war.

The machines were covered in armor, with weaponry built into their structures. The humans—soldiers, by her educated guess—were dressed in the garb of warfare. She had seen many different human warriors on many worlds, but these were the strangest she had ever seen. They held weapons of black metal that were not held like swords. She knew what they were; the most annoying of all human weapons.

Guns. Damn it, I hate those things!

Delilah looked down to the hordes at her command moving about the town, fighting everyone with whom they came into contact. Without warning, something flew by her making a horrible sound. It wasn't alone, either; a swarm of them came from behind.

Damn humans and their machines!

She had read Morgalla's reports; she had read about the vehicles of Earth. Their names escaped her for the time being, but it did not matter. The flying machines had spinning parts and she recognized the shape of "guns" attached. She became concerned that conquest of this world might be more difficult than she thought, and perhaps even futile. She had to form a plan—and fast.

Delilah saw the machines swarm the castle of Zorach. It barely stood, and bombardments from the human weapons caused it to collapse completely. In a thick cloud of dust and smoke it disappeared into nothingness.

✿

Morgalla ran through the city, keeping Delilah in sight the whole time. With the U.S. Army now in the fight, the tide turned, and many of Hell's warriors fell one by one. Earth's defenders were battling dracon and soldiers when Morgalla came running through one of many skirmishes. She ran down one alleyway and found herself between demon slayers and former comrades who all now wanted her dead.

"Shit! Kill her, kill her!" one of the human soldiers said, seeing Morgalla.

Both the Smythes and demons attacked Morgalla, but she was far more skilled than they were. She blocked their attacks and took a pair of nunchakus off one of the injured Smythes. She held up the nunchakus to all, using them far more skillfully than anyone they had ever seen.

"Oh shit, she's got the chucks!" one demonic soldier said, his terror brought forth, for he had heard stories.

The small group of soldiers took a few steps back, thinking that they were outmatched, and they were right. She battled her foes, bludgeoning them mercilessly. It was then that the other Smythes realized something strange was going on, that she was not, in fact, on the side of Hell. They looked at each other curiously as Morgalla battled their adversaries.

Only one demon remained in the alleyway. Morgalla twirled the nunchakus in her hand, ready for his assault. He lunged forward but she parried and smacked him in the head. He fell back, dazed for only a moment. They fought for a bit; Morgalla's adversary cut her forearm and she fell back, dueling with only one hand until her cut healed itself. She kicked him once in the gut and smacked him again with her weapon. He fell back, dropping his sword, but only for a moment. He looked at her, and she returned his gaze, ready to strike. He grabbed the sword as she attacked again, this time doing a spin and grasping his neck with the chain of her weapon. There was a quick twist and a snap, and he fell to the ground dead.

There was only one human civilian among the battle, huddled to the ground for protection. Taking his phone out, he tried to snap pictures but found that his device wouldn't work. He swore.

The slayers looked on, ready to defend as Morgalla panted in fatigue, breathing heavily.

"I'm going to borrow these, 'kay?" Morgalla held up her favorite weapon. She didn't wait for an answer, though, and ran off in search of Delilah.

Delilah saw that the battle was lost; it was only a matter of time before the rest of her army was destroyed. Every ally she had was gone and it would be pointless to join back in the fight. She flew off. Her options were limited at the moment, but one thing was certain: she had to flee.

Morgalla looked to the skies and saw a lone form flying away from downtown, recognizing instantly that it was Delilah. She ran after her down one street, but knew she'd need help getting to the air. Morgalla leaped into the air on top of a winged dracon. From there she leapt again and landed on another; this time it was much higher off the ground. Morgalla kept her mother in mind, the human being whose identity only Delilah knew. She might be dead, but Morgalla had to know who she was. Zorach surely was never going to tell her and he could not now. She leaped again and again, off one beast to another, every time higher and higher, keeping her eyes locked on Delilah who was flying away, oblivious to Morgalla closing in on her. With one final leap, Morgalla landed on Delilah's back, but nearly lost her footing and dropped the sword. With the nunchakus still in hand, she threw them around Delilah's neck and used the chain to choke her.

"What the...Hell?" Delilah coughed out, shocked.

With Morgalla on her back, Delilah could not fly straight and almost ran into a few beasts flying the opposite direction. She tried with all her might to keep control of her flying, with little success as Morgalla held on for dear life.

"Damn it, how many waves do they have?" James said in frustration that this battle seemed never-ending.

The people were still frightened, and they wept from both terror and exhaustion. Richard climbed up on a nearly demolished car so that everyone could see and hear him.

"Everyone! Hear me!" he yelled, and the people within earshot turned and faced him. Even those soldiers who had come to their rescue listened to this stranger, hoping that he could provide insight into what they were facing. "Your home is being invaded!"

"I think we've figured out that part for ourselves!" Meggan shouted.

"You must rally everyone and find shelter!" Richard yelled, ignoring Meggan. "These beasts will surely mean the death of you all if you do not move and try to protect yourselves! All those who are able-bodied must fight along with us or perish!"

"But wait!" one man shouted out as he stepped forward, holding up his hands to get their attention. "There must be another way! Maybe if we talk to them we can find some sort of compromise!"

Andy, Meggan, and many others rolled their eyes at what the man said.

"I don't think 'make love, not war' is in their vocabulary," Andy said.

"If they're intelligent, sensible people, we should give peace a chance," the man said. "Let's lay down our arms and talk to them!"

Richard slowly stepped down, his eyes locked on the young man and angered by his ignorance. "Son, do I sound *French* to you?" Richard expected no reply. The screeching sounds were closer and closer, and everyone then turned to the sky. *"Go! Now!"*

Many people ran for cover, seeking whatever shelter they could. Anyone with a gun fired into the air at the monsters high above. Anyone with a blade swung and cleaved their metal into the flesh of an evil brute from Hell.

Normally one would use the word *duel* to describe a spirited contest between two skilled gentleman warriors. Necrod was not a gentleman and Jasper was indeed not skilled. Destruction was left in their wake as heaps of destroyed bricks and shards of broken glass littered the ground. Both were filthy; covered in dust, debris, and sweat. Their allies were dying all around them as they battled, smashing through yet another wall of Springdale.

Jasper fell to the pavement on Main Street; the sidewalk was hard, rough, and cold. He looked to see a weapon that he had not considered. He grasped the steel embedded in the concrete, and it tore from the curb much easier than he expected. Necrod again charged forward only to be met by Jasper and his grand slam. Necrod staggered back as the top of the makeshift weapon exploded in a shower of coins along the ground. He shook off the blow and snarled at Jasper. Necrod spit out quarters as Jasper wound back for another hit.

Morgalla was still on Delilah's back, her arms wrapped around her neck, choking her. The storm above was strong and a blue flash came down. Delilah evaded and then flew low, into the park, moving among the trees. The beam that nearly hit both of them ignited the trees in the park and many burst into flame. Delilah flew through some branches, hoping they would knock Morgalla off, but her plan did not work.

Morgalla only tightened her grip on the nunchakus, the chain pressing against Delilah's neck. Suddenly, Delilah rammed headfirst into a tree, shattering it into splinters and causing Morgalla to be thrown off. She then smashed through another tree and rolled in the dirt and grass, coming to a stop. Both women lay motionless, their bodies bruised, bloodied, and broken.

✿

As Jasper fought for his life, he suddenly felt an overwhelming sensation, and realized he could feel Morgalla's pain; he knew instinctively that she was in danger. He wanted to concentrate, to zone in on the sensation and try to help her, but more adversaries attacked him, and he had no choice but to defend himself.

Downtown, the numbers of Zorach's army dwindled quickly, thanks to the warriors of Earth. The fighting stopped, and everyone looked around for more foes from Hell to battle, but there were none. They all give a cheer as victory was theirs. They then noticed that the battle wasn't quite over. They looked toward Jasper and Necrod, who were still fighting. The street seemed to go silent as they all walked up to this street brawl.

Left and right Jasper swung, crashing against the beast's skull, until Necrod fell back. Jasper looked at what was left of the parking meter, a twisted pretzel of steel. Now useless, he dropped it when Necrod got back to his feet. Soldiers of the U.S. Army all reloaded and watched the two behemoths fighting. With guns pointed at both of them Jasper and Necrod continued to exchange blows.

As Jasper hit Necrod, all guns were pointed at him, ready to fire. Then Necrod hit back and all weapons changed targets. The soldiers weren't certain just *who* the enemy was. Clearly, neither were human, but why were they fighting? They looked at each other quizzically. By now Richard and many other demon slayers had walked up. His jaw had dropped.

Everyone looked to Richard for answers, but he was just as confused as they were. Jasper finally got the upper hand with Necrod as he found his opponent against the brick wall, barely able to stand, but at the same time, every human soldier's weapon was now pointed right at him. He knew he had to convince them that he was the good guy, and that he was on their side.

"God bless America!" he shouted.

Necrod was ready to strike again, but this time he found the full power of the United States Army ready to strike against him. All soldiers turned to meet him and opened fire. Jasper had to cover his ears, along with many others, to shield from the deafening sound of gunfire. He stepped back from the barrage and found it hard to look at his nemesis being fired upon over and over again. The bullets did not pierce Necrod's hide but certainly hurt him, as he was pushed back into an open shattered window. He fell over, his body in excruciating agony.

Jasper sighed in great relief, thinking that the worst was over. But then he sensed, once again, the pain that Morgalla was feeling. He knew he had to find her.

Jasper ran past the crowd, following the irresistible pull toward Morgalla. James Smythe noticed Jasper running, and chased after him, curious to know what was happening.

James was knocked to the ground as Necrod smashed through a wall in pursuit of his quarry. James regained his senses and got up, but now everyone noticed that at least one demon was still alive. Seeing that James ran in pursuit, others followed him, including Richard.

✿

Morgalla and Delilah lay on the ground of the park; their wounds slowly beginning to heal themselves. As they regained consciousness and rose up, aching and exhausted, a pungent odor filled their nostrils. The park was on fire. Morgalla stood to see they were surrounded by flames.

Morgalla rolled over onto her stomach and looked up to see Delilah rising sluggishly. Delilah moved her wings but cried out in pain, feeling it shoot through her back. She looked at her left wing that hung lifeless. The wing was dislocated and she would have to place it back into the socket for it to heal completely. For the time being she was grounded. They looked at each other with pure contempt.

"You'll...you'll have to do better than that!" Delilah said. She was breathing hard and her ribs were sore.

Delilah reached down and from her ankle she removed a small amulet, hidden away as a secret weapon. The amulet changed into a large knife and she smiled wickedly. Morgalla saw that the nunchakus were between the two of them and knew she must get to them. She dove forward as Delilah lunged with the knife. Morgalla rolled past Delilah, grabbing the nunchakus.

Quickly, Morgalla was on her feet with the nunchakus in hand as Delilah attacked again, and the women fought. Morgalla tried not to parry her attacks, for the wood of the nunchakus was no match for the steel of Delilah's blade. She instead dodged left and right and managed to strike Delilah. Morgalla and Delilah continued their fight.

"This is pointless!" Morgalla shouted. "The portal is gone. Your forces will soon be destroyed!"

"I'll have the pleasure of killing you, filthy half-breed!" Delilah yelled, and she attacked again.

As Delilah's blade struck, Morgalla parried with the nunchakus' chain. With a mere twist of her blade, Delilah shattered the chain, gave Morgalla a kick and knocked her back onto the grass.

Jasper ran as fast as he could; he found that his new body was not only powerful but also had great stamina. He was tired from the entire day's events, but had he still been human, he wouldn't have even been able to stand. He did not know it but Necrod was not far behind, and farther back still were members of the Smythe family, including James and Richard.

The odor of smoke filled Jasper's nostrils as he saw on the horizon the blackness flowing up into the air. The night sky was dark as could be, but he still knew where to go. He reached the edge and looked down into the park, or where he thought the park was. He saw a blazing inferno and could feel the heat billowing up from the trees.

Morgalla. She's down there somewhere!

Ignoring the fire, and thinking only of Morgalla, he leaped over fallen trunks, realizing how high he could jump. With arms up to cover his face, he ran through the blazing inferno, realizing with relief that he was fireproof. Jasper arrived on the scene to find Morgalla and Delilah both worn from battle. Morgalla was ready to defend herself, though she was not armed.

"Morgalla!" he yelled in relief. He saw that she was okay, but only for the moment.

Delilah turned to see the lover of her one-time apprentice and grinned. The most evil of thoughts ran through her mind.

I'm going to make you watch your lover die!

Delilah threw her blade, aiming for Jasper. Morgalla screamed his name, running at him, and with a bounding leap she tackled her lover to the ground. Delilah's blade missed them both, but just barely. The two of them could feel the air being torn. They landed hard on the ground, Morgalla on top of Jasper.

A strange sound filled their ears, barely audible over the roaring flames. The sound was of metal embedding into the torso of a living being, a sound that Morgalla had caused more than once in her life. Brushing the dirty orange hair out of her eyes, Morgalla looked up. Jasper's eyes followed her's.

The two of them saw Necrod standing there, impaled through the chest with Delilah's blade. He had only enough energy left in his body to look down at the wound. His heart stopped beating a moment later and he was granted a very rare death for demons: his body exploded.

Jasper and Morgalla both braced themselves for pieces of Necrod falling all around them and disintegrating. Jasper stood, and he and Morgalla looked at each other briefly and then at Delilah, who was standing in stunned silence.

"Nice one," he said, now that his second demonic adversary was no longer a threat.

Delilah scowled at them with seething hatred. She leaped high in the air and to where the body of her lover was. What was left had now melted into nothingness as she gripped her blade.

Kill them both. They must suffer!

It was then, unexpectedly, that all the flames in the park blew out in one mighty gust of wind. All that remained were the smoldering cinders of the trees and some billowy smoke. Delilah looked up, seeing Richard Smythe hovering there above the ground. It was he who had, with great ease, extinguished the inferno. She looked to her right and left and noticed that many demon slayers from both families were surrounding her.

In anger she gripped her blade, her injuries still lingering and her body fatigued. She looked at Morgalla, who stared back at her. Delilah then held up her blade and brought it down into her own chest. Her weapon and clothes fell to the ground as her body changed to mist. Morgalla could feel the soul of her former friend, the only one she had, being cast to the night's wind. Jasper held Morgalla close, glad that she was all right and that their ordeal was finally over. Morgalla burst into tears. Every remaining bit of strength left her body and she melted into Jasper's arms.

Chapter Eighteen: Another Sunrise

The sun rose over a town that would never be the same. Morgalla looked at the rubble of what used to be the castle, knowing that she was never going back to the place she once called home. The sting of betrayal was still fresh, and she could not believe that her entire life was a lie. Slowly, a figure approached from behind, but she did not turn to face whoever it was.

"Are you here to kill me?" Morgalla asked with her back to the person behind her.

She did not know who it was, nor did she care at this moment. Richard was silent; he wanted to say no, but could not be sure. Morgalla turned to him and saw the look on his face. It was as if he had seen a ghost. Morgalla recognized him as the leader of the demon slayers, but knew as she looked into his eyes that he would not harm her. His eyes glistened with tears.

He set his staff on the ground as a sign of trust. He stepped a little closer to her.

"I...I don't know what to say to you," he started. "Your name is Morgalla, yes? Jasper, the young man, told me, and has filled me in on so much."

"You...you know who she is, don't you? My mother?" Morgalla asked with desperation.

"Quite well, actually," Richard said, and held up his hands.

He removed his black leather glove from his left, revealing a band of gold on his ring finger, still there even though it had been over twenty years since his wife had died. Morgalla's hand went to her mouth, agape.

"I…I never knew," she said. "What was her name?"

"Margaret."

"All this time," she said. "I always felt as if I were different." Morgalla hung her head, for at last the truth about her past came out.

"Margaret was the most beautiful and the strongest woman I ever knew. Could it be that her very spirit helped in the molding of your own?" Morgalla looked up at him, hopeful. "You are only *half*-demon, Morgalla," Richard continued. "But what does it matter? You are living proof that it is our actions, our choices that make us who we really are. You chose to do the right thing…and for that I'm grateful. You helped save us."

"Thank you," she said, managing a small smile, and he returned it.

"You honor her memory. Her spirit lives on within you!" Richard reached into his pocket and took out the golden crucifix. "This was hers. And now I want you to have it."

Morgalla was hesitant at first, but she slowly reached out and took hold of the cross, humbled by the gift. Her eyes welled, realizing that she was a woman of faith. Like with most personal possessions, especially ones that meant too much to others.

As the cross rested in her open palm, Morgalla could sense the souls of those who had owned it before her. The echo of Richard's soul was first, being the most recent, and she felt the myriad of emotions that imbued it, including the devotion he'd had to his wife, her mother. And then, she felt Margaret's soul. There were no memories; only what she felt when she died. Terrible fear was first, but then Morgalla could sense something she did not expect in a moment of death: love. Margaret's love for her husband was there, and it was powerful. She must have been thinking of him even while giving birth to Morgalla.

It only took a moment or two for this small event to occur. Richard didn't know what holding the cross did to Morgalla, but when he saw the tear roll down her cheek he was assured that it was in good hands.

"She loved you so much," Morgalla said, and looked up at Richard with red eyes.

Richard only assumed that Morgalla had powers and abilities he had yet to discover or understand.

James sat on a bench on Main Street as Jasper walked up to him, back in his human form. They both noticed that Richard and Morgalla were facing each other, standing over the rubble of the castle. The sunrise illuminated only their silhouettes on the small hill of crushed stone.

"Wonder what *that* conversation is about," James said.

"It's awkward, that's for sure," Jasper said.

Richard took hold of Morgalla's hand briefly for comfort. He then turned and walked away. Morgalla looked sad, but also a glimmer of hope blossomed in her heart. She never thought that a stranger could be so kind to her.

James looked at Jasper, who stared at Morgalla. Richard walked away from the site of Zorach's former castle. He smiled at Jasper, who smiled back. Jasper noticed that Richard's eyes were misty with tears; the memory of his late wife was fresh on his mind. At last his wife's death had been avenged and Earth was safe. The greatest of weights had been lifted.

"You were born human, yet you're one of them?" James asked Jasper. He too needed answers.

"I'm not," Jasper said. "I...I don't know what I am now."

Richard walked by Jasper and they both gave each other a small smile. Jasper somehow knew that things were going to be all right. Morgalla stood over the ruins of the castle. Hardly anything was left except rubble. Jasper walked up behind her and put his hand on her shoulder.

"You're free," he said.

"At what price?" she asked. "How many people died so that I can be free? *You* almost died."

Morgalla turned around, and she and Jasper looked into each other's eyes as they had done before, but this time it was different. Jasper looked sad, and uncertain of what to say. She rested her head against his chest and he held her close.

"But I didn't," Jasper reassured her. "Everything will be okay now, Morgalla."

Richard slowly walked away from the rubble of the castle, and James rose and moved next to his father to offer support. Both of them stood looking at the silhouettes of Jasper and Morgalla in the morning sun. Richard's expression was bittersweet.

"Smile, James." Richard said. "You have a half sister."

It was only then that James realized it. Deep down, he knew that he and Morgalla had the same mother. Rebecca then walked up, putting her hand on her husband's shoulder.

"Go ahead, you can say it," she said.

"I have no idea what you're talking about," James replied.

"You were right about her."

"Do you trust her?" James asked Richard. He did not reply at first; all he could do was stare at the young woman in the distance.

Richard wanted so much to trust Morgalla, and did, but he couldn't deny his hatred for demons. The only thing stronger, though, was his love for his wife. He refused to destroy the only part of her that still remained alive.

Jasper and Morgalla stood and embraced in the rays of the rising sun, unimaginably relieved. Jasper was happy that he and Morgalla were alive. Morgalla was also glad to be alive, but she remained uncertain about her future; she might know this world, but was a stranger to it. She could look human and have human blood flowing through her, but she was far from being one of them. When her outward appearance was hidden they saw someone else; someone they could be comfortable with. But if she revealed her true form, would they understand?

Morgalla's eyes closed and she breathed a sigh of relief. Jasper was happy for her and happy that it was finally over. He sighed, his breath visible in the suddenly chilled air, and goosebumps covered his body. He turned to Morgalla, confused.

"Why is it so cold?" he asked.

It was then that Morgalla felt the chill too; her eyes flew open, knowing what the chill meant. Suddenly, a clawed hand broke through the rubble.

"Oh no," she said.

Morgalla and Jasper looked to see Zorach emerge from the rubble. He stood, his eyes glowing red and his black cloak flowing in the morning wind. The red sunrise behind him looked like it was Hell's fire itself. He gave a roar of pure anger, and all the windows nearby shattered at the sound of his rage. Everyone within earshot was startled and covered their ears. Zorach glared at Jasper and Morgalla with hate. They felt his eyes upon them; it was as if the hand of death were on their hearts.

Zorach roared again and brought his fist down upon the ground. A shock wave moved through the ground toward Jasper and Morgalla, who dove for cover. It destroyed a couple of cars, tossing them into the air like falling leaves.

"Come on!" Richard yelled, as he and the other warriors all rushed to the scene.

Richard and three other wizards all took to the sky as other members charged in. The battle was brutal, and they used all their abilities and powers to try and defeat the demon lord.

Rubble and debris were thrown about from explosions and brute force. Bullets didn't faze the demon lord; they simply erupted into flames and crumbled to ash as they drove into his body. Zorach breathed fire to the sky and all around, paying no attention to who perished around him as a result. The wizards in the sky flew evasively to avoid getting burned.

Morgalla got up and took a sword in hand.

"Wait here," she said to Jasper.

"Morgalla, *no!*"

Morgalla ran into the battle toward her father, the sword gripped tightly in her hand. She charged at Zorach, who was unaware of her approach until he turned. With the back of his hand he deflected Morgalla and she fell to the ground. Jarvis Pelkey, a wizard of the Smythe family, landed and pointed his magical staff at Zorach and Morgalla.

"I got 'im!" he said confidently, but would soon eat his words.

"Jarvis!" Richard said, trying to stop his foolhardy friend.

Jarvis fired a lightning bolt from his staff that hit Zorach. Electricity enveloped him and Morgalla as well; she screamed in pain and fell back to the ground. Zorach gazed at Jarvis who was frozen in fear. A blast of fire from Zorach's mouth encompassed Jarvis, killing him instantly.

Morgalla came to her senses, but her entire body still felt as if it were burning. Grasping her sword, she stood on her hands and pushed up, her body leaping. She kicked Zorach in the face and he was momentarily knocked back. She flipped up in the air and landed on Zorach's head, ready to bring the killing blow upon her father. He easily smacked her with his hand and she landed over forty feet away, losing the sword in the process.

Jasper sought shelter behind a car, being careful not to be hit by any debris. Morgalla came hurtling over the car by Jasper. She landed on the pavement hard and Jasper ran up to her, concerned.

"Are you trying to get yourself killed? Just let them chuck lightning bolts at him!"

"We…we just need to keep him busy! Trust me!"

James, Rebecca, and others ran in to fight Zorach. Many were injured and their attacks completely futile. Morgalla ran back in, ignoring her pain and wishing her healing powers worked faster. Two cops carried out one of the Smythes who was injured; he was screaming, for his leg was missing. Morgalla took the sword from the wounded Smythe and ran in.

Jasper was still hiding behind a car, but suddenly he got an idea. He concentrated, hoping that he could change form at will. Just seconds later, he transformed into his demon form, filling out the large-sized pants and boots, and breathed a sigh of relief.

I wonder how strong I am?

He took hold of the car with both hands and slowly began to lift it.

Zorach brought his foot down by James, who leaped back trying not to get hit. The resulting blast knocked him back more than ten feet. Rebecca stabbed at Zorach, but his reflexes were quick and he caught the blade. He looked down at her just as she looked up to see his two red eyes glowing.

When Morgalla reentered the fight Zorach's attention shifted to her. He tossed Rebecca aside, wanting to kill the girl who he believed had betrayed him. He deflected his daughter's attacks easily with his claws and she dodged his assaults. She finally stabbed him in the leg and his hand came down, breaking the blade. He then smacked Morgalla with the back of his hand and she fell to the ground. Zorach stood over Morgalla, ready to make the killing blow.

"Hey, jerk!"

Zorach turned to see who would dare mock him in such a juvenile way. He was met by a car hurtling through the air that hit him in the face. The shock knocked Zorach back, but his claws dug into the metal and caught the car. He was not back far enough and was uninjured.

Jasper's relief that the car had hit its mark was short-lived when he realized that the impact hadn't injured Zorach at all

Get to Morgalla! Get her out of there!

Jasper ran to Morgalla as Zorach lifted up off the ground and stood with ease. He was upon Jasper and Morgalla before they could escape. Jasper punched Zorach again and again in the demon lord's torso, but did nothing to harm him. Jasper felt the pain in his knuckles and the lack of response from his adversary. Jasper saw a hand reach out for him, a hand of black armor extending out from the black cloak of Zorach. It grasped him by the throat and lifted him off the ground with ease. Jasper gasped for air, his feet kicking below him.

"Time to die, boy!"

Zorach's armored gauntlet suddenly lost a plate of metal and it fell to the ground. Zorach dropped Jasper and looked at his hand. He held up his other hand and was shocked to see the armor on his gauntlets rust and begin to fall apart.

"Your time is up," Morgalla said, getting up from the ground.

"No!" Zorach's voice was one of desperation, but he could barely speak above a whisper.

Earth was blessed never to have been touched before by Hell's evil. Zorach could not survive outside of an infernal environment for long, and his time had run out. He suddenly realized that there was no hope for his survival; his demise was inevitable unless he could get back to Hell, and Morgalla had made sure his retreat had been completely cut off. Zorach let out a roar of pain as James stabbed him in the back with his sword.

"That was for my mother you bastard!" James found satisfaction by plunging the blade into the beast and then twisting it with all of his might.

Zorach turned and knocked James back, but the sword was still embedded in the demon lord's body. With Zorach's back now facing Jasper, he drove it in deeper. Rebecca swung her sword too, slicing Zorach's midsection.

"MOVE!" Richard's voice was as loud as he could make it. Taking hold of the staff of light, he took careful aim at Zorach.

They all dove for the ground, and Jasper used his body as a shield for Morgalla. James and Rebecca both ran for their lives, away from the battle.

Margaret.

The bolt of lightning cascaded forth, striking the demon lord in the chest. His roar cut through the morning air and echoed throughout the town. His body went limp, and his cloak caught fire as he landed hard on the ground. The blue electricity hit the demon lord in the chest and he fell into a large hole over thirty feet away. Jasper slowly looked up to see that Zorach was no longer in sight. He and Morgalla looked at each other. Everyone stood, and with caution walked to where Zorach had fallen, a wall of smoke before them.

They all stood ready for the demon lord to come pouncing out, but he did not. Quivering and reaching out of the smoke, a clawed hand emerged; it was skeletal and had barely any life left in it. Zorach came crawling out from the smoke. Pieces of metal were dropping off and crumbling to dust on the ground. He looked at Morgalla; the once mighty and fearsome creature was now her height. His hand slowly reached out to her, but she looked back without flinching and showed no fear. Zorach's body then crumbled to nothing.

His cloak seemed to flow into the air with the morning wind. It disintegrated into smoke and finally into nothing at all. Only his helmet remained, empty and lifeless. Jasper stood beside his lover,

Morgalla, with his strong hand on her shoulder. In her mind, at last the mighty oak was alive and standing beside her.

✿

Back at Jasper and Andy's apartment, Meggan sat in a large chair, her hands on her temples in frustration. Andy paced the room, a cellular phone to his ear. Their clothes were dirty and torn, and their day had been long and horrific. Meggan could remember the screeching of the monsters chasing after them and coming out of the sky. The sights and sounds were fresh in their minds. They had endless questions about what had happened that day, but one in particular about which they were most curious:

Was that Jasper's voice coming out of that huge guy?

"It's ringing," she said, and Andy paced some more, waiting for Jasper to pick up.

"Damn it, where the hell is he?" Andy said to no one in particular, frustrated and worried.

"I need a drink," Meggan said. She stood and walked to the kitchen, unable to just sit helplessly.

"You don't drink," Andy said.

"Today I drink." Meggan searched through the cupboards, looking for any kind of liquor. Finally, she saw a small bottle, grabbed it, and read the label. "Schnapps!" she said, breathing a sigh of relief. "Thank God!"

Jasper finally arrived with Morgalla in his arms. He was in his human form and she in her demon form. She wore her long dark violet coat with the hood up to conceal her appearance. Morgalla felt sore all over, as if the entire army of Hell had marched over her. Every muscle of her body and every inch of her skin ached. Seeing them there, Andy and Meggan came running to the door. Meggan was in mid-drink of the bubble-gum schnapps.

"Okay, what the *hell* is going on?" Meggan demanded of Jasper.

"It's a *long* story," Jasper said, walking past them with Morgalla in his arms. Jasper carried her to his room and set her down gently on the bed. Morgalla let out a moan of pain despite Jasper's best efforts to be gentle. "I'm sorry," Jasper said, concerned for his lover and running his hand down her face.

Jasper turned around to see Andy and Meggan staring at the demon-woman on Jasper's bed. They saw the girl Jasper was dating, the young woman they had met on previous occasions. After all they had seen the day before, seeing a demon woman on their friend's bed was not that strange. Normally they would not have believed their own eyes, but they still needed to know the truth.

"Okay, start talking," Andy said to Jasper.

He didn't know what to say at first. He swallowed hard and took a deep breath, deciding that honesty was the best policy.

"My girlfriend is a demon."

Chapter Nineteen: Freedom

Shaking the snow off his coat, Mr. Kent walked into his office. The sun had just started to rise, but it was hard to tell with all the clouds in the sky. He hung up his coat and scarf, and set his briefcase down. After getting his coffee from the lounge, he went to his office to find a surprise: Jasper Davis was sitting in his chair.

Jasper was dressed differently than the last time Mr. Kent had seen him. He was wearing a long, heavy black winter coat. In fact, these days most of his wardrobe was black, as if he were mourning the loss of someone. He had stubble from not shaving for a few days and his face was serious.

"Can I *help* you?" Mr. Kent said, annoyed that Jasper had come in without invitation and made himself at home.

"You failed me," Jasper replied.

"Yes, I failed you," Mr. Kent said. "You deserved to fail. Now get out of my office before I call security."

"I already dealt with them."

"Hiya, Jazz," a security guard called. As he passed by the office, he smiled and waved.

"Hiya," replied Jasper, and then looked back at Mr. Kent. "So you were saying?"

"I was *saying* that you deserved the grade you got and there's nothing you can do to change that."

"I was wondering what your soul might be like. It took me a few classes to get to know you in a new light."

"New light?" Kent inquired, setting his coffee down. His hands went to his waist in aggravation. "Out of my chair, now."

Jasper stood up. There was a smirk on his face now, for he knew more about Kent than he had before.

"You're afraid of anyone whose opinion differs from yours. You're afraid of any student who might stand up for himself, and you think that just because you can give them a failing grade you have control over them."

"A failing grade, like I gave you," Mr. Kent replied.

"I'll get to that in a moment," Jasper continued. "You indoctrinate kids into your way of thinking. You don't teach them how to think for themselves and find their own way because you only want them to think *your* way."

As Jasper spoke, his teacher felt his pulse race and his face become warmer and warmer. A drop of sweat ran down his temple. What morality he had was being brought to light by Jasper's words. He had to admit, at least to himself, that his former student was right.

"You finished?" Kent replied. He stood and took hold of the door, ready to slam it shut. "I have class."

"No, I'm not!" Jasper put his hand on the door; it wouldn't matter how hard Kent slammed it. "I'll make you an offer. You know the work I submitted to you was good, just a difference of opinion. You know I deserve at least a passing grade."

"No," Kent said in defiance. He could feel Jasper's new powers working on him, but as much as it pained him, he still resisted.

"Feel like confessing anything?" Jasper asked. "Perhaps something that's been going on with Miss *Rider*, for example?"

"You know nothing."

"I think you wanna tell the dean everything," Jasper said, smiling.

Kent said nothing. The internal struggle now tipped in Jasper's favor. Before, what conscience he had was inching its way to the surface, but now his *job* was in jeopardy.

"A passing grade, you say?" Kent said.

✿

Jasper was bundled up as he walked through a snow-covered parking lot. His day was nearly over as he headed to meet his friends for dinner. Walking into the restaurant, he looked around to see Meggan sitting at one of the tables. She waved to him and he walked up.

"Well, well," she said with a smile. "He lives. I thought you weren't going out at all anymore."

He didn't say anything, but the look on his face spoke volumes. He wasn't in the mood for small talk. He didn't even take off his coat, which still had snow on it. He set his scarf and gloves on the table and took a seat.

"Andy?" he asked.

"Bathroom," she replied. "He told me about last week when you and he went out drinking."

"Uh-huh," Jasper replied, looking at the menu.

"So where have you been?"

"Around," Jasper said, his eyes still not meeting hers.

Andy returned, glad to see Jasper. "Hiya!" he smiled.

"Hey," Jasper said, not even looking up.

"So, what's going on?" Andy asked, taking a seat.

"Jasper was just about to tell us why he's being such a tool," Meggan replied.

It was that comment that made him finally look up from the menu.

"She's right, you're being a tool, dude," Andy said.

"You've been in a bitchy mood ever since *she* left," Meggan said.

"She had to," Jasper replied, his mood somber. "She was afraid to be here, in this town, and I don't blame her."

"And you *let* her go," Meggan said.

"I…how do I know that she truly wants me? How do I know that she didn't leave because of me?"

"Ask her," Andy interjected. "There's only one way to find out. Worst thing she can do is say no."

"If you want her, then why not go find her?" Meggan asked.

Jasper sighed. He hated it when other people were right, and honestly, they were right most of the time. He was silent and thought for a moment, then looked at Andy and Meggan. His friends smiled at him, despite his foul mood. They had strong wills and were only concerned for his health and happiness.

"Excuse me," Jasper said.

He got up and walked out of the restaurant. He stepped out into the cold night. The snow fell heavily as Jasper walked through the parking lot. As he was walking, he saw Missy and Steve heading toward the restaurant in the freezing snow.

"Well, well, well, look who it is." Missy's voice had the sound of joy in it. She needed some amusement and it had been a long time since she had seen him. "Where's your little bitch, Jasper? Oh yeah, that's right, she *left* you, didn't she?"

Jasper stood with a blank expression. He could kill or injure both of them so easily, but his conscience prevented him.

God, I hate you both.

"Let's face it, Jasper," Missy said. "You're a loser!"

"Missy," Jasper said with complete calmness, "for the first time in your life—shut the hell up!"

Missy opened her mouth again, ready to say something, but no words came out. Jasper's powers prevented her from speaking.

"Hey, watch your mouth, asshole!" Steve yelled at Jasper in a threatening manner.

Jasper merely ignored him and walked away, which only angered Steve more. Missy stood there trying to speak, but nothing came out of her mouth. She became scared and frustrated. Steve did not notice Missy's condition because he was too angry at Jasper.

"I don't have time for you, Steve," Jasper said.

"Hey, don't walk away from me!" Steve shouted.

Jasper wasn't going to stand for Steve talking back to him.

Steve grasped Jasper's shoulder and a beating was about to commence, but Jazz had dealt with greater beasts than him. When he felt Steve's hand grasp his shoulder, Jasper succumbed to his instinct. He grabbed Steve's hand and gripped it so tightly that Steve winced in pain.

"Don't you *ever* touch me again," Jasper said.

Steve swung with his other hand, which did nothing to Jasper when it struck his face. Jasper's head connected with Steve's face. Steve fell to the ground unconscious, blood trickling out of his nose. Missy tried to call for help but could not. Jasper did not look back at them as he walked away. He wished he could make them suffer a bit more, but he had more important things to do.

✻

Bagos Heights was a town not far from Springdale, about the same size in area and population. There were few places Morgalla could hide that were close. She hated the cold more than anything and she had never been more miserable. Life on Earth was now more complicated, but at least before she had a few good days.

Tonight was a typical busy Saturday night. Morgalla's raspberry hair was in a ponytail and a strand hung down over her fatigued face. Her eyes were only half-open, weary from the toils of real life. She wore an uncomfortable apron stained with beer over a green shirt, and carried a bus tub to a table covered with dirty glassware and plates. As she filled the tub a man approached her. His wardrobe was the same as every other day; he was overdressed for a night of bossing people around.

"Morgalla," he said, which caught her attention. She looked up to see him standing with his hands in his pockets. "Make sure to carry the empty bottles out to the shed."

She said nothing and nodded. If only he knew how little she respected him, and how obvious his leering at her was. His lack of morality prevented her from manipulating his soul. She took the now full bus tub back to the kitchen. The night was the same as every other night, but this one seemed to go by slower than usual.

Finally, it was time to go home. No one ever offered her a ride. She bundled up in her coat, scarf, and hat. Tonight she would have to make a stop for groceries. The snow fell heavily later, as Morgalla walked through the parking lot of her apartment complex carrying a bag of groceries. She was in her human form, with her hood up against the cold. In the dark, her features could not be seen by anyone.

As she walked along a sidewalk, she heard a whimpering. She looked around curiously, wondering where it was coming from. She looked in a bush and saw a miniature dachshund, shivering from the cold. The dog had no kind of identification around her neck. She trembled and her small, innocent brown eyes looked at Morgalla.

"What are you doing in there?"

Morgalla went to her apartment, leaving the dog there reluctantly. She opened the door to her apartment and looked back at the dachshund. The dog approached hesitantly, uncertain if she should enter, but it was obvious the apartment was much warmer than it was outside.

"It's much warmer in here," Morgalla said to her.

The dog slowly entered, sniffing the air. Morgalla set her grocery bag on the kitchen counter, and then went through her mail. She took the junk mail and dropped it in the wastepaper basket. As the dog sniffed around, Morgalla set her long coat on the couch. The dog hopped up on the couch and Morgalla wrapped her in the coat. She petted the dog gently on the head.

"You're all alone too, huh?" Her voice brought comfort to the small dog and her hand was warm.

Suddenly, there was a knock at the door. She reached for the doorknob but stopped, sensing her lover on the other side of the door. She wanted to open it and embrace him, but she was scared.

Why is he here?

Maybe he had forgiven her for leaving. The words of Delilah ran through her mind, as they had every day since her death. Jasper could never truly love her and accept her for who and what she was. There was only one way to find out for sure. She opened the door.

"Hi," he said.

Morgalla couldn't speak, feeling overwhelmed by her love for Jasper and her fear that he may not feel the same way. She knew she had hurt him when she left and she had regretted it ever since.

"May I come in?"

"Yeah," she said.

Jasper came in and his eyes explored her new home. He saw the dog on the couch and smiled.

"Got a friend, I see," he said, as he gently petted the dog.

"She followed me home," Morgalla said. "I didn't have the heart to leave her out in the cold."

Morgalla found it difficult to look Jasper in the face.

"Nice place you have here," he said. "Cozy."

"It's all I could afford, really," she replied. "As soon as I have enough money I'm moving to someplace warm."

"James called a couple of times, and Richard too. They're concerned about you, Richard especially."

Morgalla shivered. Jasper stood and walked to her as she tried to change the subject.

"I...uh...I got a driver's license," she said, taking it out and showing him. "*And* I convinced immigration to make me an American citizen!"

"I think you can convince anyone to do anything," Jasper said, smiling. He took her license in hand and looked at it. He could not help but notice that she had taken the full name *Morgalla Margaret Smythe*.

"Richard and the others will be flattered," he said. "So...why did it take you so long?" she asked timidly.

"For what?"

"To find me," she said. "It should have been easy, really."

"It took me two days," Jasper said. "It was difficult at first. But when I thought of you, and thought of the time we spent together and how good it felt, it was almost as if I could feel your soul from far away. I've known where you were for two months now."

"Why did you wait?"

Jasper sighed. He knew that lying was pointless.

"I thought you wanted nothing to do with me. But not seeing you became unbearable. I missed you and I had to see you just once."

Morgalla turned and looked out the window at the falling snow.

"I hurt you, Jasper. I know. Please believe me, I didn't mean to."

Jasper looked at Morgally curiously, sensing an entirely new emotion from her.

"You...you're afraid," he deduced. "I don't like the feel of it, either. Morgalla, why are you afraid of me?"

"I...no! I'm not afraid of *you*, Jasper. You're the greatest thing to happen to me in my life. I'm scared—scared of what is going to happen next, who is going to come for me."

"You don't know if anyone is going to come, Morgalla."

"Do *you* think I'm safe? I saw the look on your face. I was ready to kill Vex and you saw the real me. You saw the *monster* inside me."

"Monster?" he exclaimed, surprised that she would use such a word. "I was shocked, yes. But Morgalla, I know now what you've gone through and what you've had to do to survive. I've also seen you and felt your soul, and I know the good person within you."

Her back was turned to him as tears came to her eyes.

"I want to be there," he continued. "I want to be there for you, and I want to be there *with* you. I understand why you left, why you moved twenty miles away. There are inquiries, investigations which I think will never end. You were wise to leave, to run away from Springdale. But I wish you hadn't run away from me."

"But I hurt you. I didn't mean to. Please believe me."

"I believe you," Jasper said, standing close to her. He looked at her beautiful face but she did not return the gaze. His hand went to her chin, and slowly and gently he encouraged her to look up. She met his eyes. "I want to share my life with you, Morgalla. Why do you push me away? Are you afraid that I could not love the real you? Morgalla, I *do*! I'm in love with you, regardless of who or what you are. Why won't you say it?"

"Say what?"

"That you love me too."

Morgalla choked up; she could never have hidden her feelings from him even when he was human.

"We have the same powers, I can feel it, and I felt it both times when we made love. I want to be part of your life. Please let me in. I know we may face adversity, I know we may face danger, but I don't care! Morgalla, please let me be part of your life."

Morgalla was silent a moment and Jasper was patient while waiting for her response. His heart was open to her; he meant every word, and every fiber of his being was in love with her. Morgalla felt his heart *accept* her for everything that she was. She was completely different from him, but it did not matter. And Morgalla was finally discovering what true love was.

She looked up at him, tearfully, and said the words that were in her heart.

"I...I love you, Jasper," she whispered.

It was like music to his ears. Jasper's heart was full, and he smiled at Morgalla, overcome by his love for her.

"Let me see it," he said, and gently ran his hand down her cheek.

"It?"

"Your real face."

Morgalla was hesitant, but she changed into her demon self and Jasper smiled.

"You don't have to hide from me," he said.

God, please...

She did not reply with words but with actions. Jasper and Morgalla kissed, and their arms embraced each other's bodies. He could feel the joy that enveloped her soul and could tell what the answer to his question was. They released and looked at each other again. Jasper could see the crucifix, the gift that Richard gave to her, around her neck. He lifted it carefully and looked at it.

"I thought you didn't believe."

"It...*this*," she said, taking hold of the cross gently, "was important to her, and therefore it is important to me. Besides, if someone like you exists in the world, then surely there must be a God."

They heard a slight whimper and looked to see the dachshund on the couch. She had been staring at them the whole time, her eyes filled with curiosity.

✪

Dear Diary,

Sorry I have not written in a while, I'm trying to keep a low profile. I have a job, I have bills. Real life sucks. But I have someone here with me, so maybe life isn't so bad. I have to go now, but I'll drop in from time to time. For now I have a life to build.

Morgalla lay on her bed in her true form, not afraid now to show her true self to her lover. Jasper was behind her, grasping her hand; his firm and masculine grip a constant reassurance that everything was going to be okay. Her face was turned to his and they kissed passionately. Their bare skin touched under the sheets, warm and like velvet, and a glorious euphoria filled them both. No longer was her heart empty, gripped by the black gauntlet that was Hell. No longer did she feel worn beyond her years. Her soul was free, young, and wild. She was ready to journey through life with Jasper. For the first time in her life, she felt alive. They looked into each other's eyes and smiled.

"You were right," she said.

"About what?"

"The snow *is* beautiful."

Jasper lay next to his lover and she moved to rest her head on his chest. There was a cork on the sharp ends of her horns, to avoid poking him as they slept. Jasper reached over and turned out the light.

✿

Richard had slept well for the first time since he could remember. That night there was no dream, only peace. He rose with the sun, normally he would have gone to his study but instead he went to the kitchen for some coffee. He looked out to the east; the sun had risen completely and bathed his home in golden light. Many things ran though his heart and mind. His future before had been a point of light on the horizon, a singular goal that was now achieved. This question in his min now was "what now?"

With coffee in hand he walked to his study, searching through many drawers and cabinets until finally he found what he was looking for. He took out an orb made of black marble. Blowing the dust off of it he looked upon the smooth surface. The number 8 was on one side and on the other was a circular piece of glass, a window into a possible future. It had been a while since he sought out its wisdom.

He took a deep breath and shook the orb, asking his question under his breath.

"Should I trust Morgalla?"

He stopped shaking the orb and looked at the answer.

THE END